D0064997

INTERMISSION

INTERMISSION

Graham Hurley

**SEVERN
HOUSE**

First world edition published in Great Britain and the USA in 2021
by Severn House, an imprint of Canongate Books Ltd,
14 High Street, Edinburgh EH1 1TE.

Trade paperback edition first published in Great Britain and the USA in 2022
by Severn House, an imprint of Canongate Books Ltd.

severnhouse.com

British Library Cataloguing-in-Publication Data
A CIP catalogue record for this title is available from the British Library.

ISBN-13: 978-0-7278-5002-7 (cased)
ISBN-13: 978-1-78029-796-5 (trade paper)
ISBN-13: 978-1-4483-0535-3 (e-book)

All Severn House titles are printed on acid-free paper.

MIX
Paper from
responsible sources
FSC
www.fsc.org   FSC® C013056

Typeset by Palimpsest Book Production Ltd.
Falkirk, Stirlingshire, Scotland.
Printed and bound in Great Britain by
TJ Books, Padstow, Cornwall.

For HBC
a Pompey legend

'Covid-19 is the portal between one world and the next.'

—*Arundhati Roy*

PRELUDE

B ack in 2019, way before the madness began, I ran into an old friend. His name is Tim, and he lives in Portsmouth. Like me, he's a thesp, though in his case the business of being an actor – of building an entire career on pretending to be someone else – is sensibly diluted with other talents. He still plays in a band. He still coaches tennis to a very decent standard. He's maybe a decade or so older than me but he works out daily, and he has the looks and the nerve to busk his way through. Lately he's been appearing in TV commercials, which is why he found himself taking the train to London for an audition.

We met in a bar afterwards. Just now, as I write this, the notion of so many people in an enclosed space seems like an act of collective suicide, but what I remember most clearly was the expression on Tim's face. He does rueful very well. Plainly, the audition had been a disaster.

When I asked why, he shrugged. 'My fault,' he said. 'I should have listened to the casting director. All the clues were there but they passed me by.'

The commercial was for a hunky brand of off-road 4x4. Tim, a little late as usual, joined the other prospects at the production company. They were all male, and they all looked authentically outdoors: beards, lumberjack shirts, Karrimor boots. The assembled talent were to buddy up, and the thirty-second audition called for each twosome to play-act their way along a tiny ledge overhanging an enormous drop, their bodies pressed against the sheerness of the imaginary rock. Dialogue was optional. These guys, with their years of experience, were expert climbers. They knew the moves. They trusted the gear, but most of all they trusted themselves. What the casting director wanted most of all was confidence, salted by an awareness of the consequences of that single mistake.

Tim's buddy, he said, was brilliant, totally authentic, and led the traverse from the start. Tim, aware that his presence on the

rock face shouldn't go unremarked, felt obliged to say something
as the clock ticked down. With a couple of seconds left he glanced
at the office floor, winced, shivered, and said, 'God, no wonder
I can't stand heights.'

The casting director brought the audition to a brisk end. 'The
script says you have years of climbing experience,' he pointed
out. 'So how come you're dizzy all of a sudden?'

Tim, Pompey to his fingertips, had been in tight corners before.
'Ironic,' he murmured. 'The punters will love it.'

Now, in the bar, I mimed applause. Nice line, I said, but did
it work?

'Bang on.' He was grinning now. 'We nailed the job.'

At the time, that story of Tim's made me laugh and we cele-
brated with a bottle of Rioja. The commercial has aired since,
and the pair of them were great, but what really matters, nearly
a full year later, was something he told me only a couple of days
ago. We were yakking on the phone, and I told him how good I
thought the commercial had been.

He asked me first whether I was taking the piss. When I said
I wasn't, he went very quiet for a second or two. Then he told
me about the shoot itself, on a real rock face, roped to his actor
buddy. The production crew had taken every conceivable precaution against any kind of accident, and a fall, if it were to happen,
measured no more than twenty feet on to a giant airbed. But that,
Tim confessed quietly, wasn't the point. He really was terrified
of heights, of the unexpected, of that split second when gravity,
or some other force beyond your control takes charge and you
know you're in a very, very bad place.

'Fucked,' he said. 'I thought I was fucked.'

'You mean on the rock face?'

'Yeah. But afterwards, too. With the virus. And not just me.
All of us.'

I nodded, said nothing. He was more right than he can possibly
have known.

ONE

Monday, 23 March 2020

My cue to switch on the TV comes in a brief call from H. He's evidently down in Dorset, Lord of the Manor, owner of all he beholds. Hayden Prentice, aka H, owes his three hundred prime acres to adventures in the cocaine trade. This evening, unusually, he takes a moment to enquire about my state of health.

'You OK?'

'I'm fine.'

'No temperature? Cough? Nothing like that?'

'No.'

'Good,' he grunts. 'Do us a favour?'

'What is it?'

'Turn on the telly. BBC One. I'll call you back.'

I'm about to ask why, but H has already hung up. On BBC One, I have time to catch the credits for *EastEnders* before we get to half past eight. I've been out most of the day, briefing my agent and afterwards a couple of girlfriends about last month's drama shoot in Paris, and the news that the prime minister is to address the nation has passed me by. Now, I'm staring at Boris Johnson. He's sitting at a desk and looks both grave and slightly regal. Nicely cut blue suit, red patterned tie, hair unusually well-behaved.

To be frank, I'm not a Johnson fan. I've never bought the mad hair schtick, and friends of mine in a position to know tell me he's ruthless, calculating, dishonest, and congenitally lazy. One of them confided that he mislays briefing files with the same careless abandon he loses track of his numberless children. All of this I can well believe, but tonight our prime minister has something else on his mind. This evening, as he eyeballs the nation, it's very obvious that he has bad tidings to announce.

The coronavirus, he says, is having a devastating effect across country after country. It has no respect for frontiers and is with us as he speaks. This invisible killer must be brought to heel, something that will require an enormous national effort. We're all in this together, and we must all do our best to protect our amazing National Health Service.

There follows a stern list of dos and don'ts. Do stay at home. Don't go out unless it's absolutely necessary. Use food delivery systems wherever possible. All non-essential shops, he says, will be closed. As will pubs, hotels, restaurants, and public buildings like libraries and art galleries. Churches will only be open for one reason: funerals.

I'm sitting on the sofa. All of this is deeply sensible, but I can't fight the feeling that I'm back at school. This, in a way, is a tribute to Johnson's acting skills. He's playing the concerned headmaster, spelling out a series of proscriptions for our own benefit, and the performance lifts him a little in my estimation. But what rivets me to the sofa are his hands, fleshy, fat-fingered, hyperactive. At the start, they're interlinked on the flatness of the desk, but as he accelerates towards the next line on the autocue, and the line after that, each hand develops a life of its own, becomes a fist, tightly clenched – a symbol, no doubt, of resolution and furious intent. We'll nail this bastard. Believe me, we will.

Seconds after he's done, H is back on the phone.

'What do you think?'

'I think I'll check the freezer.'

'I'm serious.'

'Then I don't understand. You want me to score him out of ten? Give him performance notes for next time?'

'That's not what I meant. I had Cynthia on earlier. You remember Cynth?'

'Remind me.'

'Fat Dave's lady.' A brief pause. 'Dave Munroe?'

The name unlocks the face. Dave Munroe was a bent cop back in Portsmouth when H was a key player in the cocaine biz. According to H, Dave had his ear to every door, every conversation as Major Crimes tried to stem the city's raging thirst for cocaine. For quite a lot of money, and one or two other favours, Dave passed on a great deal of information that H regarded as priceless before sensibly cashing in his chips and electing for early retirement.

The only time I met this legend was the weekend of H's fiftieth birthday. The Pompey tribe assembled at H's Flixcombe Manor for a weekend of recreational mayhem, and one of them was Fat Dave. By now, thanks to years of committed self-abuse, he was in a wheelchair. On the Sunday, away from the wreckage of the all-nighter, we had a proper conversation. He was a balloon of a man, tiny head perched on a huge body, but he had a winning smile, and patted my hand a lot, and in truth I rather liked him.

'So, what's happened?' I ask H.

'He's only fucking got it.'

'Got what?'

'The virus. Dead man walking. That's Cynth's take, not mine.'

Cynthia, I remember, ran a boarding house in Ventnor on the Isle of Wight. Since then, according to H, she's sold up and now lives in Portsmouth.

'She and Dave moved a couple of years back. Her mum's in Pompey, proper old, and she wanted to be closer.'

'And Dave?'

'Started coughing a week and a half ago. Cynth put it down to the fags but then he got sicker and sicker, really ill, fever, the sweats, you name it. She talked to their GP and he was in QA that same afternoon.'

'And now?'

'Intensive care. Ventilator. The lot. Nightmare, darling. Cynth's in bits.'

'She's seen him?'

'No. And that's the worst of it. They won't let her anywhere near him. The closest she gets is a Skype call on her tablet and what she saw yesterday scared her shitless.'

I nod, listening to H tallying the state of the man, flat on his belly most of the time, hooked up to countless machines. The last time they had anything approaching a conversation, Dave could barely manage a couple of words between gasps for breath, and since then he's been in an induced coma.

H very rarely calls me 'darling', and this clue alone tells me he's as unmoored and adrift as poor Cynthia. Back in the day, calls from Fat Dave kept H out of the hands of the Major Crimes

Team and he's never forgotten how much he owes the man. H has many failings but loyalty to a handful of Pompey mates isn't one of them, and this conversation is the living proof.

'So what happens next?' I ask.

'We go to Pompey. Give Cynth a hand.'

'We?'

'Me, darling. And you.'

'Why me?'

'Because I could do . . . you know . . .'

'With a little support?'

'Yeah. None of this is fucking easy. Believe me.'

I nod. I understand the logic, the ageless, near-magnetic tug of Pompey for ex-hooligans like H. The city itself, what little I've seen of it, has done nothing for me, but that's not the point.

The TV is still on, the sound muted. H, too, has gone quiet.

'But what about Johnson? All these new rules?' I ask.

'Fuck 'em. The man's a twat. Just tell me you're in . . .' A moment of silence. 'Please?'

In the end, after the briefest discussion, I say yes. H gives me Cynthia's address and postcode to tap into my sat-nav and tells me to look out for signs to an area called Baffins. He'll be setting off first thing tomorrow. Should be in Pompey by mid-morning.

'You'll be coming back afterwards?' I ask.

'I doubt it. I need to see Dave.'

'They won't let you.'

'No?' He lets the question hang in the air. He wants me to think there'll be a way, that no closed door in Pompey ever resisted Hayden Prentice, but somehow I can't see it happening. Hospitals have ways and means of keeping the public at arm's length. Especially now.

'So you're staying with her? Cynthia?'

'No way. She's offered, but I thought you might fancy somewhere of our own.'

'*Our* own?'

'Yeah.'

'Is this some kind of date?'

Once again, H doesn't answer. The only night we've ever slept together was a very long time ago and H knows nothing's going to change.

'Tony Morse,' he says at length. 'I've made the call. He'll sort something.' A bark of laughter. 'This date of ours. Baffins, yeah? Around midday? Cynth's offering a spot of lunch. Be rude to disappoint her.'

I go to bed early, wondering what I've let myself in for. I first met H down in Antibes, more than twenty years ago. I was killing time on location waiting for the French scenarist to come up with a couple of rewrites. H had a lavish multi-mirrored cabin aboard a superyacht moored in the marina. The yacht, *Agincourt*, was gross in every respect. It belonged to a well-known Pompey face and he threw a party for us thesps. H, who had a serious talent for mixing killer margaritas, knew how to make a girl laugh, and – to my shame – I let the evening get the better of me.

The following day, nominated for a major award, I moved along the coast to the Cannes Film Festival, where I met the Scandi scriptwriter who was to become my husband. Berndt, alas, turned out to be a monster, but by then – over a decade and a half later – I was in all kinds of trouble. The marriage had turned both ugly and violent. Malo, whom Berndt had always supposed to be his natural son, was off the rails. Berndt elected to move in with a Swedish starlet with an enticing penthouse overlooking Stockholm harbour. All this was bad enough but Berndt, spiteful to the last, took Malo with him, leaving yours truly with a plague of persistent headaches which, after an MRI scan, turned out to be the fingerprints of a brain tumour.

It was at this point that H stepped back into my life, thanks to the tireless work of an investigative journalist who later became a friend. After a major accident on a cross-country trials bike, H was hospitalized with medical problems of his own, but when DNA tests proved that Malo was his son, and not Berndt's, he perked up immeasurably. Given what was happening to Malo, this turned out to be a blessing.

By now, as moody as ever, our boy was back in my apartment in Holland Park. H was convalescing at Flixcombe Manor, and to my delight he took our delinquent son in hand. No more drugs. No more dossing all day in bed. Tuition in rough shooting and trials riding. And finally, once Malo was clean and eager, the key role in a wild but canny bid to ship half a dozen high-rollers across the Channel in an antique trawler to the D-Day beaches to raise funds for Help for Heroes. In my view, this was a near-impossible gig, but Malo well and truly nailed it. Charm? In bucketloads. Nerveless, like his father? Definitely. Our son, I told H, has real talent.

Four years later, that judgement of mine remains incontestable. Recently, Malo has been seeing quite a lot of his dad and something he told me the other day, strictly in confidence, has snagged in what remains of my poor, feeble brain.

It's still only half past ten. Malo and his partner, Clemmie, are night birds. I reach for my mobile and give my son a ring. After years living together in a Kensington mews cottage, they're now sharing a rather nice semi in Twickenham.

We play catch-up for several minutes and then I mention H.

'The other day, you told me he was worried,' I remind him.

'He is.'

'Why might that be? You mind me asking?'

The silence that follows suggests he does. I'm about to change the subject when he's back on the line.

'Money,' he says. 'I think he's overcooked it.'

'Overcooked it' is Malo-speak for finding yourself in a very bad place, and I have some difficulty believing him. H has always been clever with money. Fresh from school, he trained as an accountant, a priceless qualification when it came to securing his place in the Pompey drug world. He understands money, makes friends with it, treats it with considerable guile as well as affection, and some of his more arcane laundering schemes, Fat Dave once told me, have been adopted by other gangs in dozens of cities nationwide. Had H stayed legit, in Dave's opinion, he'd have made himself a tidy career. As it was, thanks to cocaine, he got very, very rich.

'Overcooked?' I'm reaching for a pen and a scrap of paper. 'Tell me more.'

Malo grunts something about the Netflix movie he and Clemmie are watching. Maybe he can call me back. I shake my head. While I respect Malo's loyalty to his father, now is not the time for reticence.

'Your dad's in a bit of a state,' I tell Malo. 'Just give me a clue or two.'

'I can't, Mum, it's difficult.'

'Why?'

'You know what he's like. Too proud for his own good. If he thought we were having this conversation, he'd go mental.'

'We're not having this conversation,' I point out. 'And when we do, I guarantee he'll never know.'

'Is that a promise?'

'Of course it is.'

'How can I be sure?'

'You can't, Malo, but don't insult me. You're sounding like H. I'm your mother. Just believe me.'

'OK,' he says uncertainly.

All this time I can hear a movie soundtrack in the background, but then comes a mumbled exchange with a voice I recognize as Clemmie's and suddenly the movie's on pause.

'You remember that insurance business of Dad's? The one he called Easy-Mend to begin with?'

'Yes.'

'It's gone tits-up.'

'You mean it's failed?'

'Big time. He got major buy-in but then splurged on the advertising. That was one nasty. Then there was a rash of claims last year he couldn't cope with. Brexit isn't helping. He told me he'd factored all that shit in but now it turns out he didn't. Bad place doesn't cover it.'

'How much?'

'Seven figures. He's fighting it, of course, and it's in the hands of the lawyers, which he hates. To make it worse, he tried to offset with a couple of other investments which turned sour, good money after bad. Worst case, he might have to sell.'

'The company?'

'Flixcombe.'

'You're serious?' I put the pen to one side. 'And he told you all this?'

'He did. But that's because I kept asking the right questions which really pissed him off. He's been a dickhead, Mum. He should have asked for advice.'

'From who?'

'Me, for starters.'

'You said that? You *told* him that?'

'I did, yes.'

'And?'

'Like I say, mental, frothing at the mouth, completely out of control. I'm just glad you weren't there. At one point I thought he was going to batter me. You remember those times with Berndt? When things were really bad between you?'

'I do, yes.'

'Worse, Mum. Thank God we weren't in the kitchen.'

'What?' For a moment, this son of mine has lost me.

'Knives, Mum. Think knives. I've never seen him like that. He can be scary, sure, but never homicidal.'

This is sobering stuff. I tell him I'm sorry.

'Don't be, Mum. I can handle it.'

'I meant H. He's no angel but he doesn't deserve this.'

Malo grunts again, which I suspect might signal agreement. As briefly as I can, I describe what's happening down in Pompey.

'Fat Dave?' Malo sounds shocked. 'Fat Dave Munroe? You're serious?'

'I am, yes. According to H, he's dying. In fact, he might be dead already.'

'And Dad?'

I pause for a moment, searching for the right word. 'Crushed' would be too harsh. 'Upset' wouldn't begin to cover it. In the end I settle for 'Lost'.

'Lost how?'

'He's all over the place. He can't believe it. Normally he takes these things on the chin, sorts them himself, wouldn't dream of asking for help. Not on this occasion, though. Not now.'

'That's not Dad at all.'

'Exactly.'

'And?'

'I'm going down there to lend a hand. I've no idea what difference I can make, but it might help.'

'You want me to come?'

'No. Hunker down. Look after Clemmie. Did you hear Johnson tonight? Stay at home, all that?'

'I read it on my phone. He has to be joking, doesn't he?'

'I doubt it, Malo. What's happened to Fat Dave tells me we should take this thing seriously. And I imagine there must be lots of other Fat Daves.'

This brings the conversation to an end – my decision – but before I bow out, my son has a final question.

'What about you, Mum? That scan last week?'

'Still clear,' I tell him. 'I get another six months, lucky me.'

TWO

N ext day, I'm on the road by mid-morning. Already, our prime minister's address to the nation appears to have emptied the Bayswater Road of traffic. Purring from traffic light to traffic light, I catch glimpses of people hurrying along the pavement, heads down, hands thrust in their pockets. A couple of them are wearing face masks as they pass locked shops and shuttered pubs. Post-nuclear, I think, remembering the copy of Nevil Shute's *On the Beach* I devoured last year. The bomb's dropped, the radiation levels are climbing and we're all doomed.

The M25, if anything, is even creepier, just a scatter of supermarket trucks and white vans hogging the lane of their choice, and by the time I get to the A3 turn-off I realize how much I've taken yesterday's London for granted. I'd assumed that traffic jams, bursting cafes, and the long queue of jets descending into Heathrow were forever. How wrong can a girl be?

I'm a couple of minutes north of the Hindhead tunnel when I register the flashing blue lights in my rear-view mirror. There are two uniformed police in the front and one of them is motioning me on to the hard shoulder.

Shit.

The two officers circle the car, note the registration. Then the younger one asks me to get out. I'm desperately trying to remember Boris Johnson's very short list of excuses for breaking what the media are already calling 'lockdown', when the officer asks me where I'm going.

'Portsmouth.'

'You live there?'

'No.'

He wants to see my driving licence.

'W4 is London,' he says. 'So why Portsmouth?'

'A very good friend of mine is dying.' I bite my lip. 'His partner needs support.' This, at least, has the merit of being true.

'She has an address, this lady?'

'Yes.' I give him the address. He studies it for a moment, makes another note, and then checks his watch.

'So here's how it works.' He nods down the motorway. 'If you carry on, there's no coming back.'

'*Ever?*'

The two men exchange glances. At last, I've coaxed a smile. 'Ever,' he agrees. 'Life sentence, madam. In *Pompey*? Your call.'

Cynthia, when I finally make it to Baffins, takes me by surprise. I've been expecting someone more motherly, plumper, more Fat Dave. Instead, I'm looking at a tall woman, probably in her late fifties, well preserved, immaculately turned-out, and the house, when I step inside, is a perfect match: subtle greys and dark blues on the walls of the narrow hall, a stand of lilies on an occasional table, and an artful pattern of beautifully framed photographic prints that bring me to an admiring halt. On first sight, this place – unremarkable from the outside – has the feel of a decent art gallery. Intimate? Yes. But elegant, too.

'They're all Portsmouth.' Cynthia is nodding at the closest of the photos. 'And all Dave's work.'

I'm standing in front of a black and white shot of a landscape I don't recognize. The tide is out, and a steely light is gleaming on the exposed mud banks. On the left, the photo is framed by a crescent of footpath that skirts a two-storey clapboard house set slightly back. A Union Jack flies from the flagpole in the garden and on closer inspection, out over the water, I can see a flight of what look like mallards.

'Langstone Harbour,' Cynthia murmurs. 'You know it at all?'

'No.'

'Dave's favourite place. I used to wheel him across there whenever the light was good. It's a bit of a trek but he loved it.'

I nod, inspecting another shot, a shingle beach this time, the camera low, the pebbles shiny with recent rain. Cynthia's use of the past tense is slightly disturbing. In H's world, and increasingly mine, no one ever gives up.

'They're great,' I say. 'Dave's got a real eye.'

Cynthia spares me a glance. She looks wistful, under-nourished, and judging by the darkness under her eyes, she's not getting much sleep.

'In there.' She nods at the door at the end of the hall. 'And thank you for coming down.'

H is waiting in what turns out to be the sitting room. He's slumped in an armchair that must belong to Fat Dave because it's enormous, and he's staring into nowhere, scarcely aware of my presence.

'Trip down OK?' he mumbles.

'Fine. Perfect. I had the road to myself.'

'No Filth?'

'One stop halfway down the A3. They were charming.'

'Really?' At last, he looks up at me, then gestures loosely towards the window. 'Fucking sad, eh?'

The back garden is on the small side. A froth of early blossom brightens the single tree, and a tabby cat sprawls on a weathered wooden bench.

'What am I looking for?'

'Under the blue tarpaulin. See them?' I shake my head, then look harder.

'You mean the wheels?'

'Yeah. Dave's chair. Poor bastard.'

We have lunch around a circular table in a corner of the room. Cynthia serves a fish soup, chunks of cod floating in a thick *bouillabaisse*, with warm crusty bread and a light green salad on the side. The fish is delicious, perfectly cooked, and while H presses her for more details about Dave, my eyes keep straying to the picture that hangs over the mantelpiece. I can't make up my mind whether it's a photo or a clever piece of artwork, but either way there's no contesting the face. David Bowie, in his prime. Gelled locks, heavy mascara, killer eyes, with a deep crimson wound that seems to slice the image in half.

This, for whatever reason, comes as another surprise. My take on H's world has been based almost exclusively on mates of his who've turned up from time to time at Flixcombe. Fat Dave was one of them. Others had the same tribal markings: fading tattoos, bellies out of control, plenty of Pompey swagger. But barely an hour in the company of this woman tells a very different story, as does her quiet nod to a relationship that plainly means the world to her.

H has brought a bottle of dry sherry to break the ice. By the time we're done with the fish, the bottle is nearly empty. At this point, I'm bold enough to ask how she and Dave Munroe first met.

'Ventnor.' She holds my gaze across the table, her eyes already glassy. 'Dave was on a job on the island all week and had booked himself in, he and another guy.'

'Dessie.' This from H. 'Dessie Wren. Good bloke for a Filth. Clever, too.'

'And?' I'm still looking at Cynthia.

'He was a lovely man, Dave, you sensed that from the start. He could talk to anyone, and that's a real talent. He listened, as well, which was unheard of in my world.'

Dave, she said, was especially partial to kippers for breakfast and by mid-week she'd managed to lay hands on a supply of Arbroath smokies.

'After that, I could do no wrong. The other guy, Dessie, was out most evenings, but Dave would stay with me and we'd sit in the back parlour after I'd sorted all the other guests. There was always a lot to Dave, literally as he got fatter, but the more we talked the more I realized how unusual he was.'

'Like how?' I steal a glance at H. His eyes are half-closed, his face clouded by a frown.

'Birds, for one thing. He was mad about them, knew everything, where they came from, when to look out for them, how to recognize their calls, who they were afraid of, everything you'd ever want to know. After that first week, he'd come back when he had time off. We'd drive over to the nature reserve at Brading, spend all afternoon on the marshes. He taught me so much. He knew so much. And he was mobile in those days. The world . . .' She shrugs, a gesture of near despair. 'Our oyster.'

'That Dessie,' H grunts. 'He nearly had us a couple of times. Canny bastard. Ex-skate. Blokes like that are nearly human beings, easy to take for granted. We saw him off in the end, but only thanks to . . .' He nods towards the shrouded wheelchair in the garden. 'Dave.'

If Cynthia is thrown by this abrupt intervention, it doesn't show. Instead, at my invitation, she describes where the relationship went next, in particular the holidays they began to take together. Dave, it seems, was still married, with two young daughters, but the Job gave him every excuse in the world to cover his tracks. That first summer, allegedly in pursuit of a suspected kidnapper, Dave decamped to Greece. With Cynthia in tow.

'Corfu,' she says. 'Dave got wind of an apartment for rent in Roda. There was a little beach, tavernas to die for, music and dancing in the evenings.'

'Dave?' H looks up. *'Dancing?'*

'Indeed.' Cynthia's smile is unforced. 'Hidden talents, my Dave. He knew the moves, no problem, and if something new came along he made it up. I think "resourceful" is the word. A couple of ouzos and he'd dance all night.'

H is staring at her the way you might stare at a stranger, and I realize that this woman has the measure of him. *My Dave. Not yours.*

'And now?' I reach for my glass, knowing only too well where this conversation has to lead.

'Now is horrible. You want to see him? You want to know how bad, how *evil*, this thing is?'

Without waiting for an answer, Cynthia leaves the room. Moments later I hear footsteps overhead, then she's back with a big iPad.

'Dave's,' she explains as she opens it up and stations it between H and myself. 'He used to put all his bird shots on it.'

She stabs a finger at the screen and for the next few minutes we cycle through a series of photos while she provides a commentary. Redshanks. Tufted ducks. A lone marsh harrier. And, just look, a black-crested night heron. Then her finger strays to another icon and suddenly the sunshine and the bird life have gone. Now, H and I are looking at a hospital ward crowded with bulky figures. Masked, visored, gowned, they attend busily to patients fighting – I imagine – for their lives. They could be nurses, doctors, porters, anyone. The only clues are the names in heavy black Pentel, pinned to their gowns.

'ICU,' Cynthia mutters. 'Three days ago. These people are incredible, believe me. Twelve hours at a stretch, wearing all that? This is war. This is their armour. We're back in the Dark Ages.'

The Dark Ages. Like every other next of kin, Cynthia has been denied access to the ICU, and like every other wife, husband, mother, or lover, she'd pleaded for some kind of conversation, just a word or two, and a squeeze of the hand – anything to reach across this terrifying abyss.

'They do their best,' she says. 'You phone up and ask for the latest news, and they'll tell you straight out, no flannel, just the facts. At the start of the weekend Dave was still conscious, just. The ventilator makes proper conversation impossible, but I knew he could hear me, and that's what mattered.'

I nod. H doesn't move. He can't take his eyes off the frozen image of the ICU, and the sight of Fat Dave, already diminished, propped up on a bank of pillows. The ventilator tube disappears down his throat while a thousand other leads tether him to what's left of his life. His head is half-turned towards the camera, pale, drawn, a poor-quality version of the face I remember from H's fiftieth.

'Go on then.' H nods at the screen.

Cynthia hits the Play arrow, and then looks away. I'm guessing she must have seen this sequence dozens of times, playing and re-playing it, her last contact with the man she'd shared so many happy years with. Someone at the bedside is obviously holding up a phone or a tablet for Dave's benefit, and the moment he recognizes Cynthia he tries to muster a smile. I can see he's doing his very best, but the result is grotesque, the grimace of a man who knows the darkness is coming for him, and all the time I can hear the steady, remorseless suck and wheeze of the ventilator, Dave's chest rising and falling in tune with the machine. This is dancing with a difference, I think.

'Dave?' Cynthia's voice on the recording. 'It's me, Cynthia. Hang in there, yeah? I love you, my angel. I just want you to know that. Whatever happens, however bad it gets, just remember me. You hear what I'm saying? The times we've had? All those times to come? Just nod, Dave. I know it's hard but do it for me. For us, my angel. I love you, Dave, I really do.'

The picture wobbles a moment, and then I watch Dave struggling to manage a grunt or two, desperate to cheat the virus of its winnings, but his face has purpled the way you might react to a fish bone in your throat, a moment of panic and then the gravelly choking rasp as he tries to hoist whatever he needs to get rid of. This is a man who knows he's drowning. Not in some terrible accident, but in the swampy wreckage of his own lungs.

'Easy, my darling. Easy.' Cynthia again.

Dave looks briefly grateful, and then collapses back against the pillow, his eyes closed. Moments later, nurses are crowding around the bed, and in a moment neither H nor I will ever forget, Fat Dave raises a thin white arm and his hand trembles as he waves goodbye. Then his fingers clench and we're left with a single raised thumb. *I did my best*, he wants to say. *And I love you, too.*

We leave the house a couple of hours later. Both of us have done our best to comfort Cynthia, to tell her that there may yet be hope, that modern medicine can work all kinds of miracles, but I can tell from her face that she doesn't believe me and by late afternoon it's obvious that she wants to be left in peace.

We say our goodbyes at the door, give her a big hug, make her promise to phone the moment she needs us, but all she can manage is a tired nod. Her eyes are welling up again. She seems resigned, already in mourning. After the front door closes, H and I briefly confer beside his car. Thanks to Tony Morse, he's acquired the key to a vacant apartment down in Southsea. I'm to follow him through the city. The fact that I've given Cynthia's address as my Portsmouth lockdown address doesn't seem to bother him.

'You don't want to go to the hospital?' I ask. 'Try and talk your way in?'

The question is superfluous. H stares at me for a long moment and I can tell by the way he rubs his eyes that the afternoon around Cynthia's table has left him well and truly beached.

'God, no,' he says at last. 'Anywhere but that fucking tomb.'

We spend the evening in the apartment Tony Morse has volunteered. It's at the top of a property that overlooks Southsea Common, and the views from the third floor are sensational. The Common itself, green after recent rain, stretches away to the distant seafront. Nearer, on the left, I can see tennis courts. To the right, more distant, the Hovercraft departure terminus for the low grey swell of the Isle of Wight. This stretch of the Solent, H tells me, is prime viewing for big-ship nerds. Two generations ago you would have caught the giant Cunarders, the *Queen Elizabeth* and the *Queen Mary*, heading up towards Southampton. Tonight we have to make do with a huge container ship the size of umpteen city blocks.

The view is a godsend because the rest of the apartment, in H's phrase, is a dump. It smells of decay, of dodgy drains, of surrender to old age and maybe infirmity. The paintwork is shabby, the taps in the kitchen leak, there's a steady draught through most of the windows, and if you ever thought anaglypta wallpaper was a distant memory, you'd be wrong. There's a damp problem in the tiny bathroom and when I inspect the contents of the bucket beside the sink I find a balled prescription for, among other things, warfarin. This, I happen to know, is a blood thinner routinely prescribed after minor strokes, and this begins to suggest a picture of who might have been living here.

Another clue, more graphic, is the part-completed jigsaw we find on the threadbare carpet in the living room. The accompanying box is still brimming with spare pieces, but there's enough on the floor to suggest some kind of battle at sea.

'Trafalgar,' H grunts, turning away, and when I finally find the lid of the box, I see he was right. Admiral Nelson's flagship laid up against the French fleet. Our diminutive hero directing events from the quarterdeck with nerveless aplomb.

H and I do our best to settle in. H insists I take the bigger of the two bedrooms, while he'll doss down next door. I dump my bag on the rumpled counterpane and pull the curtains back. An inspection reveals that the big freestanding wardrobe is empty, save for the lingering scent of mothballs. Ditto the chest of drawers. It's at this point that I conclude we may be spending the night with a ghost. Warfarin probably wasn't enough. Whoever lived here, whoever began to piece together those bloody hours off Cape Trafalgar, is probably dead and gone.

Either way, I tell myself I'm only here for a single night. I can hear H in the bedroom next door. He's on the phone to a long list of local names, telling them about Fat Dave, and so I return to the living room at the front of the apartment, stepping carefully around the bones of the jigsaw, the abandoned homage to blood and treasure, knowing I have a couple of calls of my own to make.

The first goes to Malo. After I've closed the door, I tell him about our visit to Cynthia.

'Your dad's definitely in a state,' I whisper. 'It's worse than I thought.' From the sound of his voice, I can tell that Malo is disturbed. Once again, he offers to come down.

'Don't,' I tell him. 'They've sealed the borders. Police every-where. On-the-spot fines. Heavy jail sentences. Transportation, if you're lucky. You heard it here first.'

'But what about you, Mum? You're supposed to be in London.'

'I'm back tomorrow.'

'How?'

'God knows. I'll phone you if I make it.'

'And Dad?'

'I'm guessing he'll stay.'

'All by himself?'

'In this city? I doubt it.'

We part as friends. He tells me to take care and says that Richmond Park has never been so empty. My son, bless him, is back in training for his first triathlon after a succession of injuries, and now runs most nights.

'And Clemmie?'

'She comes with me.'

'Good. Keep it that way, eh?'

My other call goes to Tim. I've no idea where he lives in this place, but that turns out to be irrelevant.

'I've self-evacuated,' he says at once. 'Think the Blitz. Think

1940. I've got a label round my neck and a packet of sandwiches but they can't spell my name right.'

'As in . . .?'

'Tom. Funny thing is, I quite like it. Nice period touch. Young Thomas setting out on his big adventure.'

'This has to be a joke.'

'No way. Have you ever been out in the country? Free-range chickens at the bottom of the garden? Fresh-baked bread every morning? Home-smoked bacon? I thought Waitrose had it nailed, and you know what?'

'You're wrong.'

'Yeah. Again.'

'So, where are you?'

'Bere Regis.'

'Where's that?'

'Dorset. Ask that hooligan mate of yours. He might know.'

'I doubt it. You're there for the duration?'

'Yeah. God willing.'

'Relatives?'

'My mum. Are we getting the picture here? I'm doing it for her sake, of course. I just have to find room for all this tucker before I explode.'

Tucker. When I finish talking to Tim, I start wondering about something to eat. The fridge in the kitchen is turned off and empty. The old-style pantry offers nothing more than a little scrap of discarded muslin, the dried corpse of a sizeable bee, a packet of pasta, and a box of Oxo cubes. I look in on H but he's still deep in conversation. When I do the knife and fork mime and tap my watch, he simply nods. *Your call.* I retreat to the living room to scroll through the take-out offers on my phone and settle for an Indian restaurant that seems to be round the corner. The food is with us within half an hour, the bagged cartons left outside the front door, my card swiped at arm's length.

H is still on the phone. The gas stove turns out to be working and I manage to light the oven to keep the food warm. Back in the living room, waiting for H, I browse the books on the many shelves. The shelves themselves are DIY, poorly done. I doubt they were ever troubled by a spirit level, but the harder I look, the less that matters.

Books appeal to the detective in me because they can tell you everything you need to know about the reader, and the more attention I pay to the choice on offer, the more intrigued I become. Five Joseph Conrad novels, including *Nostromo* and *Typhoon*. The near-complete works of Patrick O'Brien. Several wartime biographies from warrior scribes on the Atlantic and Russian convoys. A rich selection of reads on the Nelsonian Navy. Books like these connect directly with the jigsaw at my feet but even more intriguing are the contents of the shelves below, most of which address crime and punishment. Famous murder trials. Legendary miscarriages of justice. *Ten Rillington Place* I happen to have read twice, not least because I was in for a part in the BBC radio drama adaptation. A fine book, deeply shocking.

'What am I smelling?' H is at the door, just off the phone. I've ordered his trusty favourites, which appear to pass muster. He has a selection of lagers in his suitcase, plucked from the fridge at Flixcombe Manor. Chicken jalfrezi with all the trimmings, plus a can or two of warm Stella, isn't a combination I'd normally go for, but under these circumstances it feels curiously apt. Tim had it right. We're all living through the Blitz again.

We eat in near silence. H is preoccupied, remote, distant, and when I ask who he'd talked to he tosses me the bones of the conversations. Wesley Kane, his one-time enforcer, is pissed off. He's watched *Goodfellas* twice in twenty-four hours and doesn't know where to turn next. Mick Pain, another stalwart back in the day, has developed Type 2 diabetes. While Gloria, an enormous Jamaican who once serviced Fat Dave in a private suite in a seafront hotel, has moved to London. In short, the passage of the years, and now the virus, are moving the Pompey story on.

'Had to happen.' H forks another cube of chicken. 'Stay put in this life and you're half fucking dead already.'

What I really want to talk about is H himself – what's gone wrong, how he's coping, and just how difficult this situation of his could get – but the last thing I want to do is betray any of my son's confidences. And so I start at the other end, with Malo.

'So what do you make of him these days? Our boy?'

'He's fine,' H grunts. 'Shaping up nicely.'

'What does that mean?'

'I had my doubts about all the Doomsday crap but hey . . .' He looks around and spreads his hands wide. 'Turns out that mate of his was right.'

Malo's mate is Sylvester Penny, the only son of our sometime ambassador in Berlin. The moment I first met him, the physical likeness to my son was uncanny – the fashionable gypsy tangle of black curls, the hint of predatory glee in his smile, his easy charm, and the sheer tightness of his focus when something interesting pops up on his radar screen. Sylvester's big idea throws the mega-rich a lifeline in the face of numberless catastrophes – anything from nuclear war to, God help us, global pandemics – and just now his superyacht packages offering sanctuary at the ends of the earth are heavily over-subscribed. Malo, through his own efforts, has become part of this adventure, winning his father's guarded approval.

'He told you about the Audi?' he asks.

'No.'

'Gone. Binned. Sold on.'

'And now?'

'He's driving a series-seven Beamer. How many twenty-one-year-olds spend that kind of money to look like a middle-aged twat?'

The Audi was a present from H after we all returned semi-intact from the D-Day beaches. Malo selling it, I'm guessing, has hurt.

'He's still running,' I point out. 'He's off the booze. He and Clemmie seem pretty tight. He's making a name for himself, thanks to Sylvester. Do I hear a round of applause?'

'No fucking way.' H isn't having it. 'That boy thinks he knows every trick in the fucking book. Fact is he doesn't, and won't for a good while, but when did he ever listen to me?'

'He loves you. To bits. Doesn't that matter?'

H has always been uncomfortable with the word 'love', but I'm sensing, once again, that something has changed.

H takes a final swipe of sauce with what's left of his chapati and then pushes the plate to one side. Only then does he look up.

'He *loves* me? He said that?' He very badly wants me to nod.
'Yes,' I say. 'He did.'

THREE

I leave Southsea next morning. H has already put a call through
to Cynthia, making sure she's OK. Dave, it seems, has had a
very difficult night and just now Cynthia wants to get her
head down before she braces herself for another call to the ICU.

'I'll go round later,' H says. 'Maybe this afternoon. Check out
exactly what she needs.'

I'm about to suggest she might want to be left alone but there's
something in H's face that tells me it would be pointless. Fat
Dave is dying and, for whatever reason, H needs to be part of
that.

'You're off then?' he grunts. We're standing on the pavement
beside my little Peugeot. In daylight, I notice for the first time
that one of the ground-floor flats is available for rent.

'Yes.' I turn back to H. 'Call me if you need me.'

'You'll be back? For the funeral?'

I nod, letting that single word, so final, settle between us.

'Of course I will,' I say brightly. 'Provided they don't arrest me.'

This isn't as fanciful as it might sound. All morning, first on my
smart phone and later on the ancient TV that belongs to the flat,
I've been following the news. Lockdown is what it says on the
tin. Every inch of the country I've always taken for granted –
Holland Park, rural Dorset, and now Portsmouth – has become
a giant set in some disaster movie: abandoned, empty, eerily
quiet.

Upstairs in the flat, I've spent nearly an hour plotting a route
north that should keep me out of trouble. This will involve a
series of detours through the leafy shires from village to village.
Given the time of year, mid-spring, I'm hoping for fields of
skipping lambs and roadside trees heavy with blossom, and as I
leave the low, grey clutter of Pompey, I realize I'm in some

danger of enjoying the journey to come. It does me no credit to admit it, but I'm glad to be out of that hideous flat, itself a kind of tomb. The virus has already cast a long shadow and last night in bed, alert for every sound, I felt I could almost touch the darkness.

By mid-morning, much happier, I've left the South Downs behind me and I'm desperate for a coffee. I know it might sound improbable but alone in the car my thoughts have strayed to my mum in Brittany. She was born in 1940, the year the Germans helped themselves to half of France. Back then, she and her family lived in Paris and, with the Germans at their heels, she and most of the rest of the city fled south. My mum was a babe in arms at the time and therefore oblivious but later, after the war, she listened to story after story about those sweltering June days, and much of this she passed on to little me.

I was in my teens by the time I mustered the patience and the interest to listen properly and what struck me then, as it strikes me now, was the sheer speed with which things can change. Only two days ago, the shuttered wayside cafes would have been open. I could have sat down with a big fat cappuccino with spoonable sprinkles on top, and maybe even a croissant or two. But now, locked down, there's nothing. How long will this coffee-less purdah last? Will I ever hear that gorgeous, anticipatory hiss of steam foaming the jug of cold milk again?

Idling in the middle of the latest village, waiting for the postman to cross the road, I think of my *grandmère* once more. Given the circumstances – milling hordes of refugees, broken-down cars, wailing kids – she would have killed for this solitude, this peace, this blissful absence of other people. But the shock of her own vulnerability she would have recognized only too well. The virus, thank God, isn't delivered by squadrons of wailing Stukas, but its sheer invisibility – death by stealth, death thanks to someone else's sneeze, death after days and nights of slowly drowning in your own secretions – is in some respects more terrifying. Boris Johnson is doubtless doing his best to play Churchill in this crisis but it's beginning to dawn on me that this virus, Dave's virus, has no respect for bombast and fancy rhetoric.

Deep in my reverie, the lone driver in an otherwise empty

village, the knock on my window comes as a surprise. The face staring down at me is oldish, female, and darkened by something I can only describe as rage. She's wearing a slash of lipstick, the brightest red, and one thin hand is trying to steady her hat in the lively wind.

The moment I lower the window, she steps back and turns slightly away. This village isn't big. I'm definitely an intruder and it's probably wise not to inquire about the off-chance of a coffee.

'Well?' she says.

'Well what?'

'Some kind of explanation? Don't you think that's the least you owe us?'

'An explanation for what?'

'For being here. When you shouldn't. Don't you listen to the wireless? To the television? Haven't you read the papers? Or don't these rules apply to you, young lady?'

Young lady? This conversation, I think, at last shows signs of promise. Wrong. My new friend wants to know where I'm going, where I've come from.

'I'm going home,' I tell her. 'To lock myself down.'

'And you've been where?'

'Portsmouth.'

'*Portsmouth?*' She's looking at me full-face now, horrified, and for a moment I'm anticipating a citizen's arrest. On the other side of the street, I'm aware of faces at windows, phones pressed to cars. Then a front door opens and a stout figure in tweeds and a Barbour jacket appears.

'Everything in order, Margery? Need a hand there?'

Margery, I suspect, would dearly love to take me into custody but dare not risk bodily contact. To spare us both any further angst, I shoot her a bright smile, engage first gear, and floor the accelerator. Two and a half hours later, mercifully intact, I'm back in Holland Park.

On the journey north, I've deliberately resisted checking my phone. Now, stepping into my own apartment, I note the texts awaiting my attention. The one at the head of the queue is from H. 'Phone me,' he's written. Nothing else. Just that. 'Phone me.'

I gaze at it a moment, and then cross the lounge to the window. From up here on the fourth floor, I can see that the car park is full, everyone tucked up for the duration. For a moment, I'm back in the borrowed flat in Southsea. Who did it belong to? Were they a couple? Had one of them died? And if someone was living there alone, was it a man? Or a woman? Given the evidence, I strongly suspect the former. No woman I've ever met would spend countless hours reconstructing the battle of Trafalgar. Neither would she let the place get into such a state.

Scrolling through the rest of my emails, I make a mental note to phone Tony Morse and find out. Tony has always been H's go-to lawyer in Pompey and over the years, when I've found myself in trouble, he's been a priceless source of both comfort and advice. He's also become a very good friend. With his easy charm and beguiling vanities, he represents yet another side of Pompey, and more to the point he's never let me down.

Tony, I think. But not quite yet. I bend to my phone again, dialling Malo's number, and the moment he answers I sense at once what's happened.

'Your dad's been in touch?'

'Yeah. First thing.'

'About Dave?'

'Yeah.'

'And?'

'He died, Mum. Early this morning, Dad says. He told me about the place he's found, the flat where you stayed last night. He's given me the address. I'm going down there tonight.'

'Why?'

'Because.'

'Because what?'

'Because he obviously can't cope. He says he can. He thinks he can. But he can't. End of story, Mum. I'm packing as we speak.'

'What about Clemmie?'

'She's staying up here. She's worried about her own folks. Her father's older than I first thought.'

'So, shouldn't you be with her? Moral support?'

'Of course I should, but Dad comes first.' He pauses for a moment, then he's back. 'Dad says you'll be down for the funeral.'

'He's right. But I don't suppose they've fixed a date yet.'

'Yeah, sure.' Another pause. 'How about tomorrow? All three of us?'

'*Tomorrow*?'

To be honest, I'm gobsmacked. H used to be a demigod to Malo. When they first met, first got to know each other, he worshipped the man who'd so suddenly turned out to be his natural father. Later that sense of awe morphed into something much closer to love, which is altogether healthier, but I'm struggling to remember a time when circumstances threw just the three of us together. Until now.

'Tomorrow?' I repeat. 'Are you serious?'

'Yes.'

'Why? Am I allowed to ask?'

'Because we should. Because we must. Because we owe it to each other.'

Each other. Such a simple proposition, I think. The retired drug-dealer, the ageing thesp, and their wayward love child all cornered by tiny fragments of RNA calling themselves Covid-19.

'Well, Mum?' Malo is getting impatient. I frown. I gaze out of the window. Then I stare at the phone. Why on earth not?

'You're on,' I say.

'Tonight?'

'Maybe tomorrow. Probably the day after.'

'How come?'

'Stuff to do, Malo. You haven't seen the state of the place. Take a sleeping bag, by the way. And whatever food you can rustle up. Oh . . . and maybe a pack of cards.'

'Booze?'

'I thought you'd given up.'

'I have. I'm thinking of you. And Dad.'

'Sweet.' I'm smiling now. 'That Italian white you know I like. Greco di Tufo? And maybe a bottle or two of Talisker. H lives on the stuff. Maybe some Rioja, as well. Are you writing all this down?'

'I am, Mum. Tomorrow would be favourite.'

'This is some kind of negotiation?'

'Of course it is.' He has the grace to laugh. 'Me and Dad banged up together? You know how moody he can get.'

He rings off after I blow him a kiss down the phone. Another first, I think, the sound of his laughter still ringing in my ear.

H, when I finally make the call, is blunt, almost aggressive. He wants to know what kept me.

'I've been on a mission.' I tell him about the scary natives in the middle of nowhere but it's like talking to a deaf man.

'Dave's gone,' he grunts.

'I know. Malo told me. And Cynthia?'

'All over the fucking place. They phoned her first thing from the ICU. You could tell yesterday she was expecting it. Poor fucker.'

'Cynthia?' I'm shocked.

'Dave. You wouldn't wish an end like that on anyone. I told Cynth he probably slipped away. I told her it was in his nature, ducking and diving all his life. Probably for the best, I said. You could see how much he was hurting in that vid.'

'And?'

'She's a tough woman. Didn't believe a word I said. Hurting's right. We need to keep an eye on her. Fuck knows what she'll do without him.'

'And now?'

'We bury him, say goodbye.'

'When?'

'Soon.' He pauses. 'Malo's coming down.'

I hang up without saying goodbye, slightly stung by H's brusqueness. Like many men under pressure, he has no time for the smaller courtesies. All that counts is the matter in hand. That and the sizeable hole Fat Dave has left behind.

By now it's early evening and I have just one last call to make. I find a bottle and pour myself a large glass of Chilean Merlot. Tony Morse answers on the second ring.

'My darling,' he murmurs. 'All well?'

'Still standing. You?'

'Third glass, alas, but nothing in the in-tray for weeks to come, thank Christ.'

We swap notes about the craziness of the times before I thank him for the loan of the flat.

'You've been down?' He seems astonished.

'Flying visit. Life's a learning curve. If you're driving, it's probably best to travel at night. Next time I'll need to remember that.'

'You're coming *back*?'

'I am.'

I bring him up to date about poor Dave Munroe and he asks me to pass his sympathies on to Cynthia. Portsmouth, in so many respects, seems to be a village and for all his villainy, Dave has won himself many admirers.

Tony wants to know more about Dave – what happened, how bad – but I quickly bring the conversation back to the flat.

'Who did it belong to? Do you mind me asking?'

'A relative.'

'He? She?'

'Both. Husband and wife until everything went wrong.'

'One of them died?'

'Something like that.'

'And now he's gone, too?'

'Couple of months ago. Massive stroke. Out like a light.'

'And someone cleared the flat?'

'I did.' He breaks off for a moment and I hear the gurgle of wine into his glass. Then he's back, as charming and playful as ever. 'I'm afraid I drew the line at the jigsaw. As you doubtless discovered.'

'No more clues?'

'It's the Battle of Trafalgar. Nelson's the little bloke with the dodgy arm.'

'I meant the flat. Who owned it? Who lived there?'

'Ah . . .' The softest chuckle. 'Maybe another day, eh? After all this nonsense is over.'

I wonder for a moment whether to press him but decide not to. Instead I ask whether he'd mind me cheering the place up.

'As in?'

'No offence, Tony, but giving it a bit of a clean? Maybe a lick of paint?'

'Do your worst, my darling.' That chuckle again. 'Break a leg, eh?'

FOUR

That same evening, I treat myself to a mental tour of the Southsea flat, room by room, making a note of what needs to be done if the three of us are to spend any time there. Top of my list is cleaning stuff: bleach, scourers, more bleach, kitchen and bathroom sprays, and something to make the place smell nice afterwards. Removing years of accumulated neglect from a stranger's final resting place was never on my agenda, but neither was the sudden arrival of the virus. In any event, whatever difference I make can't fail to help Tony Morse when he – or maybe someone else – comes to sell.

Next day, armed with my list, I join the queue at a hardware store in the back streets of Notting Hill. Everyone else in West London seems to have DIY in mind and after nearly forty minutes in the thin drizzle I finally make it inside. The business belongs to a cheerful Jamaican who must be in his eighties by now, though he never shows his age. His real name is also a mystery, so everyone I know calls him Benjy. He sorts me tins of undercoat and gloss for the woodwork, plus a big tin of emulsion for that hideous wallpaper and maybe the ceilings, plus all the other bits and pieces like sandpaper and filler. When it comes to colour, I settle for a softish white, mainly to make the most of all the sunshine that will hopefully flood in through the big front windows. Benjy, who loves a natter, is curious to know more about this project of mine, and when I tell him that it's time to give my tired apartment a spring-clean, he knows I'm lying.

'Bless you, Mrs A.' His big hand descends briefly on mine. 'Must be tough in showbusiness these days. One door shuts, eh . . .?'

The prospect of becoming a full-time painter and decorator accompanies me around the local Sainsbury's. These days I know I can rely on Malo when he makes a promise, but I happily load my trolley with a bountiful selection of wines, two bottles of Bombay Sapphire, ditto tonic water, plus a slab of Stella in case the water fails and I'm obliged to start cooking everything in Belgian lager. As well as the booze, I stock up on staples from the fast-emptying shelves: tea bags, long-life milk, tins of everything from tuna to chickpeas, plus dried herbs, stock cubes, rice, pasta, salt, black pepper . . . anything – in short – that might brighten the lockdown days and nights to come. The only disappointment is freshly ground coffee, which has run out, but I try and make up with a wildly indulgent buy I spot on the way to the checkout. I've no idea what either H or Malo will make of Palestinian freekeh, but I'll happily eat theirs if they prefer to stick to spaghetti.

Back at my apartment block, I leave the food and drink in the car, together with the paint, and head upstairs with an armful of cardboard boxes. Rosa, my tireless agent, has emailed me first thing and attached a rough-cut from last month's shoot in Paris. This is a pilot we're making for a cop series called *Dimanche*, or *Sunday*.

The script tracks a high-profile investigation triggered by a series of spectacular killings, all of which happen – you've guessed it – on the sabbath. The first of the bodies turns up without a head. The next has lost both arms, neatly severed below the shoulder. The most recent, recovered from a canal in the tenth *arrondissement*, has been disembowelled. All the victims to date have been male, young middle-aged, white, and uniformly successful. These are the Fifth Republic's dream offspring, proof of French enterprise and French virility, and logic would suggest that the killer is heading anatomically south. The next victim, at the end of a month of investigative blanks, is clearly facing castration and the executive producers are gleeful about the audience figures likely to show up for the fourth episode, should a series be commissioned.

I play a forty-something *Commissaire* called Danielle Colbert, which appears to be important in terms of the viewership. The screenwriter, also a woman, is anticipating a flood of female viewers, especially for episode four, and it therefore makes good commercial sense to put yours truly in charge of the *Brigade criminelle*. It's a brilliant part, beautifully written, and I've worked with the director before.

Nudging fifty, he's even older than me and we share the same sense of humour. His name is Remy. He's a big man in every sense: bearded, scruffy, raw-boned. He wouldn't look out of place on the yardarm of a nineteenth-century tea clipper, which is fitting because he has a sizeable yacht of his own, but the truly wonderful thing about him is the fact that I've never once heard him raise his voice. On set, he has a quiet authority that shows in the rushes, but away from the studio he has a real eye for the bizarre, the absurd, and the grotesque. He happened to be in the Bataclan theatre the night ninety Parisians died in 2015, and the image that never leaves him is the moment one of the killers leaned over a dying man and – with a hint of irritation – put two more bullets in his head.

'He had the other hand in his pocket,' Remy told me. 'He looked like he was performing a chore. He looked bored. Cool or crazy? Your call.'

I have the evening to kill before I set out for Portsmouth again, and I settle down to watch the rough cut. This will give the commissioning editor at France 2 all the clues he'll need to make a decision about the whole series, and within minutes I know I'll be spending a great deal of time in Paris, once we step back into normal life. So clever, I think. So seemingly effortless. Dialogue to die for. Surprises sprung when you least expect them.

By the time I get to the end of the pilot, it's been dark for a couple of hours. I phone Rosa. Like me, she's excited by what she's seen.

'You were *fabuleuse*, my precious. They were lucky to have you.'

'Nonsense. I'm in the best hands, and it shows. How come the French make all the best cop series?'

Rosa laughs. Good question. Then she wants to know what I'll be doing with the empty days and weeks to come, and when I tell her about Fat Dave and the flat down in Southsea, she has trouble believing me.

'Thank God you're back in one piece,' she says. 'Got enough to read?'

'Sadly not. I'm going back for the funeral.'

'When?'

'Tonight.'

'But that's illegal.'

'I know. Think enemy territory. All the best things in life happen after dark.'

It's gone midnight before I'm ready to go. I arrange the cardboard boxes I filched from Sainsbury's and fill them with my favourite pots and pans, a range of spices and pickles, some nice plates, decent towels, freshly laundered sheets, and my favourite pillow. Carrying all this stuff down to the car feels, already, like a criminal act, a harried Londoner on the run from some nameless catastrophe, except that this interpretation is the exact opposite of the truth. Up here in W4, I'm safe. In Pompey, I suspect it might be wise to take nothing for granted. Even this, it will turn out, is a hopeless understatement, but in my defence I've no idea what awaits us all in the days and weeks to come. Otherwise, no kidding, I'd have stayed in my apartment, probably in bed.

Two things happen next. The moment I get in my car and pull the door shut, a light goes on in one of the first-floor apartments. Undeterred, I start the engine, triggering another light from the floor above. I stare at it for a long moment, then I realize with total certainty that I'm going to be violently sick. I turn off the engine, kill the lights, grope for the door handle. Mercifully, I'm parked in the far corner of the rectangle of spaces, just metres away from a flower bed. I make it out of the car in time to bend double and vomit on to a stand of late daffs. I've no idea why my body should have ambushed me like this. It's never happened before, so sudden, so violent, so unannounced. At least I'm not on the M25, I think. At least I can make it back to the sanctuary of my precious apartment.

Upstairs, I lock and bolt the door. Against the virus? Against some late pay-back from my brain tumour? Against my vigilante neighbours? God knows. I make myself sick again, and then vomit a third time until my stomach has emptied. At this point, I have no option but to get undressed and slip into bed. Curled in the foetal position, I'm back in the days when a scan had found the tumour but treatment had yet to begin. Then, for day after day, night after night, I'd be on sentry duty, pacing my ruined battlements, checking for new enemies at the gate, and now – years later – I'm doing exactly the same thing.

Do I have a headache? Yes, but the feeling is strange, a burning sensation as if individual hair follicles are on fire all over my scalp. Am I running a temperature? Again, yes, but nothing alarming, nothing that's going to make me sweat and hallucinate all night, just a growl or two of fever, the way you might become aware of an approaching thunderstorm. Might I be sick again? Probably not, but my bowels are heaving and within a couple of minutes I'm back on the loo, knees clenched, eyes closed, wondering what on earth to tell Malo and H. They're expecting me to turn up tomorrow. No way will I frighten them with symptoms like these. So, if I'm still going to make it down, no matter how delayed, I'll need another excuse.

I try and kid myself to sleep and – amazingly – it works. Hours later I jerk awake to find dawn at the window. My guts are quiet. The nausea has gone. And instead of a prickly mat on top of my head, I have occasional stabs of pain behind my eyes, not thunder this time but lightning. This happened a lot when I was still fighting the tumour, and it makes me a little nervous, but the good news is that – in every other respect – I feel a great deal better.

I drift off back to sleep. Whatever happens, I tell myself, the responsible thing is to put a precautionary call through to the NHS 111 helpline. If they think the virus is trying to befriend me, self-isolation is the only option.

I phone at midday. After a longish wait, the voice at the other end is male, young, and sounds Asian. I give him my name, age and GP details. Then he starts on what is obviously a checklist of questions.

'Do you have a temperature?'

'Last night, yes. Now? No.'

'Was it high last night? Was your chest hot to the touch?'

'No.'

'Do you have any kind of cough?'

'No.'

'Nothing? A dryish cough?'

'No.'

'Shortness of breath?'

'No.'

'Does your chest feel sore?'

'No.'

'You're absolutely certain?'

'Yes.'

'Your sense of taste? Smell?'

'Both perfect.'

'I see.'

Already, to my immense relief, I feel a fraud. I tell him about the sudden attack of D&V and the strange pains in and around my head. He seems to be making notes because I can hear the soft patter of his fingers on the keyboard.

Finally, he asks me whether I have any immediate support.

'If you're asking whether I live alone, then the answer is yes.' As an afterthought, I tell him briefly about my tumour but he doesn't think that's relevant.

'You seem OK,' he says. 'Maybe it's something you ate, a bug you picked up. Stay in bed. Drink lots. Keep your fluids up. Try not to worry. Any further issues with headaches, try codeine, and if that doesn't sort it you can always phone back. Are you working just now? Do you need an isolation note?'

I say no, thank him for his time, and end the call. By now, I've come up with an alibi for the two men in my life. When I get through to Malo and try to explain the crisis with my plumbing, I can tell at once he's not buying it.

'You found *what* this morning?'

'Water all over the bathroom floor.'

'How come?'

'I think a joint may have gone, I can't really tell.'

'Just turn the water off.'

'I don't want to. If I'm to be away for a while, I need it fixed.'

'By who? No one's allowed in your flat any more.'

'I have a tame plumber. Teodor. Polish. Nerves of steel. I know he'll do me the favour.' This, at least, is true.

'Like when?'

'He says he's very busy. It could be tomorrow. Or even the day after.'

'Just leave a key with a neighbour.'

'I can't do that, Malo. These people are already watching me like a hawk. Patience is a virtue. I'll be down just as soon as I can. How's your father?'

'Don't ask.'

'That bad?'

'Worse.' He pauses a moment. 'Just give your Polish guy a ring. He'll tell you how to turn the water off. Promise?'

I stare at the phone. Then, for the first time in my life, I hang up on him.

The rest of that day, and the next, seems dreamlike. No single part of me is physically hurting and I feel that sense of floaty detachment that came with decent weed back in the day. I haven't touched the codeine, nor the Chilean Merlot, just endless cups of turmeric tea. Both days, I spend a great deal of time asleep, in wonderment that I need so much rest, but the moment I surface is the moment I'm on patrol again, looking out for signs of trouble. But nothing, literally nothing, happens.

By Saturday I've swapped the bedroom for the sofa next door in the lounge, and after a brief dalliance with the BBC News channel, I muster the concentration to get stuck into a book. An unfinished re-read of *Testament of Youth* yields gems I hadn't noticed first time round, while a couple of hours with Patrick Leigh Fermor gives me the urge to abandon everything and walk to Istanbul. Then, in no time at all, it's Saturday night and I hear a knock on my door.

It's my new neighbour, a young travel executive called Max who's just moved into Evelyn's old apartment. This is the first time we've met face to face, though naturally we keep our distance. He's a tiny man with a very bright smile and he's holding a bottle of Moët.

'For you.' He offers me the champagne. 'I shouldn't be asking this, Ms Andressen, but are you any better?'

'Better?' My loo adjoins our party wall and it dawns on me that I must have been very noisy the other night. 'Oh, that,' I say lightly. 'It was nothing. Gone. Better, like you say.'

'Great news. I'll tell Jacob. He'll be thrilled. He worries a lot, especially now.'

'Jacob?'

'My partner.'

'Ah . . .' He's still holding the Moët. 'Is that really for me?'

'Sure.'

'You're very generous, Max.' I nod at the bottle. 'But shouldn't the moving-in gifts come from me?'

'*Pas du tout.*' His smile widens even further. 'We both loved you in that Montréal movie. Another time, I guess, for a proper chat.'

With that, he's gone. Slipping back into the apartment, I glance at my watch. Nearly nine o'clock. I feel completely normal – no pain, no symptoms, no trace of any intruder. As a precaution, I check my temperature. It registers a steady 98.4 degrees Fahrenheit. Time to go, I think.

FIVE

It's gone midnight before I make it down to Southsea. I use the A3 again, slipping behind a huge Asda truck to shield me from watching eyes. I hold station like this for the length of the entire journey and mercifully it turns out to be going to Portsmouth.

My sat-nav takes me down to Southsea Common and I find a parking bay almost opposite the block of flats. Up on the third floor, I can see a light behind the mauve curtains. Malo may have been asleep because he takes an age to answer the phone.

'Sorry to wake you up,' I mutter. 'I'm across the road.'

I'm still looking up at the third floor. Within seconds, Malo's slim silhouette is at the window, the phone pressed to his ear.

'There's stuff to bring up,' I tell him. 'Lots of stuff.'

'Tomorrow, Mum. We'll do it tomorrow. I'll come down and let you in.'

'Now,' I say. 'We'll do it now.'

Ten minutes later, all the boxes are piled beside the still-unfinished jigsaw and Malo is back on his PlayStation.

'What's that?' I'm looking at the huge screen he must have brought down from London. A masked figure is abseiling down a rope from the belly of a helicopter before swinging wildly against the sheer glass cliff of a downtown office block. He smashes through the window, boots first, and seizes a startled bank employee before Malo freezes the action.

'GTA,' he says. '*Grand Theft Auto*. This is the fifth edition. You have to watch this, Mum. It's beyond awesome.'

While I've heard of *Grand Theft Auto*, I've only the vaguest notion of what the game's about. American? Definitely. But plot? Narrative? All those bothersome little tricks that keep your bum in the chair and your thumb on the controls?

Malo dismisses my queries with a shrug. The scary intruder, armed to the teeth, is setting about anything with a pulse and my son plunges into a kill-fest, with hapless bank employees exploding in every direction. Multi-tasking comes naturally to Malo's generation, something I've noticed on a number of occasions, and while he turns his attention to the bank's heavily protected vault, he briefs me on the action.

It seems we're dealing here with three characters, Michael, Franklin and Trevor, all of them psychos to various degrees, and all of them wedded to bounty hunting, auto pimping, driving very fast against the traffic flow, and – when needs must – spectacular shoot-ups. One guy begins the game as a retired gangster, another – younger, hungrier – must make his name, while the third has let the product steal his wits.

'Product?'

'Coke, Mum. He's out of his head most of the time. Occupational hazard. Great pictures. Look—'

He's done something clever with the controls and our drug-fiend hero is suddenly astride a jet-ski, heading for a cataract where the river does battle with hundreds of metres of mean-looking rocks. I'm assuming it's Malo on that jet-ski because he's jinking left and right, cheating oblivion by millimetres until he's clear of the rocks and the river tosses him towards a huge raft of logs. The logs block the passage downstream. There's no way out. I close my eyes a moment, anticipating the shock to come, but when I tune in again Malo has somehow jumped the jet-ski on to the raft and appears to be enjoying the scenery.

'That's cheating,' I tell him.

'It's ironic, Mum. You're supposed to love it.'

'But how do you win?'

'You have a target number of points. A million dollars to begin with. If you don't get wasted en route, there are harder missions and bonus multipliers. It'll go on for hours, if you let it.'

'And do you?'

'Not so far. This is the first time I've managed to get it off him.'

'Who?'

'Dad, of course. This is his game, not mine.'

I nod, taking it in. H celebrating late middle age with *Grand Theft Auto*? On the face of it, GTA is a trillion miles from the Battle of Trafalgar, but both are essays in extreme violence so maybe I'm wrong.

'You're telling me that wasn't enough?' I nod down at the jigsaw on the carpet, which appears to be no nearer completion.

'He had a go yesterday.' Malo has abandoned his father's PlayStation. 'Down on his knees with his glasses on. I timed him.'

'And?'

'He was looking for some bloke's right arm. All he could find were bits of sail. After that he was gaming again.'

'He does this stuff all day?'

'No. Most of the time he's in there.' He nods towards the smaller bedroom. 'On the phone.'

'Talking to . . .?'

'I've no idea. I don't know why he bothers. Most of the time it just makes him angry. He always shuts the door but sometimes he just loses it. This morning, he threw a glass at the wall. I'm barefoot most of the time, so I was the one clearing up.'

This is not good news. H has always been volatile, with occasional flashes of temper when he's not in total control, but something has definitely got to him.

'You think it's money?'

'I don't know. I asked him this morning, after I'd sorted the damage, but he gets in one of those moods when he just doesn't hear you.'

'Doesn't listen, you mean.'

'Exactly. We had a pizza at lunchtime and I bought him a bottle of red to go with it. I thought he might have calmed down a bit, but no chance. There's a problem with the funeral, too.'

'Cynthia's got a date?'

'Friday this coming week. Half eleven at the Crem, wherever

that is. Dad seems to think we can arrive mob-handed but you're only allowed ten people, absolute max, and they have to be immediate family. Dad isn't having it. Maybe these are the people he's phoning all the time. He wants to give Dave a proper send-off.'

'And Cynthia? Does she get a say?'

'That's the problem. Dad took me round yesterday. Nice woman. Dad's barging in, taking over, and that's the last thing she needs. I tried to explain afterwards but like I say, he never listens. It's as if Dave was a brother or something, not a fat cop who happened to be bent. Sad, really.'

'For Dave?'

'Dad. If you want the truth, I think it's all slipping away from him. The way I hear it, he used to be king of this city. Now, everybody blanks him.'

I nod. This I understand only too well. Malo holds my gaze for a moment or two and then his hands stray to the PlayStation, and he's back on the river, anticipating the challenge round the next bend. I watch while the story unfolds – more mayhem, more violence – then something very obvious strikes me.

'You said three characters . . .?' Malo nods. He's up in the mountains now, on a switch-back road with a terrifying drop. At the wheel of something red and very noisy, he's just edging a truck into the abyss below. 'So which one does H play?'

'The old retired guy.' He glances up briefly. 'Michael.'

'And?'

'He keeps fucking up. And that doesn't help, either.'

'But that's in character, surely?'

'With Michael, you mean?' The truck has left the road. Then comes a huge explosion and a blossom of flame far below.

'With H,' I murmur.

Malo simply nods, faintly amused, and I spend the next few minutes carrying some of the cardboard boxes into the kitchen. I'm on the point of storing the food in the few cupboards but on closer inspection every shelf needs a proper clean. Tomorrow, I think, leaving the boxes on the floor.

Back in the front room, Malo offers me a high five. He's made it to his first million dollars. Then he gestures towards the darkness beyond the window.

'This city is seriously weird,' he says.

'Weird how?'

'Three o'clock this afternoon, on the dot, everything went crazy. Whistles, church bells, people tooting their horns. You could even hear ships' sirens, I'm guessing from the dockyard. I looked out of the window, and there were people on the Common, not many, but they'd all stopped, just standing there, heads down, hands crossed, you know the look.'

'In mourning, you mean?'

'Exactly.'

'Why?'

'You won't believe this. I went on to Facebook to find out. This is Saturday, right? This is the first game Pompey have missed, and three o'clock would have been kick-off. So the whole city's having a sob? About *football*? I'm amazed they weren't wearing black.'

I shake my head, wondering whether Malo might have invented this for my benefit, then I hear a door opening and seconds later H has stepped into the room. He's wearing a pair of pyjamas that might be silk. They have a subdued leopard print all over them, and he looks terrible. He hasn't shaved for a couple of days and his mussed-up hair, greyer by the day, suggests he's just woken up.

He eyes us warily, offers me what might be a nod of welcome, and then stares at the big TV.

'Is this a private party?' he growls. 'Or can anyone join in?'

This joyless exchange sets the tone for the coming days. Neither Malo nor H enquire about my trauma with the plumbing back at my flat, which suggests that they never believed me in the first place, and this suspicion turns out to be well founded. It's Tuesday, and after a day and a half of non-stop cleaning I've stopped for a rest. Malo, who still runs daily, has taken to picking up a local paper on his way back from his six-kilometre loop around the bottom of Portsea Island, and I'm curled in the corner of the sagging sofa, browsing the latest news.

EasyJet has just announced they'll be cancelling all flights from tomorrow for at least two months, a development that leaves me profoundly depressed. It's not that I've booked a flight. Far from it. It's just the image of all those grounded planes. The

EasyJet livery has always represented something precious to me. Orange was the colour of whim, of an impulse decision to pack a bag and head for some exotic destination. And now even that precious door has closed in my face.

I look up to find H standing over me. He has a glass of something peat-coloured in his hand, probably Talisker.

'Who is he, then?'

'Who's who?'

'The bloke who was more important than us. The bloke you had over the weekend.'

'There was no bloke. You're fantasizing.'

'Bollocks. Just give me credit, eh?'

I abandon the paper. I know I have to draw a line in conversations like these. Thank God Malo's in the bathroom, trying to coax a trickle of lukewarm water from the shower after his run.

'There was no bloke,' I say again. 'And even if there was, so what?'

'So *what*?' H is outraged. Two o'clock in the afternoon is no time to still be in your pyjamas, and I suspect the malt isn't his first of the day.

'Yes.' I'm trying to keep my temper. 'Are you my keeper now? Or have I missed something?'

'Keeper, bollocks. I don't know whether you've noticed, but this is a fucking crisis. Not a crisis, a *war*. That's when families stick together. That's when we look after each other. Fat Dave's gone. I loved that man. I know you weren't here in the day. Neither was the boy, but that's not his fault. We bossed this city. Nothing important ever happened here without our say-so.'

'You mean your say-so?'

'I mean *our* say-so. And that was the point. We were tight. We were blood. Tasty afternoon at Leeds? Getting ambushed by those Millwall low-lifes out the back of Waterloo station? Days like that, and you're brothers under the fucking skin. That's where it all came from, believe it or not. Everything I ever earned. Everything I ever owned. Flixcombe? That wonderful view you love so much? Them Georgian windows? Somewhere the boy can call his own? Blame Pompey.'

I nod, letting the sheer force of his anger curl and break. I've played scenes like this in front of live audiences in countless theatres, sometimes Tennessee Williams, occasionally Edward Albee, and riding a wave this enormous becomes second nature. Taking any kind of stand is hopeless. Instead, like a child in the surf, you duck, succumb, keep your mouth tight shut, and finally come up for air.

H is raving now, tiny bubbles of spit at the corners of his mouth. How flogging happy pills at local raves during the summer of love paved the way to weed, and then cocaine. How he built a Class A supply network that kept everyone guessing between the Dutch Antilles and Schiphol Airport. How an assortment of Pompey mules brought consignment after consignment into the country and fed the city's appetite for the marching powder. And how, when the Major Crimes Team began to wise up, Fat Dave was the blessing from heaven.

'That lovely man saved us. Not once, not twice, but half a dozen times. The Filth can be brighter than you think. They dreamed up a sting or two, got it all nicely plotted out, made the big mistake of thinking they had us, and then Dave would call, always just in time, always with that funny little laugh of his. That meet you've got planned for tonight? Forget it. Think you're talking to a bunch of punters? Or maybe some flash investor down from London? Think again. Go to ground, H. Give it a couple of weeks. They've got fuck-all on you. You heard it first from me, yeah?'

I nod again, say nothing.

'And funny, too.' H has paused for breath. 'That man could put a smile on anyone's face. Even Wesley fucking Kane, and you know how moody *he* can be.' He shakes his head. 'Legend, Dave.'

'And now?'

'Gone.' He's staring down at me. He seems exhausted. 'Can you credit that? All the other wasters in this city, and the fucking virus picks Fat Dave? Is that fair? Is that reasonable? Just give me a clue here.'

I hold his gaze, shake my head. I've heard most of this story before, but never so angry, and never so vehement. H ran with a bunch of Pompey football hooligans while he was still doing his accountancy exams. They called themselves the 6.57 Crew, exporting chaos and mayhem to rival clubs all over the country, and all of them carry the scars of countless terrace battles to this day.

'And now?'

'Now?' H doesn't seem to understand. It's like a foreign word in his mouth. 'Now?'

'Is it different? Have times changed?'

'Times always change. We're older.'

'Wiser.'

'Richer.'

'Are you sure?'

This is a direct challenge, and H knows it.

'You've been talking to the boy,' he says stonily.

'You're right. I'm his mother.'

'What did he say?'

'He's worried about you. Like I am. Worry enough and you want to know what's gone wrong. Doesn't that sound reasonable?'

'Yeah.' He nods. 'Yeah, it does.' He looks down, slightly shame-faced, and swirls the remains of the Talisker in his glass.

'Well? You want to share whatever's gone wrong?'

'No.'

'You're sure? Only it might help.'

He shakes his head, lifts the glass to his lips, swallows the lot. Pride, I think. And maybe fear of letting us get too close.

'I was ill,' I say quietly. 'If you really want to know.'

'Ill?'

'These last few days. That's why I couldn't come down.'

'Why didn't you say?'

'Because there was no need. Sometimes it pays to keep things to yourself.' I look up at him. 'Don't you find that?'

'So what was the matter?' He's looking at me, stone-faced.

'Nothing, really, thank God. I'm over it now.'

'No bloke, then? You're telling me I was wrong?'

'Completely.' I risk a smile. 'Does that make you feel better?'

He gazes down at me for a long moment, and then cracks a rare grin.

'Yeah.' He gestures at the empty glass. 'I think I'll have the other half.'

SIX

That evening, I make an effort with a halal chicken Malo has picked up from the Bengali store round the corner. The flat, to my intense satisfaction, now smells of bleach, spiked with the incense sticks Malo has also acquired, and after we've eaten together around the wonky Formica-topped table in the kitchen, I suggest a hand or two of Gin Rummy. H brightens at the first word, and we start on one of my bottles of Bombay Sapphire. Our little *contretemps* this afternoon seems to have cleared the air, and after Malo wins for the second time, H suggests a walk.

'*All* of us?' Malo sounds alarmed.

'Me and your mum. I owe her a decent conversation.'

This is as close as H ever gets to an apology. A glance through the window confirms a full moon and a cloudless sky and we set out across the Common towards the distant frieze of fairy lights on the seafront. To be honest, I've already lost track of what we can and can't do under lockdown, but H, who's never had much time for the small print, thinks we're OK if we're a couple.

'Man and wife,' he says. 'All you have to do is pretend.'

He sounds almost happy, signs of the old H, and for this I'm very grateful. Even more welcome is his take on the couple of days he's shared *à deux* with Malo. Having a second opinion on what I've so far imagined to be a series of heavy squalls between brief intervals of sunshine is fascinating.

'He's kind, that boy of ours,' he says. 'Christ knows where he picked that up. Must be your fault.'

'You make it sound like some kind of infection.'

'Yeah? Well . . .' He shrugs. 'You speak as you find in this fucking life. I've been a miserable old bastard, I know I have, but he weathered all that grief I've been giving him, took it on the chin. Impressive, says me.'

'You should tell him.'

'Should I?' He sounds genuinely surprised. 'Why?'

'Why not?'

'Might give him ideas.' He stops to take in the silver gleam of moonlight on the sea. 'Keep the buggers on their toes. That's what my dad always said.'

'Even your own son?'

'Especially my own son.'

'And that worked for your dad?'

'Of course it did. I was out of the house as soon as I could walk, our little bit of garden first, then out in the street with my mates, up to all sorts. Gave my mum and dad a bit of peace and quiet, just the way they liked it. Look . . .' He points into the semi-darkness. 'Signs of life.'

We're on the seafront now, and I can hear the lap-lap of the waves on the foreshore below the seawall. According to H, this is where the deep-water channel dog-legs in from the Solent, and I spot something puttering along in the moonlight.

'It's a fishing boat,' H says. 'They'll tie up in the Camber. If we get a move on, we might do a bit of business.'

We hurry towards the dimmed lights of what turns out to be a fun fair, everything shuttered and locked, piles of deckchairs lashed down against the wind, a line of cars on the Cresta Run shrouded in heavy tarpaulins.

'Ghosts.' I shiver. 'Did you ever read Nevil Shute?'

'Never. There's a ghost in that khazi of a flat, by the way. I heard it last night. And the night before.'

This is very good news indeed – not about the ghosts but about H. He's never believed in the netherworld. On the contrary, whenever I've mentioned spiritualism or even the signs of the Zodiac, he just laughed. Paying to get your palm read, he once told me, is the mark of the loser.

'You saw this ghost of yours?' I ask.

'Heard it. It was a wheezing noise. I thought it might have been a kettle at first, Malo making himself a brew, but he told me he heard it too.'

'No sighting?'

'Shit, no. You want a heart attack on your hands? Just say no, even if it isn't true.' He laughs, and we stride on.

The Camber Dock, according to H, is the oldest in Pompey, tucked away behind the curl of shingle the locals call Point. This is Old

Portsmouth, and the moment we round the corner and find the fishing boat nosing slowly towards her berth, I realize I've been here before.

'*Persephone*,' I murmur. 'This is where we all went aboard.'

Persephone was an ancient Brixham trawler we'd hired years ago for the November fundraiser to the D-Day beaches. On the way back, in a rising gale, we hit a half-submerged container and, but for Ventnor beach, barely half a mile away, we would have sunk, but that's another story. Both H and Malo, that night, were nerveless in the face of near-certain disaster, an experience that did much to cement the bond between us.

H remembers, too. 'That journalist,' he grunts. 'Give him credit, he had the bollocks to make the crossing.'

'His name was Mitch, H. Mitch Culligan.'

'Yeah. Waste of fucking time, journalists, but like I say he surprised me that night. I was half-minded to chin him, and he knew that, but he didn't turn a hair.'

We circle the dock. By now, the fishing boat's tied up and H, unannounced, hops on board. A huge figure steps out of the wheelhouse.

'Who the fuck are you? Get off my boat.'

'Bass?' H has produced a ten-pound note. 'Cod? Any fucking thing. As long as it's dead.'

'Of course they're dead.' The two men are face-to-face now, H dwarfed by the skipper's bulk. 'I know you, don't I?'

'Might do.'

'HP? "Saucy" in the day? In the cocaine game? Have I got that right?'

'Might have.'

'I thought you'd passed on?'

'Died, you mean?' A bark of laughter from H. 'I went to fucking Dorset. On wet days it might be the same thing.'

'But you're back now? Is that what you're saying?'

'Just for a bit, yeah. Dave Munroe ring any bells?'

'Fat Dave? Bent cop? Fuck me.' He peels off a rubber glove and nods across the water to a block of new-looking apartments. 'He used to rent a place over there when they first went up. Bought fish every Friday. Lovely man.'

'He's dead. Covid. Last week. Funeral's Friday if you fancy it, up at the Crem. We might raise a can or two afterwards.'

'We?'

'Me and a few mates.'

'And that's why you're back?'

'Yeah. Flying visit. Bass would be favourite.'

'Wrong season, mush. I'll see what I can find.'

We leave minutes later with two sizeable skate in a plastic Co-op bag. To my knowledge, no money has passed hands, something that delights H.

'He remembers you.' I kiss him lightly on the cheek. 'Tell me you're not pleased.'

'Yeah, it's nice.' He grins at me. 'Do it again.'

'No.'

'Why not?'

'You'll only get ideas and that's not what we want.'

'Who says?'

'Me. Look over there. What's that?'

We're standing on top of the big old tower that overlooks the harbour mouth. Upstream lies the naval dockyard and I can see the looming bulk of what looks like a warship moored alongside.

'*Queen Elizabeth the Second.*' H's smile is unforced. 'Our pride and joy.'

'But what is it?'

'An aircraft carrier.'

'New?'

'Very.'

'So why do we need one of those?'

'Fuck knows. I'll bring you back here in daylight, maybe take a ride on the Gosport ferry, then you can see it for real. It's a monster, huge, must have cost a fortune.' There's fondness in H's voice, as well as pride, and when I think about it later I realize why. The 6.57 Crew were in the business of exporting serious violence. Ditto this glorious new addition to our Navy.

'It's a date,' I tell him.

'What is?'

'The Gosport ferry. Your treat, not mine.'

'Tomorrow, then?'

'Tomorrow's perfect.'

We link arms and feel our way down the stone steps and back to the street below. H is talking about his dad again. He says he set off on his bike every morning and spent his working life as a Writer in the dockyard. H inherited his desk, a wonderful piece of furniture with an ink-stained leather top in the deepest shade of green, and he has it carefully positioned in front of the view in the first-floor sitting room at Flixcombe which he uses as an office.

When I mention the desk, he laughs. 'Me and a mate lifted it from the dockyard the day Dad retired. We stuck it in the back of a white van and drove it out through the Unicorn Gate before we delivered it home for him. The bosses in the dockyard thought the world of him the whole time he was there, and they never came looking.' He falls silent for a moment, staring into nowhere.

To the best of my knowledge, both H's parents are still alive. They live somewhere in the north of the city but since I've known him he's never made the effort to drive down and see them.

'Maybe a visit?' I suggest. 'Just a wave through the front window? Just to check they're OK?'

'When?'

'Tomorrow? After the ride on the ferry?'

'Christ, no.' He shakes his head and turns away. 'You have to be joking.'

SEVEN

The ride on the ferry never happens, just one of a number of developments that tightens the virus's grip on all our lives. The following day I get up late after the disappointment of neither hearing nor seeing the ghost. There's no sign of H, but Malo is struggling out of his sleeping bag in the front room, peering at his phone. He forgot to bring an airbed and is making do with a line of saggy cushions from the sofa. He hasn't complained so far but judging by the scowl on his face, it's been a rough night.

'Shit.' He's still looking at his phone.

'What's happened?'

He says nothing, just hands me the mobile. The text is from Clemmie. *Mateo is in hospital. Maybe Covid. Nobody knows. Horrible. I'm at Mum's xxxx.*

I look up. Mateo is Clemmie's father, a Columbian businessman, fabulously rich and seriously charming. Lately, Clemmie has taken to calling him by his Christian name, rather than Papa, which feels like some rite of passage but probably isn't.

'He's older than you think, Mum. And Clem doesn't scare easily.' Malo's already scrolling through his directory, and I beat a tactful retreat the moment he gets through to Clemmie. By the time I've done last night's washing-up, and checked the skate in the fridge, the conversation is over.

Malo has joined me in the kitchen. He wants a coffee.

'Well?' I don't move.

'Clem says he's been ill for a couple of days and now he's in the Royal Free. Her mum's going crazy. She's sure he's going to die.'

'You must go up there. You have to. Moral support. Never fails.'

'Really?' Malo rolls his eyes, far from convinced. 'She's a drama queen, Mum, you know she is.'

'It's not her you should be worrying about. It's Clemmie.'

'But Clem's the only one who knows how to cope with her. And she says they're better off alone. I offered, but she doesn't want me there.'

'You made that up.'

'No, I didn't. She says having me around would be too complicated. One man in their lives is quite enough, she told me. Not that they can get in to see him.'

I nod and put the kettle on. My son, bless him, knows a great deal about the minefield of family dynamics. First Berndt. Then H. Now Mateo and his needy wife. Tread very carefully if you want to survive intact.

'Maybe a flying visit? Up and back on the train? Just to show willing?'

'No way.'

'Why not?'

'They're probably carrying the virus, too. You want me bringing all that back with me? No.' He shakes his head. 'Skip the coffee. I'm out for a run.'

He returns to his nest in the front room and by the time I've had my all-over wash, he's disappeared. I stand at the window, thinking I might catch a glimpse of him, but the Common is empty apart from two men, socially distanced from everything except their respective dogs.

The news about Mateo is deeply sobering. Fat Dave, I keep telling myself, had it coming. Abuse yourself for years on end, struggle to get by without a wheelchair, and your immune system would be hoisting the white flag within seconds of the virus knocking on your door. No wonder he ended up in ICU, and even then, there was little they could do.

Mateo, though, is different. I'm still clueless about his real age but he had a gym membership he used at least three times a week, he watched what he ate and drank, and he could still take a flight of stairs at a stylish gallop. When I was young, I once had a crush on an actor called Hurd Hatfield, who played Dorian Gray in the 1945 movie adaptation. Eternal youth is a fantasy that has stayed with me ever since, and Mateo – until just now – came very close to the lissome Mr Hatfield. If the virus can steal a man like that, what chance for the rest of us?

This is a question I don't want to answer, and the moment I turn away from the window is the moment I'm desperate for a distraction, anything to keep me from thinking too hard, and the solution, I realize, is staring me in the face. In the pungent chaos of the front room – abandoned sleeping bag, clothes strewn everywhere, empty tubes of Pringles, discarded copies of the *Portsmouth News*, plus a glimpse of the part-completed Battle of Trafalgar – it's easy to dismiss the neat line of tins I so care-fully stored in the corner, undercoat, gloss, emulsion, a line of soldiers reporting for duty. Now, I think. Now is the time to get stuck in. After the bleach, the full make-over.

Really?

I'm staring at the wallpaper. Anaglypta has always reminded me of a medical condition, interior décor disfigured by some hideous skin disease, but age and neglect make it far, far worse.

Once it must have been a brownish colour all over, hardly the best start in life, but years of sunshine through the window has bleached whole areas to give it a frankly albino feel. On top of this, it's beginning to curl at the edges and strips of the discoloured plaster underneath are appearing between the seams. To do a proper job, I need to take the whole lot off and I'm not at all sure I have the energy and the stamina to see it through. Might Malo give me a hand? I doubt it. Might H? Definitely not.

I'm rescued by a call on my mobile. It turns out to be Cynthia. I gave her my number when we paid her a visit and told her to phone any time she needed help. Now, she wants to know whether H is within hearing distance.

'No,' I tell her. 'He's still in bed.'

She says she'd like a word.

'With H?'

'No, my dear. With you. Face-to-face, I'm afraid, and I'd be grateful if H didn't know. Might that be possible?'

I tell her I can see no reason why not. When?

'This morning? Whenever you can make it.' She starts to give me her address, but I tell her I've got it stored in my sat-nav.

'Within the next hour?' I say. 'Would that be any good?'

'Perfect. I'll rustle up some coffee.'

A little guilty now, I pocket my mobile and knock softly on H's bedroom door. This is a much smaller room than mine, bare except for the single bed and a bentwood chair, and discarded bits of clothing lap the open suitcase on the floor. There's a funny smell, too, earthy, far from pleasant.

'H? Are you awake?'

The shape beneath the counterpane stirs, and a face appears. He looks terrible.

'Are you OK?'

'No. Fucking headache. Had it most of the night.'

'Have you taken anything?'

'Nothing to take.'

I nod, stepping into the room and bending over the bed.

'Do you mind?' I put my hand on his forehead. He feels sweaty, hot. 'You're running a temperature. I'll get some ibuprofen or Panadol. Whatever I can find. It may take a while because this stuff is running out. You want something to drink?'

H is staring up at me. His eyes look slightly wild in the pallor of his face. He nods, says nothing.

'Tea? Water?'

'Whatever.'

I pour him a glass of water in the kitchen and pile in the ice cubes. In truth I have plenty of medication with me, but I need an excuse to see Cynthia.

Back with H, I give him the water and tell him to try and get a bit more sleep. He seems to take it in but there's obviously something else on his mind.

He empties half the glass and hooks out an ice cube to suck. Then he mumbles something I don't quite catch.

'But what about the ferry?' he says again. 'Our date?'

'Tomorrow, H.' I haul him upright to plump the pillows and then rearrange the counterpane to make him more comfortable. His whole body is shaking. Fever, I think, stepping back towards the door. 'Back soon. Behave yourself, yeah?'

Propped against the pillow, he does his best to muster a smile.

'If only,' he says.

I'm with Cynthia barely ten minutes later. Lockdown has done us a number of favours and one of them is the almost complete absence of traffic. Cynthia's coffee, unlike the instant we're obliged to drink, smells wonderful, and I'm still eyeballing the David Bowie print over her mantelpiece when she joins me in the living room.

'I hope you didn't mind me calling,' she says. 'This probably breaks every rule in the book.'

'Not at all. Happy to help.'

Cynthia eyes me a moment, wanting to believe it, and then apologizes again, this time for the need to be blunt.

'It's about H,' she says, 'as you may have gathered.'

'Dave's funeral?'

'Of course. To tell you the truth, H has rather taken over. I'm sure he has the best of intentions, in fact I know he does. Dave thought the world of him and if he was sitting here now, he'd say I'm being a selfish old cow.'

'But . . .?'

'But it's difficult. Dave would probably tell you different, but the fact is that he'd left all the Pompey nonsense behind him. He never did all that stuff with the 6.57 Crew. He was a copper, not a hooligan, and he was a good copper, effective, clever, and you know why? Because he thought the way criminals thought. He understood their mind-set, knew how to make friends with them. He used to tell me about interview sessions in the old days, just him and some scamp across the table. He knew exactly which strings to pull, that was the phrase he used, strings to pull. Treat them right, he'd say, give them a bit of space, show an interest, make them laugh, and they'd be like putty in his hands.'

I nod. It's impossible not to wonder whether Cynthia has been rehearsing this little speech. Either way, I want to know more.

'And then?'

'And then they'd tell him everything, probably without realizing exactly what they were saying. Dave used to call it a cough. I think he meant confession.'

I tell her I understand. The last couple of years, I've been in these situations myself, on the wrong side of the table, facing seasoned detectives and their clever little traps. Thanks to Tony Morse at my elbow, and liberal use of the phrase 'No comment', I avoided giving myself away, but up against someone with Dave's talents – another league entirely – that might have been difficult.

'And all this was when?' I ask.

'Twenty-five years ago, when we first met. I gather things have changed since but back in the day, people like Dave were given free rein. All that mattered were results. We're not talking anything physical here. That wouldn't have been Dave's style at all. In fact, he once told me the moment you laid a finger on a suspect was the moment you lost him. He was clever, my Dave. Laughter, he used to say, opens any door. It certainly opened mine.'

'So what happened? How come he fell in with H and the rest of the crew?'

'Good question. That puzzled me, too, but the answer's so, so simple. The way Dave told me, the whole game changed. The police, he said, kind of lost their nerve. There were suddenly things you could and couldn't do, and that didn't sit well with people like Dave. Towards the end of his time, he was working undercover, pretending to be a disillusioned ex-cop. His bosses were trying to break up a drugs gang here in Portsmouth, and Dave was the bait. I've met mates of his who told me Dave was doing a great job, but then the people around him, the officers in charge I suppose, made a mess of the whole operation and virtually gave him away. Dave was so angry. Angry and quite bitter. These people he'd made friends with suddenly wanted to kill him. He had to hide himself away, go to ground, and he came to me in Ventnor, in the B & B. Three months on full pay until it all blew over. He was a good cook, Dave. My breakfasts improved no end.'

'And after that?'

'After that he was never the same. He stayed in the job, kept his head down, but the spark had gone. Then one day H got in touch and made him an offer.'

'To do what?'

'Keep his ear to the ground. Keep his eyes open.'

'And H was the guy he'd tried to stitch up?'

'Yes. But it was just business as far as H was concerned, at least that's the way Dave put it. H knew Dave, remember, and he had an eye for talent and he also knew that Dave had fallen out of love with the job. H was more fun. And H had a lot of money.'

'He said that? Dave?'

'Yes. To tell you the truth I was shocked at the time but, looking back, it makes perfect sense. Dave would strike you as Jack the lad, not a care in the world, but deep down that man was very conflicted and very decent. He felt those bosses of his had let him down. Badly.'

'And H was payback?'

'H was fun, like I just told you, and the money came in more than handy. Dave was leading a complicated life. He was still married. He had a family to support. There was also a problem with my B & B. It wasn't doing that well. In fact, I was in all kinds of trouble and H's money helped out, so maybe some of all this is my fault, too.'

'So, the funeral?' I query.

'H got very close to Dave, and he thinks he deserves a proper send-off. Don't get me wrong, I've been around a bit in my own life, but I've been having nightmares about who might turn up on Friday. We're allowed ten at the crematorium, absolute max,

immediate family only. I know Dave's ex is coming, plus the
two daughters. One's married with a couple of kids. The other
one's partnered with a stepson and a new baby of their own.
Including me, that's ten already. You know those mates of H. If
they're not allowed in, anything could happen.'

'You want him not to come?'

'Yes. I've no idea how you could ever make that happen, but
yes. These last few years, Dave's only belonged to me. Saying
goodbye should be private. I can't keep his ex away, and all her
brood, but deep down it's going to be just me and Dave. I know
H means well, but . . .' She gazes into her coffee. 'I'd rather he
wasn't there.'

I'm back at the flat within the hour. I haven't told Cynthia about
H being under the weather because he might well bounce back,
but in a way it would be simpler if he didn't, at least not until
the weekend. Imagine my dismay to find him out of bed and fully
dressed.

'You're better?' I enquire lightly.

'Yeah. No thanks to you.'

'What does that mean?'

'Ask the boy. He found all those tabs of yours. Having to go
out and hunt around? Where have you really been?'

Malo steps in from the shower, towelling his hair. After a run,
he glows.

'Seven-miler, Mum. Forty-three minutes dead. The people in
this city are seriously fat. That's a bad look in a shell suit.'

He pauses for a moment, scenting trouble, and retires to the
kitchen.

'Well?' H is sitting in the only armchair, nursing a mug of tea.

'I went to see Cynthia.' I see no point in lying. 'She asked
me round.'

'Cynth?' H is astonished. 'Why?'

'She wanted to talk about the funeral.'

'It's sorted. She knows that. There's nothing to talk about.'

'I'm not sure that's her take on it.' I tell him about all Dave's
relatives, and the Crem's insistence on limiting the numbers.

'But Dave's missus was a knob.'

'Hard to imagine.'

'Yeah? You think so? And those kids of his were always on the want. They robbed poor Dave blind. What's the matter with Cynth? Does she think we're gonna be an embarrassment? Pompey fucking low-life?'

This is an interesting question and pretty much nails the essence of Cynthia's reservations. A bunch of ageing hooligans? Seriously aggrieved? With the freedom of the entire car park? Stella and mourning, I try and point out, rarely mix but H isn't having it.

'Bollocks,' he says. 'I've put the word out. We'll all be there, Cynth or no Cynth. You want the honest truth? The woman's a disgrace. Did she ever really know Dave at all? Tell me I'm being harsh but I'm starting to wonder.'

This is fighting talk and does H no favours at all. In these moods, he loses control, goes way over the top, and the glimpse it offers into the man he might really be is far from comforting. Tony Morse once told me that H has been fighting demons all his life, and some days – in Tony's view – the demons win. Nicely put, I'm thinking now. And probably right.

Malo at last rejoins us. Unlike his father, he knows how to diffuse a situation.

'You need some fresh air, Mum.' He extends a hand. 'Let's get out of here.'

We walk across the Common and down to Old Portsmouth. This is exactly the route H and I took last night but in the absence of moonlight, the seafront has lost its enchantment. The promenade must have been damaged in the recent storms and is undergoing extensive repairs, while the fun fair, to be frank, is squalid: rusting machinery, salt-bitten by the wind and the weather.

In Old Portsmouth, I show Malo the steps up to the Round Tower and we climb to the top. In daylight, I get a proper look at H's pride and joy, our handsome new aircraft carrier, but when I suggest a ride on the Gosport ferry, Malo shakes his head.

'He's not well,' he says. 'Dad. He'll never admit it but something's up.'

Something's up. We both know what this innocent phrase really means, but we prefer to tiptoe round the truth. I shake my head. This nonsense has to stop.

'You really think he's got it? The virus?'

'He might. Headache? Fever? Next, he'll have that funny dry cough. Then we'll know.'

'Who says?'

'Clem. That's what happened with Mateo. It's a tick-box exercise, Mum. Eliminate everything else, and then dial for the ambulance.'

I nod, remembering my own exchange with the young man on the NHS helpline. He, too, had boxes to tick.

'H will never go to hospital,' I say. 'I guarantee it.' I tell Malo about the video we both watched on Cynthia's iPad. 'I've never seen him properly frightened the way he was then. It would take braver people than us to get him into hospital, if it turns out we're right.'

Malo nods. He's scowling now.

'He might have no choice. Not if this thing's as evil as everyone's saying.'

'Wrong. H always has a choice. That's where everything begins and ends with him. His way, no one else's. You've lived with the man, we both have. He's as stubborn as a mule. If he doesn't want to end up in ICU, he won't let it happen.'

'Then he'll die. You need oxygen, Mum. Believe me, I know about this stuff. Oxygen first, and if it gets really bad, a ventilator. All of that plus lots of nurses who know exactly what they're doing. Where on earth do you find all that outside an ICU?'

'Good question. Excellent question.' I check my watch. Nearly half past two.

'Home,' I say.

EIGHT

I phone Tony Morse that evening. H has gone back to bed, having toyed with the fish. Even a sprinkle of capers, his favourite garnish, didn't do it for him. He pushed his plate aside and left the table without saying a word. Suddenly unsteady on his feet, he looked like an old man.

Tony tells me he's watching *Casablanca*. He's got to the misty bit at the airfield where Humphrey Bogart is telling Ingrid Bergman that she has to get in the waiting plane and leave him to face whatever follows.

'I used to have a picture of that wonderful woman on my bedroom wall as a kid,' he says. 'Not many people know that.'

'Ingrid Bergman?'

'The same. The hat. The nose. Those lips. The hint of a tear. Just perfect.'

'You never told your wife?'

'Never. Not the first one, nor the second, nor the fragrant Helen. Confession was never my thing.'

'Maybe you should have been more honest. It might have saved you a fortune.'

'You're right.' The thought makes him laugh. 'What are you after?'

I tell him about H. The bottom line, the way I phrase it, is brutal. He's been in a bit of a state for a while. He's not young any more and he's at least a couple of stone overweight. Just now he's developing all the symptoms of our Covid friend and Malo and I are debating what to do with him.

'They call them hospitals,' Tony murmurs. 'Have done for a while. Lift the phone. Talk to someone.'

'It's not that simple.' I explain about the video, about Fat Dave coughing his lungs out in the ICU. 'There's no way, Tony. If it comes to it, he'd prefer to die in that lovely flat of yours.'

'You're serious?'

'Alas, yes.'

There's a longish silence. In the background, I can hear the roar of aero engines and swelling music on the soundtrack as La Bergman makes her exit from Casablanca.

'There might be something we can do.' Tony is back. 'But it'll cost.'

'How much?'

'Lots, I'm afraid. Someone will need to take a good look at him. We're probably talking consultant level. Then there's round-the-clock nursing care. We'd have to go to an agency. These people are available but they're not cheap. On top of that, there's all the extras.'

'Like?'

'Oxygen, for starters. Assuming you're right, we'll need loads, and it could go on for weeks. Then there's drugs, lots of them. To keep it neat and tidy, he's effectively a private patient. It's a seller's market, my darling.'

'Thousands?'

'Probably more.'

'Tens of thousands?'

'At least.'

'*Hundreds* of thousands?'

'It's possible. Solicitors always prepare for the worst. It's part of the charm of the job. We need to be realistic here. I'm afraid it's the old rule.'

'Which is?'

'No surprises.'

I find myself nodding. For some reason I hadn't begun to wonder how much any of this might cost but, under the circumstances, I very much like 'we'.

'You might be up for this?' I ask. 'Lending a hand?'

'I'll certainly ask around.'

'You know where to look? Who to talk to?'

'In this town? Silly question.' That laugh again, even softer. 'You need to take care as well, my darling. Keep him in bed. Wear a mask. Splash the bleach around. Give the bugger a hard time.'

The bugger, I assume, is the virus. When I mention Fat Dave's funeral, Tony says he plans to be there. He knows all about the fascists at the Crem, and he wouldn't dream of crashing the party, but he'll keep his distance and raise a solitary glass in the privacy of his car.

'And you, my darling?'

It's my turn to laugh. I've no intention of sharing Cynthia's angst about Dave's 6.57 Crew chums and I mutter something noncommittal about H not being up to it. Today is Wednesday. By Friday, anything may have happened.

'Of course, my darling. Let's talk tomorrow. In the meantime, I'll make some calls.' He breaks off again, then returns. 'Remarkable. Truly remarkable. Pure class.'

'What is?'

'Ingrid Bergman. I've still got the photo, by the way. Black and white. Wonderful lighting. The planes of her face. Her cheekbones. Those lips, again, slightly parted. An old man's fantasy, my darling. Sad, or what?'

Tony Morse, in the bleakest moments, has never failed to lift my spirits and now is no different. H is in bed. Malo is back in bad company on the PlayStation. I pour myself a hefty glass of Greco di Tufo from the fridge and settle at the table with yesterday's copy of the *Portsmouth News*.

In a strange way, this city is beginning to grow on me. It's rough at the edges, and far from pretty to look at, but the times I've ventured forth, visited a shop or two, eavesdropped on the odd conversation, tell me that the place has bred a very special kind of resilience. It's an island community. It's a bit cut-off, a bit claustrophobic. It seems to expect the worst, and I get the feeling it's rarely disappointed, but for all its stoicism, it remains oddly upbeat.

It also has a long memory. The thirst for a fight evidently lies deep in the city's DNA, and I get the feeling the Pompey tribes have been picking quarrels forever. Tim, my thespy friend, is very good on this. First, he says, Pompey's finest went to sea and took on the Spanish, then the Dutch, and then the French. Trafalgar was a great moment, a really tasty ruck, then came two world wars and shoals of sneaky U-boats. The monument on the seafront, visible from this flat, tallies the thousands of lives lost, but even so the city has never abandoned its passion for lots of blood and lots of treasure.

Now, turning the page of yesterday's *News*, I find myself reading about a fifty-three-year-old former UKIP candidate up in court. Back last year, Pompey were playing the hated Scummers in an FA Cup tie. Scummers is a word I've picked up from H. It means anyone born in Southampton. They arrived in some numbers at Fratton Park, and had the nerve to thrash Pompey 4-0. Afterwards, according to the *News*, there was a full-blown riot, two sets of supporters separated by hundreds of police, some of them on horseback. The Pompey fans couldn't wait to get at the Scummers and give them a good kicking, but the police were in the way. Frustrated, our UKIP fan instead assaulted one of the horses. Not once, not twice, but *three* times. Now, months later, the judge has gravely warned him to prepare for a jail sentence.

I shake my head, and then recharge my glass. It's a shame about the horse, but the story is richly comic. Did Mr UKIP look the beast in the eye? Did he challenge him? Ask him how hard he thought he was? And when he set about him, what did the poor horse make of it all? Pompey, I think. The gruff vigour of the place caught in a brief flurry of violence. I tear the piece out and put it to one side. If H and I are ever on speaking terms again, I suspect it might cheer him up.

Elsewhere in the paper there's a whole page of lockdown recipes. Irn-Bru fruit loaf? Mega brownies to die for? Cadbury's Creme Eggs shrouded in pavlova? This is a city that lives to eat exactly what it likes, and when it's not battering the enemy, Pompey has a very sweet tooth. Hence, I assume, Malo's amazement about all those seafront fatties.

I find him still locked in a battle of his own next door. With the last of the Greco di Tufo, I curl up in a corner of the sofa and watch a brothel sequence which is more graphic than I'd expected. Malo's character goes for a black woman with improbable breasts, and he has the tact to back out of the action before it gets too raunchy.

'Don't mind me,' I tell him. 'She'll probably eat you alive.'

Malo ignores the comment. He's been speaking to Clemmie again and it appears that the news from the hospital is good. Mateo is breathing oxygen through a mask but so far the medics see no reason to put him on to a ventilator. His vital signs are beginning to perk up and Clemmie's mum has been talking to him on Skype.

'That matters,' Malo says. 'Once you're on the ventilator, it's fifty-fifty.'

'Meaning?'

'Half of them die.'

'Christ.'

'Exactly.'

I'm thinking about H, and I suspect Malo is, too. I tell him briefly about my conversation with Tony Morse, and to my slight surprise Malo immediately warms to the prospect of keeping his dad here in the flat.

'Top idea,' he says. 'We'll all muck in and Dad can boss us about. He'll be better in no time. How many nurses, do you think?'

'No idea. Two? Three? More?'

'Brilliant. And do we get to choose?'

'*Choose?* You mean some kind of audition?'

'Of course. The Asians are the real lookers. There'll be a couple of them, at least.'

I shake my head, and nod at the screen. Too much GTA has obviously rotted my son's brain, and I'm about to launch into one of those mumsy lectures about the need to respect women when Malo lifts a finger.

'Listen,' he says. 'Did you hear that?'

'Hear what?'

He shakes his head, his finger still erect, and then – very faintly – I hear it, too. The muffled sound of a cough. From next door.

NINE

I'm awake most of the night, listening out for H. The coughing comes in fits and starts, the kind of dry rasp that fails to dislodge anything but gets progressively more irksome. I doze off around four in the morning and surface at dawn, feeling guilty. Malo has lent me his dressing gown, a Christmas present from Clemmie. It's the deepest scarlet with a black Harley-Davidson on the back and is much treasured by my son. I slip it on and go next door. H is still coughing.

'How are you?'

I'm standing in the thin grey light, peering down at the bed. H can barely raise his head.

'Not good,' he manages.

'Headache?'

'Yeah, but the cough's worse. My chest's on fire. Bloody hurts.'

He's right. His chest is hot to my touch and when I manage to get him to sit up, his back is the same. Covid, I think. For sure.

'We need help, H,' I tell him. 'Ibuprofen can only take you so far.'

'Yeah? Like what kind of help?'

I tell him about Tony Morse's offer. At a sensible hour, I'll give him a ring, see how he's getting on.

'No hospital?'

'No hospital.'

'That's a promise?'

'It is. For now.'

'What does that mean?'

'Never say never.' I bend low and tuck him in. 'Isn't that what you always told me?'

He seems relieved. His face stares up at me and every time he coughs, he winces with the pain. He's breathless, too, like a man with important news to impart. *Help me. Make this thing stop.*

'The funeral.' He tries to swallow. 'We've gotta be there.'

'No, H.'

'Yes.'

'But you're infectious. You'll put everyone else at risk. Think of the others.'

'Fuck the others. Why aren't you wearing a mask?'

Good question. The truth is I haven't got one and neither has Malo, but I packed a couple of silk scarves in my bag and I leave H for a moment to tie one round my lower face. It smells of Chanel No. 5, another life.

When I get back, H is up on his elbows.

'Bank robber,' he grunts between coughs. 'Wild West.'

I've brought him a glass of water. He sips it greedily, then wipes his mouth. He wants us to talk about the funeral again. He *has* to be there. By now, I've had a chance to think this thing through. If Tony can lay hands on full medical care at once, so much the better. If he can't, I have another proposal.

'Are you listening, H?' I settle on the bed, reach for his hand.

'Go on.'

'You need to give me all your contacts, all the people you've talked to about Dave's funeral.'

'Why?'

'Because I need to talk to them, too.'

'Saying what?'

'Stay away. Leave Dave in peace.'

'You mean fucking Cynth.'

'Same thing. If you do that for me, give me the contact numbers, I'll sort everything out.'

'There's nothing to sort.'

'There is, H. None of this is normal. Listen to the news. Three and a half thousand people have died already, and it's going up by seven hundred a day. At this rate, we'll all be dead by Christmas. Do you really want that?'

'You're kidding. Don't believe all this government crap.'

'But it's true, H.' I edge a little closer. 'If you give me the numbers, I'll drive you up there tomorrow, just you and me, safe distance, quarantine on wheels. At least you'll get to say goodbye.'

'Just me?'

'Just you.'

He's gazing up at me, frustrated, and angry, and hurt. He wants to shake his head, tell me I'm crazy, tell me I've no right to barge into his past like this, but already the virus has robbed him of the energy to put up any real fight.

'I'm fucked,' he whispers. 'My phone's on the floor there.'

I make the calls at eight in the morning. The list of names is shorter than I'd imagined, barely a dozen, and most of them are still in bed when I get through.

At first, I go on far too long about H being ill, and Cynthia wanting a little peace and quiet, and the responsibility we all have to mark Dave's passing with a bit of respect by staying away. To sweeten the pill, I throw in the promise of a get-together down at Flixcombe once all this madness is over. Stella, I say. Guinness. Whatever. Fill your boots.

This sparks the odd grunt of approval but by the time I'm in the middle of H's list, it's beginning to dawn on me that most of these people aren't that bothered. Unlike H, they're not tied hand and foot to past glories. It was good fun, they earned a quid or two, led the Filth a dance, and had some great times in between. Three of them, unprompted, remember the weekend they all descended on Disneyland Paris, spray-painted Big Thunder Mountain, gave Mickey Mouse a seeing-to and spent three nights in a Paris police cell before being deported. Another – Mick Pain – sweetly asks me to give his best to Cynthia, whom he remembers as being a bit of a looker in the day. Only Wesley Kane shows any real signs of disappointment.

'Shame,' he grunts. 'I was looking forward to it.'

'Any particular reason?'

'Yeah, Dave once grassed me up. He always thought I didn't know, but I did. Anyone else, he'd have had big trouble coming, but there was something about that guy I never quite worked out.'

'Like what?'

'Like how fucking nice he was. I blamed the happy pills to begin with, but I think it was his nature. Some people are born to be funny. I'd set out to give him a slapping and he'd end up making me laugh like a drain. That's fucking clever, know what I mean?'

I tell him I do, and when he wants to know more about H, I spare him the details.

'Not well,' I tell him. 'Gotta go.'

'Don't.'

'I'm sorry?' There's something new in his voice that I don't much like.

'We need to meet.'

'Why?'

'H's idea. Give me a ring later, yeah? He sounds rough, by the way. Really rough.'

I'm about to ask him what any of this might be about but he's ended the call. This disturbs me somewhat. H has obviously got to Wesley before I did, but why?

It's mid-morning before I get through to Tony Morse. A courtesy call to Cynthia has left her very relieved indeed, and when I tell her that there's just a possibility that H might still turn up, heavily chaperoned by yours truly, she doesn't seem to mind. H and I are very welcome to be there in the car park. Just as long as the rest of the gang don't come with us.

My last call finds Tony Morse in a queue outside his local branch of Tesco. His stash of drinkable reds has shrunk to a couple of bottles and he's badly in need of resupplies.

'Negligence or thirst?'

'Desperation, mostly. Are you sitting down?'

'I am.'

He wants to know about H. Not good, I tell him. Everything I know about this bloody virus tells me he's got it.

'OK. You want the good news first?'

'Please.'

'I've laid hands on a respiratory consultant. He happens to be Chinese, a Mr Wu, but I know how much you love irony.'

'Can he come and check H out?'

'Happy to. He's also given me the name of a nursing agency he uses. I phoned them an hour ago. If H is as bad as he sounds, Wu wants three nurses at any one time. They'll all do eight-hour shifts, so you're looking at nine nurses every twenty-four hours.'

'And oxygen? If H needs it?'

'Wu is working on that. Prices have gone through the roof, as you might imagine, and it's the same with most of the drugs.'

'And this is the bad news?'

'I'm afraid so.'

'So how much are we talking?'

'Wu wants two thousand upfront.'

'This is some kind of call-out fee?' I'm staring at the phone. 'I could get a couple of dozen plumbers for that kind of money. More if they were Polish.'

'He calls it a retainer. The two grand is a buy-in. Every house call he makes thereafter is another five hundred. He'll also need you to sign a waiver.'

'Meaning?'

'Proof that H is refusing to go into hospital. Legally, it's a sensible move. This man doesn't want to be sued if he ends up with a death on his hands.'

'Sued by who?'

'You, probably. I told Wu that was unlikely, but in his position I'd be doing exactly the same thing.'

I nod. I've never ceased to marvel at the ease with which the professional classes feather their own nests, and here's yet another example. Five hundred quid for a peek round H's bedroom door? Outrageous.

'And the nurses?' I ask.

'Fifty pounds an hour, plus expenses. I make that around four grand a day. About the oxygen and the tabs, to be honest, I'm clueless, but nothing comes cheap these days.'

Too right. This is the bill for keeping H alive, and I've been doing my best to resist calculations like these, but denial only takes you so far in life.

'You're probably looking at around seven thousand a day,' Tony says helpfully.

'And how long might all this last for?'

'Worst case, Wu thinks five weeks. H may die, of course, but let's hope he doesn't. Do the math, and you're looking at nearly a quarter of a million quid. Does H carry medical insurance?'

'He might. I'll ask.'

'If so, you'll need to check there's no clause penalizing him for not using the NHS.'

'He'll love that.'

'I bet. Listen, darling. I'm number one in the queue now, and the Tesco minder has his eye on me. Word is, there's a crisis on the booze aisle. I can cover Wu's fees for the time being, but you won't be surprised when I tell you I need some kind of guarantee I'll get that money back. Talk to H. He's a resourceful man. I'm sure it won't be a problem. *Ciao*, darling. Talk later, *si*?'

And suddenly he's gone. I'm still looking numbly at the phone when Malo joins me in the front room. He's been sitting with his dad, trying to cheer him up, but I can tell from his face that it hasn't really worked.

'Tell me he's going to be all right, Mum.' Malo sounds almost plaintive.

I try to muster a smile, and then give him a hug. In truth I can tell him no such thing. Instead, foolishly, I enquire where we might lay hands on £250,000.

'For Dad, you mean?'

'I'm afraid so. Sorting all this at home doesn't come cheap.'

'But a quarter of a million quid? You're serious?'

'Yes.'

'Shit.'

'Exactly.'

*   *   *

H gets steadily worse as the day goes on. I try and have a sensible conversation, chiefly about Wesley Kane, but H is racked by the coughing and finds it near impossible to talk. When I mention the money we'll need to find, he rolls his eyes.

'Anything,' he says. 'I'll pay any fucking price.'

'Do you have health insurance, by any chance?'

'No. No fucking need. I've been battered. This is horrible. I can't breathe any more. I'm suffocating. Just make this stop.'

I nod and leave the room. A call to Tony, with yours truly close to panic, brings Mr Wu to the door within the hour. He phones ahead to announce his imminent arrival, and Malo and I stand at the window, watching him park his car across the road. According to Malo it's a top-of-the-range Lexus, which must prove that every Covid cloud has a silver lining.

Wu gets out and opens the boot with his key fob. He's tall and slim, and looks much younger than I'd anticipated. He has PPE sealed in plastic – over-trousers, scrubs, mask, visor, surgical boots – and he dons the lot on the pavement beside the car. Then he pulls on a pair of surgical gloves, retrieves a sizeable cardboard box and a leather briefcase from the back of the car and sets off across the road.

I send Malo down to let him in and await their footsteps on the stairs. Already, this feels like a visitation from a distant planet and, looking back, the sight of Mr Wu crossing the road in his PPE gear was the moment everything began to spool out of control. He's come to banish the plague, I think. Next, he'll be daubing a cross on the door.

'Ms Andressen?' Perfect English, barely accented, accompanied by a formal bow. Then he nods at the cardboard box that Malo has carried up from the street. 'Masks, Ms Andressen. And surgical gel. And PPE for both of you. Please wear it all times when you're in contact with Mr Prentice.'

Mr Prentice. With a slight shock, I realize he's talking about H.

'Of course.' I'm watching Malo unpack the contents of the box. 'Very sensible.'

Malo and I robe up in the front room. Mr Wu is meticulous about making sure that every item of PPE is adjusted the way it should be, circling each of us carefully, peering especially hard at the fit of the mask and the plastic visor. The last time I had this degree of attention was an RSC production of *Twelfth Night* at Stratford. Playing Olivia was never really to my taste, but the costume certainly helped.

Mr Wu is happy. Next, he takes us into the kitchen and stands beside the sink, watching us while we wash our hands. First, soap. Then, gel. Malo, in particular, is impressed. When he catches Mr Wu taking a look round, he tells him about my recent efforts with the bleach.

'I know.' Mr Wu's voice is muffled behind the mask. 'I can smell it.'

A vigorous nod suggests he's pleased but my little moment of glory is short-lived. Should H have contracted the virus, Mr Wu will be insisting on something called 'deep-cleaning' daily. For a brief moment I'm trying to work out whether I have enough bleach left, but it turns out he has a specialist firm in mind. It will be £550 a visit. Nearly four thousand pounds a week. Another expense.

I take Mr Wu in to meet H. He does his best to offer a limp handshake, but even this is beyond him. Mr Wu stands over the bed, gazing down. A series of questions elicit a nod, or a shake of H's head, before Mr Wu's fingertips explore H's glands and he has a peer down H's throat. A stethoscope check comes next, chest and back, before Mr Wu takes H's temperature. The reading on his thermometer steadies at 105 degrees Fahrenheit.

Finally, our visitor produces three testing kits and asks H to open his mouth for the swab. After that, the same swab goes up his nose. The stick sealed in an airtight tube, Mr Wu makes a note of the time and the date, plus H's name. The other two swabs are for us. These, he explains, will go to a laboratory in Southampton. The motorbike is waiting outside in the street as we speak. Malo heads for the stairs to hand the samples over while Mr Wu shepherds me back to the front room, carefully closing H's bedroom door behind him. Having the swab at the very back of my throat has left me feeling slightly nauseous.

'Your friend is very ill, Ms Andressen. I'm certain it's Covid but we'll need confirmation. The lab we're using has an eight-hour turnaround. By midnight, we'll know for sure. You have questions for me?'

I ask about the nurses. First, he says, a technician will call to instal specialized bedside equipment. This is someone he evidently uses regularly, and he'll also be handling the oxygen supply. Mr H, he says, will need constant monitoring and changes of position if he's to be spared the ventilator. These, alas, are hard to acquire, and only H's own immune system will keep him out of hospital, so the challenge now is to give him a fighting chance.

A fighting chance. It's a phrase that H would normally love and I make a mental note to try and remember it.

'And the nurses?' I ask again.

'They'll be with you shortly. The first shift will last until midnight. These people are highly skilled and most of them are foreign but they all speak good English. They'll bring their own food but you might like to supply them with drinks. Make sure everything is disinfected all the time.' A crinkle around his eyes suggests a smile. 'Please.'

I nod. Malo's right. This man is seriously impressive. He's polite, organized, and – unlike me – appears to be completely unflustered. So efficient, I think, so reassuring. A quarter of a million pounds? A bargain.

At the door of the flat, still in his PPE, Mr Wu gives me a private phone number and invites me to call night or day if I need to. He lives locally and can be with me within ten minutes. In the meantime, with another courtly little bow, he tells me not to worry. Covid's only interest lies in multiplication, the most primitive of urges, and we're to hope that H's immune system will see it off.

With that parting shot, he disappears downstairs. From the living-room window, I watch him cross the road and pause beside his car to take off the PPE. Moments later, still gowned and masked, I'm back beside H.

Mr Wu, it seems, has perked him up a little. A limp wave of his hand invites me to sit on the bed. His other hand masks yet another bout of coughing and he takes a moment to catch his breath. Then he shakes his head, a seeming gesture of despair.

'What's the matter?' I'm alarmed.

His tongue flicks out, moistening his lips. Then he manages to force a smile.

'Some Scummer taking a look at that swab of mine? Hard to credit, eh?'

He's talking about the Southampton laboratory where the swabs have gone. I reach for his hand. It's damp to my touch. For the first time, it's occurred to me that all this might be my fault, that I had a brief passing tussle with the virus those few days I was ill, and that I infected H the first time I shared the flat with him. This is a horrible thought. True or not, it makes me feel worse than guilty.

I gaze down at him for a moment. His eyes have closed but when I give his hand a little squeeze, a smile ghosts across his face. Then he starts coughing again, turning his head away.

'It's going to be fine,' I whisper. 'We'll all get through this.'

TEN

From that day onwards, Thursday 2 April, our lives cease to be our own. Mr Wu decides not to wait for the swab test to confirm Covid, and within half an hour of his departure, a new-looking minibus delivers a bevy of nurses on to the pavement outside the flat. Two of them, both women, are Polish. The third announces himself as Sri Lankan.

Like Mr Wu, they quietly take charge while Malo and I lurk helplessly on the edges of this new world which seems, almost magically, to have appeared from nowhere. The older of the two Polish women, Ela, must once have been very beautiful and the sight of her face, still striking, at H's bedside sparks a definite reaction. She conducts a brief examination of H's bottom sheet, which is dark with sweat, and shakes her head. The nurses have brought armfuls of fresh bed linen, and with the help of the Sri Lankan, she gives H an all-over wash before getting rid of the dirty sheet.

The Sri Lankan, whose name is Sunil, is a slight, gentle man with an enchanting smile. He's young, still in his twenties, and he has the most beautiful hands I think I've ever seen: long, slender fingers, perfectly shaped nails, and a single silver ring on his left thumb. Slight he may be, but his physical strength is astonishing. I'm still in full PPE and offer to help with H, but he won't hear of it.

'Ways and means, Ms Andressen.' His English is excellent. 'Life is all technique, *quoi*?'

'You speak French?'

'*Un peu, oui.*'

He rolls H over and begins to wash his bottom. The third nurse, meanwhile, is clearing a space beside the bed. Her name is Marysia, and she senses my curiosity.

'We need room for the machinery, Ms Andressen, and for the oxygen. Many leads. Many switches. Then we can keep your friend here safe.'

Safe.

I believe them all. I believe Mr Wu, and now the small army of assistants – so competent, so undramatic – he's put together. As a demonstration of the sheer power of private medicine, or perhaps money, this can't fail to impress. H is in good hands. We can ask for no more.

The oxygen and the array of bedside equipment arrive soon afterwards. I'm trying, without success, to get through to Wesley Kane, and I abandon the call to watch Malo lending the guy a hand to carry the heavier items up six flights of stairs. They're both wearing full PPE, their faces bathed in sweat behind the plastic visors, and when I query the need for nine big cylinders of oxygen, the technician in charge tells me they always plan for emergencies.

'Most patients need around ten litres a minute,' he says. 'One of these cylinders contains three thousand four hundred and fifty-five litres. That's nearly six hours of constant use. Getting hold of this stuff is already a problem. What happens if we run out?'

Good point, I think. While the technician stacks the big cylinders in a corner of the front room, I turn away and try Wesley Kane again. This time he picks up.

'You,' he says.

'Me,' I agree.

Wesley and I go back a while. He's in his early forties, like me, but looks a lot younger. An old flame of H's once described him as 'sex on legs', a tribute to all those hours he puts in at the gym, and I know that many women find him irresistible. He's half-white, half-Jamaican, and his wild Afro and knowing smile have opened many doors, but there was always another side to Mr Kane that won H's attention from the moment they met.

The truth, sadly, is that Wesley Kane is a sadist, a psychopath. He loves hurting people, either to punish them or extract information, and over the years, H has used him for both. This complicity has disturbed me greatly from time to time, but Wesley can be surprisingly good company – warm and companionable – and he's always looked after me.

Now, on the phone, he's suggesting a meet.

'Where?' I ask at once.

'Not here. Not in the state you're in.'

'Meaning?'

'Infected. Carrying. A mate of mine got it the week before last. You should see the state of him. Believe me, you'll do anything to keep this fucker at arm's length.'

I find myself nodding at the phone. H, I think. Prostrate next door, newly washed, coughing his life away.

'Where, then? And when?'

Wesley has a think. When he suggests the end of South Parade Pier, I assume he's joking.

'You don't know the pier? It's on legs. It sticks out into the sea. Even in the dark, you can't miss it. Eleven o'clock, at the very end. I'm the guy in the black tracksuit. Mr Invisible.'

Night falls. We don't live in a dossy old borrowed flat anymore but a busy hospital ward. Mr Wu's nurses track back and forth, unpacking extension leads, helping the tech guy with his equipment, asking me whether we mind them using the fridge to store their juice (we don't). Malo, suddenly without a role, has retreated to the comforts of mass shootouts and gang rape, thanks to GTA, while I collapse on the sofa to enjoy my now-daily date with the *Portsmouth News*.

The stories on offer are as beguiling as ever. How to sanitize your bank cards with neat vodka. A Pompey window cleaner running 417 laps of his shared private driveway to raise money for the NHS. This news agenda offers a very distinctive take on what Boris Johnson is now calling 'our national emergency' and my jaw drops yet again as Doorway Discos sweep the city and a seventy-three-year-old retiree is jailed for assaulting his partner.

It's at this point that I realize that I really am starting to warm to the rough old community that has so suddenly taken me hostage. Academics call this reaction 'Stockholm syndrome', and in the light of the Google description – 'feelings of trust or affection felt in many cases of kidnapping or hostage-taking by a victim towards a captor' – it sounds pretty apt. Pompey, I'm beginning to realize, is a seriously quirky proposition, and if I need proof then I need look no further than our precious jigsaw.

Despite a life at stake, and medics everywhere, it's still down there on the carpet, untouched, sacrosanct, a moment of history awaiting completion. The nurses and the tech guy step carefully around it. Malo hunts half-heartedly for a particular piece when GTA starts to pall. But nobody dares tidy it all up and give ourselves a bit more space. Should this duty fall to me? Should I be the one to break this weird spell and put Lord Nelson back in his box? The answer, emphatically, is no. Already these fragments of a long-ago spilling of Pompey blood have acquired the status of an icon. Next, we'll be pausing beside it to cross ourselves, but for now I must shed my PPE and meet Wesley Kane.

He's waiting, as promised, at the end of South Parade Pier. Normally, you'd never find me alone at night in circumstances like these but I have enormous faith in Wesley's ability to keep me intact, and if I feel any real threat it comes from the weather. Despite wall-to-wall sunshine all day, it's bitterly cold now and already I'm regretting my choice of a light anorak.

At first, alone on the wooden planking, I think Wesley has – for once – stood me up, but then I sense a movement in the darkness. With it comes the faintest intake of breath, the tell-tale sign of physical exercise, and finally a figure appears. Wesley wasn't kidding about the black tracksuit, but for a moment I'm baffled by whatever else he's wearing. At first glance it looks like some kind of harness, thick stitched webbing that trails down to the two daubs of white that are his Nikes.

'Resistance exercise bands,' he explains. 'Twenty-nine quid a shot on Amazon.'

These, it turns out, have taken up the slack after closure of the city's gyms. Think big elastic bands. You hook one end to something solid, in this case a cast-iron bench, and then lunge into the darkness. Uninvited, Wesley shows me how, ever careful to keep his distance. I get the theory, but I tell him he needs more practice on the moves. Does it work? I take his word for it. Is it a good look for someone as vain as Wesley? Sadly not.

He sheds the harness and nods at the railings that fence the end of the pier.

'Two metres?' We're strolling across.

'Three,' he grunts.

Being out here in the open appears to be important. Wesley, I suspect, has thought one move ahead for most of his life and even now, under lockdown, with not a living soul around, the usual rules apply. The world is always listening, he once told me. Keep your eyes peeled. And be very careful what you say. Wesley, sadly, has been in lockdown all his life.

'This is about H?' I'm starting to shiver.

'Yeah. He's near skint. Has he told you that?'

'No, but Malo did.'

'He knows? The boy?'

'I think he's picked up a clue or two. He's brighter than you might think.'

Wesley says nothing. He's always regarded Malo as a spoiled brat and has never bothered to look harder.

'You talked to him today?' I ask. 'H?'

'Yeah.'

'And?'

'A quarter of a million quid for the meds and the care? Am I right?'

'You are. Assuming he survives.'

'That bad?'

'That bad.'

Wesley nods, but says nothing. Across the Solent I can see the lights of a town. A couple of days ago, when he was a different man, H told me it was Ryde, on the Isle of Wight.'

'H always has little projects on the go.' Wesley at last breaks the silence. 'He calls them prospects. Way back in the day, he was exactly the same. That's how all this shit kicked off.'

'Shit?'

'Gear. The marching powder. Money. Bent Filth like Fat Dave. Flixcombe. Credit to H, he was never wrong. He'd come up with some name or other, a contact or a phone number in Aruba, and we'd all be looking the fucking place up, wondering what he was on about and where the fuck it was, but do you know something? Whatever he did, whatever happened, he was always on the money.' He nods, emphatic, almost sombre. 'And it usually happened quick, too, because these things always do. Talk big enough sums, put the noughts in the right place, and you'd be amazed what goes down. H was a legend that way. He never thought small. He never lost his nerve, not once. And that's why we all ended up with a quid or two in our pockets.'

A quid or two. Watching Wesley roll himself a thin doobie, I'm wondering whether he was on the trip to Disneyland.

'And now?' I ask. 'Are we talking another prospect? Or is that something I've imagined?'

'No, you're right. It's the old dance, isn't it? Motive, first. Need, greed, whatever.'

'Desperation?' I suggest. 'The man's dying in front of our eyes.'

'OK, that'll do nicely. He suddenly has to lay hands on a lot of money otherwise he'll end up with the rest of the world in ICU. And judging from what he told me about Fat Dave, that ain't gonna happen.'

'It won't,' I confirm. 'I was there. I saw the Skype conversation. Cynthia was trying to say goodbye. Part of Dave didn't have a clue what she was talking about, but the rest did. H got it. We both got it. And Cynthia got it too, poor woman. This virus is cruel, Wes. It's unforgiving. It doesn't care who it kills or how they die, just as long as there's another victim waiting in line. H gets that, as well, and it scares him. Not an easy thing to do.'

Wesley nods, conceding the point, just a hint of respect.

'H wants back in the game,' he says softly. 'He says he's got a rainy-day fund, money he's never touched, dosh he's been saving for a time like this.'

'How much?'

'A hundred and fifty grand. Enough to make an investment or

two. H has been out of the loop for a long time now. He's got Flixcombe, you, the boy. He doesn't need Aruba and all that grief. Or at least he didn't.'

'And now?'

'Now's different. You're right, he thinks he's dying. And that's a serious proposition.'

I lean out over the rail, numb with cold now, staring down at the blackness of the water swirling around the rusting piles that hold the pier up. My lovely dead friend Pavel would hijack this metaphor at once: generations of instant fun that make piers what they are – slot machines, games arcades, cut-price bars, greasy burgers – all condemned to a slow death by sheer neglect. The country, Pavel would point out, has also run out of money. And so everything, including H, is heading for collapse.

Maybe, I think. But maybe not. I look up again, leaning back from the rail, meeting Wesley's gaze.

'You've got a job for me,' I say tonelessly. 'I can tell.'

'H has got a job for you.'

'You want me to go and talk to somebody?'

'You're right. We do.'

'Does he have a name? This guy?'

'She. She has a name. Her real name is unpronounceable. H couldn't get his tongue around it, and neither can I.'

'So, what do you call her?'

'She answers to Shanti. She runs a restaurant in Gunwharf – or used to until last week. I talked to her earlier this evening. She's expecting a call.'

'From?'

'You.'

To his credit, Wesley has devoted a bit of thought to this date of ours. He knew I'd rise to H's bait, and now we need to toast this new adventure of ours. He bends to his man sack and produces two bottles. At least one is wine.

'Why two?'

'Guess.'

'I'm that infectious?'

'Of course you fucking are. That's part of your charm. H always said you were irresistible, and he's right.'

'That was one night,' I protest. 'And I was blind drunk.'

'Makes no difference. Here . . .'

He produces a corkscrew and attends to the wine. I hear the soft pop of the cork, and then he's offering it to me at arm's length. I try and squint at the label but it's hard reading in the dark.

'It's a Gran Reserva,' Wesley says. 'From 1982. H insisted I took advice.'

I'm impressed. 1982 was a matchless year for Rioja. A hundred pounds at least. Probably more.

'And does a girl get a glass, as well?'

'Afraid not. I forgot.' He makes a playful little gesture with the bottle.

'Are you propositioning me?'

'Yeah? Is that the come-on?'

'Absolutely not. For one thing, exercise freaks bore me to death. For another, H would kill us both.'

'He might not be around.'

'He will, Wesley. And it's our job to make that happen. OK? We understand each other?' I'm trying very hard to be stern and I think it's working because Wes, sensibly, decides to tell me a little more about Shanti.

'She's a piece of work,' he says. 'She's a big woman, huge bum on her. Dave Munroe would have creamed himself.'

'And?'

'She was partnered to some guy in London before she came down here. They fell out over fuck knows what, but she scored a decent settlement and bought the restaurant out of the proceeds.'

'Proceeds of what?'

'The powder. The white. The place she bought in Gunwharf used to be Tex-Mex, crap food, worse service, but she changed the whole vibe.'

'To?'

'Moroccan. Tagines. Couscous. All that Arab shit. She's Senegalese or somewhere by birth but she spent a lot of time in Marrakesh, understands the cuisine.' He laughs softly. 'You want to guess the name of the restaurant?'

'Tell me.'

'Casablanca.'

'The *White* House?' I'm smiling now. 'A woman with a sense

of humour. Excellent. So where does she fit in all this? What do you want me to do?'

'H needs you to meet her. Word on the street tells me she's up for an investment. The right terms, H might be interested.'

'We're talking cocaine?'

'Of course. She still has the contacts and just now her business is paying her fuck all. She's put in for one of those fancy lockdown loans, but the banks blanked her.'

'All of them?'

'Dunno. Maybe you should ask. Either way, she and H are in the same boat.'

'Except that H's is sinking.'

'Exactly. And so is hers.'

'You've met her? Talked to her?'

'About this? No. But take it from me, the woman's kosher. Plus she speaks French.' He takes a long pull from his own bottle, which looks like lager, then wipes his mouth. 'Perfect, eh? Do we hear a yes?'

'We?'

'Me.' He checks his watch and yawns. 'And H.'

Before he disappears into the darkness, Wesley gives me a mobile number. Best, he says, to phone late-ish tomorrow morning. Shanti still keeps restaurant hours, and sleeps in until noon.

'I'm at a funeral tomorrow,' I remind him. 'I'll phone once Dave has gone.'

ELEVEN

G *one.*

The word alone makes me shiver. First Dave Munroe. Now, unless we can head the virus off, H.

Back home, it's nearly midnight and our nurses are at the end of their shift. The minibus is once again at the kerbside, as I cross the Common with my bottle of Rioja, and upstairs the handover is seamless. One of the new women is English, another comes from California, while the third is Bulgarian. They're all fully garbed in PPE and as I defrost I try and remember their names, helpfully pinned to their gowns. The American, Julia, emerges from H's bedroom.

'He'd like to see you, Ms Andressen. I think he wants to say goodnight.'

I nod and reach for my PPE. There's a fresh set each time we need it and I'm learning to get a snug fit for the mask and the visor. Malo is checking the back of my gown when I realize what's changed in the front room.

'Where's the jigsaw?'

'The deep-cleaning people came to check the place out. They said it was a hazard. Apparently the virus can survive on bits of jigsaw for seventy-two hours. The guy bagged the lot.'

'So where is it?'

'Behind the sofa. The bag's sealed. The guy said not to worry, it won't kill us.' Malo's finished with my gown. 'You want the good news now? Wu phoned. The results came back from the lab.'

'And?'

'We're both in the clear.'

I stare at him for a moment. Hugging anyone in full PPE isn't easy, believe me, but I manage it. Just.

'And H?'

'Covid.' He nods. 'Just as we expected.'

I find H semi-conscious, lying on his back, sweat beading on his forehead. He's breathing oxygen through a rubber mask, and his torso rises and falls as he struggles to suck at the supply. Two of the nurses are in here, keeping watch while the other is evidently in the kitchen. A cannular is dripping something into H's arm, while another tube – lower – runs into a collecting bag beneath the bed. A machine beside the American nurse is hooked up to a little peg on H's finger, recording his vital signs. I'm no stranger to high-dependency nursing, and I understand about pulse and blood pressure, but the read-out connected to his finger – currently at eighty-nine per cent – has me baffled.

When I ask the American nurse, she says the figure is a measure of oxygen saturation.

'The red corpuscles in the blood carry the oxygen,' she

explains. 'Ninety-six per cent is normal. Anything below ninety-two per cent, we have a problem. Mid to low eighties, and you're running on empty.'

'Meaning?'

'You badly need a ventilator. They do the heavy lifting, keep you alive while your immune system sets about dealing with the virus.'

'I see.' I'm looking at the read-out again. It's suddenly gone up. 'Ninety-one per cent?' I query.

'That's a good sign, best so far.' She gestures at a list of figures on a clipboard on her lap. 'I'm guessing he can hear you. Maybe you should stay a while.'

I do. After a while, the English nurse brings in a cup of tea and asks me whether I want one. I shake my head. I barely tasted Wesley's Rioja and have promised myself a proper glass before I retire.

'This bedroom's too small,' I say. 'You should move into mine. Wouldn't that be better?'

Julia's watching H. 'Small is good discipline,' she says. 'It teaches you to think everything through. We'll see how it goes.'

H begins to cough again. While the Bulgarian nurse bends over him, adjusting his head on the pillow and easing the oxygen mask to dab at the corners of his mouth, I can't take my eyes off the saturation read-out. Ninety-one per cent one moment, ninety per cent the next. With H re-masked I kneel beside him, my head beside his. Through the mask and visor, I try and talk to him, but his eyes are closed and I suspect he's barely conscious. I tell him we love him, all of us, and to hang in there. I can't be sure but the briefest flicker of movement on the pillow might just be a nod. Looking at him like this, I can't help thinking of Dave Munroe, and the likeness – his situation, the setting, his sheer helplessness – makes me feel inexpressibly sad.

I badly need to think of something else, a conversational change of subject, but talking to Julia isn't much help. When I ask her how she got into nursing in the first place, she tells me she was a medic in the US Marine Corps.

'Combat medicine teaches you everything.' She nods at H. 'In double quick time.'

*   *   *

I leave the bedroom shortly afterwards. I fetch a glass from the kitchen and retrieve the bottle of wine from where I've left it in my bedroom. The wine is silky rich and multi-layered, surprise after surprise exploding softly on my tongue, and after a while, sitting on the bed, I begin to feel better. A second glass offers another layer of comfort and by the time I've re-corked the bottle and put it carefully to one side, I've worked out how to make life a little sweeter for these remarkable women.

Back in the front room, Malo is about to get into his sleeping bag. I tell him not to bother.

'Why not?'

'You're sleeping in my room from now on. This one is for them. Somewhere to sit when the pressure's off, maybe watch the telly. It's the least we can do.'

Malo stares up at me and for a moment I think he's going to say no, but then he shrugs, stoops for the cushions off the sofa, and follows me down the hall. I'm last into the bedroom and take care to close the door very carefully, making barely a sound. The last thing I want to do, I tell myself, is disturb H. Sweet thought, but utterly ridiculous. I'm blaming the Rioja.

Next day is Dave Munroe's funeral. Malo's out of the house moments after the morning shift change, having taken the measure of the new nurses. One of them, an Asian woman, is beyond gorgeous even in full PPE and Malo clatters down the stairs, trying to master the name pinned to her gown.

'T*aa*lia?' he whispers to himself. 'Long "a"? Or Taa*lia*? Emphasis on the bit at the end?' He can't make up his mind, he tells me, but with eyes like that, who cares?

Mercifully, the morning passes without any major dramas. H is racked with bout after bout of coughing. His sat-levels have stabilized around ninety per cent and while a reading like this is definitely problematic, the nurses think he's just about holding his own. 'Just about' is far from comforting, and for the first time I'm wondering whether it isn't my responsibility to call an end to this brave experiment and get H into the ICU.

Mr Wu arrives, unannounced, mid-morning as I'm preparing to leave for the funeral. He's already clad in full PPE and he disappears into H's bedroom. I know I should be with him, gowned and masked, but to be honest I find the whole ritual so dispiriting that I make my excuses and attend to my make-up in my own room. A light blusher and just the faintest hint of lipstick is all I need. Dave, after all, won't be watching. And neither, I suspect, will anyone else.

Mr Wu knocks lightly on my door as I'm checking my bag for the car keys. I open the door and invite him in, but he insists on keeping his distance.

'You're going *out*?' he says.

I've always handled guilt very badly. All I can do is nod.

'Just a wander across the Common,' I tell him. 'The test was negative, so I think that's allowed.'

He studies me a moment, his expression unreadable behind the mask and visor. Then he makes a tiny, delicate gesture with his gloved hands which, I choose to think, could mean anything.

'As you see fit, Ms Andressen. You'll be glad to know that Mr H is putting up a fight. We need to encourage that, and we will. But the fact remains that he's very seriously ill.'

Something has been nagging at me overnight, and now – with Mr Wu – is the time to voice it.

'Mr Prentice's parents live in the city,' I tell him. 'He's never seen very much of them. Might this be the time to get them along?'

'Bring them here, you mean?'

'Yes.'

'Because you think Mr Prentice might not make it?'

'Yes.'

'I'm afraid that wouldn't be wise.' Mr Wu is looking stern again. 'They'll be old. For their sake, they should obey the rules and stay at home.'

'Then maybe a video link of some kind? FaceTime? Skype? Something like that?'

'Of course.' Mr Wu checks his watch. 'If you felt that might be appropriate.'

My sat-nav takes me to the crematorium, which is on the mainland, along the coast towards the west. I spend the drive trying to work out what to do about H's parents, but typically I fail to make a decision. On the one hand I know I'd have to live

with myself should I not make the call and H succumbs to the
virus. On the other, I have this deep-seated conviction that
somehow he'll get through. Even the sight of Dave Munroe,
helpless and dying in the ICU, has so far failed to shake this
faith of mine, but by the time I slow to make the turn into the
crematorium, I'm still in two minds about making the call.
Relations between H and his parents have been non-existent
for years, and the last thing he needs now is a family ruck
beside – God help us – his death bed. As Tony Morse might
put it, *cui bono*? Who gains?

Unlike most funerals I've ever attended, the car park is virtually
empty, but under the circumstances I imagine that's inevitable.
I find myself a parking space at least fifty metres from the nearest
car and settle down to wait. Mourners for the funeral before
Dave's have just filed into the chapel of rest, and I appear to be
the first to arrive for what follows.

Under these circumstances, it's impossible not to think yet
again about H, back in that hideous flat, fighting for his life, and
after a couple of minutes trying to raise my spirits by listening
to a French band called 'Caravan Palace', I phone Jessie. She
sorts out the housekeeping down at Flixcombe, and also serves
as a kind of secretary. She's Pompey born and bred, and H trusts
her completely, sharing decisions he'd never discuss with me.
Of all the people in the Flixcombe circle, she's known H by far
the longest, and the news that he's positive for Covid doesn't
appear to surprise her.

'I told him not to go down there,' she says. 'I told him no one
was worth that kind of risk. Not even Fat Dave Munroe. So, how
is he?'

I tell her the truth, that H is very ill.

'So, what are they saying? At the hospital?'

'He's not in the hospital, Jess. He doesn't want anything to
do with the bloody hospital. He saw a video of Dave in ICU
before he died. It terrified him, Jess. Once he's in that ICU, he
thinks he'll never get out again.'

I tell her about the army of nurses Mr Wu has supplied on
our behalf, about the oxygen and the round-the-clock care, and
about the deep cleaning that has turned Tony Morse's flat into a
hospital ward.

'That must cost a fortune,' Jessie says.

'It does. It will. But for now, it's what H wants. I've got every faith in Mr Wu, Jess. He won't let H die on us.'

'You're sure about that?'

'Yes. I'm positive.' It's a smallish lie but I have to believe it. 'I need a phone number, Jess, and I'm guessing you've got it.' I tell her I need to get in touch with H's parents, just to be on the safe side.

'Safe side how? You're telling me it's that bad?'

'I'm telling you I owe them a call.'

'In case he dies?'

'In case they've got anything to say to him.'

'Christ, it *is* that bad.'

I say nothing. Seconds later, Jessie is back with a number.

'Good luck,' she says. 'I don't think they've been in touch for years.'

'Their doing?'

'H's.'

I'm still staring at the number, my phone in my hand, when I hear a knock on the window. Startled, I fumble for the knob under the seat and bring myself up to the vertical. The figure peering down at me is heavy-set, nice coat, suit and black tie. He looks mid-fifties, maybe older, and has a big, fleshy face that belongs in a certain kind of bar – nothing fashionable or edgy, probably one of those chain pubs where you can rely on getting a couple of pints and a decent meal for your money, no fancy frills. He also has a small scar above his right eye, the relic of a wound that must once have been deep.

He's mouthing something I don't catch at first, then I recognize my own name. Enora. For a moment, I've forgotten all about H and his parents. Who *is* this guy?

He's miming for me to lower the window. I shake my head and reach for the mask I've left on the passenger seat. Once I've put it on, I say goodbye to Jessie and point at my mobile.

The figure at my window is very quick on the uptake. From his suit pocket, he produces a small notepad and scribbles a number, before flattening it against the glass. I phone the number, as invited. He has a nice voice, very male but warm, midway between a growl and a murmur.

'Dessie Wren,' he says. 'How come this thing bangs us all up?'

He means the virus, of course, and I know exactly how he feels. Meeting anyone this way, especially a stranger, is absurd.

'Dessie who?'

'Wren. As in tweet-tweet. Imagine carrying that around all your life.'

Wren. The name is vaguely familiar. I know I've heard it very recently, but Dessie helps me out.

'Dave Munroe's mucker. Cynthia may have mentioned me.'

Cynthia. Got it.

'A week on the Isle of Wight? Staying at Cynthia's B & B? Am I right?'

'Yeah.'

'And you're still a cop?'

'Sort of.'

I nod, not knowing quite where to take this conversation next, but Dessie – once again – seems to read my mind.

'You're wondering about me and Dave? You're right. We did our separate things. Dave went to the Dark Side, I stayed with the angels. Would I ever have done what Dave did? No way. Did I blame him like I should have done? Again, no. My lot can be thick, as well as vicious. The whole Dave thing was badly managed from the off and we were all the poorer as a result. Dave had real talent, gifts few coppers even know exist. He was brilliant in the interview suite, read the bad guys like a book. We were crazy to let all that go to waste.'

'And that's why you're here?' I nod towards the crematorium.

'Yeah, partly. We stayed mates, is the real story. Dave was at home in any setting, and pubs were one of them. We tied on some nights in our time, believe me. Sad to see what happened to him later. He had mischief in his bones, that lovely man. I know you've talked to Cynthia. No one deserves a death like that.'

I can only nod in agreement. Next, I suspect, we'll be talking about another Covid victim, and I'm not wrong.

'So, how's H?' he asks.

'Sick.'

'Sick as in Covid?'

'Yes.'

'As bad as Dave was?'

'Not quite. Not yet. But awful to have it, and awful to watch.'

'They let you into the ICU?'

For the second time in a couple of minutes, I explain about Mr Wu, and the arrangements we've made.

'But is that wise? Under the circumstances?'

'You'll know H. Once he's made a decision, there's no argument. The guy that made it happen is Tony Morse. Thank God he's got the contacts. You know Tony?'

'Of course I know Tony. If you happen to be a copper, he's the cross you have to bear, especially in court. But credit to the man, he can argue black is white and get away with it. Brilliant on his day, and a real piss-off.'

I smile, recognizing this description only too well. All the arrangements, I tell Dessie, were down to him.

'Tony sorted everything. We have twenty-four-hour care, oxygen on tap, and an army of pretty nurses. My son thinks it's Christmas.'

'Malo, isn't it?'

'Yes.' I blink. 'How did you know that?'

'Tony Morse told me, way back last year. Saucy's love child, he said.'

'You're right. And mine, too, if you're asking.'

This comment of mine is wasted because Dessie has spotted someone else approaching across the car park. He unbends from the window, a smile on his face.

'Look,' he says. 'The man himself.'

To no one's surprise, Tony Morse is wearing a beautifully cut cashmere overcoat, full-length, and he must have spent hours raising the shine on his black Italian shoes. The two men, against all the rules, give each other a hug. Then it's Tony's face at my window.

'H?' he mouths.

I pull a face and flutter one hand to signal 50/50. Then Dessie gives him his phone.

'Not coming over to join us?' Tony nods across the car park. 'Pay your respects before the coffin arrives?'

I gaze towards the knot of people gathered awkwardly in front of the crematorium. Cynthia, I recognize at once. She's made a big effort for the occasion: a small, stylish hat in what looks like raffia, even a veil. Her black two-piece suit has a single red rose pinned to the lapel and she's doing her best to engage with the rest of the party, an assortment of kids and adults who must belong to Dave's previous life. Despite her best efforts, conversation appears to be strained, and the thesp in me gets the impression they've all lost their place in the script.

'Well, darling?' Tony again.

I hold his gaze for a moment, the phone still to my ear.

'Can't,' I say at last. 'Your Mr Wu would have me arrested.'

TWELVE

The funeral over, I drive away, feeling utterly empty, exhausted, my duty done. I give Cynthia a little wave as I pass the thin straggle of mourners heading for their cars, but I don't think she sees me. Making my way back into the city – empty road, shuttered shops, very few people about – I'm trying to work out what to say to H about the funeral, but then I realize there's no point. Like poor Dave Munroe, he's probably past caring.

I park outside the flat and phone the number Jessie has given me for H's parents. After a while, a woman's voice answers. She sounds younger than I'd somehow expected, a Pompey accent, impatient, almost aggressive.

'Mrs Prentice?'

'Doris. And you are?' I give her my name and there's a moment's pause before she makes the connection. 'The film star? Hayden's friend?'

'Yes.'

Jessie, it seems, has mentioned me in some conversation or other. Now Doris wants to know why I'm calling. I explain as best I can. H, I know, is an only child. The news that he might be dying is something I sense I have to handle with great care, but within seconds it turns out I couldn't be more wrong.

'You're telling me he's got it? The virus?'

'I'm afraid so, yes.'

'QA?' The Queen Alexandra is the city's main hospital.

'Not yet.'

'He's gone private? Is that what you're telling me?'

'Sort of, yes.'

'Typical. Show that boy a queue, and he'd either jump it or make other arrangements. So where is he?'

I explain about the flat, the nurses, and do my best with his prognosis. Doris's take on the likelihood of her son dying is remarkably brisk.

'Not a chance, dear. If that's what God had in store for him it would have happened years ago. He'll get through it, just like he's got through everything else in that life of his. How well do you know him, as a matter of interest?'

'Well-ish. He's the father of my son, which means we meet from time to time.'

'That Malo?'

'That Malo.'

'So, when do we get to meet him? Or you for that matter?'

Talking to this woman is like trying to cope with a force-eight gale. Her bluntness, questions delivered like physical blows, leave no space for negotiation or wit or any of the other little tricks that can soften a conversation, and already I begin to understand why H has chosen to keep her at arm's length. After barely a minute I badly need shelter, and I fancy a younger H might have felt the same. Nonetheless, whatever she might think about H battering the virus and sending it on its way, I still think it's my duty to effect some kind of *rapprochement*. If H happened to die tonight, both his mum and dad deserve the chance to say *adieu*.

'You live in the city? Am I right?'

'Cosham, dear. Up on the hill. You might think it's Portsmouth but you'd be wrong. Look out of our bedroom window and you'll know exactly why we left. Filthy place. We would have gone to Chichester, if we'd ever had the money.'

I swallow hard, trying to imagine what H would make of this conversation, and then I suggest she might drive down this afternoon. We could meet beside the Common. I could fix some kind of video link and she could stay in her car, and if H happened to be conscious, they might even have a conversation.

'And you, my dear? You'd be there?'

'Of course. If that's what you want.'

'And the boy? Malo?'

'Him, too. We'd stay outside the car, obviously. We could talk like this, by phone, after you'd made contact with H.'

'You mean Hayden.' Statement, not question.

'Of course, Hayden. Does that sound like a plan? Only I'll need to make arrangements for the video.' I glance at my watch. 'Half past four this afternoon? Would that be OK?'

After a grunt of what might be assent, I give her the address. Then, without bothering to say goodbye, she's gone.

Back in the flat, I discover that Mr Wu has had a brief discussion with Ela, the oldest of the two Polish nurses, and agreed that H should be transferred into the bigger of the two bedrooms. He's also ordered a proper hospital bed, fully motorized, to make nursing easier. This will come with a state-of-the-art mattress, specially designed to minimize the possibility of pressure sores. These, Ela tells me, can easily develop into ulcers, a complication H can definitely do without.

The bed and mattress arrive in the early afternoon, conjured from God knows where. It has already been partly dismantled but it still takes three men, all wearing full PPE, to wrestle it up the endless flights of stairs. I've cleared my few possessions from H's new bedroom, and between us Malo and I haul the old bed through to the front room. A call to Tony Morse confirms that we can chuck it away, and after they've finished installing the new bed, the guy in charge of the delivery crew sweetly agrees to get rid of it. This costs me seventy pounds, but I'm in no position to bargain. The shops that are still open locally are only accepting bank cards, but my saviour has no qualms about stuffing the money away beneath his PPE and heading for the door.

Newly configured, the flat settles into the old routines, with Ela's day shift looking after H. For the time being, he's still holding his own and for that Malo and I are grateful. I despatch my son to hunt for flowers to brighten the place up and he returns with an armful of daffodils, stolen from the ornamental garden beside the tennis courts. These I arrange in a couple of jam jars

I've found in a kitchen cupboard, one for the living room, and one for the new nest I'm sharing with Malo. Here, I clamber into a new set of PPE, and then go next door to pay H a visit. My recent conversation with his mother is still ringing in my ears and as yet I've no idea how to broach the prospect of a virtual visit.

Much to my relief, H appears to be a little better. He's still coughing, still breathless, but for the time being Ela has turned off the oxygen. The mask lies on the pillow beside his head. All he has to do, he mutters, is ask.

I settle beside the new bed, which looks enormous. The agency has supplied fold-up chairs and re-stocked the kitchen fridge, and now H wants to know about Dave's funeral. I do my best to describe it but in truth there's very little to say. A tiny handful of people. Cynthia looking brave. No one talking to each other. Then home.

'And that's all?'

'I stayed in the car.' I touch my visor. 'No choice.'

'Tony Morse there?'

'Yes. And another guy. Dessie?'

'Dessie Wren? Dave's oppo back in the day?'

'That's him.'

H nods, says nothing. Over the past couple of years, I've learned to read his silences.

'There's a problem with Dessie?' I ask.

'Yeah, he's a clever bastard.'

'He seemed very nice.'

'Exactly. And that's why you shouldn't trust him. He's a shagger, too. Women love him, but I've never worked out why.'

'Maybe he makes them laugh.' I'm remembering the big face at my car window. Dessie Wren. Cursed with the surname from hell.

H begins to cough again, signalling for Ela. She arrives with a moist flannel, bathes his face, then uses the bed's remote to bring H's upper body to near-vertical. This reminds me powerfully of Pavel, whom we nursed after he was stricken with paralysis. The same reliance on technology, the same surrender to the comfort of strangers.

H is trying to hoist something from the depths of his lungs.

Ela has readied a kidney bowl and H leans forward, gasping like a fish out of water, his mouth open, his head hanging over the bowl.

'Good boy.' Ela is playing Mum. 'Again, please. We need to get rid of this stuff.'

H looks at her for a moment, his eyes watering with the effort, the thick veins in his neck beginning to bulge, and then he makes a final effort, a long spasm of coughing that clearly hurts before a thick green ball of phlegm and God knows what else appears, hanging briefly from his mouth. Ela puts her arm around him, helpless child that he is, and catches the gunk in the bowl before handing it to the other nurse. H watches her leave the room.

'Fuck,' he gasps. 'Fuck, fuck.'

Ela mops his face again with the flannel. 'Good,' she says. 'Very good.'

H, exhausted, lies back against the pillow. His face is grey, and when Ela asks about the oxygen mask he nods. She reaches across for it but his eyes have found mine again and when she tries to put the mask on his face, he shakes his head. Not quite yet.

'Anything else?' he wheezes.

'Yes. I talked to your mother.'

'My mother? About what?' He's staring up at me.

'You, H.'

'And what did she say?'

'She said she'd like a word or two.'

'Before I croak, you mean? Sort the will? Get me into the nearest fucking church? Stack up a few credits?' He's gasping for air again.

'She might love you, H.'

'No fucking way. I'd have sussed that earlier. You think I'm stupid?'

'Please? For me? And maybe Malo?'

'I wouldn't let the boy anywhere near her. She's done far too much damage already. I'm getting better. Tell her that. Fucking make her day, stuck-up bitch.'

'Your dad, maybe?'

'My dad's a lovely guy. Deserved better.'

'You mean he's dead? Gone?'

'Yeah, in every way that matters. She killed him off years ago. Husk of a man.'

'You've seen him? Recently?'

'Yeah, couple of times these last few years,' he whispers. 'Bought him a drink. Bunged him a few quid, poor bastard that he is, banged up with someone like that.' He shakes his head, leaving wet stains on the pillow slip. 'No, tell her to fuck off. Else she'll walk all over you.'

I gaze down at him for a long moment, trying to imagine a younger H staking out his territory in the badlands of Pompey. Maybe he had no choice, I think. Maybe his entire criminal career was simply a conversation with his tyrannical mother. H, in any event, has once again dismissed her. Because life, as ever, moves on.

'Wes?' He's exhausted now. 'You met him?'

'Yes.'

'Good,' He gestures weakly round: the bed, the staff, the oxygen, Mr Wu, all that expense. 'Best to get on with it, eh?'

Best to get on with it. Ten minutes later, having shed the PPE, I phone Shanti's number from the front room and get through within seconds. I'm still introducing myself when she interrupts.

'*T'as faim?*' She wants to know whether I'm hungry.

'*Oui, un peu.*'

'*T'as déjà mangé?*' Have I eaten already?

'*Non.*'

'*Six heures et demi. Casablanca. Chez moi.*' Half past six. Be there.

With a chuckle, she rings off. I'm still studying the phone. *Tu* already? When we haven't even met? Remarkable.

Sunil is sitting beside Malo, watching him on his PlayStation. Malo has abandoned *Grand Theft Auto* for another game which features hang gliders, guided missiles, and a spectacular series of sudden deaths, and Sunil is transfixed.

'Where do I find a restaurant called Casablanca?' I ask him.

'The Moroccan place?'

'Yes.'

His eyes behind the visor never leave the screen. I'm to get myself to Gunwharf. Walk towards the waterfront. I'll find it next to a bar called *Dukes*.

'It'll be closed,' he says. 'Like everything else.'

By now it's mid-afternoon, and I owe H's mother another call. This time, a male voice answers the phone.

'Harry?' I know his name from H.

'That's right. And you're . . .?'

'Enora. I talked to your wife earlier.'

'I know. So how is he, pet? That boy of mine?' Just the hint of a Geordie accent.

'A little better, but I'm afraid there's a problem with this afternoon.'

'The boy doesn't want to see her?'

'No.'

'Surprise, surprise. And me? Did you ask him?'

'No.'

'Just as well. White Vauxhall Astra. Half four still OK?' He chuckles. Then he's gone.

I now have a problem. Do I forewarn H? Spark another outburst? Raise his temperature to boiling point? Risk a seizure, or worse? Or might there be another way? In the event, all too typically, I decide to defer a decision until the two of them arrive. Malo, if it comes to it, can get into PPE and settle beside H with his smartphone. Mum and Dad, if they so wish, can make contact from their car. And afterwards, my obligations discharged, I can spend the evening in Gunwharf with a clear conscience.

By half past four, I've stationed myself beside the window in the front room, gazing down at the occasional passing car in the big road below. The white Astra appears a minute or two early and pulls into a parking bay opposite the flats. Looking down, it's impossible to see the two figures inside, but I've briefed Malo about the impending visit, and he's already getting himself into his PPE. H, according to one of the nurses, is asleep, which may be a blessing.

I check for my phone and take the stairs down to the street. The moment I step into the road, I realize that the Astra has

only one occupant. A tall figure, slightly bent, is sitting behind
the wheel. He's wearing the flat cap I've seen in dozens of black
and white archive shots from the *Portsmouth News*, and he
doesn't move as I cross the road. Beside the car, I crouch like
Dessie Wren, and show him my mobile phone. I can see H in
his face. His grey hair is beginning to thin but he still has H's
curls. These last few years, H has put on weight, a tribute to
Jessie's cooking. His dad, *au contraire*, is skin and bone, not
an ounce of spare flesh, but the moment he smiles at me I can
see H in his softer moments. Once, I suspect, this man was
handsome, and the longer I look, the greater the temptation to
think of another name. Malo.

H's dad has scribbled a mobile number for me. Moments later,
we've established contact.

'You mind if I call you Harry?' I ask.

'I'm honoured, pet.' Definitely a Tynesider. 'How is he?'

'Asleep.'

'That's for the best.'

'You want to talk to him?'

'You mean wake him up? No. I've come for a look at you,
and that boy of yours. He's around? Our Malo?'

'Our' is a revelation. Harry Prentice may be a husk of a
man in H's eyes, soaking up a lifetime of punishment from
his scary wife, but he knows exactly how to make a friend of
yours truly.

'You want me to get him down? Malo?'

'I do, pet, yes, but tell me about the boy, first.'

'Your boy?'

'My boy. He always had luck, young Hayden, and cheek, too,
and looking at you I know he's in good hands. Don't get me
wrong, pet. I know you're just friends. But he thinks the world
of you, because he's told me so, and that says to me there must
be just a little tiny candle in there somewhere.'

'Candle?'

'Between you. Heat and light. That's all we ever need, pet.
And you're talking to someone who knows.'

I nod. Despite the window between us, and Covid, and the
larger madness of the pandemic, this lovely man has kindled a
real warmth. This, in its way, is a kind of magic, increasingly

rare in most conversations that come my way, and within minutes he's sharing memories of an H I've only so far been able to picture from drunken exchanges with his Pompey mates. How he was a replacement for an earlier son who sadly miscarried. How well he did at junior school. How fearless he was when it came to scrapping. How he drove his mother crazy with his refusal to knuckle down. How a longing for bad company and the main chance finally drove him out of the family home.

'We lost him at sixteen,' he says. 'And he never came back. The little tyke would never say sorry, never apologize for any of the mess he left behind him, but he'd phone me from time to time, and you know why? Because he wanted me to understand.'

'And did you?'

'Of course I did.' He nods up at the windscreen, and for the first time I notice the little wooden cross dangling from the rear-view mirror. 'I had to live with it. He never did. Did I ever blame him for baling out? Of course I didn't. Did he lead us both a dance? Yes. Would I ever have wanted him any other way? Never. Because the lad had spirit. And he made me laugh. Fetch that Malo of yours. D'you mind?'

'Of course not.' After a final check that Harry doesn't want sight of his invalid son, I return to the flat. Malo, bless him, is still beside H, and H is still asleep. I beckon my son out of the bedroom and tell him to get rid of the visor and mask. Still gowned, he accompanies me down to the street. We cross the road, and the pair of us squat beside Harry's door.

Harry looks Malo up and down, his whole face creasing into a smile. Then comes a whirr as he lowers the window and extends a bony hand. Malo peels off his glove, and for a long moment the two men share a lingering handshake.

'Take care of our Hayden,' he says. 'And be proud of that mam of yours.'

THIRTEEN

Within the hour, still buoyed by my encounter with H's dad, I walk the mile or so to Gunwharf, which turns out to be a newish shopping and leisure complex. The promenade at the seaward end looks out over the harbour, which is as empty as Gunwharf itself, and I linger beside the water, knowing how rare it must be to have a view like this to myself. I've already spotted Casablanca on the way down, a stylish confection in light pastel shades of green, pink and light blue. One of the plate-glass windows is dominated by an extravagant palm which frames the view of the interior, and back from the waterfront, I have the opportunity to take a proper look.

By now it's nearly dark and at first all I can see inside is the bare outline of tables topped with upended chairs, but then I make out the faintest suggestion of a bar in the depths of the restaurant, a line of bottles dimly lit by the flicker of a single candle. I'm still looking for a bell or a buzzer beside the entrance when I feel the lightest pressure on my shoulder.

'Enora? *C'est toi?*' A throaty chuckle.

I glance round. This has to be Shanti. She's tall, full-figured, a commanding presence in a floaty dress with a fountain of playful stars that explode upwards towards her bosom. Her hair is cut brutally short and she's wearing a huge pair of plastic earrings. She has a bag over her shoulder but, for a big woman, she moves with the lightness of a ghost.

She's dressed for summer. I ask her in French whether she isn't cold.

'Never.' She's unlocking the door. 'Come. I must feed you.'

I follow her into the emptiness of the restaurant. She trails the scent of patchouli oil, a sweet spiciness that hangs briefly in the stale air. She collects the candle from the bar and checks the phone for messages.

'You're expecting bookings?'

'Bookings would be good.' She's speaking English now, and

she shoots me a sardonic look over her bare shoulder. 'In fact, anything would be good these days. I used to love Albert Camus, *La Peste* especially. Now I realize he wasn't joking. Days like these steal your soul.' She nods gravely, abandoning the phone. 'And the nights are even worse. You have a friend, no? One of the fallen?'

The *fallen*? H, I think, would take offence.

'I have a friend who's not very well,' I say loyally. 'Better soon, *inshallah.*'

Inshallah, if Allah wills it, raises a broad smile.

'You believe in God, my child? In the face of such evidence as this?' She gestures round the shadowed, empty space that should be so busy. Beautifully shaped hands. An interesting assortment of silver bangles on her thin wrists. When I follow her into the kitchen, she lights more candles. A little window at the back is broken and the draught makes the shadows dance on the shelves of pots and pans.

'You prefer candles to electricity?'

'I love electricity.' That throaty laugh again. 'But I haven't paid my bill. The gas people, too. They've cut me off.'

'Carelessness? You forgot?'

'Poverty. I couldn't afford it.'

'Times are that bad?'

'*Oui. Pénible.*' Cruel.

'So what happens when all this is over? And you have meals to cook?'

'They turn me on again. Because by then we'll have lots of money.'

'We?'

'You and me, my child.' She puts a finger to her lips. '*Inshallah.*'

For the time being she volunteers no more details but busies herself at the work surface beside the double sink. From her bag she produces onions, an aubergine, two small courgettes, fat beef tomatoes, and a bunch of something green I take to be coriander, and in no time at all I'm looking at the ingredients for a substantial tagine. Chopping garlic and root ginger, she tells me to take a candle back to the bar.

'The cupboard beside the telephone,' she says. 'You like Sidi

Brahim? In Marrakesh we lived on it, and you know what the locals said? Only infidels and Jews drink red wine from the fridge. Tonight, we have no choice. Either Sidi Brahim at room temperature or water from the tap. Your choice, my child.'

She turns her back and begins to layer the sliced veggies into a tagine dish before hunting for spices. I fetch the wine from the bar and by the time I return, I can smell the sweetness of the red paprika. She's cooking on an ancient-looking two-ring camping stove, dwarfed by the big tagine. The little blue tank of butane gas, she says, is nearly empty but there's a popping noise and then a blossom of flame the moment she strikes a match.

'You want another job?' She nods at a nearby drawer. 'Sidi Brahim is like us. It lives to breathe.'

I find a corkscrew in the drawer and draw the cork from the bottle. Shanti adds water to the tagine, gives it a stir, makes the sign of the cross, and then takes a sip of the wine before settling on a battered stool.

'Tell me about your sick friend. *Du coin, n'est-ce pas*?'

Du coin means local. I nod. Pompey born and bred, I say. First a hooligan. Then a trainee accountant. Then a very rich man.

'Cocaine?'

'Yes.'

'So easy. Especially now. Me? I used to love it, talk to it, make it be nice to me. More. I always wanted more.'

'This was when?'

'Not so many years ago. In Marrakesh. There you have three choices. Kif from the mountains, good kif, *very* good kif. Or cocaine. For enough, you needed a lot of money and a lot of discipline and I had neither.'

'And the third choice?'

'Sidi Brahim. Life in Marrakesh could be unkind. Red wine made me fat. Kif made me sleepy. While cocaine was going to put me in the gutter with the poor people. God invented choice to make us crazy, *n'est-ce pas*?'

'So, what happened?'

'I got fat.' She stares briefly into her glass, then shrugs and empties it. By now, I've found another stool. She looks up at me for a long moment, and then gestures me a little closer as if other people might be listening.

'How much do you need?'

'Wine?'

'Money, my child. To pay that bill of yours for your friend.'

'My child' is wearing a little thin. She's probably my age, maybe even a year or two younger, but I've been in these situations before. A lot of people I know assume that only men play power games, jostle for advantage, insist on being top dog. It isn't true.

'A quarter of a million pounds.' I hold her gaze.

'How soon?'

'Very soon.'

'You have debts?'

'I have obligations. My friend is very sick and refuses to go to hospital. It's my job to keep him alive and a quarter of a million pounds might just do that.' I offer her a thin smile. 'And you? What do you need?'

'Apart from a man?' She pours herself another glass of Sidi Brahim and offers me the bottle. 'I need enough to turn my lights back on again.'

'Maybe a man would do that.'

'Sure, my child. *Touché*. But maybe not.'

'So, we're talking electricity?'

'Of course not. *Pas du tout*. The electric will help. The electric will let me feed people, make a little money, enough to pay the other bills, but no. A confidence, my child, a secret, do you mind?'

'Not at all.'

'My life is so boring, so tedious. Take this place, this little business of mine. It was making me a living, not so much but enough. I have somewhere to live. I have amusing friends. Then everything stops, not my fault, and suddenly' – she frowns – '*tout-a-fait fauché.' Fauché*. Broke.

'So?'

'So, I look back at the days when my lights were on, when there was gas in my pipes, and do you know what I feel? What I realize? That this new life of mine was never enough. Does that make me greedy? Or just bored? In London I lived like a pirate. The man in my life was like a dog with mange, always scratching, always on the move, never still, never at rest. But at least every day was different.'

'You were dealing?'

'He was dealing. And he was very, very good at it. We made a lot of money, stayed out of trouble. And we were laughing all the time.'

'Until?'

'Until he met someone else. Never trust Italian journalists, no matter how often they smile at you.'

'She stole your man?'

'He, my child. *He* stole my man. And that was a surprise, not just to me but to him as well. The morning he told me he'd never been so happy in his life was the morning I left. Not "happy". He used a different word: "complete". He said Giuseppe made him complete, and you know what that means? It means I'd been living with half a man, not a whole man at all.' She shakes her head. 'Nearly ten years. Unbelievable.' The tagine is simmering now, bubbling softly under the thickness of the glazed lid. 'You like couscous? Of course you like couscous. The whole world likes couscous. God is kind. I have a second ring on my little cooker. All I need is a little water and maybe a drop of olive oil.' She leans forward, her hand on my knee, and gives me a playful kiss on my cheek. '*Inshallah.*'

The tagine is delicious, full-bodied, perfectly spiced. I have a list of questions I know I ought to be asking her. About exactly what H's investment might buy us, about how the cocaine might be sourced, and – most important of all – about how we turn all these uncut kilos of pure white into the umpteen deals which will multiply H's stake into the kind of money he so badly needs. If he's ever well enough to listen, these are the details H is going to demand, testing whatever Shanti has to say against his own experience, but whenever I try to pin this woman down, the only thing that appears to interest her is H's cash.

'How much? Exactly?'

'A hundred and fifty thousand pounds. I thought I told you.'

'Tell me again.'

'One hundred and fifty K.'

'And it comes directly from him? He has this money now?'

'Yes.'

'How?'

'I don't understand.'

'How will he pay? How will I get the money? Bank draft? Cheque?' She shrugs. 'Cash?'

'I've no idea. I've never done this before.'

'So, it's always been him? This H? Is that what you're telling me?'

'Of course. I'm an actress, not a drug dealer.'

'A favour, then? You're doing him a favour?'

'Of course. Because he's sick. In fact, he may be dying. No one seems to know, not yet, but I'm doing my best to help with all the bills we have to pay.'

'Otherwise?'

'Otherwise he'll end up in hospital, in the ICU.'

'But the ICU is free.'

'I know, but a friend of his just died there. And H thinks he'd be next on the list.'

Shanti tips her head back, expels a long blue plume of smoke, says she doesn't understand. Whoever turns down free health care? The kitchen stinks of weed now, but I've declined her offer to roll me a doobie of my own.

'There's more wine, my child.' She nods towards the empty bottle and then checks her watch. 'Me too, please.'

I leave the kitchen to hunt for more Sidi Brahim and return to find her reading a text on her mobile. A sudden scowl clouds her face.

'*Merde*,' she says. 'He's at the door already.'

'Who?'

'You go. His name's Sean. He may need help.'

'With what?'

'The generator. The little man's always hungry, too. Thank God there's still tagine in the pot.'

Sean is waiting outside in the street, a pale, thin face shrouded in a grey hoodie, his hunched back turned away from the wind blasting in from the harbour. I open the door, and for a moment, looking at the blankness in his eyes, I assume he's drunk. Wrong.

'Yeah?'

I'm staring at him. Two of his teeth are broken at the front. His question is meaningless.

'You're after Shanti?' I ask him.

'Yeah,' he says again. Exactly the same intonation. This vagrant has bits missing, I think. He's not entirely, to coin a phrase, complete.

'She mentioned a generator,' I say.

'It's round the back. You're offering? Or what?'

He doesn't wait for an answer, just turns his back and limps off. He's wearing grey trackie bottoms beneath the hoodie, and a shoelace trails from one of his runners. I follow him down the alley beside the restaurant. At the back of the premises, he stops behind a white van parked next to a builder's skip. He opens the rear door. Peering inside, behind the generator, I can see a mattress, and a grubby duvet, and a couple of cushions. Also, deep towards the back, the outline of a bicycle. Together we manhandle the generator out. Sean smells of something sour, of damp and neglect, but his strength takes me by surprise. Together, we manhandle the generator to the restaurant's back door, Sean doing most of the heavy lifting. Shanti is waiting for us.

'You brought fuel, too?' She's looking at Sean.

'Yeah. Tank's full. Plus two cans extra. Enough to get the fridge cold.'

We carry the generator through to the kitchen. The draught from the door has blown out most of the candles, but when Shanti opens the big fridge-freezer there's enough light to make out trays of meat joints, still oozing blood.

'Venison,' Shanti says. 'Cheap if you know where to go. You place an order. The poacher does the rest.'

Sean fires up the generator, finds the plug and the fridge begins to purr.

'You sell this stuff?' I'm still looking at Shanti.

'Of course. This city lives for meat like this. Spread the word and it sells itself.'

She shuts the freezer door and busies herself with the tagine while Sean rolls himself a doobie. Conversation between the two of them is sparse, no more than a grunt or two on Sean's part, but I get the impression that they've known each other for a while. She seems to treat him with respect, even caution. The last thing she's ever going to call him is 'my child', and that, too, is interesting.

Over the next half hour or so, while Sean wolfs the tagine and a couple of stale baguettes, Shanti is bent over her smart phone, firing off a volley of texts. I, meanwhile, work steadily through the second bottle of Sidi Brahim, listening to the howl of the wind through the broken window and trying not to think too hard about H back at the flat. There may, or may not, have been a third bottle of Moroccan red but by midnight I'm past caring. Not once has Shanti shown the slightest interest in resuming negotiations over H's investment, and for that, I'm grateful.

Instead, I find myself listening to Sean. He's evidently taken a bit of a shine to me and the weed has opened him up. He does most of the talking, an exercise in free association that takes in everything from the millions of undeclared corpses he's heard about in the basement of the local hospital to the promised screening of Pompey's epic 2010 FA Cup tie against the hated Scummers.

'Fucking classic,' he says. 'Listen to those old guys who were at the game that day and you'd think we'd got to Wembley. You know what else happened that season? Four changes of owner, most of the ground staff sacked, thousands of other redundancies, the tax man knocking on the fucking door, and on top of all that we get relegated at the end of the season.' He peers at me, as if I'd just arrived. 'You from around here?'

'Afraid not.'

'No?' He reaches for my glass. 'I don't fucking blame you.'

At the end of the evening, Shanti puts her phone away and declares she's had enough. She looks at the empty bottles and shakes her head.

'Sean will walk you home,' she says. 'He'll be back to sleep in the van. Right, Sean?'

Sean nods, and moments later we find ourselves out in the darkness again. The wind, if anything, is even stronger and between flurries of rain I can taste salt on my lips. Saying goodbye to Shanti, she holds my hand for a long moment, then gives it a little squeeze.

'À plus tard,' she murmurs. See you later.

Quite what this means is a mystery but Sean, who must be freezing inside his thin hoodie, plays the gentleman and squires me back through the tangle of waterside battlements that have always, he says, kept the fucking French out. The Round Tower. The Square Tower. Garrison Square. Long Curtain. Each of these Pompey landmarks sparks a grunt or two of explanation from Sean, and I peer into the windy darkness as we stagger past, trying to imagine the roar of cannon and the glint of unsheathed cutlass blades in the fitful moonlight. Say what you like about this hooligan city but stuff has happened here, important stuff, stuff that ends up in a list of names on countless monuments, and Sean is telling me about the sinking of the *Mary Rose* untold years ago when we find ourselves wandering through the fun fair.

I pause a moment, staring up at the bones of the helter-skelter ride, trying to get my bearings. Then I become aware of Sean bent over the door of the nearby games arcade. I've guessed his age at late twenties, early thirties, and by now I know that he's a self-taught electrician, taking money off anyone who'll put work his way. One of his clients, he now tells me, has the franchise for the games arcade, and only this morning he's been doing maintenance on some of the older machines.

He has the key to the door and moments later I'm following the torch on his smart phone through the muddle of slots and games machines. At last, in the bowels of all this tat, he stops. The place has already spooked me. I'm far too drunk to be seriously frightened but the place has the feel of a certain kind of film set, full of artful menace, and the howl of the wind outside supplies the perfect soundtrack.

Ahead of me, Sean has stopped. The beam of his smart phone sweeps left and right and then steadies on an array of stand-up mirrors. I last saw mirrors like these half a lifetime ago on the cheaper end of the promenade at Cannes. They're malformed to make you look seriously weird, offering wildly distorted images that used to make me laugh. Us thesps would pay them a visit after partying at the film festival, the cherry on the cake after an evening's boozing, and those surreal moments – fat in one mirror, thin in the next – became a kind of tradition. Now is no different. In the light of Sean's beam, I throw a few shapes, pout, smooch, blow myself a kiss, and then attempt a final twirl that sends me crashing into Sean's arms.

Again, much to my surprise, he has the strength to carry my weight. I'm totally relaxed, staring up at the shape of his hoodie.

'Brilliant, yeah?' He's grinning fit to burst and the torch beam spills briefly across the wreckage of his mouth. 'I knew you'd fucking love it.'

We say our goodbyes at two metres distance back outside. I can see the Common from here and, thanks to H, I know my way home.

'Good to meet you,' I say. 'Do you really sleep in that van?'

'Yeah, some nights.' He gives me a strange smile. 'Next time, eh?'

FOURTEEN

Malo is still awake by the time I get back. I let myself into the building, negotiate the six flights of steps with some difficulty, and turn the key in flat number seven as quietly as I can. The place smells even more like a hospital than I remember from only hours ago, but I manage to make it to our new bedroom without meeting any of the nurses. H's door is closed, and I can hear a low murmur of conversation from inside.

Despite my best efforts, Malo knows at once that I'm drunk. The light is on and he's reading a copy of *Top Gear* magazine.

'You're pissed,' he says. 'Where have you been?'

'Out.'

'Yeah. I get that. But where?'

I shake my head. He's still wearing his PPE gown, his mask and visor lie beside his sleeping bag and there's no mistaking the reproach in his voice. While H is fighting for his life, I've been out partying.

'How is he?' I've shed my wet anorak and I'm trying to unbutton my top. I feel about twelve.

'He's out of it. Has been all evening.'

'You were with him? All that time?'

'Of course.'

I nod. I don't know what to say. Hopeless. I manage to wrestle the rest of my clothes off, and collapse into bed in my knickers and bra. Malo has gone back to his magazine, which is a blessing of sorts, but as my eyes close and I drift away I'm starting to wonder where this bizarre spell of incarceration, a prison sentence with no release date, will leave us all.

Next thing I know, it's the middle of the night and the room is in darkness. I lay perfectly still for a moment. The wind seems to have dropped outside the window and I can hear the steady breathing of my son on the floor beside the bed. Then, with a sudden gust of nausea, I realize my head is bursting, along with my bladder. This is urgent.

I manage to get out of the room without waking him and make my way, still semi-naked, to the bathroom. After I'm done on the loo, I look in the cupboard over the sink in the hope of finding tablets. Nothing. Maybe the kitchen, I think. Ibuprofen, paracetamol, aspirin. Anything to stop me throwing up.

I'm on my knees in the kitchen, searching a cupboard full of assorted crockery, when the door opens. It's Julia, the American nurse. She looks surprised.

'You OK down there, Ms Andressen?'

'You wouldn't have a tablet, by any chance?'

'For what? Precisely?'

'A headache?'

I can tell at once from the expression on her face that this is a big mistake, and I'm right. She wants to know what else is going on with me. Do I feel hot? Have I been coughing at all? Is my sense of smell impaired? In short, should I be tucked up next door with H?

'I'm afraid I had too much to drink. My fault. Let's call it self-abuse.' I force a smile. 'Ibuprofen? Maybe two?'

Judgemental is generally a word I try to avoid but looking at Julia, here and now, I can think of no other. I'm employing this woman. However temporary, this is our territory. Yet the way she stares at me, that tiny, unforgiving shake of the head, tells me I'm completely out of order. Lockdown means lockdown. Just who do I think I am?

She steps out of the kitchen and returns with a packet of ibuprofen.

'These are two-hundred-milligram capsules,' she says briskly. 'Never more than two at a time, and never more than six in twenty-four hours. Drink lots of water and we'll see how you are in the morning.' She begins to back out of the room as I reach for a glass, but then stops. 'He's awake, by the way. Shall I give him your best?'

Bitch, I think, swallowing the tablets. I stay in the kitchen for a couple of minutes, letting my guts settle down, then make my way back to bed. Malo, thank God, is asleep. Suddenly cold, I slip between the sheets and pull the duvet up around my neck. Moments before I drift off again, I hear laughter from next door.

Next morning, I sleep late and awake to find myself alone. Last time I checked, Malo's runners were tucked away beside his sleeping bag. Now, they've gone. My phone tells me it's nearly ten o'clock. My headache has disappeared, but I'm left with a shaky sense of not knowing exactly what to do next. I feel nervous, adrift from my moorings. I used to have a life, a place to call my own, little freedoms I took for granted. Now I'm never living with less than six people, in a tiny space, and four of them think I'm a drunk.

I find Taalia on the sofa in the front room, half-watching TV while she makes notes on an important-looking form. She confirms that Malo has gone out for a run.

'Nice boy,' she says. 'You must be proud.'

'And H?'

'He's asleep again.' She flips back through what appears to be an hourly log. 'His sats were better last night. Julia was pleased with him.'

'And now?'

'Not so great.'

'But OK?'

'Yes.' She nods. 'Sort of.'

Sort of. Her tone of voice does nothing to raise my spirits, but I'm still too jumpy to push her for the details. Good days and bad days, I tell myself. And three of these scary nurses to keep H alive.

I make myself a cup of tea and retire to the privacy of our bedroom. I need, very badly, to talk to someone who represents the other bit of my life, the part I realize was so precious. Rosa, my agent, normally reserves Saturday morning for a tour of her favourite café-bars, mainly around Covent Garden, but like everyone else in the world, she's banged up.

It's her husband who answers the phone. His name is Kurt. He's German, a huge bear of a man. He trained as a lawyer but now helps Rosa at the agency, taking care of the legals.

'*Alles gut?*' I enquire. This more or less exhausts my store of German and he's kind enough to stick to English.

'Never better,' he says. 'We managed to get down to the coast. Snuck under the wire and avoided the Fun Police by the skin of our teeth.' This, coming from a German, I find seriously amusing.

Kurt and Rosa have a beautiful house in Deal, as well as a *pied-à-terre* in Camden, a tribute to her earning power. She made her fortune years back, feasting off the meteoric rise of a handful of young actors who – thanks in part to her canniness – truly made the big time. I was never one of those, but we've always been close.

'My precious?' It's Rosa.

'Me,' I agree.

'All well?'

'No. Since you ask.'

I bore her with a brief account of life in Southsea. Nurses. PPE. Covid-talk. Plus the company of umpteen strangers, most of them foreign.

'Sounds wonderful,' Rosa says. 'I hope you're keeping notes.'

'Sadly not. Any news from Paris?'

'None, my precious. I gather things are even stricter over there. Macron plays Napoleon in this production and everyone hides behind their shutters. I'm afraid we might have to brace ourselves for a bit of a wait.'

'Seriously?'

'So I'm told. Everything's come to a halt. We might even be talking about next year, assuming they OK the series.'

'Shit.'

'I knew you'd be pleased. Anticipation is everything, my precious. Look on the bright side.'

I nod, unconvinced. I phoned for a bit of a lift. Now this.

'And you?' I say brightly. 'How's it going?'

'Brilliant, since you ask.'

'Brilliant how?'

'Everything's so *quiet.* No tourists. No boy racers. No pollution. On a clear night, like last night, we can put on our coats and sit on the balcony and see the lights of France. Just think of all those French punters just gagging for *Dimanche.* Fear not, my precious. All will be well.'

With that, and a cheerful aside about the imminent collapse of live theatre, she's gone.

Deflated, I lie back on the bed, wondering who else to phone. Tim, I think, my actor friend who aced the 4x4 commercial on the rock face. He, at least, understands the darker side of Portsmouth.

Moments later, I find myself talking to his mum. Tim, she says, is in the garden transplanting rows of early peas. For some reason, I find this seriously impressive, so rural, so *real*, so un-Pompey.

His mum hands the phone over. Not just peas, it turns out, but broad beans, and cabbage, and some promising heads of romaine lettuce.

'Sounds idyllic,' I tell him. 'You'll never come back.'

'You're right. I've worked this bastard virus out. It thrives in confined spaces. It hates fresh air. I read yesterday that the Vietnamese haven't had a single death. And you know why? Because they're all out there in the paddy fields, doing the rice thing. Covid's payback for living indoors. Where did we go so wrong?'

The question floors me, so concise, so *right.* Not just where but *why*, and *how*, did we go so wrong? I start to tell him about H, about the agency, about a new set of faces every eight hours, and finally about me and my son negotiating a new relationship in a bedroom no bigger than a prison cell. Tim, bless him, understands exactly where I'm headed.

'You should get out more,' he says at once.

'I did. Last night.'

'Where?'

'Gunwharf. You know a place called Casablanca? It's a resto, newish, Moroccan cuisine.'

'Yeah. And the woman's off her head.' Tim's laughing. 'Good cook, though. And decent weed.'

'You know her?'

'Yeah. Everyone knows her. She's become a bit of a legend. Shanti. Keeps rough company but you'd never blame her for that, not in Pompey. I once saw her drink an old 6.57 hooligan under the table. They were celebrating his divorce and there was nothing but Bourbon on offer. This was a couple of years back. She once tapped me up for tennis lessons, but she didn't want to pay. Not in money.'

'She's been around for a while?'

'Off and on, yeah. The way I heard it, she had some minted bloke in London, but I'm guessing that's history now.' He pauses. 'You're telling me you met her last night?'

'Yes.'

'So, what did you make of her?'

'Crazy, like you said. We drank far too much. Way over the top. I met another guy, too. Sean? Thin, terrible teeth, drives a white van? Calls himself an electrician?'

'Could be anyone in this city.' Tim's laughing again. 'Especially the teeth. What was he like?'

'Strange.'

'Strange interesting? Strange horrible? Strange scary?'

'Just strange. I haven't made my mind up yet.'

'You're seeing him again?'

'I hope not.'

'Why's that?'

'I don't know.'

'He's got a surname, this Sean? You want me to ask around?'

For a moment, I don't answer. Then I hear footsteps outside and the sound of Malo's voice. He's talking to Taalia, the Asian nurse, telling her what a brilliant day it is, how they might get a run together, when she has time off.

'Gotta go,' I tell Tim.

'And this Sean?'

'Sure, by all means ask around.'

'No problem. Listen, something else, this khazi of a flat you're all in. If you need to escape, to get your head down someplace else, just ring.'

'Like where?'

'Chez moi. I'm round the corner from you. The woman next door has a spare key. I can always phone her if things get heavy.'

Heavy? I want to know more, but Tim's gone already and it's Malo's face at the door.

'Surprise, surprise,' he says coldly. 'You're awake.'

FIFTEEN

The rest of the day, I'd prefer to forget. Within minutes, Mr Wu has arrived. He goes in to see H, and emerges a while later. I'm dressed by now, waiting for him in the front room. He says that H is pretty much the same, no real change. The good news is that there's no sign of the infection spreading to his liver and kidneys, which appears to be happening in ICUs up and down the country.

'And the bad news?'

'He's exhausted. He's a strong man, but he'll need our help for a while yet.'

'Are you telling me he's getting better?'

'Not at all. He's holding his own, and believe me, Ms Andressen, that's a compliment. Twenty years older, he might be dead by now. We have to be very careful, one day at a time, sometimes one hour at a time. The virus never gives up. And neither will we.' He might be smiling behind the mask and the visor, I can't tell, but either way it doesn't matter because Mr Wu has something else on his mind. 'We've been here three days now, Ms Andressen. I understand the nursing agency delivered an envelope last night.'

'They did?'

'Yes. There's a note on the log. Your son signed for it.'

'Malo?'

'Yes.'

'So, what was it? In the envelope?'

Mr Wu doesn't answer for a moment. Then he suggests, in all our interests, that we have a conversation.

'All three of us?' I'm lost.

'Yourself and your son, Ms Andressen.' He checks his watch. 'I'm late for the ICU already.'

Malo always takes an age in the shower. I'm still on the lumpy sofa in the front room when he finally emerges. He's wearing a fresh pair of jeans and a Womad T-shirt I've never seen before. He looks wonderful, and I'd normally tell him so, but not this morning.

'The agency sent us a letter last night, is that right?'

'Yes.'

'So where is it?'

'In the bedroom.'

He's staring down at me. I can smell toast from the kitchen and there's a smear of butter on one corner of his mouth. He doesn't move.

'Are you going to get the bloody thing?' I'm staring up at him. 'Or what?'

He shrugs and leaves the room. Seconds later, he returns with a white envelope and drops it on my lap.

'Why didn't you mention this last night?'

'Read it, Mum.'

'I asked you a question.'

'You were off your head. Just read it.'

I do his bidding. The letter comes from the agency's financial director. As Tony Morse has already warned, we're running up a substantial bill. The daily roster of nurses is costing us £3,600 per day. Other charges, including medical supplies, oxygen, and the new hospital bed, so far total £4,567. The deep-cleaning company have yet to invoice for their services, and this sum will appear in the next account. Under normal circumstances the agency would have asked for a deposit before the commencement of care, but time was short. Now, having talked to Mr Wu, they would appreciate an initial payment of £20,000, with ongoing care to be invoiced at the end of every week, the first payment due on Friday 10 April. Should the patient stage an early recovery, or be transferred to hospital, any outstanding monies will, of course, be reimbursed, but in the meantime, early payment – preferably by BACS or a credit card – would be much appreciated.

I look up. I knew a reckoning like this was inevitable, but I feel physically sick. The £20,000 I could just about manage myself, but these are early days. What happens when the next bill arrives on Friday? And all the Fridays thereafter?

'You should have told me, Malo.'

'Last night, you mean? Why? What would have been the point?'

'This morning, then. Before you went for that run of yours.'

'You were asleep. And in any case, it's sorted.'

'*Sorted?* How?'

'I talked to Jessie last night. She's got access to Dad's rainy-day fund, and she also got on to the people at the agency first thing. You never pay their first demand, ever. That's just the starter for negotiations. Taalia told me the block-rate they get for ICU nurses from the NHS. It's way below what they're charging us, so they've got every incentive to keep us on the hook. In the end we settled for fifteen.'

'Fifteen thousand?'

'Yeah.'

'And your dad? What did he have to say?'

'Nothing. He's out of it.' He shrugs. 'Just like you, Mum.'

With this parting shot, he retrieves the letter from my lap and leaves the room. I hear the slam of our bedroom door, and then the opening bars of an Ed Sheeran song, first very loud, then softer. Malo, like me, needs time to calm down.

I get up and go to the window, fighting to get a grip, to get everything back into some kind of focus. Jessie we can depend on. Jessie, I know, will do Malo's bidding and come up with whatever sum he thinks we'll need to keep the agency sweet. She has a lot of time for this son of ours. Hence, I assume, last night's conversation.

Twenty thousand pounds. Fifteen thousand pounds. Four thousand five hundred and something pounds. Plus the deep-cleaning bills. Plus whatever we owe Tony Morse for taking care of Mr Wu.

I'm trying to compute all these figures, trying to understand the sheer scale of what all this will cost us. H's bid to turn his rainy-day fund into cocaine is, I realize, the purest fantasy, the old Pompey reflex, and it's a relief that Malo's taken charge. I'm also impressed by how savvy he is. I would never have bargained on the phone like that, never have saved us five thousand pounds on the deposit. If I ever wanted proof that Malo carries H's DNA, then here it is.

But what about H himself? Shouldn't someone have a word? Share what's going on? I'm still at the window, still staring out, still hearing the contempt in my son's voice. *Out of it*, he'd said. *You're out of it*. Drunk. Pissed. Incapable. MIA. Missing in action. A video game gone hopelessly wrong. No, I think. I'm better than this. That someone has to be me.

It's late morning before I put on my PPE and venture into H's bedroom. The sight of his face on the pillow stops me by the door and, looking at him, I know exactly what he'll be like in twenty years' time. Is this why Malo is so angry with me? Did he sit here all evening, wondering where his mother had gone, watching his precious dad grow visibly older? Sicker? More vulnerable? The virus seems to have given H's sagging flesh the texture and the colour of parchment. He looks like a much-thumbed book, read and re-read, and now in the box for the charity shop.

I'm aware of the nurses eyeing me with some interest. There are obviously no secrets left in this tomb of a flat, and today's headline has handsome young Malo falling out with his feckless mother.

'Would you mind leaving us alone for a moment or two?' I ask.

'He's asleep, Ms Andressen.'

'I know. I can see that.'

There's an exchange of glances before the oldest of the nurses gets to her feet. The other two follow her out of the room. They'll leave the door an inch or two ajar. If anything happens, just shout.

If anything happens? Fat chance, I think, drawing up one of the chairs and settling beside the bed. H isn't on the oxygen just now. His mouth is open and every time he breathes out, there's a gust of something sour and slightly chemical, which must have to do with his meds. Looking round, I notice a bottle of warfarin tablets on the nearby trolley. In concentrated doses, this stuff kills rats.

'H?' I take his hand, stroke it. 'Can you hear me?'

Nothing happens. I ask the question again, my lips barely inches from his ear on the pillow, and I notice a tiny tremor of recognition beneath his eyelids.

'H? Are you in there?' I ask for a third time. 'Can you hear me?'

He nods, and then his spare hand comes up to cover his mouth just moments before a spasm of coughing racks his upper body. Each successive cough triggers a kind of jack-knife reaction. He forces himself forward before the next one arrives, his whole body tense. He's trying to get there first, I think, before the virus wreaks yet more havoc, and the wreckage from his ruined lungs begins to gather and clot in the back of his throat.

I lay hands on the kidney bowl I've seen the nurses use, and hold it under his chin, cradling the back of his head as gently as I can.

'Get it out, H. Do it for me.' I don't want the nurses back in the room. I can do this. For H's sake. And Malo's. And mine.

Another bout of coughing, more pain, his whole face contorted, and then – with a giant effort – H deposits a sizeable gob in the kidney bowl, snail-green, viscous, almost alive.

'Jesus,' he gasps. I wipe his face with a towel, kiss the hotness of his cheek. His eyes are open now and he's looking for the nurses. This must happen a million times in his waking day, I think. It's something primitive, the instinctive reaction of a frightened man. *I'm not well. I'm worse than not well. Don't go away. Help me.*

'H?' His eyes are wild. I'm beginning to suspect he doesn't recognize me. 'It's me. Enora.'

This seems to calm him. He wants to know where he is, what's going on.

'You're in Pompey,' I tell him. 'We're looking after you.'

'We?'

'Me. Those nurses of yours. Malo.'

'Malo?' He's frowning now.

'Your son. Our son.'

'Yeah?'

'He worries about you, H. We all do. But we're here. We truly are. And we're not going away.'

He nods, and then his eyes close again before his breathing starts to quicken. A face has appeared at the door, and moments later I'm watching one of the nurses re-fitting the oxygen mask. The supply restored, his heaving chest begins to slow. He's gone again, I know it, this indomitable figure who – at least in his own account – was once king of this unruly city.

Outside, in the narrow hall, I pause beside the other nurses. 'Warfarin?' I query.

'It's a blood thinner, Ms Andressen. In case Mr H gets a thrombosis.'

'You mean a stroke?'

'Yes.'

Malo, sensibly, has gone out again and I spend the afternoon trying to rescue something, *anything*, from the wreckage of the day so far. A trawl through back numbers of the *Portsmouth News* reveals just a glimmer of light in my darkness. I'm not up for neighbourhood singalongs or a YouTube training video once again featuring the local bare-knuckle boxing phenomenon, but my eye is caught by the news that the Chichester Festival Theatre is streaming its production of *Flowers for Mrs Harris*. The play is based on a very affecting novel by Paul Gallico, and I once caught a French adaptation in Paris, where a lot of the action takes place. Streaming starts this coming week.

I make a note of the date, phone one of the nurses to check whether they want tea or not, then have another look at the bookshelves in search of something to read. A couple of books catch my eye, and one of them is *Typhoon*. I've always had an on-off passion for Joseph Conrad, not least because he wrote such powerful novels in a language that he'd only just learned, and the very title of *Typhoon* is an almost perfect match for my darker expectations. We're adrift on the ocean and a storm is about to break. Best to find out what happens next.

I'm halfway through the first chapter, my feet up on the sofa, when my mobile begins to ring. A glance at the screen tells me it's Wesley Kane. He wants to know how it went with Shanti.

'It didn't,' I tell him. 'We got blind drunk and then I walked home.'

'That's not what she says.'

'Then why ask me?'

'Because I want your version.'

'What's hers?'

'She really liked you.'

'She was pissed. Like me.'

'No, but she says you discussed . . . you know . . .'

'What? Discussed what?'

'H's dosh. Ways and means. You with me?'

'Not really. She cooks a lovely tagine. I'll never drink Sidi Brahim again. That's about it.'

There's a brief silence. My finger is still anchored in the first chapter of *Typhoon*. Captain MacWhirr doesn't like the colour of the sky. Then Wesley is back with me. He says he wants a meet. The verb he actually uses is 'needs'.

'Why?'

'We've got a proposition for you.'

'We?'

'Me and Shanti. I'll be under the pier this time. And it's low tide.'

SIXTEEN

The shadows under the pier are beginning to lengthen by the time I make it down to the beach, and the sunshine has once again lost its warmth. Shanti is wearing a pullover and a pair of jeans. The pullover might be World War Two vintage, one of those roll-neck sweaters the crew used to wear on black and white Atlantic convoy movies.

She's sitting on the damp shingle with her back against one of the thick encrusted pillars that hold up the pier, and her Doc Martens are fashionably unlaced. She's smoking a spliff and the smoke hangs in the still air while Wesley paces around. The news that I've been certified Covid-free has loosened him up somewhat, and he dares to come much closer. He has the same look as last time: trainers, trackie bottoms, smart blue hoodie with the hint of a Barça top beneath. Despite the promise of a sensational sunset, there are very few people around.

'Look.' Wesley points a derisive finger. 'Filth in their fucking element. Two metres distance. Else we'll do you for making conversation.'

Wesley's right. A man and a woman, both uniformed, both wearing hi-vis jackets, have stopped a couple on the promenade. One of them is making notes, while the other is shaking his head. After a while, the couple stroll away, hand in hand.

'So how does that fucking work?' Wesley again.

'They're married,' I mutter. 'That makes it legal.'

'Yeah? And they can prove it?'

'I've no idea. So what's this about?' I'm looking down at Shanti. The spliff is dying between her fingers. She appears to be half asleep.

'We have a plan,' Wesley says. 'All we need is a downpayment.'

'From?'

'H, of course.'

'That could be a problem. He's not really up to it just now.'

'Too busy dying?'

'Very funny.' I turn to look him in the eye. 'Maybe it helps to make a joke, I must try it more often. Loosen up. Not be so much of a gloom bag. Is he cogent? Talkative? Sadly not. Does he cough a lot? I'm afraid he does. Is he in pain? Yes. Is the outlook grim? Maybe terminal? Yes. You know how many people have died in this city so far? Fifty-six. One of them's Fat Dave. The next, you're right, could be H.'

Shanti, more alert than I'd thought, is miming applause. She likes my little riff and she thinks – rightly – that it's aimed squarely at Wes.

'This lovely woman is an actress,' she says to Wesley. Then she looks up. 'You write your own scripts? If not, then maybe you should.'

'I thank you.' I perform a stagey little bow.

'Fifty grand upfront,' Wes says. 'I'm freezing my bollocks off here. The only question is how it gets paid. I'm suggesting cash. Shanti doesn't care. Fifty grand will buy you treble that by the weekend after next. You want it in writing, no problem. You want it in blood? My fucking pleasure. People in this city are dying of boredom. A twenty-quid toot puts a smile back on your face. Two hundred quid for the weekend of your dreams? Perfect.'

'So who's doing the selling?' I'm looking at Wesley.

'*Moi.*' Shanti stirs and gets to her feet before having a stretch. She moves like an animal, full of languor and quality kif, crossing the pebbles towards me. 'You think I go door to door? Wrong. Orders come in on the phone. Kids deliver. If they get funny with the money, my friend here' – she nods at Wesley – 'has a word.'

I can well believe it. When I tell her *plus ça change*, she beams with pleasure.

'We're all the victims of habit.' She stifles a yawn. 'Wesley especially. A reputation like his, you can run a decent business. You and me? The kids would die laughing.' She shoots Wesley a look. 'Eh, *chérie*? Do I have that right?'

Wesley nods, accepting the compliment, and for the first time I start to wonder whether these two have become a couple. Shanti and Wes. The Couscous Queen and her loyal Enforcer.

'Go on,' he tells her. 'Hand it over. It's bloody cold.'

Shanti digs in the pocket of her jeans and then offers me a folded piece of paper.

'Bank details, my child. It's a business account in the name of the restaurant. The money is to fund me through the hard times, which has the merit of being true. Wesley's idea, not mine.'

That night, back in the flat, I share this encounter with Malo. For the time being, he appears to have forgiven me for criminal neglect and for whatever else I haven't done, and this comes as a relief. He's also spent a couple of hours with Taalia as soon as she came off shift. There's nowhere to go, of course, for coffee or a proper drink, but that doesn't seem to matter. They went for a walk, talked a lot, and he made her laugh, never a good sign.

'You're halfway married,' I tell him sternly. I have to get my own back.

'Clem won't ever know.'

'You're right, but I will. Listen to your mother. Clemmie's one in a million. Odds like that, you'd be mad to screw it up.'

'I'm not screwing it up. You want the truth? This place is driving me nuts.'

'Pompey? Or the flat?'

'Both.'

'Then welcome to the club. I used to have a really nice life. Once. Share and share alike? Can we at least agree on that?'

I change the subject, and tell him about the conversation under the pier, and last night's revelries in Casablanca. The more he learns about Shanti, the less he believes me.

'This woman belongs in a movie,' he says.

'She *is* a movie. Larger than life in every sense you can possibly imagine. I half-believe half of what she says.'

'And the rest?'

'Fantasy. Fairy tales. She's making it up.'

'And she and Wesley? Are they shagging?'

'Might be. That's what she wants me to believe so it's probably not true.'

'And Wes?'

'He'd love it to be true.'

Malo nods. A couple of years back he got way out of his depth with a bunch of wild Somali drug dealers, and Clemmie was kidnapped as a direct result. Wesley had a hand in digging him out of all that, and Malo has been grateful – as well as slightly awed – ever since. After the deafening make-believe of *Grand Theft Auto*, Wesley Kane is very definitely the real deal, and Malo knows that.

'So, what are they after? Exactly?'

'Your dad's money. A couple of days ago, when H could still think things through, he thought that was a good idea. That's why I went to the restaurant last night.'

'And what do you think now? Be honest.'

'I don't like it at all.'

'Why not?'

'Because it doesn't smell good, taste good.'

'But the investment, the multiplier. If I understand those figures from the agency, we have to double Dad's money. Isn't that a factor? Otherwise, we'll run out.'

'You mean you think it's a good idea?' I'm staring at him now. 'We invest what little H has got left in a drug deal? In this city, that sounds seriously retro to me. What if it all goes wrong?'

'It never did. Not in the day. You know Flixcombe as well as I do. Pompey bought all that, every last acre. You're still looking at a huge market here. If Wes and this woman have got it sorted the way they say they have, Dad could be banged up here for months and we'd still be able to pay the bills.'

'And if they haven't got it sorted?'

'Then we'd crash and burn, obviously, but what makes you think they're dodgy?'

'They may not be dodgy, Malo, but they're definitely old. This is a young man's game. As you well know.'

'That's unfair. This is Pompey. Everything's different.'

'You say.'

'I say. How do they want the money?'

'I've no idea.' I'm lying now. I've still got Shanti's bank details in my jeans pocket, but I think a little caution might be wise. 'All this is too easy,' I tell him. 'The best scripts make it tough on the protagonist.'

'The what?'

'H. The main man. I know it's tough on him already, but I'd hate for him to get set up. Especially in this city.'

'Set up? You're telling me you don't trust Wesley? After all that stuff he's done for Dad? How close they've been?'

'Trust is a funny thing, Malo. Money unpicks everything, and you're talking to someone who knows. Berndt was a good man when I met him. Money and fame turned him into someone else.'

'Wes isn't Berndt,' Malo insists. 'Wes is Wes. Berndt was a twat.'

'I see.' I nod, trying to sense where this conversation is taking us. 'So you'd go with Wes? Is that what you're saying?'

'Yes, I would.'

'Why?'

'For Dad's sake, obviously.' His long frame is curled at the other end of the sofa, but now he leans forward, suddenly intense. 'Dad's money will last three and a half weeks. I've worked it out. After that he'll have to go into hospital and he's sure it'll be the end of him. Wu is talking seven weeks, max. A deal with Wes would cover that. Don't the figures speak for themselves? Or have I got this wrong?'

He hasn't, of course. I double check the figures, and he's got them absolutely right. H's rainy-day fund might take him through to the end of the month. After that, there's nothing left.

That evening, we both sit with H, in full PPE, while two of the nurses retire to the front room to watch TV. Malo has yet to pay the £15,000 deposit, and has heard nothing from the agency since talking to them this morning. Tomorrow is Sunday, which might give me a little leeway to try and think this thing through. Ideally, of course, we'd explain the whole situation to H and await his decision, but just now that option doesn't exist.

The hours tick by. From time to time, the nurse still with us checks the oxygen flow, and the various tubes and catheters that tether H to his vital signs. She makes notes on the daily log, while Malo nods along to Ed Sheeran on his ear buds, and I plunge ever deeper into *Typhoon*. At around eleven, towards the end of their shift, Malo and I make a discreet exit while the nurses muster round the bed to roll H on to his belly ahead of the coming night.

Out in the corridor, we're thinking about a last coffee when we hear a commotion from the bedroom. H is half-yelling, half-coughing, and we step back inside to find him bolt upright in bed, lashing out at the nurses around him. Malo gets there ahead of me, and there's space for him to enfold his dad in a gigantic bear hug. Moments later I'm there too, trying to soothe him, trying to tell him that everything's going to be fine.

'We're here for you, H. There isn't a problem.'

He stares at me for a long moment. One of the nurses is looking badly frightened. Then H, without warning, breaks down, shaking his head, trying to smother yet another cough.

'Sammy,' he whispers. 'Fucking Sammy.'

'Who, Dad?' This from Malo.

'Sammy. Help me, son. Tell me it's going to be OK. You'll do that? Sort all this Sammy business?'

He's staring at Malo, then at me, then at the other faces around his bed, and tears are pouring down his face.

'I got it wrong,' he says finally. 'So fucking wrong.'

SEVENTEEN

S sedated, H sleeps like a baby. Or that's what Mr Wu says when he turns up first thing on Sunday morning. Both Malo and I, anxious about this latest development, want to know what might happen next.

'Your father is very disturbed.' Mr Wu is looking at Malo. 'This virus can trigger hallucinations. You get an idea in your head, it can be anything, come from anywhere, but there's no letting it go.'

'Something real?' I ask. 'Something from his past?'

'Only you would know that. Sammy? Have I got the name right?'

'Yes.'

'You know who this person might be?'

'I'm afraid not. I'll ask around, make some enquiries. He's certainly never mentioned any Sammy to me.'

Mr Wu nods, trying to be sympathetic, but I sense there's something else that's bothering him.

'Naturally, I've talked to all three nurses separately, just to make sure we're all absolutely clear about this thing. One of them was very upset. She told me she'd felt the violence in your Mr H. That was the word she used. Violence. Is this something you recognize, Ms Andressen?'

The question is troubling, and very direct. Of course, H can be violent. That's where all his money came from.

'That's news to me.' I muster a smile. 'He's always been the sweetest man.'

'So, can you account for my nurse's apprehension?'

'I'm afraid I can't. I can only apologize. If it's a question of blame, maybe we should be thinking about the virus. Once he gets back to normal I'm sure he'll try and make amends. The last thing he'd ever want to do is frighten anyone.'

'Good to hear, Ms Andressen. I'd be foolish to downplay an incident like this. Nurses are trained to take account of the unexpected, but it would be irresponsible on my part to put any of my nurses at physical risk, as I'm sure you'd agree.'

'Of course.' I force another smile. Mr Wu, with his perfect manners, is telling me that H is on a final warning. Any more lashing out, and he'll be in the back of an ambulance, heading for the ICU. 'More sedation?' I suggest lightly. 'Might that be a good idea?'

Malo and I spend the rest of the morning revisiting the figures we discussed last night. By midday, there's no room left for argument. Unless we can put H's money to work, his care will run out before the end of the month. And that date makes no allowances for anything unexpected that might fatten the bill.

It's at this point that I feel an overwhelming need for outside advice. I'm the last person to underestimate the challenge of becoming a player in the Pompey cocaine game, and the person I should be talking to is Tony Morse. He knows this city better than anyone. And more to the point, he's been looking after H's best interests for most of his working life.

I find him at home, here in Pompey. I've no appetite for sharing the contents of this call with any of our three nurses who might be listening, so I suggest a discreet meet.

'*En plein air?*' he says at once. 'No can do.'

'It's a beautiful day.' I'm standing beside the window. 'Half the city's on the prom.'

'Then bless them. Me? I have a tiny problem. The last time I caught flu wasn't pleasant. This is far worse.'

'You've got it?' I'm horrified. 'Headache?'

'Tick.'

'Temperature?'

'Tick.'

'That horrible dry cough?'

'Thankfully not. I'm telling myself it's something else. You're right, it's a lovely day. I've got a pile of fresh veg here I'll never eat. Come round and pick it up. I'll leave it in a bag on the front doorstep. We can talk on phones. I'll pose in the window in the silk jim-jams I stole from the Hong Kong Mandarin. It won't tell you anything you didn't suspect already, my darling, but I like to think it's still a good look.' He laughs rather mirth-lessly and gives me an address.

'Craneswater Park?' I query.

'It's the closest this town gets to posh. Beware of the dog.'

Malo and I set out in the early afternoon. He's found the address on his phone and we set off along the seafront and around the grey spread of Southsea Castle. I'm trying to remember Sean telling me about the *Mary Rose* coming to grief under the gaze of Henry VIII, but Malo knows all about it already.

'Too many people on board,' he says briskly. 'Too much weight. Capsized without firing a shot. Christ, look at that.'

We've skirted the castle now, and he's pointing at the long stretch of beach below us. Little clots of people are gathered on rugs, enjoying the sunshine. Blue smoke curls upwards from dozens of barbecues, and up on the prom a litter of empty cans surround a brimming waste bin. For early April, this is truly remarkable. Pompey is in the rudest health. Bugger the virus.

Ten minutes later, we've reached the pier in time to watch half a dozen police officers getting out of the back of a van. The sergeant in charge bends to his radio and then sends his troops into battle. They disperse among the alfresco picnics, taking names, dousing fires, breaking the party up.

'Shame,' Malo says. 'This feels almost normal.'

Tony Morse's place is round the corner from a pitch and putt course, a little further on. It's a handsome Edwardian villa, an essay in red brick and impossibly tall windows. There's one of those cutesy French warnings hanging on the double gates – *Attention aux chiens* – and looking at the house, I can only wonder how many people live here.

Tony has always been discreet about his private life. H swears there were at least three wives, and he thinks there might be a couple more tucked away somewhere, but even he was never really sure. In any event, it doesn't matter. The moment we step on to the brief crescent of gravel drive, a woman stirs at one of the front windows. She's young enough to be Tony's daughter, and she's extremely pretty, and moments later my phone begins to ring. It's the man himself. He promises he's on his way.

He appears within minutes. By now, I've retrieved the Waitrose bag from the front door step, and taken a peek inside. New potatoes, salad stuff, celeriac, new season carrots. Brilliant. Tony's standing at the window, his phone to his ear. He's wearing a three-quarter-length dressing gown, with a lively dragon motif, and he looks a bit unsteady before he sinks gratefully into a rather nice 1940s-style wingchair his companion has brought over. She gives us a little wave, and then disappears.

'Corinne,' Tony says. 'Don't ask, don't get.'

This could mean anything, which is probably the point, and when I ask how he's feeling, he's equally unhelpful.

'Malt whisky and hot lemon,' he says. 'Never fails. How's H?'

I tell him the truth. I tell him that H has left us.

'Left?' He looks startled. 'Died, you mean?'

'Taken his leave. Moved temporarily on. I get the impression this Covid thing wants your undivided attention. H was raving last night. Lost it completely, poor man. Thank God for your Mr Wu.'

'He's looking after you?'

'Absolutely. You've done us all proud, Tony. Mr Wu's the perfect gentleman. Unlike H.'

'You mentioned money on the phone.'

'I did.'

'And?'

I run through the math. These figures originally came from Tony himself, and nothing seems to surprise him. Not going into hospital was always H's choice, and – as he points out – every decision has consequences.

'So H may have a liquidity problem?' he suggests. 'Is that what I'm hearing?'

'If you're asking whether he's going to run out of money, the answer is yes. That first invoice you picked up from Mr Wu is covered, Tony. The cheque's in the post.'

'I'm obliged, my darling. And the rest?'

This, of course, is the crunch. Do I play coy? Do I artfully seed the conversation with hints that H might be tempted to revive an old association or two? Or do I simply tell him the truth? Tony already looks like he wants to be back in bed, so I opt for the latter.

'H wants to set up a cocaine deal,' I say carefully. 'He thinks that's the best way of settling his debts.'

'He's still got the contacts?' Not a flicker of surprise on Tony's part.

'He says he has.'

'Locally?'

'Yes.'

'And precisely how does he plan to do this? Given the state he's in?'

'We handle the details.'

'And you think you can do that?'

'I think we have no choice.'

'So why talk to me about it?'

'Because you understand the way these things work, Tony. That dressing gown, incidentally, is sensational.'

Tony smiles, and gives us a slightly wobbly twirl. Then he reminds me that the drugs biz in Pompey, like everything else, has moved on.

'For the record, my darling, this is a conversation between friends. Whatever advice I might offer is just that, a conversation. If you were coming to me professionally, you'd never get past the door. I know that's lawyer talk for covering my arse, but I mean it.'

'Of course. And?'

'Be bloody careful, the pair of you. I'm not going to ask who you're dealing with, and I don't want you to tell me, but this place is a swamp now, new players on the block, and if your guys get it wrong, the consequences could be ugly.'

'For us?'

'Of course. But for H, too. Our friends in blue haven't closed the file and they never will. H led them a dance, and they have very long memories. So if you or your new friends fuck up . . .' Another smile, chilly this time. '*Attention aux flics, quoi?*'

I nod. I think I know exactly what he's saying. Don't go near any drug deal. Find some other way. I'm about to say our good-byes but I'm distracted by my phone. It's the nurse in charge on the current shift back at the flat. With a sinking heart, I signal an apology to Tony, and ask her what's up.

'Bit of a crisis,' she says. 'The electric has gone off.'

'*All* of it?'

'Yes. Lights. Sockets. The lot.'

'What about the oxygen?' I'm trying to think this through.

'That, too. The pump's gone.'

'And H?'

'Short term, he may be OK, but if we can't get the power back on we'll have to call an ambulance.'

'You mean ICU? The whole deal?'

'Yes.'

I'm panicking and for a brief moment I don't know what to do. Then Malo steps in. He's heard the whole exchange.

'Ask Tony Morse about the control board. It's his flat. He should know.'

Brilliant. I make contact with Tony again. He's disappeared from the window and when he picks up, I can hear him wheezing.

'I'm halfway up the stairs, my darling. Going to bed should never be this tough.'

I explain about the power failure. The meters and control boards for all the flats, he says, are in a cupboard on the ground floor just inside the main door.

'I imagine you'll need to get back sharpish. Borrow my car. Corinne's got the keys.'

Tony drives a BMW. Malo takes the wheel and we're back outside the flat within minutes. The front door is open, as is the big cupboard with all the control boards. There appears to be no one around.

Malo has already located the board for Flat 7. He squints up at the rows of switches but can see no problem.

'They're all down.' We're on the stairs now, heading upwards. 'That's the way they should be.'

The door to the flat is also opened, and the moment we step inside I can hear H. He's yelling for Malo. Not me, Malo.

We're standing in the open bedroom door. We have no time to bother with PPE, but it's a relief to hear the mutter of the oxygen pump. All three nurses are gathered around the bed, trying to get the mask on to H's face, and the one who phoned me glances round.

'Thank God.' She's looking at Malo. 'He thinks we're taking him to hospital. Just tell him everything's going to be OK.'

Malo joins them around the bed. One of them hands him a paper mask. He bends to his father and tells him that everything's going to be all right. No ambulance. No blues and twos. No ICU. H stares up at him, his big face shiny with sweat, an old man now, befuddled, witless, frightened.

'Yeah?' he mutters. 'You called the bastards off?'

'There were no bastards, Dad. Everything's fine. Maybe you've been dreaming. Here, let's get that mask on you.'

H succumbs without further protest. His head is back on the pillow. His eyes are closed. His lungs are filling with the precious oxygen. Malo looks down at him, and then kisses him lightly on the forehead. Two of the nurses are smiling. The other one is on the phone to the agency.

'We need someone to take a look at the electrics here,' she says quietly. 'This place is a nightmare.'

EIGHTEEN

Back in full PPE, I sit with H for a couple of hours, partly to offer comfort if he gets agitated again, but mainly to keep abreast of the situation with the nursing agency. I suspect that their patience with us is beginning to wear thin, and this latest near disaster with the electrics won't have helped.

It hasn't. In the mid-afternoon, a face I've never seen before appears. She introduces herself as Natasha, and says she's the agency's relief manager, holding the fort over the weekend.

'You have a minute, Ms Andressen?'

I peel off my visor and mask and join her in the front room. She comes straight to the point. A call to Southern Electric has brought an emergency call-out crew to the flats. They're downstairs now, checking the control box. According to the nurses, the power was off for around six minutes, then restored itself. As soon as extra PPE arrives, the engineers will be doing a sweep of the apartment. So far, she says, they haven't been able to locate a fault downstairs. Do I have any idea what might have gone wrong?

I say I can't help her. I've talked to the nurses and they've all told me that the power simply failed, no warning, no fizzing from a dodgy socket, no sign that they'd overloaded any of the circuits. Just the sudden realization that all the bedside equipment had stopped, and that the unwavering green digits that track H's vital signs were no more. And then, equally unexplained, the power went on again.

'It's the oxygen that bothers us most,' she says. 'That's something we can't afford to lose.'

The call-out crew from Southern Electric appear, full PPE plus lots of diagnostic equipment. They test every socket, every circuit, and while much of the wiring is old-ish they can find nothing wrong. This appears to appease Natasha.

'Just one of those things?' I suggest.

'Must be.' She's checking her watch. 'One of the girls thinks there's a ghost here. Maybe that's the answer.'

A ghost. She might be right. Since we all moved in, and both I and H sensed a presence in the place, it's gone a bit quiet on the poltergeist front. But I know that ghosts thrive on attention, and this one's certainly got ours. Either way, Natasha seems happy enough, which is a blessing, and once she's gone, I settle down with Joseph Conrad, wondering vaguely what might have happened to Malo.

He's back at dusk, looking pleased with himself.

'Taalia?' I query.

'Shanti. Your friend from the restaurant. I managed to track her down.'

'Why did you do that?'

'You said she wanted fifty grand. I got her down to forty.'

'I see.' I'm starting to get angry again. 'So, am I redundant here? Have you taken over completely?'

'Not at all. It's for Dad's sake, really. I don't want to see him ripped off.'

'Getting ripped off isn't the issue. Weren't you listening to Tony Morse? *Any* drugs deal is a bad idea. Ripped off would be the least of his worries. The moment we say yes is the moment we put his life in someone else's hands.'

'His life? That's why we need the money, Mum. To keep him alive.'

'I meant his freedom. You know what Tony said. There are animals out there, reptiles in the swamp, anything could happen. Just suppose he gets through this. Just suppose we all do. He's getting better, he doesn't need this kind of care any more. We all start leading a normal life again. Then it turns out that one of those deals has gone wrong, someone's been hurt, the police have started sniffing around, and guess whose name is on the cheque?'

'There is no cheque. I'm not stupid, Mum.'

'I'm not with you.'

'I talked to Jessie today, explained everything. It turns out that Dad's rainy-day fund is in cash, fifty-pound notes, a whole stack of them. I told Jess about the agency bills. She's bringing fifty-five grand down tomorrow. Fifteen goes to the agency to keep them sweet. That's what we've agreed.'

'And the rest? The forty grand?'

Malo doesn't answer. In certain situations he can be utterly shameless and this is definitely one of them.

'No,' I say firmly. 'No way are you giving that woman that money.'

'Why not?'

'Because we've taken the best advice, and the best advice says don't.'

'Tony's off the pace. He's also ill.'

'So that makes you some kind of expert? Do you remember *anything* about your last dealings in the cocaine trade?'

This is ruthless on my part, but I don't care. Getting Clemmie kidnapped should have taught my son a thing or two about career gangsters, but I'm obviously wrong. By now, alas, he's as angry as I am.

'Let's get real, Mum. When it comes to making the decision you can't stop me.'

'I can't? How does that work?'

'Because I'm Dad's nearest next-of-kin.' He shrugs. 'And you're not.'

* * *

That night, in silence, we watch the Queen addressing the nation. She's speaking from Windsor Castle. The turquoise dress is offset by three rows of pearls and a rather nice brooch, and there are few surprises in what she has to say. The debt we owe to the NHS and care workers. The need to look after our families and neighbours. The place the nation should make in its heart for something she terms 'a quiet, good-humoured resolve'. And finally, her personal conviction that we shall all, surely, meet again. This dignified nod to Vera Lynn brings the address to an end, and live pictures show cul-de-sacs erupting around the kingdom.

Malo, of course, hasn't a clue about Vera Lynn, but that's not really his fault. As for me, I find the broadcast oddly affecting. The Queen's own son, after all, has had his personal tussle with the virus and those couldn't have been easy days chez Windsor. Covid will never bow the head or bend the knee to anyone.

I can tell that Malo wants to bring this evening to an end, but I'm determined not to let him go until we've made some kind of peace with each other. This, naturally, will require him to agree with me, but as the argument gets more and more heated, I realize that he's as headstrong and stubborn as his father. He tells me he has an instinct about decisions like these. He wants me to believe that he's good at sussing people he's never met. And in the shape of Shanti and Wes, he insists we're looking at H's salvation. I don't believe in any of these propositions, and say so, but Malo – again like his father – has mastered the art of not listening. We're still at loggerheads when breaking news appears on the TV.

We both fall silent. Malo brings the sound up on the remote. First Windsor Castle, now 10 Downing Street. Prime Minister Boris Johnson has been taken to St Thomas's hospital for routine tests. This announcement is accompanied by a shot of him joining the Thursday evening clap on the doorstep of Downing Street.

Routine tests? Malo isn't fooled for a moment.

'He's got it, Mum.' He's pointing at the screen. 'Just look at him.'

My son's probably right. Johnson looks stooped and drawn and haggard, with dark shadows under his eyes. I recognize this look, largely because we're living with it, and it gives me no comfort to picture the days and nights he has to come.

'You think he'll die, Mum?' Malo's generation has no time for nuance.

'I've no idea. He'll get the best treatment, bound to. If they can't save him, what chance do any of us have?'

'Exactly. And you believe that?'

'I do.'

'Then we have to keep these people here. Keep Dad out of hospital. Give him a fighting chance. You know how many people have died up there? At the QA?'

The QA is Pompey-speak for the Queen Alexandra Hospital, up on the hill.

'Fifty-six,' I say numbly. The figure is engraved in my heart.

We're in bed by half past ten. All I want to do is go to sleep but Malo, suddenly solicitous, asks me whether I mind the light on. He's in the middle of a feature in his *Top Gear* magazine and can't wait to see what happens when you drive a Porsche Carrera flat out on a stretch of Welsh beach at low tide. Mercifully this comes without sound effects, unlike *Grand Theft Auto*, and I'm asleep within minutes.

I awake to hear a knock on the door. It must be hours later because the room is in darkness and Malo is sound asleep. Not wanting to wake him, I feel my way around his sleeping bag and slip out of the room. One of the night-shift nurses is waiting in the corridor. For some reason the lights are out here, too.

'It's happened again,' she says. 'The power's off.'

I stare at her. She's carrying a torch. I'm wearing nothing but a pair of pyjama bottoms and a Caravan Palace T-shirt, but I know exactly what I must do.

'Do you mind?' I ask for the torch.

'Where are you going?'

'Downstairs.'

I let myself out of the flat. There are security lights in the stairwell, motion-sensitive, and they're still working as I hurry down. On the ground floor the lino feels cold on my bare feet. The big cupboard with the control boards is on the wall beside the front door and I'm praying it's not locked. One tug, and it opens. Our control board is at the top, just within my reach, but I need the torch to check on the switches. I track the beam slowly left to right along the switches controlling various circuits until I find the black master switch. I have exactly this set-up back in London, and I know how it works. I hold the beam steady, making sure I've got this thing right, then I reach up and flick the switch back down. No doubt about it. Someone has been here in the last couple of minutes and cut the power to our flat.

This realization, incontestable, ices the blood in my veins. I start to shiver, a deep feeling of dread, wondering what might happen next. Then I check the front door. It's closed, but the deadlock isn't on. Someone's been in, I think. Someone's watching us, waiting outside, waiting to seize his moment. First yesterday afternoon, in broad daylight, now in pitch darkness in the middle of the night.

I open the door, barely aware of the thin drizzle. The loom of the streetlights reaches on to the Common but I can see no signs of life. Neither, in either direction, is there anyone on the pavement. I gaze out into the darkness, and as I do so proper rain begins to fall, sweeping in from the Solent, driving me back indoors.

Half-thinking I must have made the last five minutes up, I check on the control board again, making sure everything's back in order. It is. I close the door, put the deadlock on, and climb the stairs to the flat. The lights are back on in the corridor, and when I put my head around H's bedroom door, everyone's looking relieved.

I return the torch to the nurse who woke me up. She wants to know what the matter was.

'We've got a ghost,' I say lightly, hoping this might keep the incident off the log, but knowing it won't. I nod at H. 'What about my lovely friend?'

'Never noticed a thing,' she says. 'He's been sleeping like a baby for hours now.'

NINETEEN

This, on the face of it, is good news but it doesn't last. After a disturbed night, on edge in case the power fails again, I get up early, still trying to tease a little sense into what's happening to us. Helpless doesn't begin to do justice to the way I'm feeling. We seemed to have offended the gods of Covid, and probably untold others. One power outage you might put down to rogue mice, or bad karma, or even a ghost. Two takes us into another dimension completely. Someone out there is determined to hurt us, H in particular. But who? And why?

It's still early, barely seven. To the best of my recollection, Jessie gets up early in her little cottage on the Flixcombe estate. First things first. No way will my son lay hands on £55,000 of H's money.

To my relief, she's already on the road. Malo, she says, has given her the address and the postcode of the flat. She knows Pompey well. She should be with us by eight at the latest.

'There's no traffic at all,' she says. 'I can't believe it.'

'Don't come to the flat,' I tell her. 'In fact, don't come into the city at all.'

'Why not?' She sounds suddenly wary.

'They're stopping people on the motorway. Unless you've got a very good excuse, they'll send you home.' This is a lie, but only just. According to the *Portsmouth News,* the traffic police have begun to pilot random checks.

'So, what shall I do?'

'I'll meet you outside the city. You know Fort Widley? On Portsdown Hill?'

'Of course I do.'

'There's a big car park on the hill across the road from the fort,' I tell her. 'Malo took me up before we did that trip to the D-Day beaches. I'll meet you there.'

'No problem,' she says. 'But what about you? How come you can drive around?'

'I've got a friend's car at the moment. He's a defending solicitor in court. So he has an exemption.'

'Right.' She's sounding brighter now, evidently pleased to be spared the trip into the city itself. 'And how's H?'

'Much the same. Not great.'

'And Malo?'

'Still asleep. Tell me you're surprised.'

She laughs. She drives an old Land Rover, and I hear the clatter of the engine in the background.

'About half an hour, then,' she says. 'I've still got a flask of coffee I haven't touched.'

Twenty minutes later, I'm up on Portsdown Hill, parked across from the red-brick battlements of Fort Widley. There isn't a soul around up here, and even down in the city it felt like the quietest of Sundays. A handful of delivery trucks, the occasional postman on foot, and the beginnings of a queue – mainly older people – patiently waiting for a Londis to open.

Tony's car smells of cigars, and I get out for a stretch. The view from up here on the hill I remember as sensational, and now – pollution free – it's even better. In the distance, beyond the empty blue of the Solent, I can see the low swell of the Isle of Wight, while the grey sprawl of the island city lies beneath me, the early sun gleaming on the harbours that surround it. Traffic on the motorway that loops into the city from the west is sparse, hundreds of metres between vehicles, and as I watch I catch the faintest howl of a siren from somewhere deep in the muddle of streets that is Portsmouth. Probably an ambulance, I think. Another Covid victim heading for the hospital immediately below me.

I shake my head, remembering yet again that moment in the chill of the entrance hall last night when I checked out the control board. Someone knows about the battle we're fighting to keep H alive. They've got into the property. They know where to look for the electricity supply. And they know the number of our flat. Without oxygen, H will be in serious trouble and I suspect they know that too. This is creepy enough, but the sheer size of the city below me makes it far more troubling. In his day, given the scale of his ambition, H has probably made hundreds of enemies. So how on earth do I even start to narrow the field?

Jessie appears within minutes and carefully parks ten metres away. I somehow thought we might be sharing the coffee at touching distance but she's scrupulous about obeying the rules. She's only brought one cup and when I insist she keeps it for herself, she looks relieved. She and Andy, she says, have been watching far too much telly. The virus has so far spared country areas like West Dorset but it's obvious that it's gone mad in the cities. It's chilly up here in the wind, and she's hunched in her quilted green anorak, nursing the coffee, staring down at the acres of rooftops that are Portsmouth. Jessie has spent most of her life down there but doesn't appear to have missed it.

'Fifty-six dead.' She shakes her head. 'Hundreds of confirmed cases. I checked. You're saints, both of you. Thank God H is in good hands.'

She wants to know about Malo. I tell her about the flat, how intimate it is, and how things can occasionally get a bit difficult. The news that we're living with three nurses night and day amazes her. Once again, she's worried about what it must be costing H. All I can do is agree.

'How much does he have left, incidentally?' I enquire. 'In cash?'

'Just over one hundred and ten thousand. I had a count last night. Malo says you might be needing that, too.'

'He's right. We might.'

She nods, then looks me in the eye. 'So why won't he go into hospital? Like everyone else?'

'Because he watched Fat Dave die in there, and it scared him witless.' I tell her about our lunch with Cynthia, and the sequence we watched on her iPad. Already, that afternoon the three of us shared seems to belong to a different life.

Jessie nods, and says she doesn't blame him. 'Apparently you have to sign a form before they put you on the ventilator. By that time you've got a fifty-fifty chance of not making it, and they need consent. They often put you into an induced coma, too. H would hate that.'

He would, indeed. Jessie's finished her coffee now, and when I ask for the money she goes back to the Land Rover and fetches a dark-green kit bag which probably belongs to Andy. Fifty-five thousand pounds weighs more than you might think.

'Malo said it was in fifties.'

'He's wrong. It's mainly twenties, some tens. I've counted it twice. If it doesn't tally, give me a ring and I'll sort it.' She's eyeing the city again. 'Give H my love, eh? And Malo, too. That boy's suddenly grown up, hasn't he?'

I nod, saying nothing, watching her climb back into the Land Rover. She pulls the door shut, starts the engine, and blows me a little kiss. Then she's gone.

* * *

Fifty-five thousand pounds is a lot of money. I put the kit bag in the boot and sit behind the wheel, listening to a local news station that Tony Morse has pre-tuned. There's lots of reaction to the Queen's little pep talk last night, and one caller regrets that her mum wasn't around to hear it. Every crisis has a silver lining, she says, and that amazing speech would have been hers. Amazing? I'm not sure.

Next comes an update on our ailing PM, who appears to be sicker than Downing Street have been prepared to admit. He's now in ICU but has so far been spared the ventilator. Finally, on a happier note, there's news of a pink supermoon which will be appearing for most of the week. Tomorrow offers the best viewing opportunities, and we should all be looking east as it rises, if we want to catch it in its pomp.

Pink. Supermoon. Even a simple idea like tomorrow.

I shake my head, realizing how easy it is to lose your bearings in a crisis like this. Watching H succumb so quickly to the virus was one thing. Trying to protect him from some vengeful stalker, quite another. What I need is a conversation with someone I trust, someone with detailed knowledge about the craziness of those days, someone who might be in a position to protect us all.

It's nearly nine o'clock now. Not too early, I think. Especially given the circumstances. I reach for my mobile.

'Dessie? Dessie Wren?' An answering grunt tells me he's still in bed. Shit.

'Who is this?'

'Enora. Tony Morse's friend. We met at Dave's funeral. Sort of . . .'

'Ah . . .' He's apologetic now, fully conscious. I am, it seems, just what an old man needs on a Monday morning.

'Old?' I query. 'Am I phoning the right number?'

'You're too bloody kind. What can I do for you?'

'It's a bit tricky . . .'

'On the phone, you mean?'

'Yes.'

'You want a meet?'

'I do. Might that be possible?'

'Of course. My pleasure. You've got wheels?'

'I can do better than that. I've got Tony's wheels.'

'He's sick. Do you know that?'

'I do, yes.'

'Then watch what you touch. Wipes, you need wipes. Steering wheel, auto shift, radio controls, the lot.' A moment's pause. 'So where do you want to meet?'

'Your call. It's a great car. And I've got Tony's exemption.'

'Come here, then. My place. You know Cowplain?'

I don't. He gives me an address and a postcode, then asks whether I've eaten yet. When I tell him I haven't, he chuckles.

'Full English then, unless you're a veggie.'

'I'm not.'

'Excellent. Better and better. I'll get the bacon on.'

Something's not quite right here. Eagerness definitely has its place, but an invite like this from someone so fastidious about lockdown hygiene is odd.

'Won't it bother you?' I ask. 'Having a stranger in your house?'

'God, no. To tell you the truth, I'd murder for company just now, and in any case –' another chuckle – 'I've got plenty of wipes.'

TWENTY

Cowplain is fifteen minutes away, a collection of suburban properties off the old main road north. Number 101 Gladys Avenue turns out to be a bungalow, half concealed by an out-of-control hedge. A newish VW is parked on the cracked hardstanding, and a drift of empty take-out cartons have been trapped by the rusting foot of the wrought-iron gate. I wonder for a moment about the wisdom of leaving the kit bag in the boot, and decide to take it in. I open the gate and ring the bell beside the door. The tiny bay window beside me badly needs attention, as does a mangy tabby cat on the inside sill.

Dessie opens the door. He's wearing jeans that must be at least one size too big, and a rather nice denim shirt that looks new. He seems pleased to see me, then catches sight of the take-out boxes.

'Bloody kids,' he says. 'There's a Chinese up the road. No one cooks any more, not round here.'

'You've got a bag? You want me to get rid of them?'

'Bloody hell, no. Christ knows who's touched that lot. I'll sort it later.' He stands to one side. 'Come in.'

I can smell bacon the moment I step inside. Dessie's also gone overboard with the aftershave.

'Nice.' I'm looking at a stand of framed photos on a grand piano in the walk-through lounge/diner. Both come as a surprise in this setting. 'You play?'

'I'm afraid I do.' He settles briefly at the keyboard and I watch his big fingers dancing over the keys. He offers a series of riffs on a theme I can't quite place, but his playfulness reminds me of long-ago evenings in a jazz club Berndt and I used to frequent in Notting Hill.

'"Stormy Weather".' Dessie is on his feet again. 'No offence if you didn't recognize it.'

'I did,' I lie. 'Who's that?' I'm pointing at one of the shots on the piano, a young face in naval uniform. Heavily posed and carefully side-lit, it has to be a studio shot.

'Me,' he says. 'My dad paid to have that done. I'd just joined up. He'd abandoned all hope before then.'

'Wild child?'

'Lazy. And not very nice. I hated school, chased the wrong girls. I'm sure you're getting the picture here.'

He offers to store my kit bag outside in the hall. Breakfast is nearly ready. One egg or two?

I tell him I'd prefer to leave the bag where it is, and settle for one egg. He departs to the kitchen, telling me to help myself to the piano if I fancy it. Instead I glance at the rest of the photos, the youthful face getting steadily older, mates appearing from time to time. In one of the shots, Dessie stands in the middle of a group of matelots on what looks like the hull of a submarine. There are mountains in the background, beyond a stretch of grey water. The tallest of the guys in the shot is holding a sizeable teddy bear, and I've read enough editions of the *Portsmouth News* by now to recognize the blue and white Pompey scarf around its neck.

I can hear Dessie clattering about in the kitchen. He's whistling

'Stormy Weather', and then starts on the lyrics as something hits the hot fat in his frying pan. I'm eyeing my kit bag. Jessie has been careful to secure the drawstring, and I loosen the double knot and take a peek inside. Thick bundles of notes are bound together with blue elastic bands. I bend to the bag and give it a shake. There must be dozens and dozens of them. Fifty-five thousand pounds, I think. I've never seen so much money in my life.

I re-tie the double knot and leave the bag beside a piano leg. Moments later, Dessie is serving up, and I join him at the table. Full English, indeed. After eggs, bacon, sausage, hash browns, tomatoes, and beans, I stop counting the ingredients. Even the bottles of sauce and jars of show-off pickles have a little tray of their own.

When I ask him whether he eats like this all the time, he shakes his head.

'Only when I have company,' he says. 'Which these days means never.'

'Mrs Wren?'

'Lives elsewhere. Was our parting messy? Not really. Was the divorce my fault? Yes. Did I get screwed financially? I'm afraid so.' He stabs at a sausage. 'You're gonna be asking about kids next. They never happened, thank God, though we spent a lot of time trying.'

'Thank God?'

'Kids and divorce don't mix. And believe me, I should know.'

I love his candour. It carries a hint of recklessness. So far, Dessie hasn't expressed the slightest interest in why I'm here, and for that I'm grateful. Best to get to know him first. Pavel, as ever, had a word for this moment in the script. He used to call it 'foreplay'.

'Those pictures on the piano.' I'm chasing a mushroom round my plate. 'Were you on submarines?'

'I was. It was an accident, really. When you join up, they give you preferences. Someone put my name down for submarines. I never sussed who it was, and he probably didn't mean well, but in the end he did me a favour. Ordinary Seaman Jenny Wren? Submariner? I loved it.'

'Really? Being underwater all that time? You're telling me you're some kind of agoraphobe?'

'Christ no, quite the reverse. It was the blokes, really. You're right, you're banged up for a long time and none of it feels very natural to begin with but get the right mix in a boat like that, and you really bond. Submariners are the best of the best. We had to depend on each other, and we did. Think fighter pilots underwater. Bottom Gun.'

Bottom Gun. *Top Gun* was one of Berndt's all-time favourite movies and I must have seen it at least three times. This man is quietly very funny.

'Did they really call you Jenny?'

'Of course. The Navy runs on nicknames. Jenny Wren. Dusty Miller. Smudge Smith. You call a bloke by his nickname for so long you forget his real name. Jenny Wren. Just think about it. If you survive that, you can survive anything.'

'And your job? What were you actually *doing*?'

'Mainly nailing the Russian subs. It's a game. Cat and mouse. We'd go to sea for three months and get up to all kinds of stunts.'

'I meant you personally. What were *you* doing?'

'I was a sonar operator. Underwater you do everything by sound. Navigate. Make life tough for the Russians. You're staring at a screen, and listening very hard, and trying to make sense of all the clues. What are these guys up to? What does this manoeuvre tell you? Why has he gone to that depth? How come he's stopped dead in the water? It's chess. It prepares you for anything. Everything that helped me in the Job, I learned in submarines. Motive, patterns of behaviour, weaknesses. The lot.'

'The Job?' I'm full already and barely halfway through my plate of food.

'I left the Service in '94. Put in ten good years but everything was changing. My old girl was put out to grass.'

'Out to grass?' I'm getting seriously lost.

'Decommissioned. *Courageous* was knackered, falling apart, way too noisy, bit like me. My dad was a copper and he had a great time in the Job, so it seemed the obvious move. You join as a probationer, learn the ropes, wear the uniform, get the boring shit done, but I was CID within a couple of years. Never looked back after that.'

'Motive? Patterns of behaviour? Weaknesses?'

'You've got it. I was still on that bloody sub. And in some

respects, I still am. First, hunt for the clues. Then work out what they're trying to tell you.'

Work out what they're trying to tell you.

'Someone told me you were on Major Crimes for a while.' I'm toying with the rest of my egg. 'They said you were in charge of intel.'

'Who was that?'

'It doesn't matter.'

'H?'

'Yes.'

'He's right. That's exactly what I did. Ex-skate Jenny Wren. The guy with his fat ear to the ground.'

'And now?'

'Now I've retired. Again. First the Navy. Now the Job.'

'But you'll still have contacts?'

'In the Job? Of course. Coppers are getting younger by the day and a lot of them aren't to my taste but there are still some players in there, and you're right, we still have a pint or two.'

'Socially, you mean?'

'Sometimes. Sometimes not.'

'Not? Meaning you still do . . .' I shrug, hunting for the right word. 'Business?'

'No comment.' He holds my gaze. I can't take him an inch further. Pavel, I know, would be disappointed.

At length, he pushes his plate aside. To my relief he, too, has been defeated.

'So why did you come here?' he says. 'Why the call in the first place?'

I tidy my plate and take my time. Something tells me I'll only have one decent chance at getting this right.

'How well did you know H?' I ask. 'Be honest.'

'I knew him very well. I knew him much better than he ever suspected.' He taps one ear. 'That was my job.'

'So why didn't you . . .' I shrug. 'Arrest him?'

'Take him down, you mean?'

'Yes.'

'Because he was very clever, very sharp, and because he knew most of our moves way in advance. He owed that little favour to Dave Munroe, but he's dead now so I guess there must be a

God. Believe me, we tried very hard to put H back in his box but it never quite worked out.'

'And that frustrated you?'

'It pissed us off. I know all about you and H. I know about Antibes, and that superyacht where it happened, and that boy of yours. I know what H did with most of the money he made, and I have a shrewd idea what happened to the rest but proving all that stuff in court is what matters, and he knew we never had quite enough to make it stick. I hear good things about Flixcombe. The views, the estate, the house itself. Am I right?'

'Flixcombe is beautiful. There are friends of mine who'd call it divine.'

'I bet. It's also bought with the proceeds of crime, which I know is a tiresome detail, but it's true nonetheless.'

'You may be right.' I concede the point with a smile. 'But the same would be true of most of the National Trust properties H and I have ever been to. Slavery? Piracy? Taking what's not yours from Johnny Foreigner? This is H's line, not mine.'

'H is right.' Dessie's smiling now. 'Blood and treasure? Never failed. Especially in a place like Pompey.'

At this point comes a strange pause in the conversation. Pavel would call it a caesura. My Breton mum would talk of an angel passing. What both of them meant was a moment when you stop, take stock, and then – just maybe – take the opportunity to nudge the conversation in a new direction. I quite like this man, and he knows it. I like how open, how trusting, he seems to be. I like his playfulness, and he has the kind of artful patience I've learned to associate with big men. He's also an acute listener, which is very rare in either sex, and even more unusual if you've built two careers on that single talent.

'You'll remember names from the old days,' I suggest.

'You're right.' He taps his head. 'All filed away.'

'And now? How much do you know about what's going on now?'

'Here, you mean? In Pompey?'

'Of course.'

'Try me.'

I nod. From here, I tell myself, there's no going back. *Fais attention*, as my mother might say. Take care.

'A woman called Shanti?'

'Go on.'

'You know her?'

'Of her, yes. Beyond that, no.'

'So what do you know *of* her?'

'That she's in the game, or has been. Is she any good? I've no idea. Does she have the connections? I gather she does, though maybe not down here. Would she be on H's radar? Assuming he's after a punt or two? Very probably. Beyond that, you'd know more than me.' He pauses for a mouthful of cold beans. Then his head comes up again. 'You're here to tell me that H is in touch with this woman? I'm amazed he's got the time. I thought he was dying.'

'No comment.' I lightly touch the corner of my mouth. 'Tomato sauce. Not a good look.'

We both look at each other, and we both laugh. This is a moment of genuine complicity, and I take maximum advantage.

'The name Sammy,' I murmur. 'Ring any bells in that big, big memory of yours?'

Dessie frowns, making a real effort, but he knows I know he's faking.

'Nothing,' he says. 'Sammy? Complete blank. You've got a surname?'

'Sadly not.'

'So why Sammy? Why table the name?'

'No comment.'

'Is it something H said?'

'H is out of it most of the time, and what he says is mostly nonsense.'

'Most of the time?'

'Most of the time.' I nod. 'You know why I'm really here?'

'Tell me.'

'Someone's trying to get at H, and I've no idea who.'

'Get at?'

'Kill.'

I tell Dessie about our two power failures, someone fiddling around with the master switch in the control box, someone ill-disposed to Mr Hayden Prentice.

'Christ.' This time Dessie isn't faking it. He wants to know more.

'There is no more. Not until he does it again and gets a result. Catch H at the right time, turn off the oxygen, and he's dead within minutes. At least that's what they tell me. I'm frightened, Dessie. If you really want an explanation, that's why I'm here. Frightened and – to be frank – a little helpless. Malo and I have been doing our best under the circumstances. Now, Pompey seems to be getting the better of us.' I push my chair back and stand up.

'You OK?' Dessie sounds alarmed.

'I need the loo. Not your fault. Mine for being so greedy.'

'Door on the right before you get to the kitchen.' He nods at my plate. 'Can I take it you're done?'

'I am. It was delicious.'

I make my way down the corridor. The loo is like a sentry box and I squat for a minute or two of the purest relief. There are more photos on the wall, in clip frames this time, and I'm guessing that these come from Dessie's CID days. In one of them, whoever took the photo has caught him at his desk. He's crouched over his phone, making notes on a pad with his other hand, and I stare at it for a while. Whoever he's talking to, whatever he's just learned, may well have been in connection with Malo's dad. H was, for a long time, one of Major Crimes' prime targets in Pompey, a source of some pride for H himself, and it's very strange to be sitting here, in this same listener's bungalow, imagining how that conversation might have gone. What's the little bastard up to now? How come he knows so much about us? What the fuck's going on?

Back at the table, to my surprise, the plates are still there. Dessie has evidently been on the phone because his mobile lies at his elbow.

'Better?'

'Immeasurably. And I mean it. If all else fails, you could run a café. Fabulous breakfast. Absolute classic.'

He nods. The smile strikes me as genuine. Then, in a way that feels entirely spontaneous, he reaches for my hand.

'You mind me asking you a question?' he says.

'Not at all.'

'Why are you carrying all that money?'

I look away a moment, robbed of an answer. I should have guessed that he'd take a peek in the bag, but I didn't. My hand is still in his and I've no great desire to reclaim it.

'It doesn't matter,' I say at last. 'H is running up debts. They have to be met.' I start to tell him about the nursing agency, and Mr Wu's fees, and all the rest of it, but he interrupts me to say he knows all this already.

'How?'

'Tony told me. The rest I could work out for myself.' His big hand briefly tightens around mine. 'I expect you're en route to the nursing agency.'

'I am, of course.'

'Really?'

'Yes.'

'No other plans for all that dosh?'

'No.'

'You're absolutely sure?'

'Yes.'

'So it's all going to the nursing agency?'

'Yes.'

He looks at me a moment longer, a smile on his lips.

'Just as well. Do it now. It's probably more than you owe them but that doesn't matter. Call it an investment. Call it whatever you like.'

An investment. How ironic.

'You mean that?' I have to be sure.

'I'm afraid I do. One other thing.'

'Yes?'

'This Sammy. I'll have a bit of a think, maybe make a call or two.' He studies me for a moment, then nods back towards my bag. 'You owe me already.' He gives my hand the softest squeeze. 'It might be nice if we met again.'

I nod, say nothing. He shepherds me out into the narrow little hall and opens the front door. As he does so, I notice a wooden plaque on the wall. It features two golden dolphins, meeting head-to-head beneath a regal crown. Nothing else.

When I ask what it is, Dessie studies it a moment, then tells me it's the badge you get when you pass your Part III exams to become a submariner.

'Like aircrew wings?'

'Exactly.' I know he wants to kiss me. 'Bottom Gun.'

TWENTY-ONE

B ack in the car, Jessie's bag stowed safely in the boot, it takes me no time at all to get through to the nursing agency. Happily, Mr Wu is on the premises, in conference with the agency's Director of Operations, and the woman on the switchboard assures me he'll still be around if I come at once.

'And this is in connection with . . .?' she asks.

'The money we owe you.'

'Excellent. I'll pass the message on.'

The agency is in Port Solent, a marina I've only seen previously from the motorway. The car park that serves the commercial area is virtually empty, and I retrieve the bag from the boot and walk to the row of office units that overlook the marina basin. This space, unlike the car park, is overflowing with craft, most of them smallish yachts – a consequence, I'm guessing, of lockdown. Until further notice, owners are forbidden to use their boats.

I'm about to take the stairs to the first floor, when I notice a boat at the far end of the marina. It's much bigger than everything else in the basin and has an entire pontoon of its own. Unlike the surrounding yachts, this is a motor cruiser. The last time I saw anything of this size was two decades ago in Antibes. I've got the kit bag hoisted over one shoulder, and the sheer weight of the money is starting to wear me out, a rich metaphor that would have delighted Pavel. Later, I think, making a mental note to check out the boat.

The agency's offices are at the very end of the timber walkway on the first floor. There's a list of directors on the brass plaque beside the entry bell. The three names are in alphabetical order, and Mr Wu is at the bottom of the list. Not just a respiratory consultant, I think, but a businessman as well.

I give my name to the speaker phone and get buzzed in to

find Mr Wu sitting beside the receptionist, going through a list of must-do items. Within seconds, I'm next door in an adjacent office, saying yes to coffee and no to biscuits. Mr Wu, as ever, is the soul of discretion. I sense at once that he wants to discuss the second power failure, but now I've realized his larger financial interest in H's care, I'm working to a different agenda.

The office appears to belong to the Director of Operations and has a conference table as well as a desk. I untie the drawstring on the bag and empty the contents on to the table. Half a dozen bundles of notes end up on the floor and Mr Wu is still gazing at all that money as I retrieve them.

'Where does it come from?' he says quietly. 'I have to know.'

'A property sale in West Dorset.' With Dessie's help I've anticipated this question.

'You have all the paperwork?'

'Of course. Not now, but later.'

'I see.' He seems happy enough and summons the receptionist to help with the counting. The receptionist used to work in a building society. Her fingers are a blur as she counts the notes, and she fetches more elastic bands and sorts them into wads of a thousand pounds. Twenty minutes later, we're looking at £55,000, bang on. *Chapeau* to Jessie. She's played a blinder.

By now, it's quietly obvious that Mr Wu is very pleased indeed. From his pocket, he produces an up-to-date account of exactly how much we owe. Including his own fees, per-diem charges for the nursing cover, plus a trillion extras, it comes to nearly £23,000. Add the fee for the deep cleaning, and we're looking at £24,500.

'Perfect.' I carefully separate twenty-five wads of banknotes and put them to one side. This sum will clear our current debt. Mr Wu is watching my every move.

'And the rest?' he asks.

'You have a safe here?'

'Not here. Elsewhere would be better.'

'Then you keep it. Let's call it a deposit against your next invoice. I'll need a receipt, obviously, and the liability for storage is obviously yours.'

'Of course.' He's eyeing the rest of the cash on the table. He tells me that this should take Mr H through to next weekend, but after that we're once again on the meter.

'Not a problem, Mr Wu.'

'You have more?'

'Of course.'

'In cash, like this?'

'Yes.' I try to warm this exchange with a smile. 'Land in Dorset is worth a fortune. You'd be amazed.'

He nods. He looks briefly pensive. If I'm thinking all this money has spared me a discussion about the electricity supply at the flat, I'm wrong.

'You're happy with the care to date, Ms Andressen?'

'Very. Being able to see H every day makes it all worthwhile, and he probably feels the same way. All we can say is thank you.'

'A pleasure, Ms Andressen. We have to talk about the incident last night. Do you mind?'

I shake my head and listen patiently while he outlines the obvious dangers. His duty, he says, is to safeguard our Mr H, and for that to happen he has to be sure that there will be no more surprises.

'Surprises, Mr Wu?'

'Someone breaking in. Someone turning off the power.'

'Of course.'

'You have plans in that respect?'

'We do, Mr Wu. I was taking advice only this morning.'

'From? Do you mind me asking?'

'Not at all.' An even warmer smile. 'The police.'

'Good.' He nods. 'Very good. Then I think we can agree that the matter is resolved.'

'And if it isn't?'

'Then we must find alternative accommodation.' He nods at the table. 'Which will doubtless incur further cost.'

Mr Wu, as delicate and tactful as ever, is once again marking my card. No more power outages. Else H will be on the move.

I extend a hand and tell him I'm grateful. He gives me that lovely little half-bow and looks forward to our next meeting. I leave him in the office to sort out the money and pause on my way out to check one last detail with the receptionist, now back behind her desk. I've no idea whether she'll know the answer to my question, but it's worth a try.

'There's a superyacht moored at the end of the marina,' I tell her. 'Much bigger than everything else.'

'White? Shiny? Plastic? Just a bit loud? No sails? No mast?'

'That's the one.'

'It's brand new, arrived just before Christmas. I'm trying to remember the name. Are you good on battles?'

'Agincourt?' My heart is sinking.

'That's it. *Agincourt.*'

'And the owner?'

'Guy called Dennis. I'm afraid I don't know his second name. He's big in construction.'

'And he lives here? In Pompey?'

'Somewhere close by, I think. Not sure exactly where.'

I thank her for her help and don't bother with the walk to the end of the marina. I can tell from here that this year's *Agincourt* is an even grosser toy than the last one. Twenty years ago, a smaller version was berthed in the marina at Antibes. It was full of the owner's mates, most of them from Pompey, and H was one of the less shouty guests on board. I only stayed a single night but that was enough for us both to conceive Malo.

Agincourt. Dennis.

I make my way back through the city, wondering how on earth I'm going to handle the wrath of Malo. I've intercepted the money he was counting on. I've lodged the whole lot with Mr Wu. I suspect I've kept H out of big trouble, assuming he ever gets better. But none of that will count with my son because I've wrecked whatever plans he's been cooking up, and like his father he hates being second-guessed.

Back at the flats, I pause beside the big cupboard that contains the meters on the ground floor. Someone's secured it with a padlock, a combination rather than a key. I study it a moment, then head for the stairs. Malo is in the front room, talking to Taalia. He ignores me at first but then Taalia gets called away to attend to H. Malo watches her leave the room, and then turns back.

'I phoned Jessie,' he says. 'Why didn't you tell me? Why didn't you wake me up? I would have gone. I could have handled it myself.'

'Handled what?'

'The money. Did you find Shanti?'

'Of course not.'

'You're telling me you've still got it? Fifty-five grand?'

'No.'

'So where the fuck is it?'

'I gave it to Wu. We're paid up until the weekend.' I drop the empty kit bag on the floor. 'Do I hear a thank you?'

He's staring at me, shaking his head. He can't believe what he's just heard, how stupid I am, how perverse, how *devious*.

'She's expecting that money,' he says. 'She's got everything else set up, the contacts, the distribution, everything. We could have had all of it back within ten working days. *Trebled.*'

'And you believed her?'

'Of course I believed her.'

'Really?'

'Yes.'

'Then you owe me two thank yous. One for keeping the agency off our backs. And another for saving you a great deal of embarrassment.'

'Like how?'

'Like losing fifty-five grand of your father's money. Why don't you try it in French? *Merci, maman.* There. So easy. No embarrassment. No shame. Just do it. For me. *Merci, maman.* I won't hold any of this against you. I promise.'

Malo rolls his eyes. He's had enough. Abruptly, he gets up from the sofa and heads for the door, and the staircase beyond. I want to ask him about the lock on the cupboard downstairs, whether it's his doing, and if so whether he's shared the combination with everyone else in the building, but now is not the time. I've no idea where he's going and I suspect that he doesn't, either.

He must have left the building now, because I hear the crash of the front door as he pulls it shut behind him. The whole building seems to shudder, and Taalia must have heard it too, because she's back in the front room, looking concerned.

'My son,' I explain briefly. 'You get used to it in the end.'

She nods. She has an envelope in her hand. It's got my name on it and for a moment I assume it's yet another bill that needs paying, but I'm wrong.

'Julia left this for you,' she said. 'She said she doesn't want it lying around any more.'

'What is it?'

'I don't know.' She shrugs. 'She didn't say.'

Once she's left the room, I open the envelope. I recognize H's mobile at once. It's still got charge, and out of curiosity, I start to scroll through the texts he's obviously missed. The most recent arrived yesterday afternoon, at 17.03. It comes from a number I don't immediately recognize. *Assume balance also available?* it reads. *110K?* I stare at it a moment. £110,000 must refer to the balance of H's rainy-day fund. The expected forty thousand has yet to arrive, but the texter needs to be sure about the rest as well. In which case, he won't have been disappointed by the reply. Sixteen minutes after receipt of the text, H has offered the clearest of answers.

Yes. Just that. *Yes.*

This is puzzling. These last few days, to my knowledge, H has been in no state to take part in any SMS exchange. I glance at my watch. By now, it's late morning and the next shift change is due this afternoon. Ela, the older of the two Polish nurses, would have been on duty yesterday afternoon and might be able to shed light on the mystery.

She arrives on time, and I wait until the handover is complete and the outgoing nurses have departed. H, according to Taalia, is a little better this morning and has even eaten a small bowl of porridge.

'You think he's on the mend?'

She shakes her head and says it's far too early to be sure. She has two girlfriends who are working on the ICU at the QA hospital and they're finding that the virus makes life tough for everyone. One day, she says, a patient is making real progress. The next, he might be dead.

'So, no promises?'

'None, I'm afraid, Ms Andressen. He's asleep again at the moment.'

As soon as Taalia's gone, I ask Ela to come through to the front room. We talk now via mobiles, which seems strange when we're only a room apart but makes perfect lockdown sense.

Ela has taken off her mask and visor before she joins me and confirms that H is still asleep.

'And yesterday?' I ask.

'The same. Most of the time he was on the mask. The coughing was definitely better, just a little from time to time, but he was exhausted. You saw him yourself, Ms Andressen. You sat with him until Natasha arrived.'

She's right. I did. And H was definitely in no state to bother with his smart phone.

'Around five o'clock yesterday afternoon,' I begin. 'Can you remember exactly what you were all doing?'

Ela raises an eyebrow. She doesn't understand what I'm trying to say.

'Looking after Mr H, of course.'

'All three of you?'

'Most of the time, yes.'

'Sometimes just two of you?'

'Occasionally, yes.'

'But might there ever be only one of you?'

'Never.'

'You're sure?'

'Of course I'm sure. We have to be ready for anything, Ms Andressen. And that means at least two of us. Always.' She's frowning now, a little disturbed. 'Why?'

I do my best to make light of it. Just a silly question from a confused client. I probably need more sleep, I tell her.

She nods, far from convinced, and reaches for her mask and visor. Moments later, she's gone.

I pick the phone up, checking the text again. *Assume balance also available? 110K?*

The temptation to ring the number is overwhelming, but my finger hovers over the screen for a moment before I do it. The number rings and rings, and then I'm suddenly listening to a voice I recognize.

'H?' He sounds surprised. 'You're better?'

My finger strays across the screen. I don't say a word.

'H? You there?'

I end the call, still staring down at the phone.

Wesley Kane.

TWENTY-TWO

Malo returns after dark. I'm sitting with H in full PPE, sharing a crossword with Sunil, when I hear his voice outside the door. He's talking to Marysia, one of the Polish nurses, before he disappears into our bedroom, and when she joins us again, she says he's getting ready to go out for a run. Running in the dark has become routine for my son, and I'm glad because exercise always puts him in a better mood. Maybe, after he comes back, we can be friends again.

Wesley? Getting in direct touch with H? When he probably knows H can't respond? It makes no sense. None at all. I stay at his bedside, the crossword abandoned, occasionally checking to see whether he shows any signs of waking up. The little peg-like oximeter has now been attached to his right middle finger and, according to the bedside read-out, his sat level has steadied at 93%. According to Sunil, this is way better than some of the earlier readings, and will keep his blood well oxygenated. His cough, however briefly, also seems to have disappeared.

Malo departs for his run and I leave H in the hands of the nursing team. Once I've shed the PPE, I go from floor to floor, knocking on doors, wanting to check about the new combination lock on the cupboard downstairs. There are eight flats in all, and I only manage to get a response from three of them. Two of the residents are old, both women, and they confirm that a nice young man had explained about the new lock on the cupboard and given them the combination. Neither of them are at all curious about this sudden need for security, thinking it must somehow be linked to the virus, but one of them is curious about the constant comings and goings to our flat upstairs. I don't want to alarm anyone, and so I mutter something about a protracted family celebration and leave it at that.

On the ground floor, there are two flats, one of them owned by a man in his seventies with a lopsided walk, watery eyes and four-day stubble. He's wearing a yellow life jacket with a plastic whistle over a pair of pyjamas and I can hear the blare of the TV from somewhere behind him. When I apologize for the intrusion, he says it isn't a problem. He's been up for ages and – yes – he too has the combination for the new lock. Unlike the women upstairs, he wants to know why the lock was necessary in the first place, and without going into details I mention problems we're having with the supply. He seems to lose the thread after that and when I enquire whether he's been aware of any intruders, he shakes his head.

'Can't help you,' he says. 'I'm deaf as a post.'

I linger for a moment longer and nod at the door opposite.

'Is that the flat that was let recently?'

'What, dear?'

'Has someone just moved in?'

He frowns, looks vaguer than ever, then shakes his head. 'It's for sale,' he says. 'I think.'

I thank him for his time and knock on the door opposite, but nothing happens. Back upstairs, my duty done, I collapse on the sofa. Malo has bought today's edition of the *Portsmouth News,* and I start to thumb idly through, deferring the call I know I have to make.

A longish piece offers advice on keeping sane over the imminent Easter break: dream up a card, plot an indoors egg hunt, sew an Easter bonnet, or convert an empty egg carton into a bunny-themed draughts board. All of this is mildly depressing. It reads like a newsletter you might circulate to a bunch of lifers on 'B' wing, and when I turn the page it gets worse. How to deal with dry skin or even eczema after repeated handwashing. Plus a cheerful guide on ratting out your neighbours when they break the lockdown rules.

Finally, I can delay the call no longer. I phone Wesley on the number I always use, and he picks up at once.

'You OK?' he grunts.

'Never better. Not interrupting anything, I hope.'

'Chance would be a fine thing. I used to like this place. Now it's driving me nuts.'

I tell him I understand. Then I ask him about the text he sent to H yesterday afternoon.

'You know about that?'

'Yes.'

'He showed you?'

'Of course he didn't. He's sick, Wesley. You must know that. He's in no state to read anything. He can barely put one word after another.' I pause. 'So why did you send it?'

For a second or two, he has no answer. Then he's back on the line, voluble, almost offended.

'I had Shanti on, didn't I? Pissed-off doesn't cover it. She was expecting forty grand and nothing happened.'

'That's because I took it elsewhere, Wesley. As you know, that money belongs to H. It pays for all the care he's getting.'

'Yeah, but it won't last, will it? You know that and so does that boy of yours.'

'It might. We don't know yet.'

'And if it doesn't? What do we tell H, then? When they cart him off to the ICU and stuff a tube down his throat?'

'We hope that won't happen. These girls of his are doing their best with him. As far as I can gather, the word is stabilized.'

'Yeah? That's not the point though. We had an agreement.'

'We?'

'Me, and Shanti, and the boy. This is for H. That's why we've been putting out for him, all of us. It was sweet. We had it nailed. Now you come along and the party's fucking over. Sweet dreams, my love. When the shit hits the fan with H, and we're all back at the Crem, you might be thinking different.'

I blink, holding the phone at arm's length. I've never heard Wesley as angry as this, and I wait a moment or two hoping the diatribe might come to an end. At last, he seems to have run out of expletives.

'Enora? You still there?'

'I am. And I need to ask you something.'

'Sure. Ask away.'

'How well do you know this woman?'

'Shanti?'

'Yes.'

'Well enough.'

'Well enough for what?'

'Well enough to know she's kosher.'

'That's not an answer. Are you fucking her?' I pause a moment. 'Is that a yes?'

'In my dreams.' For the first time, he laughs. 'You saw the arse on her? What choice does a man have?'

I'm staring at the phone again, robbed of an answer. Just sometimes, even seasoned thesps like me lose their place in the script.

'You men are all the same,' I manage at last. 'You all think with your dicks. Listen, I have a really neat little trick for turning an egg carton into a draughts board. Hours of happy fun. If you're short of things to do, just give me a ring.'

My finger finds the off button, and Wesley is no more.

An hour later, Malo has yet to return. It's nearly nine o'clock and I'm beginning to fret. The last thing I want to do is disturb Taalia, but in the end I have no choice. I know that one of the nurses next door has her mobile number and she's happy to part with it.

'Trying to find Malo?' the nurse enquires.

'Something like that.'

I retreat to the privacy of the front room again and ring the number. Taalia turns out to be in the bath. And no, she hasn't seen my son.

'Is there a problem?' she says. 'Can I help?'

I thank her for the thought and hang up. I've no idea what might have happened, but the more I think about it, the more I'm certain I have to get out there and start looking. He might have tripped up in the dark, pulled a muscle, hurt himself. Worse, he might have decided to pay Shanti a visit, try somehow to make amends. If he wants to blame his interfering mother, so be it. Just as long as he's safe.

I happen to know the route Malo takes every night, largely because he's told me so often. Out across the Common, left on the seafront, up and over the battlements next to the Castle, then down to the promenade on the other side. After that, it's a straight run past the pier, a couple of miles at least, until there's no more seafront left. Then back again, same route.

I fetch my anorak, and check to make sure I've got my mobile. Sunil is in the kitchen, making himself a sandwich, and when he asks where I'm off to, I tell him I need the fresh air.

'And Mr Malo?' He knows I'm lying.

'Him, too.'

The Common, as ever, is deserted. There was rain in the air earlier, but the clouds have parted now and a huge creamy moon hangs over the Solent. The tide is high, and I pause on the seafront, gazing at the rumpled silver eiderdown lapping at my feet. Pompey's supermoon. As predicted in yesterday's *Portsmouth News*.

So far, I've seen no sign of Malo. I hurry on, head down against the keenness of the wind. The brilliance of the moon sheds a magical light on the castle, the harshness of the shadows lifting it into another dimension, and once again I marvel at the simple pleasures of looking at the world with no one else around. Sooner or later, I think, this wonderful sense of exclusivity, of being an audience of one, will have gone.

The path crests a little hill that leads around the nose of the Castle, and then I'm looking at the long stretch of the empty promenade under the loops of coloured lights. Wave after wave, silver beneath the moon, curls on to the pebble beach and when I look up again, I can see the brief shapes of seagulls, white-bellied, riding the wind. Hallucinatory. Wondrous. Beyond special. I shake my head.

I'm back on the promenade now, walking quickly to stay warm, one eye on the beach. Maybe Malo's tripped and fallen sideways on to the pebbles. Maybe he's gone beachcombing. Maybe he's as enchanted by the moonlight as his mother. Whatever. On the left of the promenade, away from the beach, are a series of shelters with benches inside. The first three are empty. The next one isn't. I slow, then stop. A long shape occupies the bench. I can't be certain but, in the half-darkness, it might be wearing running kit.

I steal a little closer, nervous now. The body is inert, no sign of movement. It's turned away from the sea and the promenade, and one arm hangs down, a gesture of helplessness that chills me to the bone. I stop again, staring down. It's Malo's watch, definitely, on his thin wrist, and there's something black-looking on his knuckles that could be caked blood.

'Malo?'

No response. Already I'm fearing the worst. He's dead, I

think. Something's happened, a fight, an ambush, some feral presence lying in wait. Or maybe something simpler, the wrong word to a passing stranger, the wrong place on the wrong night, and a sudden flurry of violence with God knows what consequences.

'Malo?'

He's within touching distance now, just a fingertip away, and I reach forward, cradling his head. His flesh, thank God, is still warm and I find a pulse in his neck. Then, very gently, I turn his head, and what I see, the face I find, brings a hot gust of something bitter and viscous bubbling up from the very middle of me. Both eyes are closed. His nose has been broken. And through his swollen lips I can see the wreckage of his perfect teeth. I step back and throw up. Twice.

'Malo?' I've wiped my mouth. 'Malo?' I'm kneeling beside him. 'Speak to me. Please God, speak to me.'

At length, very faintly, I get a reaction. It could be a groan. It could be anything. But at least he's still alive.

I look at him for a moment longer, and then fetch out my phone. Dial 999. So simple.

'Your name, caller?' A woman's voice. 'And which service do you require?'

TWENTY-THREE

The ambulance is with me within minutes. One paramedic bends over Malo, inspecting his facial injuries with a torch, while the other one takes me aside.

'And you are . . .?'

'His mother.'

'Name?'

'Enora Andressen.'

'I meant your son.'

'Malo.'

He nods, scribbles himself a note, and then asks for a contact number.

'But I'm coming with you.' I gesture towards the ambulance at the kerbside. 'Aren't I?'

'It might be possible, Ms Andressen, but we'll need to be certain that you haven't been in close contact with anyone infectious.'

I blink. It's a matter of record that I'm sharing a flat with a confirmed case of Covid. Pointless, therefore, to pretend otherwise. As briefly as I can, I explain the situation.

'And your son? He's living there too?'

'Yes.'

'So how come he goes out running?'

To this I have no answer but the other paramedic has conducted some brief checks and is tapping his watch. Malo needs a hospital. As soon as.

They fetch a stretcher from the ambulance and I watch, aghast, as they ease Malo's limp body off the wooden bench. So far, no one has mentioned the police. I follow the paramedics as they wheel the stretcher across the pavement and lift him into the back of the ambulance. Before they leave, I give them my mobile number and in return I get a direct line that will take me straight to A&E. If I phone tomorrow morning, someone will be able to fill me in.

'On what?'

'Your son's status, Ms Andressen. We'll obviously be logging the incident so someone needs to be talking to the police.'

'You mean me?'

'Of course. As next of kin, I'm afraid they'll need a word with you.'

Next of kin. I've never liked this phrase, so ominous, so potentially final, and just now it promises nothing but bad news.

'So what do you think?' I'm looking at my son. His head is half-turned from the harsh glare of the lights inside the ambulance, and a thin trickle of saliva from the wreckage of his mouth is pinked with blood.

'It's hard for us to say, Ms Andressen. If you can wait until the morning, they'll have taken a proper look at him.'

'And the police?'

'You can do it now, or you can report it tomorrow morning.

You might not want to hang around here waiting for them to turn up. It's your call.'

With that, the rear doors slam shut on Malo. One of the paramedics has stayed with him, while the other one clambers into the cab and settles behind the wheel. The paramedic in the back is already on the radio but I can't hear what he's saying. Does an incident like this have some kind of priority code? Do they call ahead, briefing the people in A&E on what to expect? And if so, how do they really think he is?

I'm still watching the tail lights of the ambulance disappearing into the city. He's only hurt, I keep telling myself. It'll take a while for all of us to get over it, and he'll certainly need attention at the hands of a good dentist, but no way is he going to die. Not Malo. Not my son.

Deep down, though, I'm not at all convinced. I know far too much about the lottery that can so suddenly put your life in danger. I know about brain scans, about the patience and skill of the people who stand between you and the Grimmest of Reapers, but I also know that there comes a point beyond which nobody, no matter how clever, can help you. Malo has obviously taken a beating. Maybe his skull is fractured. Maybe he has a bleed on the brain. Maybe, assuming he survives at all, he'll be permanently damaged. *Please God*, I whisper, *keep my son intact*.

I'm still at the kerbside, numb with the kind of aftershock that steals up on you. Utterly helpless, I seem to have lost the power of decision. The thought of going back to that horrible flat, to that cell of a bedroom I've been sharing with Malo, is unbearable. This city, this situation, this evil, evil virus has stolen the person I love most in all the world, and I haven't got a clue what to do next.

Booking into a hotel would be tempting, but they're all closed. Phoning the police would at least give me company for a while but how do I explain breaking quarantine? Not just my son, but me as well? Maybe I should phone Wesley. I know he'd drive down here and fetch me, and he'd very definitely give me a bed for the night, but on what terms? No, there has to be another way. I need someone who'll lend a listening ear, someone who might be able to make sense of what's just happened, someone familiar with what Pavel always called the Dark Side.

I walk slowly back to the promenade and spend a long moment staring down at the bench where I found my poor, broken son. Briefly, I try and picture the chain of events that put him at the mercy of whoever set about him, but the thought of Malo so alone, so suddenly vulnerable, is too painful to bear and so I tear myself away and cross the promenade and lift my head until I can see nothing but the rags of scudding cloud that soften the harshness of the moonlight.

The temptation now is to curl up on the pebbles, tucked in beside the seawall, and make myself the smallest possible target for whatever disaster awaits me next, but I know that this is the purest fantasy. If the last few days have taught me anything, it's the need to keep my wits about me and to try – somehow – to anticipate life's next move. Pavel would have talked sternly about the importance of holding my nerve, about thinking things through, and now – hearing his thin voice in the chilly darkness – I know he's right.

My call to Dessie Wren finds him, once again, in bed. The moment I tell him about finding Malo, he's trying to remember where he put his car keys.

He's down on the seafront to collect me within half an hour. I wave him down from the kerbside and get into the car.

'You OK?'

'No.'

'Cry if it helps.'

'It doesn't. I tried.'

'So where do you want to go?'

'Anywhere but that bloody flat.'

He suggests we go back to his place and I agree. It's a huge relief to be out of the city, and I tell him so. By now he's got the whole story – Malo's injuries, the ambulance coming, my exchange with the paramedic – and when it comes to the police, he tells me to leave everything to him. Gratitude, or maybe relief, is too small a word. I'm still terrified by what tomorrow's call to the hospital might reveal, but at least, fingers crossed, I won't be arrested.

At home, in his bungalow in Cowplain, Dessie pours me a large glass of brandy. By now, it's occurred to me that I'm already on a police file somewhere for breaching lockdown rules, but when I tell him about being stopped on the motorway that first time I drove down, he doesn't seem to think it matters. Hindhead, he says, is in Surrey, different force, different database. No one talks to anyone else these days, and there simply aren't enough bodies in or out of uniform to start chasing around after delinquent film stars.

If the latter phrase is designed to cheer me up, it works. Calling Dessie, I've already concluded, was a good decision. There's something about him, maybe his sheer physical presence, that is deeply comforting. This man, I suspect, has been in some very tight corners and has learned a thing or two about getting by. I also like the phrase 'delinquent film star'.

'You've Googled me?'

'Of course.'

'Should I be flattered?'

'Christ, no. I'm a nosey bugger. I do it all the time. It used to go with the Job. Now it's become a habit.'

He wants to know about my favourite film, my favourite location, actors and actresses I admire, scenes I regretted having to play, and what difference the Frenchness in me makes when it comes to – in his phrase – 'scoping' a particular part. This is a more acute question than it might seem, and one that no one else has ever asked me before, and after a second glass of brandy I find myself telling him about the work I've already done on *Dimanche*, and how right it feels to be playing a French cop.

This latest scalp on my belt absolutely gets his attention. He nods in all the right places, laughs at the funnier bits, and it's a while before I realize exactly why our conversation has taken this turn. He wants me to stop thinking about Malo, about what tomorrow might bring, about having to phone the hospital, how circumstances have so suddenly kidnapped my precious boy. This, to me, is a very Christian act. More to the point, it takes some guile to pull it off. *Chapeau*, I think.

'Do you regret not having kids?' I ask. 'Be honest.'

'What's that got to do with any of this?'

'I'm just curious. You're a gifted listener. You've got a great deal of patience. You'd make a terrific dad.'

He shrugs – a gesture, I sense, of mild embarrassment. Maybe I've just touched a tender spot. Or maybe he's faking it. Either way, I want to know more.

'What about your wife? Did she want kids?'

'Definitely.'

'But they never happened?'

'No.'

'And did that become a problem between you?'

'Yes, one of many if you're really asking. Having your husband away at sea for three months was never an easy gig. You get extra pay on submarines, and she loved that, but she needed someone around to moan at and I was never there.'

'And afterwards? Once you'd left and become a cop?'

'I was still on the lam, still going absent without leave. CID is the perfect alibi, believe me, if you never want to go home.'

'And that happened?'

'Yes.'

'So, where were you?'

This time he won't answer, simply shakes his head, but my question has sparked a playful little smile which, after the second brandy, is all I need.

'H says you were a famous shagger. Is he right?'

'No comment.'

'He *is* right?'

'More?' His hand has found the bottle of Armagnac.

I shake my head, conscious that I've gone way too far, broken every rule in the book. This kind of dialogue with the likes of Wesley Kane would give him the green light to take any number of liberties, but here and now, cocooned by the brandy, I can't imagine anyone less predatory than Dessie Wren. Nonetheless, I tell myself I have to draw the line. Tomorrow, for better or worse, I'll find out about Malo. I'll also press Dessie for clues about who could possibly have hurt him so badly. But for now, safe in this man's hands, I badly need a good night's sleep.

The sofa on which I'm sitting looks like it might convert into a bed, and even if it doesn't, all I need is a blanket and a cushion, but Dessie shakes his head. He has a spare bedroom, everything I could possibly need, and he insists I use it. While he hunts out a towel and a brand-new toothbrush he's stored somewhere, I wash out the glasses in the kitchen.

Hunting for a tea towel, I notice a small, framed photo of a little boy, propped against a line of cookery books. He looks no more than seven or eight. He's wearing football kit, black and white stripes, and the camera has caught him half-kneeling while he re-ties a lace. He's looking up, and there's something so spontaneous about his grin that it takes me back to my early days with Malo.

'His name's Stuart. Everyone calls him Titch.' Dessie is standing in the doorway, a folded towel in his hand. 'He's my godson.'

'And you took the photo?'

'I did, yes.'

'Recently?'

'Years ago. It was just before Christmas. They were cocky as hell and they lost four–nil.'

'You went to every game?'

'Christ, yes. That little boy would give me serious grief, otherwise.' He smiles. 'He played striker. He was good, too, he had all the moves, and he was brave, given his size.'

'He lived locally?'

'He lived in Southsea. I got to see him most weekends, especially in the winter.' He hands me the towel. 'If I were you, I'd put a call through to the flat and tell them what happened. It might get awkward if they report you both missing.' His gaze returns to the photo of his godson, and he smiles again. 'Who'd have thought, eh?'

Who'd have thought?

I'm looking at him, wondering exactly what doors this little boy might have opened in Dessie Wren's life, but when I raise an enquiring eyebrow, it's obvious that he doesn't want to take the conversation any further.

'Second door on the right,' he says. 'The toothbrush is on the shelf over the hand basin.'

TWENTY-FOUR

I seem to spend most of the night dreaming. The dreams, to begin with, are incoherent, wildly associative, my memory and my imagination ganging up on the rest of me, something I can only put down to the aftershocks of finding Malo last night. The first sequence of dreams feel like a meteor shower, sudden spasms of intense light tracking across the darkness inside my head, and it finds me at a house I've never seen before. It's big, as big as Tony Morse's place but somehow different, and the moment I step inside – don't ask me how – I know with complete certainty that it belongs to H. This is Pompey in the early days, I tell myself. Probably Southsea, maybe even Craneswater Park. This is how he spent those first millions he was making from the cocaine trade. This is the way he announced his arrival in this teeming city.

In the basement of this house is a swimming pool that also serves as a dining table. The water is imperfectly hidden beneath a spread of folding wooden panels, highly polished with a deep grain, but they don't fit properly. There are blue bits around the edges where he's added dye to the water, and there's a powerful smell of chlorine. Characters come and go around this table, swimming briefly into focus like rogue chords on Dessie's piano. With the exception of a younger version of Wesley Kane, whom I recognize immediately, these men are all huge and heavily tattooed, cheerful Pompey braggarts running to fat, most of them versions of Dave Munroe before obesity and liver disease put him in a wheelchair. I circulate among them, unseen, unremarked, ghost-like. I want to find my son, I explain. But none of them are listening.

Upstairs, the house is empty, though I can still hear laughter from below. I wander from room to room, calling Malo's name, telling him that everything's fine, that he'll be safe, that he should trust me, but there's no sign of him. A huge staircase winds upwards from floor after floor, exactly the kind of statement H would have relished making. No one's bothered to carpet it, another of H's fingerprints on the crazy abandon of this house, but when I get to the very top I suddenly find myself in a room walled entirely in glass. It's broad daylight by now, and sunshine floods across the bare boards. There are trees outside, and lots of wind, and in the far corner of the room, very briefly, I think I spot a jigsaw. The Battle of Trafalgar? I've no idea because the moment I take a proper look, it's gone.

Then I hear a voice. It's slightly muffled but it's definitely Malo. Not only that but I can date it exactly. At thirteen, his voice started to break, something I remember with absolute clarity because it coincided with the first time he started to truant.

'Mum?' He's lost. He wants me. Needs me. But where is he? He calls again, more urgent this time, a thin piping plea that cracks under the sticky assault of all those adolescent hormones. The next floor down, I tell myself. Not here.

And so I take the stairs again, dizzied by the urgency of this mission, telling him to hang on, to be brave, not to give up. The door to the room is open. It's suddenly dark again but I can see a cupboard, hard up against the wall. This is the only item of furniture in the room. There's nothing else.

I approach the cupboard. Every step I make echoes in the darkness. I'm trying to be as quiet, as light-footed as I can but it's like I'm wearing heavy boots. There's nowhere to hide. The ghost in me has gone.

The cupboard is the exact replica of the cupboard back in the flats, the one that Malo has padlocked, the one that holds all the meters and control panels. I stare at it a moment. No padlock. Just Malo inside it, begging me to let him out.

And so I reach forward, and open the door, and the moment I do so, a tiny little spotlight settles on the figure inside. The theatricality of this moment, the suddenness of the reveal, is deeply shocking but what's worse is the sight of Malo himself. He's not thirteen any more, in fact he's not even born at all. Naked, curled in the foetal position, the tadpole eyes in his huge head are staring out at me, and he has a tiny thumb in his mouth.

'Mum?' he's trying to say. 'Are you there?'

I awake with a start. It's daylight again. I'm howling my eyes out, and once I manage to mop the tears with a corner of the sheet, I find Dessie standing beside the bed. He has a mug in his hand, and a bowl of what turns out to be sugar cubes. He's wearing the same jeans and same sweatshirt as last night, and he's looking deeply uncomfortable.

'Tea?' he says.

I phone the number at the hospital an hour or so later. I couldn't face Dessie's offer of another breakfast, but a long, hot shower has made me feel a little better. The number I ring takes me to a desk in A&E. The nurse must be at the end of her shift because the moment I mention Malo's name, she remembers him coming in.

'Black curly hair?' she says. 'Been out running? Bit of a state?'

I say yes to both, fighting the urge to cry again. Malo in that hideous shelter. Utterly ruined.

The nurse is telling me that he's been admitted. She'll transfer me to the ward where he's being looked after. Someone up there should be able to help. I hang on, waiting for the new voice, praying that my son is still alive. Finally, a male voice answers. I want to know about a young man called Malo Andressen, I tell him.

'And you are?'

'His mother.'

'I'm looking at him now, Ms Andressen.'

'And?'

'He can't manage anything more ambitious than Complan, I'm afraid, but there's nothing wrong with his appetite.'

'You're telling me he's OK?' I can't believe it. 'He's *eating*?'

'Sipping would be closer. But he's still very much with us.'

My new friend, my saviour, has a light Irish accent and turns out to be a registrar on the ward. Malo, he tells me, has already had a series of X-rays. There's no damage to his skull, but his jaw is broken in two places and will need to be wired. He's also got hairline fractures on three ribs. Facially, the registrar has seen worse on Saturday nights. His nose will need a re-set, and his teeth will need sorting when dental surgeries open again, but apart from that, he's pretty much the full deal.

'You've talked to him?'

'I have, sure. He's a bit of a mumbler, that son of yours, but that's not entirely his fault.'

'Does he remember anything?'

'Nothing. He remembers setting out for the run, and he tells me he remembers the moon on the water. Apart from that, it's all a bit of a mystery.'

'So, is he in pain?'

'A little. Not much. I'm blaming the gods of medication, Ms Andressen. Drugs are a wonderful thing, as I'm sure our young Malo will agree.'

Our young Malo. Wonderful. I'm still reeling from the news, but in a good way. I have a million other questions to ask but I know that this man's time is precious.

'Can I come in and see him?'

'I'm afraid not, Ms Andressen. You're in touch with someone carrying the virus? Would that be right?'

'I'm afraid so.'

'Then the answer's no. But *nil desperandum.* We should have the lad home within a couple of days.'

A couple of days? Ten minutes ago, I was dreading another visit to the Crem. Now this.

'Thank you,' is all I can say.

'It's a pleasure, Ms Andressen. Might you have an address for delivery, by any chance?' He laughs. 'I expect they'll give you a time slot.'

It's late morning. At Dessie's insistence, I've managed to tuck away a little scrambled egg on toast and now he's been kind enough to make a brief detour on our way back into the city. For the second time in a week, I'm parked on the top of Portsdown Hill, staring out at the city below. The surge of relief sparked by my phone call to the hospital has gone. The knowledge that Malo is in good hands remains a comfort, but I want to know who hurt him.

Dessie nods. He's been nothing but kindness since he picked me up last night. He's been patient, and – for a man – he seems to have a remarkable understanding of the more vulnerable bits of the female psyche. This is the first time I've troubled him with a direct question about how and why Malo ended up in that bus shelter, and when it comes to an answer he's showing signs of hesitation.

'You need to help me here,' he says. 'I need to know who you and your boy have been talking to.'

'About?'

'Money. You arrived with a sack full of notes the other day. Parked it in my front room. You asked me about Shanti, and I suggested you take that money to the nursing agency. Why did I do that? Because either you or your boy had other plans. None of this is subtle, I'm afraid. But people get hurt in this game, and you're looking at someone who knows. Old habits die hard, and I'm guessing that H wanted to grow whatever money he had left. Am I right?'

I nod, and say nothing for a moment before asking him how much he knows about H's financial affairs.

'You mean now?'

'Yes.'

'I know enough.'

'Enough for what?'

'Enough to know he's made a couple of crap investments and that he's lost what most of us would regard as a fortune. Face him with a huge bill, just to keep him alive, and he's got a problem. I've been around long enough to know that people rarely change. H was always a risk-taker. Your Mr Wu may end up wanting hundreds of thousands of pounds. H has to find that money in double-quick time to avoid the ICU, which he dreads, and the only way he knows takes him straight back into the game. Except that the game has moved on.'

'You know about Mr Wu?'

'Yes.'

'Why? How come?'

'Because I'm still in the game, too. I'm employed as a civilian adviser now, which means I never really left. You'll know that H upset a lot of people back in the day, and I'm telling you the file remains open. There are very senior policemen in this city who would kill to see H behind bars.'

'Kill?'

'Poor choice of words. But I'm guessing you know what I mean.'

'And you think there's a chance of that? Of putting H away?'

'I do, yes. You never say never. Not in my little gang.'

I nod. A sudden shaft of sunlight has speared through the tumble of clouds over the grey sprawl of the city and settled briefly on the forest of cranes in the dockyard.

'Your little gang?' I say softly.

'My little gang,' he confirms.

'So where do you sit in all this? And how come you're being so nice to me?'

'You want the truth?' He turns to look at me. 'I don't want to see good people hurt.'

'That's a bit late, isn't it? After last night?'

'I meant you.'

'You think these people will come for me, too? As well as H and Malo?'

'I do, yes.'

'And who might they be?'

Once again, there's a moment of hesitation and that same playful little smile I'd noticed last night. Then he beckons me a little closer, as if someone might be listening.

'I'm going to drop you off at Tony Morse's flat, yes?'

'Yes.'

'And my guess is that you'll be paying your respects to H, yes?'

'Of course.'

'Then you might do both of us a favour. You mentioned a guy called Sammy. You said H had got in a bit of a state about him. I've done a bit of asking around.'

'And?'

'I suspect his second name is McGaughy. You might try that on H and see what happens.'

'Just that? Just the name? Sammy McGaughy? Nothing else? No more clues?'

'Not yet, no. Have a chat, if he's up to it. And let's see where it takes us.'

'Us?' I can't help smiling. For someone so subtle, so deft, so full of guile, this is unusually blatant.

'Us,' he agrees, reaching for the ignition keys and firing up the engine. 'And don't worry about the police. I talked to some people this morning. They may still want to talk to you, but not yet.'

TWENTY-FIVE

D essie drops me down in Southsea, and asks me to phone him once I've talked to H. He also, he says, would appreciate another conversation, this time about Wesley Kane. By now, I'm becoming aware that Dessie has cast me in a particular role in this developing drama, and I'm far from comfortable about the implications. At the kerbside, outside the flat, I decide to level with him.

'Just how many people do you want me to rat out?' I ask him.

'Rat out?' he says mildly. 'Is that what this is about?'

I hold his gaze for a long moment. Then I put my hand briefly on his arm.

'Thanks for looking after me,' I say. 'And I mean that.'

I get out of the car and let myself into the flats without a backward glance. The sight of the meter cupboard, still padlocked, brings me to a sudden halt but I fight a rising sense of panic, and make for the stairs. Up in the flat, I must have been in the front room for no more than half a minute before the door opens and Taalia joins me. I phoned last night and told one of the duty nurses about Malo.

'How is he?' she says at once.

'That was going to be my question.'

She looks confused, hurt even, then realizes that I'm talking about H.

'He's pulling through,' she says. 'Mr Wu was here this morning. He says it's still early days but the signs are good. Maybe even better than good. We're all really proud of him.' She pauses. 'And Malo?'

I tell her what little I know, glossing over the more horrible bits. Some people must have set about him. He ended up in hospital. He's not looking his best but it's down to all of us to bring him through it.

'He's coming back?'

'In a couple of days. Maybe even sooner.'

'Here?'

'Of course. Round-the-clock nursing? What more could he want?'

This prospect puts a smile on her face. She departs to look for a fresh set of PPE, while I settle on the sofa and put a call through to Tim, down in Bere Regis. When he answers, I ask him whether he was serious about the loan of his flat. He says yes, and gives me a phone number for the neighbour who has a spare key. He'll phone her now and tell her to expect a knock on her door.

'Everything OK?' he asks. I can hear the concern in his voice and decide, once again, to tell him the truth.

'No,' I say. 'It isn't. Long story. Thanks for the flat. Speak later, eh?'

Taalia is back with the PPE. She stays to help me into it, belt the gown at the back, and make sure the mask and visor are a good fit, and feeling her hands dancing lightly over my face I can't help wondering whether she'll be doing this for Malo, as well. I've no idea how long wounds like his take to heal, but they're bound to be sensitive.

H, when I finally make it into the bedroom, is sitting up. He's not wearing the oxygen mask, and there's a definite blush of colour in his face. He's pleased to see me, too, and after the events of the last twelve hours, this comes as a real tonic.

'Here.' He pats the side of the bed, ignoring Sunil's plea to observe the two-metre rule. 'Where the fuck have you been?'

'Out.'

'Why? Where?'

There's a vigour, even a slight menace, in these questions which I take to be a very good sign. I'm looking at the old H, wrestling back control. I tell him that a girl deserves a break from time to time, and that cabin fever is something new in my life, and he has the grace to smile.

'And the boy?'

This is trickier. I glance at Taalia and the faintest shake of her head tells me that H doesn't know he hasn't been around. For just how long can I sustain a white lie before Malo returns? One glance at his face would tell H everything he needs to know, and so I edge a little closer on the side of the bed and tell him that our boy has met with a bit of an accident.

'Accident? Like what? How?'

'He was out running,' I say lightly. 'You wouldn't believe the state of that promenade.'

'You're telling me he fell over?'

'Yes. Hurt himself quite badly. Up here, and round here.' I touch my face, then gesture at my ribcage. 'They're keeping him in for a couple of days. When all this is over, we should think about finding a good dentist.'

'His teeth?'

'And his jaw, H. Broken in two places.'

'Because he *fell over*?' H doesn't believe this fiction for a moment. 'Because of some paving fucking slab?'

I nod, say nothing. Taalia's right. H, as we say in France, *est en plein forme*, firing on all cylinders. Is this the moment for me to mention Sammy McGaughy? I suspect not.

'So what really happened?'

'He got hurt.'

'I know that. You told me that. But *how*?'

I shake my head, put a finger to my lips, do the thespy thing, try and make light of it, but this simply angers him more.

'Get Wesley round,' he says. 'I need someone to tell me the fucking truth. Someone's had a go at the boy. It's all over your face. I'm not blind, and I'm not dying any more, so do me a favour. Get Wesley. Phone him. Drive round. Pick him up. Any fucking thing. We have to sort this. All of us. Even you.'

This is a step too far. After the events of the last twenty-four hours, I deserve more than this volley of abuse. I'm angry now, probably more angry than he is, and I can sense the atmosphere in the room getting tense. None of these nurses signed up for a full-scale domestic. Saving someone's life is one thing, putting up with H at full throttle is quite another.

'Sammy McGaughy?' I enquire.

H is about to launch into another tirade, but the name stops him dead. He's staring at me. He doesn't know what to say, can't believe his ears.

'Again?' he whispers.

'Sammy McGaughy.'

'Where did you get that name?'

'It doesn't matter.'

'It fucking does.' He tries to lunge at me, tries to grab my
arm, but I'm too quick for him. Sunil is on his feet, trying to
restrain him, trying to spare me another furious assault. H does
his best to fight him off but Sunil, who seems to have the weight
of a feather, is much stronger than he looks. There comes the
beginnings of a serious scuffle, H trying to land a blow or two,
but Sunil has him in an arm lock and isn't letting go. He's also
very good at calming H down. I'm aware of the other two nurses
exchanging glances, and Taalia – in particular – is visibly frightened. But then the fight goes out of H and he slumps back against
the pillow, his eyes closing, one hand crabbing across the sheet
in search of the oxygen mask. Seconds later, Sunil is helping
him fix the mask to his face, making sure the elastic is comfortable around the back of his head.

A relapse, I think. Thank God.

Shaken, I take the PPE off, make my excuses, and leave the flat.
I have the address of Tim's place, barely a five-minute walk
away. His neighbour has been speaking to Tim and hands me a
key. Knowing Tim, she doesn't think there'll be much in the
fridge but there's a branch of Waitrose just across the road and
if I'm desperate, she can spare a jug of milk. I take the key,
thank her, and let myself into Tim's flat.

After the damp squalor of our perch on the seafront, Tim's
place is a different proposition. It feels warm and lived-in. Thesps
have a bad habit of collecting various trophies from numberless
locations, and Tim is no exception. I spend a very happy fifteen
minutes, trying to calm myself down, admiring a pin board of
location snaps featuring many faces I happen to know, and
wondering what on earth possessed him to volunteer for an
evening of belly laughs in *The Navy Lark* at the Torch Theatre
in Milford Haven.

Tim's bookshelves are interesting, too. He's always nursed a
feeling that he really should have been Dennis Hopper, astride
a Harley-Davidson, growling his way south along California's
Highway One, and he has a rich selection of alternative reading
from early James Baldwin to Jack Kerouac and Tom Wolfe. I'm
taking a peek at the flat's only bedroom, which features a set of
Tim's drums, when my phone starts to ring. It's Dessie Wren,

and for a moment I'm tempted to ignore it, but then have second thoughts. In some important ways, I owe this man at least a conversation, if only for taking me in last night.

'Are you OK to talk?' he asks at once.

'Yes. Why do you ask?'

'You're not with H?'

'Not at the moment, no.'

'But you've talked to him?'

'Yes.'

'And?'

I don't answer. In the background, at Dessie's end, I think I'm hearing seagulls. Then he's back on the phone again.

'It's probably best if we do this face to face,' he says.

'Do what?'

'It doesn't matter. Except I'm about to do you a big, big favour. I'm parked on the seafront. Just where I picked you up last night. Sooner rather than later, eh?'

He ends the call without a further word of explanation, and I'm left staring at the phone. Favour? Seafront? I shake my head, aware that after this brief moment of solace at Tim's, events have once again taken charge.

I'm getting to know Southsea by now and I take a slight detour that would suggest I'm coming from the direction of Tony Morse's flat. Dessie leans across and opens the front passenger door as I approach. He's listening to a concert on Radio Three, and I recognize the second movement of Beethoven's *Eroica* symphony. There are crumbs on his lap and when he notices my interest, he offers me the untouched half of his egg and cress sandwich.

'Lunch,' he says. 'Compliments of Londis.'

I nod absently, taking the sandwich, absorbed by the music. It was Berndt who introduced me to this symphony, the one gift of his that came without strings of any kind, and even after all the wounds we inflicted on each other I still, in my heart, thank him for it.

Dessie reaches for the volume control but I tell him to leave it alone. There's a passage for the brass midway through the second movement, taken up by the strings, and it never fails to touch me. Dessie's sitting back now, his big hands clasped over his belly, his eyes closed. Once the movement has flickered and died, I let him have his way with the volume control.

'Well?' he says.

'Sublime,' I tell him. 'And it's his year, too. Two hundred and fiftieth anniversary. I could listen to music like that for the rest of my life and die a happy woman. In fact, I nearly did just that.'

I tell him briefly about my tussle with the Grim Reaper. After the operation, when chemo took me to places I never want to revisit, it was music like this that kept me going.

'Shit,' he says quietly. 'I didn't know.'

'Why should you? It's a detail. Cancer is ugly. The virus is ugly. Our bodies let us down. The world belongs to the microbes. They're the ones who'll survive. Not us.' I look at him, forcing a smile. 'How many clichés in all that? Are you counting? Should you be? I mean it. In the end, nothing much matters.'

'You're kidding.'

'Am I? How do you know, Mr Jenny Wren? How can you ever be sure?'

I'm gazing at him now, offering him the time and space to frame some kind of answer, but unless I've got this little scene completely wrong, he genuinely doesn't know what to say.

'You mentioned a favour,' I remind him. 'What is it?'

'Fuck the favour. You're a very unusual woman. And that's a compliment.'

'Thank you.' I do my best to force a smile. 'And the favour?'

He stares at me a moment, still wrong-footed, and then shakes his head as if to get all the bits inside back in working order. I recognize this gesture, this little tic, because I do it myself, especially when I've drunk too much. For now, though, I couldn't be more sober.

'That money you brought to my place,' he says. 'I'm guessing there's more.'

'You guess right.'

'How much more?'

'A lot. You never embarrass a lady by asking for specific figures, but a lot.'

'Six figures?'

'Yes.'

'And where is it?'

'Why do you ask?'

'Because you need to get out of this car, and make a call to whoever's looking after it, and tell them to put it somewhere very safe.'

I blink. After Beethoven and half an egg sandwich, this man has my full attention.

'You're telling me this person, these people, are under threat?'

'The money. The money is under threat. Make the call now.' He nods towards the pavement. 'I promise you won't regret it.'

'We're talking the bad guys here?'

'We're talking however much H has got squirrelled away. Just do it. Please. I'll wait.'

'You mean there's more?'

'I'm afraid so.'

'We haven't finished? We're not through?'

'Far from it.'

Bloody hell. I get out of the car and find Jessie's number on my directory. She's down at Flixcombe and she answers at once. When I mention H's rainy-day fund, she assumes I need another instalment to pay the nursing agency. I tell her she's wrong.

'He's getting better, Jess. My guess is we'll probably need another fifty grand but fingers crossed we might not want the rest.'

'So, what do you want me to do?'

'Hide it.'

'*Hide* it? What is this?'

'To be honest, Jess, I'm not at all sure, but a man I think I trust insists you make it very hard to find. Take it to the woods and bury it. Ask Andy, he'll have some ideas. Just as long as it's away from the house.'

'Jesus, Enora. You're starting to frighten me.'

'I'm sorry. I don't mean to. This is for H, really.'

'And Malo? What does he think?'

'Malo's another story. I'll phone you later. Byeee . . .'

I end the call and return to the car. Dessie half mutes the Beethoven again.

'Done?' he asks.

I nod, glad he wants no more details.

'Next?' My smile this time is unforced. 'How can I help you, Mr Wren?'

'Wesley Kane.'

'What about him?'

'He has two phones, at least.'

'You want me to steal them? Destroy them? Clone the SIM card? Pop them in a Jiffy bag and send them to Cowplain? Just name it, Mr Wren.'

Watching his face, I know I'm on a roll. For the second time, he's not quite sure how to handle this.

'You can get to see him?' he asks at last.

'Any time I like. He very badly wants to get into my knickers. As long as it's daylight, and somewhere public, I stand a fighting chance. Otherwise I'm afraid it's *rideaux.*'

'It's what?'

'Curtains. With a little flurry at the end when I take a bow.'

'This might not be so funny,' Dessie murmurs. 'There are photos on one of those phones we need. We're not asking you to steal it. Just give us a clue where he might keep it.'

'So you can seize it?'

'One way or another, yes. It needn't be obvious. It needn't be in his face. There are other ways. Here . . .'

'What's that?'

Dessie has produced a cube wrapped in silver foil. He slips it into a plastic sachet and hands it across.

'It's a little present for Mr Kane. The man has a nose for good skunk and this is the best.'

'You're serious?' I open the sachet and sniff inside.

'We are, yes. We've done the biz on Mr Kane a number of times over the years and got nowhere. You have collateral.'

'You mean something he wants? *Needs?* Nicely put.'

'Not at all. My pleasure. I've just saved you at least a hundred grand, so I'm guessing you might return the favour.'

'By meeting Wesley?'

'Yes.'

'And afterwards?'

'Afterwards?' He nods down at my mobile. 'Phone your friend again about the money. Do it tomorrow afternoon. By then, she should have news for you. Tomorrow evening, if restaurants were open, I'd treat you to something lovely. As it is, it might be home cooking again. You're going back to that shitty flat?'

'Of course.'

'Then phone me when you need picking up.' He holds my gaze. 'Deal?'

I say nothing. The pronoun he's been using is starting to bother me.

'We?' I ask.

'We.' He confirms.

'Meaning?'

'My little gang.' He nods at the radio. 'The final movement nails it.' A thin smile. 'Stay tuned, eh?'

TWENTY-SIX

Wesley Kane isn't hard to get hold of. I phone him mid-afternoon, and he insists I come over at once. Daytime television is driving him insane. Banged up with this shit all day, he tells me, does weird things to your head. He sounds friendly, even warm, and after our previous exchanges this comes as a surprise.

I've never been to Wesley's place, never had the pleasure, but he's given me the address. Fratton is just one of the many jigsaws of terraced Victorian properties that make up this city, and I've noticed that estate agents are doing their best to rebadge it as a little urban village, but you'd need more than clever marketing and a fancy label to brighten these streets. The parking is impossible, and some of the houses look beyond redemption. Despite lockdown, and the rain, kids are kicking a ball around in the street while ageing faces, many of them Asian, tut-tut behind falls of grimy net curtain. It's a world scored for satellite dishes and dripping gutters. Fratton, I think, could do with a Doorstep Disco.

Wesley's front door is painted a deep purple. I've heard H

telling stories about this house of his, chiefly on those evenings when half a dozen of the tribe made the trek down to Flixcombe for an evening of Stella and gentle reminiscence. H claims to have bought it for Wesley years ago when trade was booming and he needed an enforcer to keep the competition in their place. Wesley, so H would have us believe, had a special room in the house for the application of serious pain, and by and large it worked a treat. At the time, I dismissed most of this as boys' talk, but since then, knowing Wesley a little better, I've realized how much he enjoys violence. Which, given the way he's decorated the place, is truly remarkable.

Everything is pink: the narrow hall, the tiny cave of the front room, the diner at the back. He's laid deep-pile carpet everywhere, a cheesy white to offset the pinkness of everything else, and when Wesley takes me through to the kitchen, I find myself looking at a Barbie wall calendar. Wesley's April, like everyone else's, is near-empty but that's not the point. If I was a psychologist, this entire house would be Exhibit One. Wesley's either taking the piss or he has a big problem.

'What do you think?' It's a serious question.

'Have you got daughters upstairs?' I ask him. 'Are there any other secrets I should know about?'

'Pink's good for the blood pressure,' he says. 'It's very calming. The inner me loves it.'

'The inner you, Wes? I didn't know you had one.'

This kind of banter goes down very well with Wes. I sensed we could be friends from the moment I met him, and he's always looked after my best interests. From the start I realized there was something slightly childlike about him, a winning naivety at odds with his fearsome reputation, and this little house of his seems to prove it. He wants us, above all, to be mates. For real, if at all possible, but otherwise just buddies.

I watch him uncorking a bottle of Côtes du Rhône he must have bought specially. In return, I present him with the little cube wrapped in silver foil. The gesture, which I try to make as artless as possible, feels like the grossest treachery. What links me and H is Malo, nothing else. But that alone, Pompey flesh and blood, is enough to make me one of the tribe.

'Where did you get that?' Wesley has unwrapped the cube

and is sniffing it. Then he applies a wetted forefinger and gives it a lick. 'Nice. Very nice.'

'Good. I got it from an actor friend. He didn't want any money but I gave him a tenner in the end. Too generous, do you think?'

'Fuck, no. A *tenner*? For this?'

The resin is the deepest black. Wesley fetches a pouch of loose tobacco and some papers and begins to skin up. His hands, I notice, have developed the faintest shake. He crumbles the resin over the spliff and seals it with another lick before finding a match. He holds the first lungful for a long moment before expelling a long blue plume of smoke. Then he nods towards the front room.

'This deserves a bit of a sit-down,' he says.

I follow him through with the bottle and a glass. Over the mantelpiece is a framed print of what looks like a gazelle in some forest glade. As an image, it belongs on the birthday card you'd give your granny, the winsome creature's innocence caught in a haze of golden sunshine, and it reminds me of a railway journey Wesley and I shared a while back. The train went through edges of the New Forest, and Wesley couldn't tear himself away from the scruffy little ponies grazing beside the track. He thought they were sweet, and that was his word, not mine.

'You like it here?' I gesture towards the window.

'It's seriously crap. The area, the fucking neighbours, the low-life who keeps trying to nick my bike round the back, but – yeah – I love it. They've brought a speed limit in now. Twenty miles per hour. The kids won't get run over any more and we'll all die of disappointment.' He shoots me an inane grin. 'How does that sound? I'm blaming the weed. You want a toke? Help yourself.'

He offers me the spliff, but I shake my head. This is a small room, airless with the windows closed, and the smell of weed is overpowering. At this rate, we'll both end up stoned.

'Don't you want to know about H?' I ask him. 'I think he might be getting better.'

'I know. That's what he said.'

'He's been in touch?' This comes as a surprise.

'Yeah. He phoned me half an hour ago, banging on about that boy of yours. He's hurt. Have I got that right?'

I nod, and tell him about finding Malo on the seafront.

'He took a slap or two?'

'More than that. They set about him, Wes. What happened put him in hospital. That's why I'm here. I want to know why, and how, and who bloody did it. I told H it was an accident but he wouldn't have it.'

'Of course he wouldn't. He knows this city. They weren't having a go at Malo, they were getting at H.'

'That's the other thing.' I tell Wesley about the meter cupboards at the flats, and about some stranger breaking in to turn off the supply.

'Just your flat?'

'Yes.'

'That's seriously bad shit.'

'Exactly. H was dying at the time. Without oxygen, without the pump, it would have been over. Someone wants to kill him, Wes. And you're right. If they can't get at him, Malo will be more than acceptable. H can look after himself. Malo can't. For me, that's where it begins and ends. I'm serious, Wes. This has to stop.'

'Yeah, that's exactly what H said. Word for fucking word. Me? I'm a tough old bastard. The boy? There for the taking. You're right. This is out of order. Next, they'll be up the hospital to finish the job.' He stares at me for a moment, and then suddenly leans forward, his hand on my knee. 'Pompey joke, love. No offence.'

It doesn't feel like a joke, far from it. A glass of Côtes du Rhône and a lungful of Dessie's skunk are beginning to do very bad things to me.

'So, who'd want to kill H, Wes? Who'd want to go to all that trouble?'

'You want a list?' He throws his head back, seemingly delighted, but there's not a shred of warmth in his bark of laughter. 'That man pissed off everyone, and I mean everyone. Not me. Not Johnny In-Yer-Face Mr Hurt-You. But lots of others. People have long memories here. No one ever forgets. And when the chance comes, you know what? They fucking take it.'

That man, it occurs to me, is H. This is a new Wesley – a Wesley I've never heard before. He sounds aggrieved, even resentful, and I'm starting to wonder exactly what Dessie might have added to his little cube of skunk. I'm still feeling guilty about being here at all, but if this is the truth I want to know more.

'You've got names?'

'Of course I've got names. Faces from back in the day? Blokes he stitched up? Tossers who thought he'd got far too big for his fucking boots? H's problem was success. Lay your hands on that kind of money, and half the fucking world's gonna come after you. That's why he needed someone like me. That's why he *still* needs someone like me. And you think I really get off on that kind of gig? You don't think it becomes a pain in the arse in the end? Having to dig H or his fucking boy out of some hole or other? You want the truth? I'm getting past it, love. Some things I can still handle, that would be a real pleasure, not just for me but for you, too, and that's a fucking promise, but the rest of it . . .?' He falls silent for a moment, staring at the spliff. 'The problem in this city is way simpler than I ever thought. No one gets away. Ever. Not me. Not Fat Dave. Not even H. You think you do, but you don't. And you know why? Because it becomes a state of mind. When you're young it doesn't matter, nothing fucking matters, and that's because everything's a laugh. Now's different. We're all sick, and that's got nothing to do with the fucking virus. It eats away at you, this place, and in the end there's fuck all left.' He nods, suddenly grave. 'You're a lovely woman. You're a lovely gal. H doesn't deserve you. No way. Ever.'

'H hasn't got me,' I point out. 'All we have is Malo.'

'That's not what he thinks. You know it's not. I've watched the pair of you sometimes. H thinks he's clever, and he is, but I can read him like a fucking book. In that evil little head of his, he's all over you. He thinks you belong to him, he thinks he has sole rights, and one day he figures that you'll get it, that you'll say yes.'

'To what?'

'Every fucking thing. Eight times a night. Upside down. Whatever.'

'You're stoned, Wes. You're talking nonsense.'

'Stoned? Yes. Nonsense? Never. You have to be around people

like H to understand him, and I was, and I do. Back in the day I'd put out for him, and he knew it. I worshipped the man. Not the money, the man. Why? Because he'd got it all so sorted. Because he was so clever, so evil, so fucking *brave*. There was no one in this city he was frightened of. There was no stroke he wouldn't pull, and some of them were genius, everyone said so. Get alongside a bloke like that, my love, and you were doomed. He pulled the strings, all of them, and you didn't have a fucking prayer.'

'And that matters?'

'Now? Yeah, big time. Then? I loved the man. I loved everything he did, everything he touched, and that made me Mr Lucky. Wes Kane. Breaks yer leg for half a crown, and gives you a battering afterwards, and why? Because Mr Hayden fucking Prentice tells him to. That was me, that was my reputation. H says jump, I jump. H slips me a couple of grand and a whack of toot, I put the lot up my nose. H says there's a problem, I sort it. Gladly. Mr Efficient. No fucking comeback. End of.' He takes a deep suck on the spliff, and lies back in the armchair, staring up at the ceiling.

Skunked or otherwise, this is deeply revealing. Never have I suspected this kind of darkness in Wesley's soul. But there's more to come.

He peers at me for a long moment, and then gets to his feet before making his way unsteadily towards the door. Despite the trackie bottoms, and all those sessions with the resistance bands, and the wild explosion of hair, he looks like an old man. Then, from the kitchen, comes the scrape of something metallic, and a muttered curse. Moments later, he's back in the room, holding a mobile phone.

He settles in the chair again, scrolling slowly through what I sense is a gallery of photos. Some put a smile on his face. At the sight of others, he shakes his head. One in particular makes him visibly wince. Then he finds the shots he's after, and joins me on the sofa. A week in Tenerife, I wonder. Maybe some cruise or other?

At first sight, the image makes no sense. Then, with a hot jolt of recognition, I realize I'm looking at someone's face, upside down, on what must be the bottom sheet of a bed. Strands of greying hair are matted with blood against the whiteness of the scalp. The nose and the mouth have lost all definition, like a piece of Photoshopping gone horribly wrong, and the bottom lip has become entangled with a blackened row of broken teeth. It could be a man, just, but something very heavy has cratered this face, and the surrounding sheet is a lacework of spilled blood, strangely delicate.

'Swipe to the right.' Wesley has rolled himself another spliff.

I do his bidding. No sheet, this time, but an entire body, semi-clothed, jeans, torn grey T-shirt, grubby plimsolls, bare ankles. I stare at the screen until I have to turn away.

'He's dead, this guy?'

'Very. My fault. Went a bit over the top.'

'*You* did this?'

'Yeah. Not my idea, not to begin with, but I got H's point, saw no other way. The guy had been grassing us up for years. How else do you fund all day in the pub? Pathetic, I know, but he had it coming to him. Probably a release in the end. Look on the bright side, eh?'

I shake my head, trying – unsuccessfully – not to look at the screen again. This could be Malo, I think. The briefest spasm of violence. Or maybe something more protracted, more considered. On some days, I suspect Wesley Kane took his time.

'This happened where?'

'Upstairs. Spare bedroom.' He's smiling now. 'Pink every-where. You'd love it.'

'And afterwards?'

'We put him in a van and buried him.'

'We?'

'Me.' He sucks at the doobie. 'And H. There's woods every-where on the mainland. You're spoiled for choice.'

I nod, sickened by how banal, how obvious, this is.

'And he had a name?' I gesture at the screen. 'This poor man?'

'Of course he did. Everyone's got a name.' He's staring at the doobie. 'Sammy. Sammy McGaughy.'

TWENTY-SEVEN

can't wait to get out of that house. I return the phone, abandon my glass, leave the bottle on the carpet by the sofa, and flee. I'm sure there's a whole gallery of trophy shots, souvenirs from the days when H bossed this city, but I've seen enough. Sammy McGaughy? I shake my head. No wonder H was haunted by the name. But at least he has some kind of conscience, felt some kind of terror in the darkness the other night before he prepared to meet his Maker.

Sammy McGaughy.

At moments like these it's always one tiny detail that sticks in the memory, an image that will torment me for far too long, and in Sammy's case it's the bareness of his skinny ankle against the blood-soaked sheets. Neglected, I think. Wasted. Washed up. And finally disposed of.

I'm still driving Tony Morse's car, and it's parked two streets away. I've phoned him twice, speaking to Corinne on both occasions, and she says there's no hurry to bring it back. Tony is still under the weather but responding to TLC.

Now, sitting behind his steering wheel, I have one eye on the emptiness of the street in the rear-view mirror, half expecting Wesley to lurch into sight. Maybe he, too, is burdened by his many sins. Listening to him through the fug of skunk, it certainly felt that way.

My phone begins to ring. It's Tim. He wants to know whether I've picked up the key to his flat, and whether everything's OK. I tell him everything's fine, or nearly fine, or maybe just a little bit fine, and ask him about Milford Haven.

'*The Navy Lark*?' I ask him, trying to forget about Sammy McGaughy. 'Did you do it for the money? The reviews? Or what?'

'The money? They paid buttons. I did it for the laugh. They were lovely people. It was a nice place, too. West Wales in the rain? Life was never so sweet.'

He wants to know what I made of the flat. I tell him it's beyond perfect, exactly what I need, and he says that's just as well.

'Why?' My heart is sinking already.

'You remember you asked me about a guy called Sean? Thin? Terrible teeth? Drives a white van? Calls himself an electrician?'

I half-nod. I'm trying very hard to focus, to claw my way back through the madness of the last few days. Sean? Some kind of electrician? Then I have it. The games arcade in the fun fair. Following the light on the mobile through the darkness. And finally that set of funny mirrors at the very back of the arcade, me in one, Sean in the other, one fat, one even thinner than normal.

'Got him,' I say. 'Little guy. We got very pissed together.'

'So why the interest? Am I allowed to ask?'

'It's complicated.' I know I sound defensive but that's the way I'm feeling just now. 'You know this city way better than me, Tim. I should have done an induction course. I should have had the jabs. But I'm guessing even that would have been pointless. Nothing, literally *nothing*, could have prepared me for the last few days.'

'Bloody hell.'

'Exactly. So tell me about Sean.'

'He's a local. Locally hatched. Born and semi-bred. Went away in his late teens for a very long time, joined the Pompey diaspora. From what I can make out, he's only just come back.'

'From where?'

'Germany, mainly. And lately Poland. That's where he became an electrician.'

'And?'

'Word on the street says he's carrying a grudge. People also say he's a bit of a headcase, with us some days, AWOL the next. Too much weed? I've no idea.'

'This grudge. What's that about?'

'I get the impression it's family. Beyond that, I haven't a clue.'

Family? I shudder. Please God, no. But when I ask Tim about a surname, I know at once we're all in big, big trouble.

'McGaughy,' he says. 'Sean McGaughy. Does any of this stuff help? Or am I wasting your time here?'

'Not at all,' I mutter.

To Tim's slight disappointment, I end the call, and stare numbly through the windscreen, letting the obvious conclusions settle

like dust. It was Sean who broke into the flats, Sean who found
the supply to our flat, Sean who turned the power off. Maybe he
followed me across the Common that night after we'd visited
the games arcade. Maybe that's how he knew where we all lived.
Either way, he's still out there, still waiting, still watching, still
biding his time. Yuk.

I find directions to Cowplain on my sat-nav, before threading my
way through the badlands of Fratton and heading for the
motorway out of the city. Sean McGaughy, I'm thinking. One
way or another, I have to talk face to face with Dessie. If he isn't
in, I'll simply wait.

I've just passed what turns out to be a large police station,
with the motorway flyover in sight, when I get flagged down.
I'm still looking under the dashboard for Tony's exemption when
a uniformed figure bends to my window.

'Your name, Madam?'

I give him my name and when he asks where I'm going, I tell
him I'm en route to a meeting.

'This is work, Ms Andressen?' His eyes have strayed to my
sat-nav.

'Yes.'

'What sort of work?'

'Legal work.' I've found the exemption now, and I hand it to
him through the open window. He scans it quickly, and then steps
away. Seconds later he's checking something on his radio before
reappearing beside the car, squatting to get a proper look at me.
He returns the exemption and hopes I have a pleasant evening.

'And that's it?' I can't mask my surprise.

'That's it, Ms Andressen. Take care, now.'

Weirder and weirder. The motorway is empty. I take the Cowplain
exit off the motorway ten minutes later and follow my sat-nav
to Dessie's place. His VW, thankfully, is parked on the hardstanding beside the bungalow and his front door opens before I
even ring the bell. By now, it's occurred to me that I probably
have a police file all of my own.

'They phoned ahead? Warned you?'

'Of course they did. Belong to the right gang and life's a breeze.'

This is creepy. I'm aware of Dessie closing the door behind me. 'I used to think that Kafka made it all up,' I tell him. 'Now I'm not so sure.'

He takes me through to the lounge. The sheet music on his piano suggests he's been having a go at a Schubert Impromptu, but by now I'm hard-pressed to believe anything.

'Young Wesley?' he asks. We've barely said hello.

'No foreplay, then?' I say lightly. 'We get right down to it?'

'I'm afraid so.'

'And is there a reason? Or am I just the messenger here?'

Dessie refuses to rise to the bait. I'm still trying to work out whether we've ever been friends, or whether our previous conversations were no more than role-play on his part, but then he spreads his arms wide. This appears to be the invitation to a hug.

'You look terrible,' he says. 'Am I allowed?'

'No.' I shake my head. 'You're not. You mentioned a name this morning. Sean McGaughy. I don't know whether the taxes I pay stretch to police protection, but I'm guessing you're probably *au fait* with the details.'

'You're telling me you know Sean?'

'I've met him. Once.'

'And?'

'He struck me as . . .' I shrug. 'Not quite all there. At the time, I didn't know why. Now, I think I probably do. His dad was Sammy McGaughy, yes?'

Dessie nods, says nothing.

'And Sammy's dead. Am I right?'

'Sammy was a Misper. Not quite the same thing, unless you're telling me otherwise.' Misper is police-speak for Missing Person, as I know from previous dealings with the men in blue.

'So, when did he go missing? This Sammy person?'

'Late July, 2003. He lived in a doss in Buckland. The woman in the flat below kept an eye on him and filed the report. He spent most afternoons at a pub called the Druid's Arms. Called it a day after that. Career alcoholic. Sad man.'

Sad man. All I can think of is that bare ankle, no socks, and the blood all over the sheets.

'So how did he get the money? For the pub?'

'He was a grass. This city is full of them. They pick up a quid or two here and there for information they normally make up. Sammy was so gone by the time he got lifted that he'd probably lost all track of the lies he was telling.'

'Lifted?'

'He upset some powerful people.'

'Like H?'

'We think so, yes.'

'But you've just told me he was lying most of the time. What harm did that do?'

'We had no idea. And he probably didn't, either. All it took with people like H was a whisper or two, just the possibility that Sammy might have grassed him up. A waster like that was barely a candle. If you smelled any kind of threat, you snuffed him out.'

'Horrible.'

'You're right.'

'And you were . . .' I frown. 'You were on the case, way back then?'

'I was, yes. I handled intel on Major Crimes. I was four years into the Job and it was my first proper assignment. We all knew what had happened but proving it was a nightmare. H was no fool. And neither was Wesley. A psycho? Definitely. But he knew how to cover his tracks. So –' he nods at the sofa – 'you want to tell me what happened with Wes?'

'No. Not yet. I want us to talk about police protection.'

'You mean for H?'

'Yes.'

'Against who?'

'Sean McGaughy. He's been away a while and now he's back in the city, as I'm sure you know. His dad's been missing forever and now he thinks he knows why. Script-wise, we'd call this a settling of debts. One life for another. Are you with me?'

'That implies that Sammy's dead.'

'It does indeed, Mr Wren.'

'And you *know* that?'

'Yes.'

'How?'

I don't answer. *Won't* answer.

'You've seen Wesley?'

'No comment.'

'You won't tell me?'

'No comment.'

He studies me for a long moment, then tries to warm this conversation with a smile.

'Technically, I could have you arrested for obstruction of justice. You know that, don't you?'

'Go ahead,' I tell him. 'I'm probably safer in a police cell just now.'

He nods, conceding the point.

'This is beyond irony,' he says at last. 'We start with H. Back then we were certain he'd either killed Sammy himself, or had a hand in it. He certainly makes a great deal of money in the drugs biz and lives like a bloody prince on the proceeds. Twenty years later, you're asking me for police protection. Just in case McGaughy's surviving son comes knocking on H's door.'

'Sean's an electrician,' I point out. 'He understands how power feeds work, and he's tried to kill H twice already. Last time I checked, murder was a crime. He might well have another go. Shouldn't you be stopping him? Or would a dead H be a blessing? If the virus can't help you out, then maybe Sean McGaughy can. Isn't that what this is about? Or have I been in showbiz for too long?'

Once again, our conversation comes to a halt. I'm here for one thing, and one thing only. I want to keep H, and by extension Malo, safe.

'Well?' I say at last. 'Can you take care of the situation? Or am I wasting my time?'

TWENTY-EIGHT

I drive back to Southsea. Dessie has refused to make any commitment to protect H, but that's probably because he needs to make a call or two. I park outside the flats and climb to the third floor. It's early evening by now and Sunil is on the sofa in full PPE, watching the BBC News. He barely stirs when I step into the room, but simply nods at the screen.

'Nine hundred and thirty-eight deaths in a single day? That's unbelievable.'

He's right. Recent events seem to have walled me off from the wider world, and this is a sudden reminder that the entire UK, indeed the entire planet, is losing its nerve as well as its bearings. An emergency COBRA meeting has been called for tomorrow to review the lockdown measures and scientists are warning that they may be in force until early June. The Prime Minister, meanwhile, is steadily improving and may soon be out of intensive care.

'How's H?' I enquire.

'Fretful, Ms Andressen.'

Fretful is a word loaded with menace if you know H as well as I do. I ask Sunil exactly what he means.

'Mr Wu came to see him this afternoon. His physical signs are good. We've all been surprised, and so was Mr Wu, but H is worrying about something and none of us seem to know why.'

'You've asked him?'

'Of course.'

'And?'

'He wasn't very polite. That's another problem. Mr Wu wasn't impressed.'

I bet. H hates being trapped in any kind of corner. The virus has banged him up for a while, but he's been too ill to do very much about it. Now he's getting better, his mind clearer, he's emphatically back at the wheel. Mentioning Sammy McGaughy, now I understand the full implications, was a big, big mistake.

'You think I might be able to help?' I'm remembering Sunil's role after our last ruck.

'I do, Ms Andressen.' He nods at my carefully folded pile of PPE. 'Shall we try again?'

H receives me in silence, but it turns out that he's half-asleep. I settle beside his bed and wait for him to surface. He peers up at me, recognizing the face behind the mask. His breathing, at last, is virtually normal. Neither is there any trace of a cough.

'You've seen him? Wes?'

'I have, H. Of course I have.'

'And?'

'He's making enquiries as we speak. Putting the word out.'

'About the boy?'

'Absolutely.'

'Good.' He nods. 'About fucking time. He was always lazy, Wes. He always delivered in the end, but it took forever to get him going.'

Delivered. I try to mask an inner shudder, but H hasn't finished.

'Well done.' He pats my arm. 'And the boy?'

'On the mend. He's eating porridge, can you believe that?'

'Serves him bloody right. He'll be back soon, yeah?'

'I hope so. Couple of days, max.'

'And you say Wes is sorting it?'

'Yes.'

H nods, happy now, and I catch a discreet thumbs-up from Sunil before I make my excuses and depart. Forty minutes later, as I'm about to leave the flat, I get a call from Dessie.

'Two guys will be with you within the hour,' he says, 'both uniformed. They'll be outside covering all the approaches, one fo'rrard, one aft. They'll be there all night. You don't have to owe me, but it might be nice.'

I smile, and start to thank him, but he's gone.

I spend the night at Tim's flat, feasting from a Chinese takeout I've ordered by phone. This feels like life under occupation. No one but Tim knows where I am, not H, not Dessie, not Wesley, and that knowledge buys me a little peace. I know very little about jazz but Tim has a huge collection of CDs and I pass what's left of the evening with Miles Davis, John Coltrane, and a bottle of Argentinian Merlot I find at the back of one of Tim's cupboards. What I need to do above all is somehow build a dam against those images on Wesley's phone, and *Kind of Blue* nearly does it. With music like that in the world, I conclude, things can't be all bad.

Thanks to the Merlot, I sleep like a baby. By the time my phone wakes me up, it's gone nine o'clock and sunshine is flooding over Tim's map-of-the-world duvet. It's Jessie. She's calling from Flixcombe. I have trouble working out whether she's excited or angry, and in the end I settle for the latter.

'Two vans,' she says. 'They've been here all night, and they've

only just gone. Fucking liberty, says me, and if you want the full
SP you should listen to Andy. He says they're threatening to be
back tomorrow, can you believe that?'

'Who are we talking about, Jess?'

'The police. The Filth. Who else? They drove up from Pompey.
I even knew one of them. Little tyke called Jason. Last time I
saw him he was a trainee at Asda.'

She's telling me the whole story, how they turned up yesterday,
thrust a warrant at her, and then tore H's study apart before
starting on the rest of the house.

'What did they take?'

'Financial records, mostly. Stuff going way back.'

'And the money?'

'Safe, tell H. How is he?'

'Much better. Answering back. I think I preferred him ill.'

'You think he can do without the nurses?'

'I think he might. He's beginning to test their patience. I told
them it was bound to happen, but no one listens these days.'

'Is he there? Can I have a word?'

'Later, Jess. He's asleep just now.'

'And Malo?'

'All good. He's asleep, too. Same DNA.'

I say goodbye and ring off. Two more lies, I think, but who's
counting?

Dessie is the next on my list. A good night's sleep has done
wonders. I ask him to meet me outside Tony Morse's flat by the
Common, and to my surprise he agrees. I suggest eleven o'clock.

'Not sooner?'

'No.'

'Busy?'

'Always.'

I down a mug of Tim's instant coffee and make for the door.
Parking in Wesley's street is no easier than it was yesterday, and
I end up leaving Tony's BMW on double yellow lines round the
corner. I'm calling by on a mercy mission, I tell myself, an
explanation that Tony Morse will be welcome to use in court if
he chooses to contest the parking ticket.

Wesley takes an age to come to the door. Normally, he treats himself to a variety of aftershaves but today he looks – and smells – rank. Bleary doesn't do justice to his eyes. The whites have a yellowy tinge to them, and I was right about his hands. He's nursing what looks like a cup of tea, and it's slopping around as he tries to steady the saucer.

'You,' he grunts, 'can fuck off.'

'No, Wes. Do yourself a favour. Just listen to me.'

'Yeah? I buy you nice wine? We're in for the evening? And you just bugger off?'

'That phone of yours, the one with the photos . . .?'

'Yeah?'

'I need it, Wes. Now. I'm doing you a favour here. If you don't believe me, if you don't trust me, so be it. Good luck inside. Ten years goes in a flash, you'd be amazed.'

He peers at me, and I sense he's trying to work out my angle.

'So, what's this about?'

'You, Wes. And H.'

'He sent you here? To get those fucking pics?'

'No one sent me here, Wes. Not H. Not the Filth. No one. Believe it or not, I've got a mind of my own. Take it or leave it, Wes. Your call.'

I've never spoken to him like this before, and he's finding it hard to take. Women should know their place in Wesley Kane's life, and I suspect none of them – to date – have had the right to be so blunt.

'So, what happens to the phone? If I give it to you?'

'I'll get rid of it.'

'Why can't I do that?'

'Because you won't, you can't. For whatever reason this stuff talks to you. You need it, Wes. You'll promise me to bin it, then you'll take one last peek, and you'll have a bit of a think, and tell yourself you'll sort it later. But later will be too late, Wes.'

'Why?'

'Because.'

'That's not a reason.'

'It is, Wes. There's stuff going on here that you don't want to be part of, believe me. Give me that phone and I'll leave you in peace. It's a no-brainer, Wes. Just give me the fucking thing. Then it's gone. Forever.'

He studies me for a long moment as if I'm here to offer him therapy, which in a way is true. Then, at last, he cracks a smile.

'Does this mean you might be back?'

'One day, yes. I care about you, Wes. And I care about H, too, which I'm guessing won't be music to your ears. But that's what being a woman means these days. Men have a habit of leaving a mess, always did, always will. Just ask yourself who does the clearing up.'

'You?'

'Me,' I agree.

He nods, less hostile now. Does he buy into all this mumsy stuff? Does he really trust me? I've no idea but after a couple of minutes waiting on his doorstep, he's back with the phone.

'Just give it to me, Wes.' I extend my hand.

'You'll really come back?'

'One day, yes.'

'And maybe stay?'

'That depends.'

'On what?'

'On whether or not you've removed the SD card.'

'I haven't.' He finally gives me the phone. 'Deal?'

I've got the phone. I've done it. Too easy? Yes. But Wesley Kane is beyond strange.

I'm back at the flat beside Southsea Common with an hour to spare before Dessie arrives. I'm glad of the thinking time I've saved for myself but the moment I park, I recognize the top-of-the-range Lexus several bays away. Mr Wu, I think.

I find him upstairs, taking off his visor and mask with one hand while making a phone call with the other. The moment he sees me, he abandons the phone.

'Please.' He nods at the sofa. 'We need to talk.'

He tells me that H is making excellent progress. He says that his sat levels are back to normal, that he shows no signs of fever, and that the cough that has plagued him for so long seems to have disappeared.

'Should I blame the drugs, Mr Wu?' I'm trying to make light of it. 'All that medication you've given him?'

'We've given him very little medication, Ms Andressen. Some

antibiotics, some anti-inflammatories, but that's all. What made the difference was the oxygen. That gave him time for his immune system to win the battle.'

'So, the battle's over? Is that what you're telling me?'

'I doubt it. He'll be very tired, and maybe a little weak. He'll have to rest, and he'll need to recover properly. There's always the chance that the virus will flare up again, but we all have our fingers crossed. Any sign of more infection, of course, and we can always review the situation.'

'You're *leaving*?'

'We are, Ms Andressen. I'm withdrawing all the nurses with the exception of Taalia until four o'clock, and Sunil until midnight. This is for our benefit, as well as yours, Ms Andressen.'

'What does that mean?'

'It means you'll be saving yourself a great deal of money. In fact, there may even be some modest reimbursement from the money you've already paid us.'

'And you? The agency? Your wonderful nurses?'

Mr Wu plainly doesn't want the rest of this conversation, but when I insist, he sighs and puts his phone carefully to one side.

'Mr H has been difficult from time to time. I suspect you're aware of that.'

'I am. He's been a sick man.'

'Indeed. But there are other issues, too, and to be frank I'm not sure it's in our best interests to continue this association. For one thing, the hospital are crying out for more nurses, trained nurses, nurses with ICU experience. We have an obligation here, and I'm afraid we can't duck it. You know how many people have died in this city so far? Just in hospital? Eighty.' He nods gravely. 'Eight-oh,' he says again.

'And?'

'And what?'

'You said other issues.'

'I did, yes.' He nods, studies his hands, then looks me in the eye. 'There are rules here, Ms Andressen, things you can and can't do. You've been living with someone infected by the virus. Yet you're seldom here. This morning? Last night?' He holds my gaze. 'Where were you?'

'I'm afraid that's none of your business.'

'But it is, Ms Andressen. Or at least it was.' He checks his watch and gets to his feet. He'd like the oxygen cylinders and the bedside equipment to remain in the bedroom until all nursing cover ceases tomorrow morning. After that, he says with the ghost of a smile, the equipment will be removed and the flat will be ours again.

'And H?'

'Mr H is getting better. Let's look on the bright side.'

TWENTY-NINE

B y the time Dessie arrives, only Taalia remains in the flat. I've been standing in the window in the front room, and the moment I spot Dessie's VW slowing to nose into the parking space opposite, I descend to the street. Dessie watches me emerge from the flats in his rear-view mirror and leans across to open the front passenger door.

The moment I'm settled, I ask him about the promised police cover. This morning I could find no trace of a uniform either to the front or rear of the property.

'They were withdrawn first thing, at the end of their shifts. We did the risk assessment and decided not to replace them.'

'How come?'

'We have grounds for believing that Sean McGaughy has left the city.'

'This is intelligence?'

'I'm afraid I'm not at liberty to say.'

Really? Why so formal, I want to ask him. Why this sudden outbreak of corporate speak? Instead, I tell him that I've been in touch with Jessie again.

'She told you we paid a visit?'

'She did. "Mob-handed" was the phrase she used, plus a couple of expletives. What was the point? What were you doing?'

'This is a Major Crimes operation. To get the full story, you should be speaking to someone else.'

'But you'd know, surely?'

'I work as a civilian adviser, as I think I explained. They tell me what they want to tell me.'

'But your gut feeling? That instinct of yours?'

'My gut feeling is that H is in the shit. They're doing a full forensic audit. They're piecing together every deal he's made, every pound he's spent, every investment he's risked since he left this city. They're looking for laundered money, and months down the line, who knows, they might find it.'

I nod, look out across the Common and watch a lone figure bending to clean up after his dog. Something's very wrong here, and now I know exactly what it is.

'That money you asked me to hide. You're a cop, or you used to be. So how come you're suddenly so kind to me?'

'We would have seized it. All of it. Without that money, H would be in the ICU. You know the rest of the story better than I do.'

'You're telling me you've personally spared him the ICU?' I'm incredulous. 'Why on earth would you ever do that? You owe H nothing. In fact, your lot would probably be dancing on his grave the moment he popped it.'

'No.' Dessie shakes his head.

'No, what?'

'No, I wouldn't want him dead. Not if I could help him in the meantime.'

'I don't believe you. There has to be a why. There has to be a reason. H happens to be getting better.' I nod towards the flats across the road. 'That's great news for us, probably less so for all the cops he wound up. I get the impression you laid trap after trap back in the day. I understand you'd pull any stroke to put him away. Am I right? You were there, Dessie, you'd know.'

Dessie says nothing. I await some clue, *any* clue, but he won't even look at me. Finally, just the hint of a nod.

'You're right,' he says. 'H was a pain.'

'So why help us out with the money? Why see it our way?'

'I just told you.'

'You told me nothing. Unless you're another Dave Munroe.'

The suggestion puts the ghost of a smile on his face. Then he turns to look at me.

'Where were you last night?' he asks. 'I saw the overnight log. The blokes we put in saw you leave. Technically, that's breaking the lockdown restrictions, but we can live with that. More importantly, you never came home. Am I right?'

'Yes.'

'So, where were you?'

I shake my head. No comment.

'Wesley, was it? All night?'

The question comes as a surprise, not least because it seems so suddenly personal.

'Say you're right. Would that matter to you?'

'Yes, it would.'

'Why?'

'Because that man has done some evil things. He's hurt a lot of people. Physically, mentally, any way he can. He's not a nice person. Lunatic would be close. Psychotic, even closer.'

'He's damaged, Dessie.'

'You know that?'

'Yes. And I've known it for a while. Did I spend the night with him? No. Would I? Never in a million years. He thinks I might one day, and that's sweet on his part, but it won't happen.'

'But you saw him? Last night?'

'Yes. Briefly. I don't know what you put in that skunk but Wesley loved it.'

'And?'

'And nothing. I made my excuses and left.' I nod across at the flats again. 'H needs a bit of company. Are you up for this?'

With some reluctance, because Dessie would prefer this conversation of ours to continue, we get out of the car and climb the stairs to the flat. The tall cylinders of oxygen are still stacked in the front room, awaiting collection. For the first time, with their white tops and black bases, they remind me of a line of nuns awaiting word about what might happen next, but without the usual gang of nurses, the place seems empty and neglected and sad, exactly the way we found it.

Dessie looks round and spots the tins of paint I've never opened.

'They belong to Tony?'

'Me, I'm afraid. I arrived with good intentions but never got round to it.'

'It's a doss.' Dessie shakes his head. 'Tony should have sorted some of this.'

Mr Wu has left half a dozen sets of PPE and I hand the biggest to Dessie while I, too, ready myself for our visit to H's bedroom. I've done this so many times now that I know all the moves by heart, and once Dessie has gowned up, and tugged on a pair of plastic gloves, I fuss with his mask and visor, making sure the fit is snug. His eyes behind the visor are following my every move, and when I tell him he'll do, he catches my hand and gives it a little squeeze.

'Don't be nervous.' My hand is still in his. 'It's only H. He won't eat you.'

The bedroom door is half open and I can hear Taalia trying out a list of Easter jokes on H.

'What do you get if you pour boiling water down a rabbit hole?'

'Dunno.'

'A hot cross bunny.' She giggles. 'And here's another one. How does Easter end?'

'With an "R".' It's Dessie this time. He opens the door wide and steps in. Taalia looks round. She's sitting on the edge of the bed with an open copy of the *News* on her lap. Then she sees me.

'Taalia.' I'm doing the introductions. 'Dessie.'

H, at first, is bemused. He can't quite work out what's going on, and this annoys him. Then he takes a proper look at the big face behind the mask.

'Dessie fucking Wren,' he grunts. 'What are you doing here?'

I can tell at once that H is far from unhappy at having this man step back into his life. Against all the rules, he extends an arm for a fist-bump. Very Pompey, I think.

Taalia folds the paper and asks whether we'd like tea. H says yes for all of us.

'And biscuits,' he adds. 'Them ginger chocs.'

Taalia disappears while H nods at the little dent she's made in the blanket. Not for me, but for Dessie. Already, I'm way out of my depth. These two men appear to be friends. The Drug Baron and the Intel King. Only in Pompey.

'You still with the Filth, Dessie? Scratching around for a living?'

'I am, H. A pleasure, as always.'

'I had my housekeeper on just now, Jessie, Pompey gal . . .' His hand crabs towards his phone. 'Your lot were all over us last night. Hooligans in fucking uniform. Jess says she's got a list of stuff we'll have to put right. Where do I send the bill?'

'Usual address, H. It might be a while, though.'

'Great. Nothing fucking changes. One day it might occur to those dickhead bosses of yours that they're wasting their time. Never put anything on paper, Dessie, unless it can't hurt you. The way I hear it, your lot are stuffed for money, haven't got the bodies any more, so how come you're pissing all that budget away? No hard feelings, mate, but I'm a taxpayer now, and I have views about all this.'

The conversation goes on, variations on the same theme, H seizing every opportunity to have a dig at the men in blue. I can see he's buoyed by having this face from the past at his bedside. He's playful, amused, and not the least bit threatened or aggressive. After Taalia has served tea and biscuits, Dessie at last gets round to asking him how he feels.

'Knackered, Des. But fucking glad to still be here. A word in your ear: anyone who says this virus is like catching flu is off the planet. It's a bastard. It's evil. I kid you not, there were days I'd had enough, more than enough, but you know what?' He nods towards Taalia. 'That lovely lady and her mates kept me going. Cost a fortune but I expect it's tax-deductible. I'll need to talk to my accountant. Unless you've fucking locked him up.'

'Tomorrow, H. He's on the list. Give him a call. Tell him to leave the country.'

'No can do, Des. It's fucking closed for the duration. We've shut up shop. No more Torremolinos. No more Disneyland. All we've got now is crap TV and jokes about Easter bunnies. You got any more in that rag of yours, Taalia?'

'What kind of jewellery do Easter bunnies wear?' Taalia looks from face to face. We all shrug. 'Fourteen carat gold,' she says, delighted.

It's nearly midday before Dessie decides to leave. He and H exchange another fist-bump, and then H peers up at him.

'What about that boy of yours? Titch? Did he ever make it big time? Pompey? The Scummers? Man U? Liverpool?'

'No, H, he didn't.'

'So what happened?'

'He joined the Navy. His decision, nothing to do with me. Doing OK, though, so far.'

'Subs?'

'Maybe one day, who knows.' Dessie pauses, looking down at the face on the pillow. 'He still remembers you, H. And he's still grateful. Like me.'

Back outside, I ask Dessie for a lift down to Old Portsmouth. The sun is out at last and, despite a blustery wind, there's a hint of warmth in the air. At my suggestion, Dessie lets me off at the foot of the Round Tower that overlooks the harbour entrance. He says he has a meeting at the Major Crimes suite, otherwise he'd join me for a walk.

'Shame,' I say. 'It's a lovely day.'

We look at each other for a moment. There's a question that's been bothering me since we left H's bedroom, but I'm not quite sure how to put it.

'You mind if I ask you something?'

'Not at all.'

'H mentioned that godson of yours, Titch. Were they close?'

'In a way, yes.'

'How come?'

'Titch developed a problem down here.' He touches his knee. 'It was unusual – the lad was really unlucky. There was nothing the NHS could offer but I found a surgeon in Turin who knew how to deal with it. He'd developed this operation. Cured dozens of kids. Cost a fortune, though. Thick end of five figures including all the extras, and at the time, what with one thing and another, I didn't have that sort of money.'

'So, what happened?'

'H stumped up. After Dave Munroe told him all about it.'

'H covered the lot?'

'Yeah, and a bit on top to make me and the lad happy out there.'

'You were with him? In Italy?'

'I was, yes.'

'And his parents? Where were they?'

Dessie looks at me a moment, then checks his watch. 'One day, yeah? When all this shit is over?'

I get out of the car and make my way to the top of the Round Tower. Once again, there's no one in sight. The wind is blowing a gale up here and already I'm regretting the lack of a coat. The tide is flooding in below me, and upstream I can see H's pride and joy, the looming shape of our latest aircraft carrier.

I gaze at it a moment, remembering the fierce pride in H's voice when he first laid eyes on the monster, and the longer I reflect, the more I realize that this battered old city was bred for violence. Pompey blood, I think, in exchange for foreign treasure. Spanish doubloons? French brandy? Colombian cocaine? The story rolls on from generation to generation, ships plundered, foreigners put to the sword, rival football fans battered, and all in the name of a hooligan England masquerading as the nation's soul.

I fumble for a moment in the pocket of my jeans, and then extract Wesley's mobile phone. I fire it up and swipe my way into his gallery. I recognize Sammy McGaughy at once, and there are more shots that – mercifully – I didn't see last night. They rolled him into a tatty old carpet, and secured it with binder twine, and drove his thin little body out of the city and buried him in woodland. I never got a proper look at the body on the phone because they never untied the carpet to take a shot, but there were dozens and dozens more pictures, as graphic as the photos I saw last night, violence elevated to an art form: different faces, different angles, different lighting, different takes on Wesley's brand of sadomasochism.

None of these people appear to be dead, just Sammy, but you can see fear in a man's eyes, and then pain, and then anguish, and after a while, I back out of the gallery, and turn the phone off, and check to make sure there's still no one around before going to the very edge of the top of the tower that overhangs the boiling water beneath. At school, in Brittany, I was exceptionally good at the French version of rounders. Now, after a practice swing or two, I hurl the phone out into the tidal stream.

The wind catches it for a moment, just a glint of sunshine on the little glass screen, and then – with a tiny splash – it's gone.

Back at the flat, I let myself in. At first, when she doesn't respond to my call, I think for one awful moment that Taalia must have left us. Like Mr Wu, I assume, she's had enough. Then I hear H's bedroom door opening and closing, and suddenly she's with me in the living room, getting rid of her visor and untying her mask. She looks, for some reason, radiant.

'What's happened,' I ask. 'What's up?'

'Malo.' Her smile widens. 'They're bringing him back.'

THIRTY

I t takes both paramedics on the ambulance to help Malo up the stairs. They obviously know about H and the virus because they leave him with Taalia and me on the top landing, and one of them offers Malo a farewell pat on the shoulder before they clatter back downstairs.

'Good luck, son. Stay safe, eh?'

Malo looks terrible. The swelling around his mouth and jaw has begun to subside but his whole face seems lopsided, and the mass of bruising has yellowed and purpled. I know a trendy couple who run a cutting-edge gallery in Primrose Hill, and they call this particular combination of colours 'swamp art'. The rightness of the phrase has always eluded me, but now I know exactly what they mean. My son, with his bloodshot eyes and missing front teeth, is a creature from the deep.

We get him into the front room and sit him down. Walking, he says, is difficult, and talking is a no-no. His jaw is wired in two places and I imagine he'll be avoiding the longer words for a while. Taalia attends to him on the sofa, holding a plastic mug while Malo sucks fresh orange juice through a bendy straw. She has an extraordinary gentleness – part nurse, part someone else, someone much closer, fonder, needier – and watching them together I can't help thinking of poor Clemmie. This virus, I realize, is changing everything in front of our eyes. Not once, since Taalia's arrival, has Malo lifted the phone to the woman he intends to marry.

'Do you remember how it all happened?' I ask him.

He shakes his head while Taalia sponges the last of the juice from his lower lip.

'Nothing at all?'

'No.'

'And the hospital?'

'Good.' He nods. 'Good people. Kind.'

Kind? Taalia and I debate whether or not to expose H to his battered son, but it's Malo who takes the decision out of our hands.

'Dad,' he says, struggling to his feet.

We help him into a PPE gown, and Taalia does her best to slip a mask on, but Malo won't have anything near his lower face. One of the paramedics told me that he tested negative for Covid at the hospital but – to be frank – I've lost the plot about whether H is still contagious. Taalia thinks not but insists we shouldn't be taking any risks and so I garb up before helping Malo along the corridor to H's room.

H is sitting up in bed, reading something on his tablet. No one has breathed a word about Malo being discharged from the hospital, and when he first glances up from the tablet he doesn't seem to recognize his son. Given the circumstances, this isn't a surprise. The PPE gowns make everyone look the same, and the old Malo has disappeared behind a mask of lacerations and bruising.

'Dad?' We've steadied Malo beside the bed.

'Son?' H looks shocked. 'Is that you?'

'Me.' Malo extends a hand and H takes it, looking closely at the scabs around his knuckles. 'You fought back? Landed some decent shots? Good boy. Sit.' He pats the bed. He might be talking to his dog.

Malo does his bidding and perches himself awkwardly on the side of the bed while H bombards him with questions. What, exactly, happened? Who were these low life? How many of them? And he asks, finally, whether Malo might have recognized a face or two.

'Well, son? Help me out here?'

'He remembers nothing, H,' I explain as gently as I can. 'And I get the impression that talking hurts.'

'Bound to for a while. Only natural. Jesus, they did a job on him, didn't they?'

This is the moment I realize that H is as aghast as the rest of us. Behind his gruff ultra-maleness, there lurks a real sense of disbelief. You can see it in the tiny shakes of his head, in those small moments of silence when he runs out of things to say and can only stare up at his ruined son. Who could possibly have done something like this? Who'd ever have the *nerve*?

After not very long, Malo wants to go. He looks exhausted. He plaits both hands together, a cushion for his head, miming sleep, and mumbles something about how hard it is to kip in a hospital ward. Taalia understands at once. She's made the bed up for him next door and I watch them leave before turning back to H.

'We need Wes.' His face has darkened. 'We need him here, round the clock, twenty-four hours. Ring him, yeah? Tell him there's money in it, tell him any fucking thing, just make it happen.' He gestures for me to use his mobile, and the message couldn't be plainer. He's taken a long, hard look at his son, and he doesn't want strangers at his door. 'Under siege' is a big phrase, but that's exactly how it feels.

'We could leave,' I suggest. 'We could all go back to Flixcombe.'

'Over my dead fucking body,' he growls. 'Not yet, anyway.'

'You mean you want to stay here? Take whatever's coming?'

'Yeah. One way or another, yeah. Since when did I ever do a runner from this city? There's a time and place for calling it a day and it ain't here and it ain't yet. Wes still has the contacts, he'll know which buttons to press. We have to get this thing sorted. Else they'll piss all over us.'

There's a brutal logic in all this and it isn't hard to spot. It goes with giant aircraft carriers and the masts of HMS *Victory* in the historic dockyard. It explains why thousands of men from this city ended up as names on the seafront war memorial. Never waver. Never bend the knee. Never, in Dessie's phrase, jack it in.

'You're mad,' I tell H. 'They nearly killed our boy. The virus has nearly killed you. Tell me I'm being girly, but isn't there a lesson here, some decision it might be time to make, like pack our bags and leave?'

'No way,' he insists. 'You want to go back to that lovely pad of yours, fucking London, all the rest of it, then fill your boots. Me and the boy . . .'

'You're different?'

'We're staying put. Make the call. Get Wes round. Put some Stellas in the fridge. This is war, my love.' He gestures vaguely towards the door. 'End of.'

Talking to Wesley again is the last thing I want to do. The thought of him moving in full-time, having to share so intimate a space, fills me with dread. I know exactly what that man's capable of. Dessie Wren, wittingly or otherwise, has nailed it completely. Wesley Kane is a lunatic. A madman. A psycho.

To my relief, when I finally get through to Wesley, he hasn't the slightest interest in coming to H's defence. His days of snapping to attention and rallying to the fucking colours, he says, are well and truly over. This is nicely put, and makes my heart briefly sing, but it's what he says next that stops me in my tracks.

'I owe you,' he says. 'I just want you to know that.'

'Owe me what?'

'A thank you. You did the job on that phone of mine?'

'I did, yes.'

'Seriously?'

'Very seriously.'

'Then thank you. I'm binning the snuff movies, too, getting rid of the lot. I just want you to know that. I trust you completely, and it's all working out.'

I happen to know about snuff movies. I've even watched a sequence or two from the days when Berndt, my equally psychotic ex, used to get hold of a couple to get in the mood for his next screenplay. People die on camera in all kinds of graphic ways. For real.

'I've reformed you?' I ask lightly. 'Is that what I'm hearing?'

'Completely. I've turned the corner, seen the fucking light.'

'Glad to hear it, Wes. I'll tell H. He'll be thrilled.'

'Do that.' Wesley's laughing now. 'And tell the old bastard he's better off out of this city.'

'Any particular reason?'

'No, but you heard it here first. One good turn? All that shit? I'm watching *The Sound of Music* just now. That Julie Andrews is something else.'

Another cackle of laughter, and then he's gone.

Back in H's bedroom, H has trouble believing the news from Wesley. 'You're telling me he said no? Why would he do that? You talked money?'

'He didn't let me. He thinks I've turned his life around. God knows why.'

'Turned his life around? Wesley fucking Kane? Is he ill? Temperature? Bit of a cough?' H rolls his eyes and settles back against the pillows. 'What the fuck's going on here?'

What, indeed? I spend the early evening in the living room, watching TV. H has, once again, refused to abandon the flat until he's good and ready. This means being out of quarantine and having the energy to face the journey home, and so I comfort myself with Channel Four News. Another 786 people have died in the last twenty-four hours. Transport for London has announced new protective measures for its drivers after a spate of virus-related deaths. And a rather fetching psychologist shares the news that Covid-19 views us all as 'big, yummy chunks of food'. Half an hour of this stuff is deeply dispiriting, not least because I appear to be banged up in this hideous flat until further notice, and in the end I turn off the TV and opt instead to try and finish *Typhoon*.

Full-length on the sofa, I catch up with the story, the essence of which is very simple indeed. Huge storm. Tiny ship. Every prospect of coming to grief. Conrad himself was at sea in vessels like these, poorly maintained, hopelessly vulnerable, and the writing is beyond vivid. Then comes a paragraph that seems to echo – with an alarming exactness – our own predicament. I read it for a second time, then a third, filleting Conrad's prose for the choicest morsels. *Excessive tumult. A numbness of spirit. A searching and insidious fatigue that penetrates deep into a man's breast to cast down and sadden his heart.*

I lie back for a moment and close my eyes. How come
Conrad, so long ago, should have put his finger on the way I'm
feeling now? Was it prescience? Did he hear voices? And if he
was here now, a survivor from the storm, what would he suggest
in the way of advice?

'Ms Andressen?'

I look up, startled. It's Sunil, and he's arrived for his last shift
with us.

'What's that?' I'm looking at the bottle in his hand.

'It's for you, Ms Andressen. From all of us.'

'A present, you mean?'

'Yes.'

Quite why I deserve a bottle of Prosecco is beyond me, but
it's a lovely gesture. While Sunil puts on his PPE, I explain
about Malo's return. Taalia, I explain, is insisting on staying the
night to keep an eye on him. Given that she can check on H at
the same time, Sunil might as well have the evening off.

Sunil gives the proposition a moment's thought, then shakes
his head. He's been on the phone to Taalia already, apologizing
for being so late, and he's sure that she and Malo will have lots
to catch up on. No, H will remain his responsibility. Despite
everything, he's grown very fond of the man. Difficult, yes, but
definitely worth it.

I shrug. Maybe we could share the bottle later? Together? Just
the two of us?

Sunil looks at me, suddenly thoughtful, and then nods. He's
brought something else with him and he unpacks it from his day
sack. It turns out to be a baby alarm, Wi-Fi linked to a tiny
monitoring screen.

'It might be useful, Ms Andressen. When we're not here
anymore.'

It's a nice thought, deeply practical, and I love the idea of H,
our grouchy curmudgeon, finding himself at the business end of
a baby alarm. Sunil disappears to set up the alarm and sit with
H while I get to finish *Typhoon*. Thanks to Captain MacWhirr
and the gods of the China Sea, Conrad makes landfall intact, the
kind of deliverance I can only dream about.

I put the book aside and fetch a couple of glasses from the
kitchen. One peek around Malo's door finds my son asleep in

Taalia's arms. Poor Clemmie, I think again, but what on earth am I supposed to do?

Sunil joins me in the front room a little later. Mr H, he says, has gone to sleep. All his vital signs are still good, but Sunil warns me not to expect miracles.

'We're finding this virus goes on and on.' He accepts a glass of Prosecco. 'You think you're through it, and the worst is definitely over, but then you get wave after wave of something not feeling right. Muscle pains, getting hard to breathe again, being fit for nothing? I'm just letting you know, that's all.'

I'm watching the little black and white screen of the baby alarm, H's sleeping face on the pillow, and I tell Sunil I'm grateful. The Sri Lankan has excellent English, totally idiomatic, and after I ask a question or two, he starts to tell me a little about his background. He was raised in Sri Lanka, attended a top school in Colombo. His father, a merchant, had money but Sunil needed to get away from the sub-continent and spread his wings. He went first to Paris, and then Berlin, but finding work in Europe wasn't easy, until he made it to the UK. At this point, I'm scenting problems.

'You've got a visa? A work permit? Permission to be here?'

'Sort of.' He looks shamefaced. His glass is barely touched.

'What does that mean?'

'It's easy to get jobs here. The pay's not so great for people like me, but no one asks too many questions if the paperwork looks right.'

'You bought fake permissions?'

'Something like that.'

'So, you're an illegal?'

'Nearly. I'm a fully qualified nurse. I passed the exams at home. I've never put anyone in danger.'

'But the paperwork you mentioned?'

He shakes his head. He doesn't want to talk about the paperwork, or the Home Office, or the need to keep his head well down.

'There's something else, Ms Andressen.' At last he's taken a sip of the Prosecco. 'Something I should tell you.'

'Like what?'

'I got the job at the agency only very recently. This was my first assignment.'

'How? Why?'

'I had a call. It came from no one I'd ever heard of before. It was very sudden, very urgent. They told me to go to the agency offices. Everything would be taken care of.'

'Port Solent? The marina place?'

'Yes. I went, of course, and they gave me the job.'

'Here? With us?'

'Yes.'

'And?'

'I had to speak to this person, this stranger, every day.'

'About what?'

'About you, Ms Andressen. And Mr H. And everything that was happening.'

I'm staring at him now, and I put my glass to one side.

'A spy in the camp? Is that what you've been?'

'Yes. But there's more.'

'Tell me.'

'At the start of the week, Monday I think, I got more instructions. Mr H has a phone. He was very ill. I knew where the phone was and I was to expect a text at a particular time. It was late afternoon. I don't remember exactly when, but all I had to do was to reply to the text. Just one word. Yes.'

I nod. I remember the text arriving. It came from Wesley Kane's phone, and it asked whether H wanted to send the balance of his rainy-day fund to Shanti.

'This stranger asked you to expect the text? And then to answer it?'

'Yes.'

'So, who was he?'

'I never had a name but that didn't seem to matter. He said he was a policeman, and he said he'd look after the Home Office people if I did what he asked.'

'He'd arrange for you to stay? Legally?'

'Yes.'

'And?'

'The Home Office say they want to see me to discuss my status. Maybe next month. Maybe next year. Maybe never.'

I nod. The hunt for intel, I think. Major Crimes. So devious. So ruthless. So simple.

'This stranger. What did he look like?'

'He was a big man, older than you'd expect for a policem. He had a little scar on his face.' He taps the skin above his rigt eyebrow. 'And he always wore a jacket. There was a little badge on that jacket, just here on the lapel.' He touches his chest. 'Two fish with a crown in the middle.'

I sit back against the lumpiness of the sofa, wondering whether to be surprised, or horrified, or outraged, or simply resigned. Leading Seaman Jenny Wren, I think. Unmasked at last.

'So why are you telling me all this?' I'm looking at Sunil again. 'Aren't you worried about these people? About this stranger?'

'No.' He shakes his head. 'I've decided to go. Just as soon as I can.'

'Go where, Sunil?'

'Home. This country isn't for me, Ms Andressen. Not anymore.'

I nod, telling myself it makes sense. I'm thinking fast now, steps I have to take, precautions I have to make. A couple more questions establish that Sunil is sharing a bedsit in the city with two other Asians. Dessie Wren will know this. I find the key to Tim's flat, and give it to Sunil. Marmion Road, I say. Red door. Second floor. Opposite Waitrose. Then I check on the baby alarm, and tiptoe into H's bedroom. He's left his mobile on the little bedside table. I go back to the front room and give it to Sunil. Any calls he needs to make should be on this phone, not his own. Otherwise they'll know exactly where he is.

'How?'

'It's complicated. They can track you, follow you, pick you up, so don't use it. Don't even turn it on. Yes?'

Sunil nods. He's had enough of this game, this job, this country. Everything's ganged up on him. He's out of his depth, totally lost. He really does want to get home, and I suddenly feel very, very sorry for him.

He's still wearing his PPE, and I turn my head away as he peels it off and folds it into a neat pile, which he leaves on the armchair by the window. I give him a hug at the door and tell him I'm very grateful.

'It was a pleasure, Ms Andressen. I told you. I like your Mr H.'

'I meant the story you told me.'

e nods uncertainly, saying nothing. Moments later, after
other hug, he's gone.

THIRTY-ONE

With H asleep, and Malo tucked up with Taalia, I decide
to spend the night on the sofa, stretching full-length
beneath an eiderdown I find in one of the cupboards
in H's bedroom. The eiderdown smells musty and damp, but the
Prosecco helps no end and I'm asleep within minutes.

When I jerk awake, I have no idea what time it is, absolutely
none. I lie motionless in the chilly half-darkness, aware of the
occasional gust of wind whining through the gap in the sash
window. Then I hear the noise that must have woken me up. It's
metallic, a feral scratching, and I think it's coming from the front
door. I'm rigid beneath the eiderdown, barely moving, barely
breathing, every nerve stretched tight. After a while, maybe a
full minute, I move very cautiously to check my mobile. It's
02.44. I'm hearing things, I tell myself. Too much Prosecco. Too
much going on. A mouse. A ghost. Anything.

I close my eyes again, and then it happens a second time,
much louder. Metal against metal, and definitely from the
darkness that cloaks the front door. I'm frightened now. Berndt
once told me that everyone in this life has a certain allotment
of courage, a store of rationed pluck on which he or she can
depend. These last few years, I've drawn heavily on that
account, and I know it's nearly empty. Every instinct tells me
to shut my eyes and hope the noise goes away. What remains
of my courage suggests that I should get out of bed and
investigate.

And so I do. It's cold in the flat, much colder than I'd anticipated, or maybe sheer terror has iced the bits of me I can still
feel. Either way, still fully clothed, I pick up the empty bottle of
Prosecco. One glance at the baby alarm tells me that H is still
asleep, and so I tiptoe towards the darkness that hides the door
and feel my way across the tiny space that serves as an entrance

hall. Just four of us left in this tomb of a flat, I think. And I'm the last man standing.

I'm beside the door now, immobile, stock still, simply listening. Here, unlike the front room, with its spill of light from the streetlamps, I can see nothing. I try and remember the door from the inside, the Yale lock that needs fixing, the bolt at the top that doesn't quite slot in properly, the letter box with its squeaky flap. The letter box, I think. I extend a hand and trace its outline with one fingertip. The flap doesn't fully close and when I put my eye to it, I can see the thinnest strip of something lighter out on the landing.

For a long moment, nothing happens. Then the something lighter moves and I hear that same noise, that same scratching. It's very close now, almost intimate, and then comes the softest intake of breath. Someone's out there. And that someone is trying to get in.

It has to be Sean McGaughy, I think. He's tried twice and failed. In his deranged little brain, this will be third time lucky.

Shit.

I'm still on one knee. The neck of the Prosecco bottle is clammy in my hand and I haven't a clue what to do next. The noise happens again, louder this time, and I feel the physical presence, intensely disturbing, of this madman at our door. I tell myself I have only one choice, one option. I need to do something Sean McGaughy least expects.

And so I very slowly ease the flap of the letter box open, put my lips to the gap, and summon my fiercest stage whisper.

'You,' I hiss, 'can fuck off.'

There's a moment of absolute silence. And then comes a stir and a shuffle of movement before I hear footsteps, light, receding down the stairs. I release the deadlock on the Yale and open the door. Nothing. Not even a stir of air, or a noise downstairs as the front door opens and shuts. Shaky but relieved, I lock the door again, bolt it at the top, and then return to the front room. From the window, the streetlights reach deep into the Common.

Once again, nothing.

It takes an age to get to sleep again. The slightest noise, even a tiny rattle from the sash window as the wind begins to rise, sets

my pulse racing and I lie there in the dark, the duvet knotted
beneath my chin, trying to make myself invisible should Sean
McGaughy return and somehow get into the flat. Trying to picture
him is no problem. My memory serves up image after image
from the evening we briefly shared at Shanti's resto. The thin
pale figure in the grey hoodie as he waited for me to let him in.
His unexpected strength when we manhandled the generator out
of the back of his van. The way one of the mirrors in the games
arcade bent and shrank his skinny outline until he was nothing
more than a slash of grey, a first mark an artist might make on
a blank sheet of paper, full of unspoken menace.

Out on the landing, he was obviously breaking in. What if I
hadn't shooed him away? What if I'd stayed asleep? What would
have happened to the two men in my life, one of them still groggy
from Covid, the other a casualty of this city's darker side? The
longer I think about Malo, the more I'm convinced that Sean
McGaughy must – in some way – have been responsible. Wesley's
right. Hospitalizing Malo was yet another way of getting at H,
and tonight Sean planned a final settlement of accounts. H had
to answer for his father's death. And it would be Sean's job to
make sure that bill was paid in full.

A knife? Some kind of bludgeon? A gun? I've no idea. All I
know is that this script holds nothing but the darkest of surprises,
and that it probably falls to little me to keep us all safe. I shake
my head, close my eyes, hug the duvet a little tighter. No one
can ever audition you for a role like this, I tell myself. And
the worst possible news would be the realization that the part is
yours. No second thoughts. No backing out. Just learn the lines,
take a deep breath, and get on with it.

The next thing I know is Taalia standing beside the sofa, a mug
of tea in her hand. She apologizes for waking me up and I try
to tell her that it's no problem but the words come out in the
wrong order. I'm still frightened, still confused, still groggy. That
bloody letter box, I'm thinking. And the presence on the landing,
barely feet away.

'How's Malo?' I manage at last.

'Tired. And I think he's in pain.'

'H?'

'Not so good.'

This absolutely gets my attention. How? Why? Is H sick again? Has the virus found somewhere else in his body to nest?

'There's no temperature, Ms Andressen. He's not ill like he has been. He's just tired and . . .' She's got a lovely shrug. 'You know?'

'Grumpy?'

'Yes. These things take time. He has to understand that. I tried just now but he never listens. Maybe if you had a moment . . .?' She's nodding at Sunil's pile of PPE.

'Of course.' I'm on the move already, swallowing the remains of the tea and wondering exactly what to say, how to put it. I'm cogent now, back in control of myself. Unless I was dreaming, a lunatic with debts to settle tried to get in during the middle of the night. Should I tell H? Would that get us anywhere useful? By the time Taalia has helped me on with the PPE, I've decided that the answer is no. Instead I pull up a chair beside H's bed and pass on the good news I've just heard on the radio.

'Tonight, we all clap for the NHS,' I tell him.

'We?'

'The entire nation, H.'

'Why?'

'Solidarity. Eight o'clock, on the dot. Make a note. You can stand at the front window and join in, but only if I can get the bloody thing open.'

'Clap?' He still doesn't understand the concept. 'How does that fucking work?'

This is laughable. 'It's about people like you, H. People back from the dead. Think gratitude. Without all those lovely nurses, you'd probably be dead.'

'Bollocks,' he snorts. 'I paid for all that, and it cost me the fucking earth.'

Leaving H in these moods is like retreating under fire. Nothing is right. Not the night's sleep he's barely had. Not the tea that Taalia's delivered. Not the brief sight of his precious son making his way towards the bathroom, disfigured by scum who need teaching a lesson. Then comes the moment when he can't find his mobile phone.

'Where the fuck is it?' he says.

I shrug. I say I haven't a clue. Plainly, he doesn't believe me. The whole world is against him. Something must be done.

'Wes,' he grunts. 'Try again.'

Yes, H. Leaving a delighted Taalia in charge, I take a lukewarm shower, get dressed, and step onto the Common to make the call. I tell Wes briefly about last night. I don't mention Sean by name because that might provoke yet more violence, but this morning, unlike last time we talked on the phone, Wesley's kind enough to hear me out.

'There was definitely someone trying to get in?'

'For sure. I swear it. I don't make these things up, Wes. I'm not that clever.'

'And you think it might happen again?'

'Yes. This is the third time someone's had a go at us. There's a pattern here. The nurses have gone. Except for one of them, we're pretty much on our own. H is still sick, sicker than he thinks he is, and Malo's a basket case. We're there for the taking, Wes. It's help-yourself time.'

'You're telling me you told him to fuck off? Whispered in his ear? That that's all it took?'

'Yes, and thank God it worked. I never did violence. Not at school and not afterwards.'

'Shame. You might have missed out.'

Wesley promises me he'll have a think and phone me back. Standing guard will obviously mean staying the night. Am I cool with that?

'I'm cool with anything, Wes. When H gets nervous, I do, too.'

'You've told him about last night?'

'No.'

'Just as well.' Wes rings off.

My second call catches Dessie at what he terms a difficult moment.

'You're doing something unspeakable?'

'I'm at work. In your book, and in mine too, it's probably the same thing. We need a meet.'

'My thoughts entirely. When? Where?' Dessie mentions a car

park on the seafront beyond the fun fair. I happen to know it
well because it's en route to Old Portsmouth.

'Eleven o'clock on the dot,' he says. 'I'm the good-looking
one in the knackered VW.'

Very funny. Twelve hours gives you a fighting chance to revisit
assumptions you'd begun to believe, and already I'm relishing
the chance to get one or two things off my chest. First, though,
I must check on Sunil.

By now, it's nearly ten o'clock. En route to Tim's flat, I make
a precautionary call to H's mobile number. When Sunil answers,
I ask him whether he's OK.

'I'm fine, Ms Andressen.' He says he's about to go out and
pick up a few things at the supermarket across the road.

'Don't,' I say at once. 'Just give me a list.'

He wants milk, bread, and eggs. Then he asks how long he'll
be staying in the flat and when I tell him I don't know, can't be
sure, he adds rice and a collection of fresh veggies.

'Nothing else?'

'Nothing.'

The queue in the car park for the supermarket is longer than I'd
anticipated, and it's twenty to eleven when I finally make it to Tim's
flat. I hand over the shopping and tell Sunil I'll be back later.

'Don't go out.' I'm doing my best to be stern. 'And remember
not to use your own phone.'

I'm down in the car park by the fun fair with three minutes to
spare. Dessie, for the first time in our brief relationship, is late.
I linger by the railings, looking at the greyness of the sea, still
catching my breath as a fishing boat putters past. It might be the
same skipper who gave H the skate, but already that transaction
belongs to a different life.

Dessie at last turns up. He spots me at once and flashes his
headlights. I join him in the car.

'Nightmare,' he says at once. 'Run two operations with the
same target and you're looking at serious confliction. Back in
the day, we'd blow all the tanks and dive. I was silly enough to
suggest it and took a hiding. Never cross a detective superinten-
dent. The rank turns them all into monsters.'

'Same target?' I ask. 'So who might that be?'

'H, of course.'

'And you're going to tell me more?'

'Only if you're nice to me.'

'What does that mean?'

'I'm looking at your face. People in your trade are supposed to be good at hiding their feelings. Am I getting warm here? Or is there a good reason you're so pissed off?'

I've made the mistake of over-preparing for this conversation, which I suspect is the last we'll ever have outside a custody suite, but already Dessie has torn up my script. Clever, I think.

'Sunil?' I enquire. 'Does the name ring any bells? Sri Lankan boy? Very suggestible?'

Dessie gazes at me and for a moment or two I think I recognize something close to admiration in his smile.

'It's what we do,' he says. 'Infil, exfil, plant the canary in the mine and see what happens.'

'You recruited him. Put pressure on him. Bribed him.'

'We did. You caught us on the hop, I'm afraid, getting all that help in so quickly. The lad was on the radar already. We knew all about his dodgy status, and the nursing qualification was a bonus. He's been a good little soldier. Served us well.'

'Us?'

'*Operation Plover.* That's my baby. We call it a cold case.'

I nod. I've heard the term before. 'This is Sammy McGaughy?' I enquire.

'The very same. Sad old guy, like I told you. No one missed him but that's not the point. People disappear and you have to wonder why.'

'And that's why you're after that phone of Wesley Kane's?'

'Of course. If you're a proper psycho you keep trophy snaps. It goes with the territory. We call it a marker.' He pauses. 'Any luck?'

'None. I'm afraid I didn't even ask.'

'You're serious?'

'Always.'

'Might I ask why?'

'Because your gang's not my gang. A week ago, maybe longer, I had no idea about this city of yours. Now I'm getting to know how it ticks.'

'H has been asking the same question for most of his life. That's why he's so rich.'

'And that's why you have to bring him down? Lock him away?'

'Of course. It's our job to tidy up after people like H. He's helped himself to whatever he fancies for years, decades, and there's every sign he's about to do it again. Do we simply watch? Applaud the clever bits? Help him on his way? Or might we do something about it?'

It's Dessie's turn to get angry. He's on the defensive now, and it's showing me another side to the man.

'You leaned on Sunil,' I say. 'You took advantage. How does that make you feel?'

'It's a tactic,' Dessie shrugs. 'Small print. Means and ends. If he'd kept his nose clean it might have worked out for the lad. He's bought himself some serious credits. The right word in the right ear can work wonders.'

'At the Home Office?'

'Of course.'

'And now? After this conversation?'

'Now he's a dead man. First, we'll bang him up. Then, if he's lucky, we'll deport him.'

'There's another option?'

'Of course. In our game, there's always another option. Thanks for the tip, though. Happily, we know where to look.'

I nod, wondering whether I shouldn't be recording this conversation.

'You said two operations. What's the other one?'

'*Avocet.* This is live, ongoing. My masters think H was about to get back in the game. There are ways of turning that suspicion into evidence.'

'All that material you seized at Flixcombe?'

'That's part of it, sure. *Avocet* is driven by the figures. You'd be amazed at what a decent forensic accountant can unearth. People like H are good at burying the stuff that matters. It's our job to dig it up.'

'And?'

'We have meetings. Endless meetings. Not everything goes to plan. There's lots of shouting, more than you might think, and Detective Superintendents shout loudest of all.'

I raise an eyebrow, wondering just how rough a morning Dessie Wren has really had. He's so plausible, so easy to be with. In another life, he'd have made a decent actor.

'You'll have that dreadful flat of ours under surveillance. CCTV maybe? People in cars? Am I right?'

'You know that? You've got the evidence?'

'No,' I admit. 'But tell me it isn't true.'

Dessie says nothing. Then looks away and shrugs again.

'H is a high-value target,' he says softly. 'He's also an obvious flight risk. Believe me, we're doing the nation a favour.'

'By keeping him banged up?'

'Yes.'

I nod, relieved and even proud that I've at last got to the question that really matters.

'They keep a log? Those surveillance guys of yours?'

'Of course.'

'And you get to see it?'

'Sometimes, yes.'

'This morning maybe? At that meetings of yours?'

'Yes.'

'So what did it tell you about movements in and out of the building?'

'When?'

'Last night. Between midnight and dawn.'

Dessie eyes me for a long moment. Another trace on the sonar screen, I think. Something unexpected.

'Is this important?'

'Yes.'

'Am I allowed to ask why?'

'No.'

He nods, and I watch his fingers stray briefly to the little scar above his eye.

'One note,' he says at last. 'At twelve fifty-eight. The boy Sunil leaving to go home.'

'Nothing else? No one in or out?'

'No.'

THIRTY-TWO

'm back at Tim's flat within the half hour. I'm not at all sure where Dessie and I now stand, but that's probably deliberate on his part. Am I still a bit player in this little drama, an innocent bystander who needs the comfort of an encircling arm? Or have I become a suspect in my own right? To both questions I have no answer, but in a way that no longer matters. For the first time, like Captain MacWhirr, I think I might have glimpsed a way of surviving this typhoon.

Sunil is pleased I've come back. He asks again how long I think he may be staying here.

'For a while, I'm afraid. You've really made up your mind? About going home?'

He nods, and when I ask him whether he has any money, he says yes. He has a little saved up, not much, but it's all in the place where he's living.

'Don't go there. Don't be tempted. Here.' I give him all the money I've got in my purse to cover any emergencies that might crop up. It comes to less than forty pounds. He takes the money with some reluctance but when I ask him for another shopping list, he shakes his head, says he's got plenty enough to get by.

I nod, holding his gaze, hopelessly aware of how much guilt we share. On his part for ratting us out. And now, on mine, for adding him to *Operation Avocet*'s arrest list. Ghosting him away under lockdown won't be easy – no ferries, no planes – but I know I have to find a way.

'We need to be patient, Sunil.' I give him a hug. 'But I'm guessing you're good at that.'

I return to Southsea Common and pick up Tony Morse's car. It's a ten-minute drive through largely empty streets, and then out along the spur motorway that loops across the upper harbour. Port Solent is a little pocket of masts and apartment buildings tucked into a corner on the mainland. I park up and retrace my steps to the nursing agency. Mr Wu, it turns out, is up at the hospital just now, but when I explain what I'm after, the receptionist lifts a phone.

Zophia is Mr Wu's Director of Operations. She handles all the day-to-day financial stuff and helps him stay abreast of what she calls 'the bigger picture'. Like many of the nurses, she's Polish, a big, handsome woman with an air of easy command. She insists on brewing us both a pot of fresh coffee, and cheerfully admits that business has never been so good.

'Nearly a hundred nurses,' she tells me, 'and every one of them employed. Mr Wu must have seen this coming. He doubled the staff after Christmas, which is just as well. The right people are impossible to find now. If this country of yours isn't very careful, you'll run out.'

I explain about the £55,000 I left with Mr Wu only days ago. I'm about to ask for some of that money back, but Zophia is already studying our account on her PC. I watch her eyes as she scrolls through entry after entry, an interminable list of line items that hauled H back from the near-dead. Finally, a blur of keystrokes produces a figure. Then she frowns.

'You want a last deep-clean?'

'No, thanks.'

'Then we owe you twelve thousand, one hundred and twelve pounds.' She looks up. 'And the patient? Am I allowed to ask?'

'Fighting fit.' I'm on my feet already. 'Thanks to you.'

We agree that she'll transfer the money into one of H's business accounts, and I promise to phone with the details. On my way out through reception, I linger briefly beside the desk.

The receptionist is gazing at her PC screen.

'You remember I mentioned a yacht when I was last here?'

'*Agincourt*,' she says at once. 'Dennis Mortimer.'

'You know him?'

'I looked him up when you'd gone.'

'You wouldn't have any contact details by any chance?'

'Playfair Construction.' She's back to the PC screen already. 'Google it.'

Curiosity takes me along the edge of the marina to the pontoon near the entrance where *Agincourt* is berthed. My memories of her earlier namesake are sketchy, a tribute to H's margaritas down in Antibes, but the moment I'm close enough, I know that this latest trophy buy is bigger, sleeker, and even whiter than the last one.

Back in Tony Morse's BMW, I Google Playfair Construction. The website is nicely designed, quietly boastful, and showcases completed projects, chiefly in Reading and Basingstoke. These properties are modest commercial units, artfully sited, and come with state-of-the-art security, plus a whole list of other must-have gizmos. A portfolio of premises like these, I imagine, will have brought him serious wealth. Hence *Agincourt*.

There's a listed contact number on the website and I ring it, only to get a pre-recorded message about Covid, lockdown, and the regrettable suspension of normal service. I'm about to hang up when a woman's voice cuts in.

'Justin? Is that you?'

'I'm afraid not. I'm after Dennis Mortimer. Might he be there?'

'You've come through to his direct line, God knows how. Who are you?'

I give her my name and wait to see where it gets me. Then comes a muttered conversation in the background, and – abruptly – a new voice on the line.

'Enora? Enora *Andressen*?' This is a voice I remember, Pompey-rough, full of mischief. H used to call him Den.

'The same,' I say.

'Still at it?'

'At what?'

'Hooking all those punters? We had a little film festival, back last year. I'd found a buyer for the old boat and we wanted to give her a proper send-off and so we laid hands on a couple of DVDs and pushed off for the weekend.' He names a couple of my more commercial films and then laughs. 'The missus wasn't amused but we had some of the Antibes crowd on board so who cares. Tooled around the Isle of Wight all weekend, and then got wrecked in Yarmouth. Quality movies. Great outing. What can I do for you?'

I explain briefly about H and confirm that he seems to be on the mend. This appears to be good news.

'I tried to get hold of him last year but he's a hard bugger to nail down. Shame. He'd have loved that weekend. So why the call? *Que pasa?'*

I tell him it's hard to explain on the phone. Maybe a meet?

'No problema.' He gives me another number. 'We're at home at the moment. Bosham. Ring any bells? Lovely spot. Nice view of the harbour. Come to lunch one day. We're on lockdown at the moment, but no one's watching.'

Agincourt. Antibes. I put my phone to one side, bits of that evening beginning to swim up through the silt that is my memory. Dennis Mortimer, according to H, had always been a reliable client when it came to quality cocaine, and threw wild parties at his Craneswater mansion as his business career went from strength to strength. He worked hard, and played even harder, and H – who always had an eye for phonies – thought the world of him. In return, Den relished his arm's-length rapport with Pompey's *demi-monde*, and made a quiet investment or two which served both men extremely well. Hence his invite to H to join the cruise down to Antibes, and hence – two decades later – his warmth on the phone.

My next call goes to Jessie, at Flixcombe. I tell her about the rebate on the agency fees and give her the contact details so she can sort out the BACS transfer herself.

'And Malo?' she asks.

'He's back with us, Jess.'

'In that flat?'

'Yes.'

'That must be nice.'

Nice? I'm staring at the phone. Either she's being wildly ironic, or she simply can't imagine the squalor of the place, plus the added challenge of trying to keep H in one piece. The latter, I suspect, probably hits the mark, and I end the conversation with a promise to get H home safe.

'No hurry,' she says. 'Apart from the Filth, it's been really peaceful down here.'

THIRTY-THREE

Tony Morse, when I make it to Craneswater, is a little better. I park on the street outside his villa, and raise him on the phone. It's early afternoon now. Last night's rain has gone, the clouds have parted, and it's a truly glorious day. There's a softness in the air, and I can taste the sea in the fitful breeze.

'I'm in the garden, my darling. Take the path round the side of the house. The summerhouse is made for convalescents like me. Corinne has even found a plaid blanket. Can you believe how kind women can be?'

I lock the car and follow his directions. The summerhouse looks new, a testament to the earning power of talented defence solicitors, and Tony – exactly as billed – is sitting in a wicker *chaise*, reading a copy of *The Times*. He has a cheroot in one hand, and a glass of what looks like brandy in the other. He glances up at my approach and shades his eyes against the glare of the sun.

I stop the regulation two metres away and dangle the keys to his BMW.

'I've brought it back,' I tell him. 'I can't thank you enough.'

'My pleasure, my darling. German engineering? Never lets you down.'

'I meant the exemption certificate. It spared me a great deal of bother.'

'You were pretending to be me?'

'I was pretending to work for you. Next time I have to audition for a legal secretary, I'll knock it out of the park.'

He finds this news amusing. Corinne has appeared with one of those chairs you take on camping expeditions. She unfolds it, and then asks me whether I want full sun.

'Of course,' I say. 'Who wouldn't?'

'And a little Armagnac? Just to be sociable?'

'Why, yes.'

She disappears and I settle into the chair, which is much more comfortable than it looks. I update Tony on the state of H's health, and I'm about to go into a great deal more detail when he puts his fingers to his lips and gestures at the nearby hedge. His neighbour, it appears, is a Crown Court judge. Best to be on the safe side.

'Safe side? You want me closer?'

'God, yes. As close as you like, my angel, but not quite yet. Just phone me. If we need to exchange confidences, best to keep quiet. *Capisce?*'

Capisce is Brooklyn gangster-talk for 'get it?' and has recently served as a running gag between me and Tony. I get out my phone. He does the same. Bizarre.

'Right-oh.' He's on the phone now. 'How bad is it?'

'How bad?' I whisper. 'You know about all of this already?'

'Most of it, I suspect, but let's pretend otherwise. Start at the beginning. H is in the shit. It's payback time for the Filth, and there's a long queue of even dodgier characters at your door. H was crazy to come back here at all. Thanks to our bloody virus friend, he can't leave, and so now the past has returned to haunt him. I get the sense that's page one in the script. Deeply promising, if I may say so. Over to you, my darling. I await your instructions.'

Bravo. I mime applause, which he accepts with a graceful nod, and then tell him exactly what's been happening these last few days. Tony Morse is the one person in this city I'd trust with my life. Over the last few years, he's dug me out of a series of holes, but this is by far the deepest, and so I tell him almost everything, every last detail bar one.

The evening I spent at Shanti's resto in Gunwharf, my blossoming relationship with Dessie Wren, the efforts of the nurses to keep H alive, strange messages to H's mobile, the snuff pics on Wesley's phone I dumped off the Round Tower, Malo coming to grief on the seafront, the efforts by some stranger to get at H, and finally the role of a sweet, gentle Sri Lankan called Sunil.

'That Dessie's a snake,' I tell Tony. 'A woman my age should have known that from the start.'

'Dessie's doing his job,' Tony says mildly. 'I could introduce you to some truly evil coppers, my darling. He's not one of them.'

'You say.'

'I say. As a matter of fact, he's one of the good guys. *En passant*, he also fancies you.'

'I noticed that. Is this something you discussed?'

'He phoned me at lunchtime to check I was OK. The jungle tom-toms had passed the word. Possible Covid. Morse might be a goner. I assured him that wasn't the case, of course, and we ended up talking nonsense, as men do.'

'About me?'

'I'm afraid so. He thinks you're wasted up there in London. A decade younger, he told me, and you'd see the error of your ways.'

'There's something wrong with being forty-two?'

'He was talking about himself, my darling. Dessie does charm for a living, as you probably sussed. Ten years ago, he took some remarkable scalps in this city, and only some of them were villains. Women I credit with exquisite taste fall for him. Lately, I suspect it's been more difficult. I get the sense he's feeling his age. You're definitely on his radar, prime target, but you'd know that already. Ten years ago, he would have pounced. Now he's not quite so sure of himself. I told him not to be silly. Everything sorts itself out. Even a mid-life crisis. Was he grateful for my advice? I doubt it. Why? Because men never listen. Not even Dessie.'

I can't help smiling. This is a *tour de force*, I think, on Tony's part, proof that he's very definitely getting better, and the real clue – the clincher – lies in the pay-off. *Men never listen. Not even Dessie.* What an acute judgement. Leading Seaman Jenny Wren, hunched over his sonar screen, hunting for those tell-tale echoes that will take him to his prey. Russians? Villains? Me? I'm in good company.

'And has he given up?' I ask. 'As a matter of interest?'

'I fear not.'

'From my point of view?'

'His, my darling. I warned him about you. I told him how discerning you are when it comes to the important things in life. I told him I've been trying my very best, my very hardest for years and years, and still no result.'

'And?'

'He wasn't listening. Consistency is normally a virtue, my darling, but I just hope Mr Wren can cope with a major disappointment.'

'Me?'

'Of course.'

'You're marking my card?'

'I'm telling you this is a wicked, wicked city, much more complex than you might imagine. At its heart it's a village, just a handful of players, movers and shakers who might make a difference, and H used to be one of them. Dessie, believe it or not, is another. He and H were close once. It wasn't a corrupt relationship, far from it, but H helped Dessie out over that kid of his, the one you mentioned, and Dessie is the kind of guy who never forgets a gesture like that. It doesn't disturb his aim for a moment, not Dessie's, but you have to factor it in.'

'You said *his* kid.'

'I did.'

'Not his godson?'

'Christ, no. Dessie's missus couldn't have children. She was barren, my darling, and Dessie always loved kids. As far as Titch is concerned, he's always been coy about the details, but I gather he was shagging another man's wife and she obliged him with a son.'

'And this woman's husband?'

'He's history, now. Prostate cancer. She lives alone in North End. I get the impression she's done with men.'

'Including Dessie?'

'The jury's out on that one. Dessie is a loyal little soul. I know it sounds odd when he's a serial shagger, but there's definitely something big and red and glistening in that chest of his. Dessie's all heart. Whatever he says, whoever it might be, he normally means it. The really devious stuff is for the bad guys. Dessie is a man of limitless appetite. Given the chance, he'd eat the whole world.'

I'm not quite sure what to make of this phrase, chiefly because I suspect he's got the verb wrong, but Tony has an enormous respect for the English language and values precision above everything.

'You're telling me I should trust him?'

'Christ, no. You've got our Dessie in a bit of a pickle. He once forbade me to mix business and pleasure. It turned out to be very good advice but just now he should be listening to himself. A week ago, you were the mother of H's son. You had the decency to give H a little moral support when he came down here to say his goodbyes to Fat Dave. You've also stood by him when he got sick himself. That earns you credits in Dessie's book. He doesn't think you're shagging H, and he's right, but loyalty goes a long way with Dessie, and on top of that, like I say, he fancies you.'

'Should I be flattered?'

'Yes.'

'Because?'

'Because I think he means it, which – just now – is somewhat ironic.'

Tony asks me whether I'm familiar with the phrase 'Crazy Ivan'. When I say no, he insists there's no shame because he'd never heard of it either, not until lunchtime.

'Today, you mean?'

'Yes. As I explained, Dessie phoned. You've definitely got him worried.'

'How? Why?'

'He wouldn't say, wouldn't spell it out, but then he mentioned Crazy Ivan. It goes back to his time in the Navy. They'd be tracking some Russian submarine for days on end. This is the Cold War. The games they played really mattered. So, they'd lurk and lurk and make all kinds of recordings that would come in handy later, then the Russians would finally twig that they had a Brit boat up their backsides.'

'So, what happened? What would they do?'

'Russian subs are apparently built like the proverbial. Double hulls? Does that make sense? In any event, they'd pull a hundred-and-eighty-degree turn and just come straight for you, kamikaze stuff. You had to dive, go left, go right, surface, anything to get out of the way. It wasn't subtle but it worked.' He nods. 'Crazy Ivan.'

I try and imagine this piece of submerged theatre, two rival gangs, suddenly head-to-head.

'So what's any of this got to do with . . .' I shrug. 'Now?'

'He thinks you're pulling a Crazy Ivan.'

'On who?'

'Him. Ah . . . resupplies . . .'

It's Corinne. She comes gliding over Tony's immaculate lawn with a laden tray. A brandy on ice for me. A big plate of canapes in case we get peckish. And an open bottle of Armagnac for seconds. She's wearing a rather fetching straw hat which she settles on Tony's head.

'That naughty sun, darling. With no pollution, we have to take care.'

She bends to give him a kiss, and then heads back towards the house. For a moment, I'm tempted to enquire further, but Tony wags a finger.

'Don't,' he says. 'I've adopted a new rule. Never make assumptions. If you ask me where that wonderful woman is taking me, I'd tell you it's for real. Three marriages would argue otherwise. Best to count your blessings and enjoy the moment. *Capisce?*'

I nod. I get it. Conversations like this, especially with Tony Morse, are always a delight but I need to get back to *Operation Avocet*. Tony, after all, is a defence lawyer. It's his job to weigh the strength of the enemy's hand and offer the appropriate advice.

'*Avocet*'s a Major Crimes thing,' I suggest. 'Am I right?'

'You are.'

'And Dessie seems to think they've got H where they want him.'

'That's wish fulfilment, my darling. Nothing happens in court without evidence. They'll spend a great deal of time and money trawling through all the paperwork they seized at Flixcombe. H isn't stupid, far from it. I doubt they'll find anything. That's partly why they tried to fit him up with Shanti. They knew he needed a lot of money in a great hurry, and they tried to make it easy for him. Thanks to you, not a penny went her way, and we can prove that.'

'And the text that Wesley sent?'

'That was clumsy. If they're stooping to a stroke like that, then they're getting desperate. In any event, my darling, they'd need both phones – Wesley's and H's – and I'm hearing from you that one's gone off the Round Tower, while the other's in the hands of young Sunil. A word in your ear. When you get H's phone back, bin it. We agree?'

'We do.' I lift my glass. 'So, *Avocet*?'

'They're playing games. It'll come to nothing. Trust me.'

'You're sure?'

'Absolutely. Our real challenge is *Plover*.'

'The cold case? Sammy McGaughy? Dessie's baby?'

'Exactly. I suspect Dessie thought he was close to a result. The key here is Wesley. That man was never Mr Stable and the way I'm hearing it, he has a grudge against H.'

'That's probably true. He also killed Sammy McGaughy. I've seen the evidence.'

'Which no longer exists.'

'Indeed.'

Tony Morse nods, toying with his glass.

'Dessie has been playing Wes. That's my assumption. For whatever reason, Wes has agreed to help lay the bait for H. That takes us to Shanti, the Casablanca, all that. In return, Dessie might have agreed to drop the cold case.'

'And meant it?'

'Christ, no. Dessie thinks Wes is vermin. Sadly, Wes has yet to work that out. Dessie will stitch him up royally and see him in court. That's the way it's been shaping.'

'And now?'

'Now, my darling, there's something you still haven't told us. Not me, and certainly not Dessie.' He raises his glass. 'To Crazy Ivan,' he says, 'or whatever else you have in mind.'

THIRTY-FOUR

Google tells me about Flat 2 on Clarence Parade. I'm standing outside an estate agency in the middle of Southsea. It is, of course, closed, but according to my internet search, one of the two ground-floor flats in our property overlooking the Common is still listed for rental. I can see the details in the window. Sea views, two bedrooms, retro kitchen, £775 per month, part furnished. The accompanying photo shows the front of the property, which includes a For Rent board wired to the railings.

A typed notice on the door of the agency advises clients to contact a telephone number in the event of urgent enquiries. The number answers on the third ring, a woman's voice. I explain that I'm after a rental with sea views. I've seen Flat 2 on the agency's website and want to know if it's still available. The woman puts me on hold while she checks.

I spend a couple of minutes outside the agency, idly browsing other properties while I wait for her to come back to me. I'm more than aware that I'm getting out far more than I should, but this has given me a ringside seat on the real consequences of lockdown. Life has suddenly come to a complete halt, whole businesses – like this one – suddenly frozen in a moment of time. Locked doors. Remote phone numbers. Employees banged up with their screaming kids on furlough schemes that will probably have to last for months.

This is game, set and match to a tiny speck of virus too small for any of us to picture, and one of my real regrets is that Pavel died too soon to be part of it all. We shared conversations during that last year of his life which were truly apocalyptic. Paralysed, physically helpless, he was still tuned into media he trusted, and he had an almost gleeful conviction that the developed world was writing itself cheques it would never be able to cash. Too many people. Expectations wildly out of line with anything the planet can sustain. And a slow, remorseless melting – not just of the icecaps but of the glue that keeps us all together.

Pavel, bless him, was putting his own money on one of those big headline events that kick off most disaster movies – a nuclear war, killer hurricanes – and like most of us he'd dismissed quiet warnings from concerned scientists that the real threat might be far more primitive. But Covid is here now. It doesn't have a conscience. It doesn't mind how many millions it kills. And the moment a vaccine arrives it will doubtless change its name, adopt some artful disguise, and reappear to create yet more havoc. This, I suspect, would have put the ghost of a smile on Pavel's face. The world will end, he'd whisper, not with a bang but a cough.

'Ms Andressen?'

The woman from the agency is back on the line. She tells me that the property is currently tenanted on a rolling monthly contract. To the best of her knowledge, the occupier has every intention of moving on and I'm more than welcome to register an interest if I anticipate renting the place on a more permanent basis. I tell her that this is very much my intention and wonder whether I might take a peek.

At this point, she laughs. To the best of her knowledge, no one's allowed to do anything anymore, but if I fancy knocking on the young man's door, who knows what might happen.

'He has a name? This young man?'

She departs once again to check the contract. Then she's back.

'A Mr McGaughy,' she says. 'Sean McGaughy.'

It takes me a while to fully absorb this news, but the longer I think about it, the more sense it makes. I wander across the Common in the early-evening sunshine, and then turn to look back. Sean McGaughy was indeed the feral presence at our door in the middle of the night, and he never left the property because he lives there. Hence the interference in the meter cupboard, and hence – as well – the permanently closed curtains in the front windows of his flat. He's been in there in the gloom, biding his time, awaiting his chance. H killed his father. And H, in turn, must pay.

The thought of sharing a house with a killer is truly chilling. The virus we can sort of cope with. Sean McGaughy is a threat of a different order. I remember the night we reeled back from Gunwharf, three bottles down, and the way he paused on every bastion, every redoubt, telling me what had happened here, why the muddle of fortifications had been built, how you never trust a foreigner. The blood of this city runs in his veins, just as it still fuels H, and later – in the darkness of the games arcade – I remember his thin little body shrunk even more by the distorting mirrors. A wisp of a man in his skinny jeans and threadbare hoodie. Pompey warps you, I think. It twists you out of shape. It feeds an insatiable appetite, first for violence, and now revenge.

I phone Wesley on the one mobile he has left.

'You're still coming tonight?' I ask him. 'Just say yes.'

Back at the flat, Taalia is still in residence. More importantly, she's decided that we should all join the rest of the nation in clapping for the NHS at eight o'clock. This invitation includes H, which means we must all wear PPE. H is now using the toilet in the bathroom, but only with help from Malo. He's unsteady on his feet, having to pause for breath before making it down the corridor, but Taalia thinks it will be good for him to take a look at the world outside.

With five minutes to go, I've finally managed to get the sash window in the front room at least half-lowered so we can hear what's going on, and Taalia shrouds H in a blanket before Malo and I help him through to the front room. The oxygen cylinders have now been collected, revealing a mirror on the far wall, blackened in one corner. H pauses to study himself for the briefest moment before turning away in disgust.

'Who's that old bastard?' he grunts.

Malo has fired up the TV, and already the news presenter is preparing us for the big event. He promises live pictures from every corner of the kingdom and as we watch, the coverage cuts to Belfast where families are flooding out of a row of terrace houses. Mothers are carrying babies. Kids are waving Union Jacks. One pensioner offers her neighbours slices of sponge cake. In the background, a pair of giant yellow cranes.

I join H at the window. Below, in the street, knots of people are beginning to gather. Among them, I recognize the old man downstairs. He's looking as wild as ever, and he's still wearing the lifejacket I saw before. There's a plastic whistle attached to the lifejacket and the moment eight o'clock comes, he raises it to his lips and starts to blow while everyone around him claps. Then comes the wail of ships' sirens from the dockyard, and a couple of toots from a passing car, and when I look out across the Common, I can see a couple of policemen in hi-vis jackets, stock-still except for their gloved hands. Maybe they've come to deal with Sean McGaughy, I think. Or maybe this is part of *Operation Avocet*'s surveillance operation. Either way, they're wasting their time.

H, hunched in his blanket, is having difficulty taking any of this in and for the first time, I sense the weariness in him. It was Sunil who warned me about Covid's reluctance to call it a day, about the mess it leaves behind, about the weeks and maybe months when patients like H will have to cope with recurrent bouts of exhaustion. To his credit, he stays at the window for the full five minutes, and towards the end he even deigns to clap, but I can tell his heart isn't in it.

Finally, the noise of clapping from the street below thins and dies. On the TV, families are once again closing their front doors on the world. Kids appear in front-room windows, mugging for the camera beside yet another crayoned rainbow. Then it's over, and Fiona Bruce has joined us to present a semi-virtual edition of *Question Time*.

H stares at her for a moment, then he shivers and turns away. 'Wes?' he says.

Wesley doesn't turn up until gone ten. Taalia lets him in downstairs, and he appears in the front room. He's wearing jeans and a tracksuit top tonight, and he's carrying a small rucksack. He gives me a brief nod and says he wants to talk to H. When I offer him PPE, he shakes his head.

'No need.' He smells of whisky.

H is glad to see him. 'Sit down, Wes.' He pats the side of the bed. 'You want something to drink?'

Wesley produces a bottle of Jack Daniel's from his day sack. I fetch a couple of glasses from the kitchen. 'Where's yours?' Wes is staring up at me.

'Later, Wes.'

'Later when?'

'Later when we've got this thing over.'

'Thing?' H is sharper than I'd thought. 'What thing?'

I tell them about our new tenant in Flat 2. In my view, I say, this is the guy who turned off the power, and tried to get into the flat last night.

'Why the fuck would he want to do that?' This from H.

'Because he's got a grudge, H.'

'How come?'

'Because you killed his dad. Sean McGaughy? Sammy?'

H is staring at me. Then he reaches for Wesley.

'Get down there, Wes. Sort the little fucker out.'

This happens to be my plan, too, but the night is still young and a conversation with Sean can wait. In the meantime, I need to clarify another issue.

'The police think you were going back into the cocaine business, H.'

'They're right. I was.'

'With Shanti. And Wes, here.'

'Right again.'

'But it turned out to be a set-up, H. A trap. Enticement.' I'm looking at Wesley now. 'So how much did you know about all this? Be honest.'

'All what?'

'Setting Shanti up. Getting her to source drugs. Getting H to pay for it.'

'It was H's fucking idea. He just told us.'

'Yes, but you helped it along. Maybe at the invitation of our police friends.'

'You're telling me I grassed H?' He's staring at me. 'Is that what you're saying?'

'Asking. I'm asking. That's all.'

'Then wash your fucking mouth out. I don't need any of this. I came here to do you guys a favour. I've been digging H out of the shit all my fucking life, and tonight's no different. You want me to sort this situation? No problem. But never use that word again.'

'Grass? That was your word, Wes, not mine.'

H is watching us carefully. He's always read these situations very well, far better than me. He can smell a lie at a thousand metres and just now, he's looking very hard at Wesley.

'Is it true, Wes?' His face is a mask. 'You tried to fit me up? For money, was it? Or some deal you had going with the Filth? Did they know about Sammy already? Made you an offer you couldn't refuse? Home safe in return for little me? Was that the way it happened?'

H's voice has sunk to a whisper. Even now, even old, even sick, he's full of menace, and one glance at Wesley tells me something I've never before suspected. H's tame psycho is terrified of his master.

H puts the question again. Has Wesley been talking to the Filth? Just a yes or a no.

'Bollocks, no,' Wes is sweating now. 'No fucking way. Ever.'

'You mean that? I can trust you? Just the way I've always trusted you?'

'Of course.'

'So, you'll do what we ask?'

'Yeah. A pleasure, H.'

'And no hard feelings?' There's no warmth in his smile. 'Mush?'

I discard the PPE and explain exactly what I want to happen next. The ground-floor flats have rear entrances. I know this because I checked this evening before I went upstairs. Outside the rear door of number two, I found a bicycle, chained to a fence post. I suspect the bike belongs to Sean McGaughy, the one I saw in the back of his van, and I suspect as well that he used it at some point to follow my son on one of his evening runs. Once he knew the route Malo always took, it would have been child's play to recruit a couple of mates and stage an ambush. If he couldn't get to H himself, then putting his son in hospital would be the next best thing.

'You want him to admit it?'

'I want him to tell me about it.'

'Same thing, no?'

We exchange looks, then make our way downstairs. I show Wesley the rear entrance and leave him there. Back in the hall, I knock on the door of number two. First time, nothing happens. I knock again, louder, then try the door handle. It's locked.

'Sean?' I call. 'Sean McGaughy?'

Again nothing. I'm beginning to think he might be out for the night, but then I put my ear to the door and catch the faintest stir of movement inside. For a long minute, nothing happens. I call his name again, and then a third time, and suddenly there comes a shout from the depths of the flat, partly surprise, partly alarm. Wesley, I think. Waiting in the darkness outside Sean's back door.

I can hear footsteps now, and raised voices. Then the door opens in front of me and I'm looking at Sean McGaughy. Wesley has him in a chokehold. His head is back against Wesley's chin and he's gasping for air.

'Kick me again,' says Wesley, 'and I'll kill you.'

I slip into the flat and close the door behind me. 'Partly furnished' is wildly optimistic. The layout of the flat is similar to ours: a front room, two bedrooms, and a squalid galley kitchen, complete with Formica worktops, that reeks of old fat. The front room is bare, except for a TV and a two-seat sofa. There's a mantelpiece over the blocked-up fireplace, and Sean has made an effort to cheer the place up with an untidy grid of snaps blu-tacked to the wallpaper above the mantelpiece. Most of the photos show a naked woman in her mid-forties. Shanti has an arch smile for the camera and the poses she strikes leave nothing to the imagination. Wesley has seen them, too.

'Shagging her, are you?' His grip tightens around Sean's scrawny throat. 'I always fucking wondered who was up that arse of hers.'

Sean says nothing. He can barely breathe.

'Steady, Wes,' I murmur. I'm looking at another face on the wall that I recognize. Last time I saw Sammy McGaughy was on Wesley's phone, and he was probably dead.

'This is your dad, Sean?'

'Yeah.'

'And that's you?'

'Yeah.'

I take a closer look at the shot. Sean is much younger in the photo, barely in his teens. He's wearing a scruffy pair of jeans and no top. He and his dad are sitting on the pebbles, and Sean's thin chest is pinked with sunburn. Sammy has a can of Guinness raised to the camera while Sean is attending to a choc ice. I recognize the pier in the background, and the scatter of families on the beach suggests high summer.

'What about your mum, Sean? Did she take this shot?'

'No.' He shakes his head and when he tries hard to swallow, I tell Wesley to ease off.

'So, where was she? Your mum?'

'Back home. She'd thrown Dad out. Me and Dad met when we could. Sometimes he was even sober. Yeah . . .' He nods, looking at the photo. 'Lucky me, eh?'

'So where was he living?'

'He had a doss in Buckland. He lost it completely in the end. Pissed himself most nights, and never changed the sheets. The place stank.'

'But you missed him?'

'Yeah. Funny that, but I did.'

'And he just disappeared?'

'Yeah. I was away after that, had enough, went abroad, then a mate got in touch, told me what happened. In this city there are people you don't upset. Dad never got that.'

'And you?'

'I'm his boy.' He nods at the emptiness of the room. 'And this is another fucking doss.'

I nod, taking my time. 'There's a man upstairs you've been trying to kill,' I say softly. 'It never quite worked out and so you set about his son. On the seafront. Monday night. I was the one who found him, Sean, because he happens to be my son, too.'

'Yeah?' Sean feigns surprise, or perhaps indifference.

'You're denying it?'

'I don't know what you're talking about.'

'You didn't turn the power off? You didn't come upstairs in the middle of the night?'

'No. Neither have I touched that son of yours. Why should I? What's in it for me?'

I study him for a long moment. Then I tell Wesley I'm off for a proper look at the rest of the flat. Back in a while. Wesley nods.

'Take your time,' he says. 'We've got all night.'

There are two bedrooms, and my guess is that Sean occupies the bigger one. The bed has been slept in, the duvet thrown back, one pillow on the floor. A sagging wardrobe is empty except for a discarded hoodie and pair of muddied boots, while a scruffy holdall in the opposite corner of the room yields a collection of dirty underwear and a balled T-shirt wrapped in a pair of jeans. I take out the jeans and give them a shake, hearing the clink of what I assume to be money in one of the pockets. The jeans are stained on both thighs – splatter patterns that I recognize from a number of film sets. The stains are dark and have stiffened the denim and I'm guessing they could be blood. The same is true when I take a proper look at the T-shirt. Blood, definitely.

It's at this point that I hear first a gasp, then a muffled scream from the front room. To my shame, I don't react. Like father, like son, I think. A couple more minutes, then I'll intervene.

I'm going through the jeans pockets now. Expecting coins, my fingers curl around something snub-nosed and cylindrical.

Moments later, I'm looking at a palm full of bullets. There are five in all, the brass cases glinting in the overhead light, and I empty out the holdall. No gun. I step next door. Wesley is still at work in the front room, but this story has suddenly acquired a whole new dimension. Sean McGaughy, last night, may well have been armed. So where is the gun?

Stop. Think. Work it out. The second bedroom is bare except for a mattress on the floor and a badly painted chest of drawers. The drawers are empty and there's nowhere else to serve as a hiding place. Back next door in Sean's bedroom, I'm about to abandon the search when I notice the single pillow still on the bed. Underneath, wrapped in a plastic bag, I find the gun.

I pick it up and carry it carefully next door to the front room. Wesley has Sean between his knees, the way you might pin a sheep you want to shear. This pose, Sean's mute helplessness, has stayed with me ever since. I can see no visible signs of damage, no blood, but the slightest pressure from Wesley draws gasps of pain.

'Well?' I dangle the gun in front of Sean. He closes his eyes, shakes his head. He doesn't want to know. This is disappointing, but the gun has definitely impressed Wesley.

'Fuck me,' he says to Sean. I think he means it as a compliment.

I go back to the bedroom and return with the jeans and the bloodied T-shirt, handling both with great care.

'And this stuff?' I ask Sean. 'Were you wearing it on Monday night? Is that my son's blood?'

His shake of the head is half-hearted and Wesley squeezes even harder.

'You want a cough? The full confession?' He's looking up at me, and then winks. 'It's possible but it'll cost.'

Sean is terrified now. I can see it in his eyes. I tell Wesley to back off and return to the bedroom. My first call goes to Tony Morse, who turns out to be in bed. I start to apologize, but he's already sensed that this might be urgent.

'What's happened?'

I tell him about Sean McGaughy, and the gun, and the blood stains.

'Where is he now? This Sean?'

'He's in safe hands.'

'Meaning?'

'Wesley's taking care of him. What do we do next?'

Tony takes a moment to think it through, then he's back on the phone.

'Call Dessie. Tell him you've found the T-shirt and tell him about the gun. You have ammunition, too?'

'Yes. Five bullets.'

'Excellent. Dessie will cream himself. Firearms on the premises? Expect the TFU at any moment.'

'TFU?'

'Tactical Firearms Unit. The full Ninja gig. Enjoy, my darling.'

'And the jeans?'

'Make sure you keep them. We're talking serious DNA here and exhibits sometimes go missing. Independent analysis. Never fails. Nighty-night.'

He rings off, and moments later I've raised Dessie. Same story.

'Christ,' he says. 'And this guy's *armed*?'

'I'm afraid he is, Mr Wren,' I'm back in the front room with Sean and Wesley. 'Don't tell me that's a surprise.'

The TFU, as promised, arrive within the half hour, four enormous policemen clad in body armour. They're all toting guns handed out from the boot of a black BMW, and a sergeant takes charge as I lead them into the flat. The sight of Wesley draws a nod of recognition.

'Helping out, Wes?'

'Always.'

'And this is?'

'Sean McGaughy,' I explain.

'And the gun is yours, son?'

'No comment.'

Sean is handcuffed and led away. I've taken the precaution of removing his jeans from the holdall and leaving them upstairs in the top flat. Then comes a stir of movement in the open doorway, and I see Dessie Wren's big face peering in. As an attached civilian, he has no real role here but he's driven down from Cowplain just the same.

'Have you got a moment?' He nods towards the street.

We cross the road and stand in the half-darkness on the Common, just beyond the throw of light from the street.

'Clever,' he says.

'Sean? Renting the flat?'

'You. Sussing him. When I told you I thought he'd gone to London, I meant it. If we could have put him in that flat, if we'd known he was there, there's no way we'd have left you so exposed.'

'That's sweet,' I say.

'You don't believe me?'

'Of course I don't. You lie and lie and lie, Mr Wren. I know a lot about truth and I know a lot about fiction, but in your trade, I'm guessing it gets harder and harder to spot the difference. That makes you very post-modern by the way.'

'Is that a compliment?'

'No. We were friends once, and I was getting to like that.'

'And now?'

'Now?' Upstairs in our flat the light is on in the front room and I can see the outline of Malo peering down at us. I give him a little wave before returning to Dessie, and beckoning him closer. 'Now is different, and you know why? Because I pulled a Crazy Ivan . . .' I kiss him lightly on the cheek. 'And it worked.'

THIRTY-FIVE

The next few days, to be frank, pass in a blur which I quickly diagnose as relief. Major Crimes despatches a young female detective who interviews both myself and Malo. Taalia, by now, has had to return to work and my son, to my alarm, strikes up an immediate rapport with the new cop in his life. He makes the most of his injuries, which isn't difficult given the yellowing bruises on his face, and when asked he maintains that he can remember nothing about the incident on the seafront. At this point, the DC produces a mug shot of Sean from the custody suite. Malo spares it a glance, and then another, and at length something sparks a slow nod of recognition.

'The teeth,' Malo says. 'I remember those teeth.'

This turns out to be lucky on our part because most custody sergeants insist on keeping your mouth shut when they take photos, but this one clearly slipped through. Once the interview is over, the DC bags the bloodstained T-shirt and swabs Malo's mouth to try and get a DNA match. If this works out at the forensic lab, she says, then Sean McGaughy may be looking at a lengthy prison sentence. GBH? Possession of a firearm and ammunition? The latter charge, of course, will raise all kinds of other issues, including Sean's belief that H had his dad killed, but yet another call to Tony Morse after the DC has gone helps put my mind to rest.

'They have to prove it,' Tony points out. 'And from where I'm sitting there's absolutely no chance. Chiefly because they have no evidence.'

Before we hang up, he wants to know about H. I confirm that no one has yet interviewed him, something that doesn't surprise him in the least.

'They're keeping their powder dry,' he says. 'They'll wait for the forensic accountants to have their say and see what kind of case they can make. I doubt very much it'll come to anything at all. H was always very tidy when it came to serious money.' He pauses. 'H's mobile phone? The one you gave to Sunil? The one with the message from Wesley about the money? You need to get rid of it.'

'*All* of it?' Stupid question, but I'm thinking of H's huge directory of contacts.

'Save the SIM card. Bin the rest.'

'And Sammy McGaughy?' I ask one last time.

'Forget it. Cold case? Dessie's wasting his time.'

From Dessie himself I hear nothing. I know he's probably looking for Sunil, because Mr Wu has been calling from the nursing agency, asking whether his newly recruited Sri Lankan has made contact at all, but I say no. In truth, I'm paying Tim's flat regular calls, always checking to make sure I'm not being followed. I've also bought Sunil a cheap cell phone from an Asian store, swapping it for H's mobile, and Sunil and I get used to spending a little time together.

From my point of view, this is more than welcome. I'm very happy to leave H in Malo's hands, now my son is getting his strength back, and after Sunil unearths a chessboard in one of Tim's cupboards, Sunil and I pass whole afternoons playing game after game, with one eye on the TV. Tim's subscription runs to Al Jazeera and CNN, as well as all the UK channels, and this is the first time Sunil has had the time and opportunity to discover just what a pickle the world has got itself into.

'Pickle?'

'Mess, Sunil. Covid? Falling out of love with China? Trump? The Israeli land grabs? Johnson? More Covid? I'd go back to Sri Lanka if I were you. Grow coconuts. Sit in the sun and ponder. Start a family.'

'I'd love to.' He's wiping me off the board. 'But it's not that easy.'

'No?'

'No. Being different here was never a problem. At home?' He shrugs and lifts my queen.

I'm normally good at reading sexuality, but this is the first time I've realized that Sunil is gay.

'You didn't guess?' He seems amused.

'Too busy, I'm afraid.' I'm looking at the dire situation of my king. 'Other things on my mind.'

By now it's the Easter weekend. I borrow a wheelchair from a local branch of the Red Cross and take H for longish walks along the seafront. On one of these walks, early on Good Friday, I find him shelter from the wind at the end of the pier before disappearing round the corner to the rails on the other side. The tide is sluicing round the barnacled feet of the pillars that support the pier, and I stare down at the grey water for a moment or two before dropping H's mobile into the waves. By the time I re-join him, hunched beneath a blanket in the wheelchair, he looks cold and slightly resentful, a coach-trip OAP the driver forgot to collect.

'Took your time,' he grunts, staring into nowhere.

In truth, H is getting stronger by the day, which is a relief, but I think the events of the last three weeks have taken him to a place he's finding deeply uncomfortable. H, like many self-made men, has a profound belief in his own immortality. Serious disease was something that happened to other people, while life's other calamities would simply avert their gaze and pass him by. After Covid came knocking at his door that's no longer true, and when he joins us in the evening to watch TV, he gets up and totters back to bed at the first mention of the virus. The implications of this aren't lost on either myself or my son, but it's Malo who puts it into words.

'Do you think he'll ever be the same, Mum?'

I give the question some thought, not least because it's something I've been asking myself, and in the end, I shake my head.

'No, I don't. I think all this has changed him, but you know what? That might not be a bad thing.'

Do I truly believe that? I don't know. H's appeal has always been the sheer voltage he brought to any conversation, any enterprise. I've seen him stare down impending disaster on occasion after occasion, never once losing his nerve, and the tightest of these corners was often occupied by our errant son. Malo, thankfully, has grown up at last, but Easter Sunday brings an abrupt reminder, for me at least, that we should never take anything for granted.

As part of the Easter celebrations, the local diocese is livestreaming a service from the comfort of the Bishop of Portsmouth's home. All three of us are sitting in front of the TV, but H has gone to sleep. The bishop is telling us that in these days of national lockdown, the resurrection message is more potent than ever. Light after death, he intones. Light after darkness. Hope from despair. He makes the sign of the cross in front of a wall washed with a rather subtle shade of grey, and there follows a choral performance of an Easter hymn by three brothers from the Portsmouth Cathedral choir. The hymn is 'Jesus Christ is Risen Today', which I happen to know well. It's a wonderful anthem to pain, loss, death and salvation, and I'm singing quietly along when I glance sideways at Malo. He, in turn, is gazing at his father, his cheeks wet with tears.

Three days later, we're all beginning to suffer from cabin fever, and I know that Sunil – still at Tim's flat – feels the same way.

H, unusually, seems desperate to get out of Pompey, even for a day, and I run the idea past Tony Morse.

'Does Major Crimes still have us under surveillance? If we do a runner for a couple of hours, will anyone notice?'

Tony thinks that's highly unlikely. H is still – technically – in quarantine, and it might be wise to stay in the city until the DNA results arrive for Sean's T-shirt, but Tony sees no problem with us taking a brief spin in the countryside.

'Anywhere nice?' he asks.

'Bosham.'

'Ah.' Tony's laughing. 'Give my best to my first wife. She's married a very rich chap there. Worth a fortune. Happy as Larry.'

'The new husband?'

'My ex-wife.'

I put the phone down and break the news to H. The realization that I've spoken to Dennis Mortimer, and that he's invited me to lunch, puts a broad smile on his face.

'Den?' he says. 'Are you kidding?'

I phone the Bosham number and broach the idea. All Dennis needs is the assurance that neither H nor I are infectious. Not for his benefit, he says, but for his missus. Sunil, I know, has hung on to half a dozen test kits and I pick them up that same afternoon. By nightfall, both swabs are in the post, en route to the labs in Southampton. The service is priority turnaround and within twenty-four hours, both of us are in the clear.

I phone Dennis again with the news and promise to bring the lab certifications that have arrived on my phone.

'Tomorrow, then,' he says, giving me an address. 'Lovely pad, bang on the water. Big fat flag on top of the pole. The missus is offering sea bass or steak and ale pie. Your call.'

I put the choice to H. These last few days, his appetite has well and truly returned.

'Steak and ale,' he growls. 'With roast potatoes.'

I've never been to Bosham, but the moment we get to the end of the road that leads down through a straggle of bungalows, I recognize the harbour. This much-photographed stretch of water laps against a crescent of pebble beach, strewn with seaweed and driftwood. Houses of uncertain age, many of them in cobble and flint, look directly on to an amazing view. The place feels intimate, as well as beautiful. We're only fifteen miles from the sprawl of Pompey but it's like a different world. Even H, sitting beside me, is impressed.

'Trust Den,' he mutters.

Finding chez Mortimer is easy. The road bends round to the right, running beside the row of houses, and there's only one property with a flagpole flying the St George's cross in the garden. I leave H in the car and push through the garden gate. A face in the window sees me coming and the door opens before I get there.

'Enora?' This must be Den's wife. Her name is Cathy. She's my age, maybe a year or two younger. She has a big, open face and the beginnings of a decent tan. She wants to see the lab certificates and she's still peering at my mobile phone when Den appears. No one's shaken my hand for weeks, and it's nice to have physical contact with a stranger again.

Den has to be at least a decade older than his wife, and I'm still trying to place the ready smile in my memories of long-ago Antibes when he spots H in the car. Den is wearing what I imagine must be *de rigueur* in these parts: salmon-pink chinos, and a nice shirt with a light blue cashmere sweater draped around his shoulders. Also, a battered pair of deck shoes, no socks. He's a big man, tall, thinning sandy hair, not an ounce of fat, and he lopes down the path to help H out of the car. For a long moment, the two of them embrace in the sunshine, and when H comes limping slowly up the brick path, he looks genuinely moved. Back from the dead, I think. Den's phrase, not mine.

We eat in a glorious room at the rear of the property. This is, in essence, a cottage and was probably built for fishermen. None of the rooms are big but this one has been artfully extended and has ample space for a table in front of the window. The view is framed by balls of coloured glass suspended in cradles of tarry rope, a lovely idea, and while Den serves drinks, and Cathy busies in the kitchen, I gaze out at the glistening mud flats.

In Brittany, we have a bird you often see on the foreshore. It's a speckled brown and white, nothing remarkable, and it spends most of its life hunting for tiny specks of something to eat. We call them *tournepierres*, or turnstones, and out of this window I can see dozens of them pecking busily away among the tangle of debris washed up by the tide. As a kid, I always admired their persistence, which seemed to me to be wildly optimistic, and in this setting – especially when you add a nearby raft of shelducks – they perfectly complement the view.

Cathy serves the steak and ale pie, no hors d'oeuvres. By now, H and Den have done a thorough job on the last twenty years of their respective careers, and I sense that nothing much has changed since we all so briefly met that evening down in Antibes. H has cashed in his winnings from the Pompey cocaine trade and retired to the comforts of Flixcombe Manor. Den has made a fortune from developing out-of-town commercial sites and is looking, he says, for new opportunities in Spain. The spanking-new *Agincourt* is ready for her maiden voyage, and Den says he can't fucking wait. There are worse places to weather lockdown than this glorious cottage but him and his missus, they both agree, are getting on each other's nerves, and he's gagging to put to sea.

My favourite stage plays always feature a perfect entrance cue, and this is mine.

'Anywhere particular in mind?' I ask.

'Marbella. Hand on heart, it's more business than pleasure. These days you can't move for fucking Russians down there but if you can put up with the bling, they're worth getting to know. Most of them are so minted they don't know what to buy next.'

'And that's where you come in?'

'For fucking sure. Fancy it, H? Spot of proper sunshine? Seafood to die for?' he shoots me a look. 'Margaritas?'

H is grinning. He has a smear of gravy around the corner of his mouth. I want to lean across and give it a wipe but I know he'd never forgive me. Instead, I try to discreetly semaphore the problem, but he hasn't a clue what I'm trying to get at.

'You could come, too.' Den is looking at me. 'Old times, yeah?'

I smile and do my best to act disappointed. Alas, I tell him, I still have a career. I explain briefly about Paris, and *Dimanche*, and Commissaire Danielle Colbert. This sparks real interest from Cathy, who wants to know more, but there's something else I need to raise while we're all getting on so well.

'There's a young guy called Sunil,' I say. 'He was one of the nurses who saved H's life.'

'That's right, Den.' H stabs a last cube of steak and pops it into his mouth. 'Cracking kid. You'd love him, Den. In fact, you'd love them all. Spoiled to death, I was. Or fucking nearly.'

This makes Den laugh, but he's still looking at me. I've met people like this before. One of the reasons he's so rich is that he's always ahead of the game.

'So how can I help?' he asks softly.

'Sunil has visa issues. It's complicated, but that's what it boils down to.'

'He's an illegal?'

'He's a fucking nurse, Den, and he saved my life.' This from H. 'That's all you need to know.'

'And so?' Den's eyes have never left my face.

'I thought you might take him to Marbella,' I say brightly. 'When you go.'

Cathy, I can sense at once, isn't happy. She catches her husband's eye and gives him a little shake of the head, but Den ignores her.

'That's more than possible.' He reaches for his glass of Rioja. 'We won't be going until they say we can, but if he can wait that long . . .' He shrugs. *'No problema.'*

THIRTY-SIX

This news gladdens me more than I can say. Sunil has been on my conscience from the moment I confronted Dessie about his role in our flat, and now – provided he keeps his head down at Tim's – I can get him safely out of the country.

It's early evening before I'm sober enough to drive back to Pompey. The afternoon at Den's place has been an orgy of reminiscence, story after story, and I know it's done H immeasurable good. He needs to rebuild his bridges to those buccaneering glory days, to reframe the legend he still believes in, and Den – with amazing deftness – has made that happen. H, he told me quietly before we left, always had that special touch. In any trade, any profession, he'd have hit the motherlode. That it happened to be cocaine was incidental. And they all had a lot of fun.

Now, H wants to know more about Sunil. I've never told him about the way he ratted us all out, and I'm not about to start now. H has never had much time for paperwork, and even less for any arm of the government, but his admiration for people who get off their arse and make a new life for themselves is unfeigned. As is Sunil's decision to bail out of the UK.

'Fucking country's on the skids,' he grunts. 'Who'd blame him?'

Back in the flat, I decide to wait until the morning to pass on the good news to Sunil. I spend a very happy couple of hours in front of the TV, watching a National Theatre production of *Jane Eyre*. Taalia is staying the night once again, but her presence cheers Malo up no end and I've decided to stay in denial about poor Clemmie. Thanks to a call from Tony Morse, moments after the end of *Jane Eyre*, I now know that Sean is banged up in the remand wing at Winchester prison, and that knowledge makes for a perfect night's sleep.

Next morning, I get up early to beat the queue in the Waitrose car park and buy a small mountain of food to keep Sunil going over the next month or two. Weighed down with two bags of shopping, I make the usual call from my pay-as-you-go phone before I climb the stairs to Tim's flat. Sunil takes an age to answer, and when he finally picks up I know at once that something bad has happened.

'What's the matter?'

'Come,' he says. 'Please.'

Sunil has the key to the flat, and has to let me in. He stands uncertainly in the open doorway. He's wearing a pair of scarlet boxer shorts and not much else. His bare feet are curling on Tim's sanded floorboards, and his face is shiny with sweat.

'You're ill, Sunil?'

'Sick.' He nods.

'Since when?'

'Yesterday.' He begins to cough. 'Maybe the day before.'

'Why didn't you phone?'

He shrugs and turns away. He doesn't know.

I follow him into the flat, bolting the door top and bottom, and leaving the shopping on the floor to sort out later. Sunil has already gone back to bed. He's dropped the blinds against the brightness of the morning sun and he's lying on his side, his face to the wall, his hand to his mouth as he tries to stifle another bout of coughing. I've seen H like this, exactly the same symptoms, the day I phoned Tony Morse for help.

I fetch a wet flannel from the bathroom, circle the bed, and settle beside him. His flesh is hot to my touch. I bathe his face and tell him that everything's going to be fine.

'PPE,' he mutters. His eyes are closed, and as I watch, his whole body begins to tremble. When I ask him what hurts, and where, his hand strays across his body. Legs. Belly. Head. And especially his chest. 'It's like sunburn,' he says. 'Inside.'

Like sunburn. Inside.

I shudder. H was never this graphic but I know exactly what Sunil means. As a trained nurse, he knows. Covid has stolen into yet another corner of our lives.

I make Sunil as comfortable as I can. I leave him with iced water at his bedside and open the window to get a little air into the room. Back at our flat, we have two complete sets of PPE left over and I manage to get them both into Malo's rucksack. There's no sign of Taalia, but when she finally emerges from Malo's bedroom, I swear her to silence and then break the news about Sunil. She wants to help, and she promises to get more PPE and maybe drugs from the agency. Also, if possible, more priority testing kits. When I press her about the drugs, it turns out that she's talking about ibuprofen. We still have lots of these and I add two packets to the rucksack. As an afterthought, she returns to Malo's bedroom and emerges with a thermometer. Anything above 105 degrees, she says, and I must call for an ambulance.

H joins us in the front room, the first time he's made it without help. When he asks what's going on, I tell him about Sunil. Somehow or other, he's picked up the virus. In less than forty-eight hours, he's become a very sick man.

'The boy needs help,' he says at once. 'Get the agency in. I'll pay.'

I shake my head. For the time being, I'll do what I can. If he gets any worse, I'll definitely have to seek proper advice. I bend for the rucksack, and half-turn to make for the door. H is staring at me.

'How long?' he says. 'How long will you be gone?'

I shrug. I tell him I don't know. Sunil is heavily infected. Quarantine lasts two weeks. Who knows? It might even be longer.

H nods. Then turns on his heel and totters back towards his bedroom.

'You need food?' This from Taalia.

'No.' I shoot her a wry smile. 'That's the least of my problems.'

I shoulder the rucksack and say my goodbyes. I feel, in this moment, like some soldier off to fight a foreign war. Then H is back. He thrusts a Waitrose bag at me. Inside is his tablet, plus a charger.

'Take it,' he says. 'You'll go mad otherwise.'

Back at Tim's, Sunil appears to be asleep, his cheek on the pillow, his beautiful hands folded between his thighs. I stand by the bed for a while, looking down at him, knowing that I need to get into the PPE, then his body convulses with a fresh spasm of coughs, and he's left gasping for air. H, I think again, just hours before the oxygen arrived.

I retire next door and sort out the PPE. Gowned and masked, I'm soon back beside Sunil, pulling on a pair of rubber gloves. This is almost second nature now, my default setting, but what's different is the total absence of everything else I came to take for granted when H was so ill. No bedside equipment to tell me about his saturation levels. No drip for the antibiotics. And no oxygen to feed the mask on his face. Instead, it's just him and me against the virus. I gaze down at his long body curled on the damp sheet. He's found a perch on the cliff face that is the UK, and he's doing his very best to hang on. God knows what happens if his grip begins to weaken.

Around midday, after a fitful sleep broken by fits of coughing, he opens one eye. The sight of me beside the bed seems to come as a relief.

'You're staying?' he whispers.

'For as long as you need me.'

He nods, swallows, winces. I sense he's got something to tell me, and it turns out I'm right.

'HIV,' he mutters. Talking clearly hurts.

'Yes?'

'Me,' he points to his chest.

'You've got it? HIV?'

He nods, swallows again, closes his eyes. Another cough is coming, and I lean back in anticipation. What little I know about HIV and AIDS tells me that it does no favours to the immune system. Having it leaves you wide open to any passing infection – the worst possible news if an intruder as clever as Covid happens by.

While Sunil tries to sleep again, I retreat next door. I take off my visor and face mask and check out HIV on H's tablet. I'm right. If you're positive for either HIV or full-blown AIDS, you're strongly recommended to take special precautions under lockdown. I sit back, wondering if Dessie knew anything of this when he made friends with Sunil and shepherded him towards the nursing agency. In the first place, it would have been grossly irresponsible for any patient Sunil happened to be nursing. And in the second, it might well turn out to be a death sentence for Sunil himself.

I shake my head, slumped in Tim's armchair, and for the first time I become aware of the last chess game Sunil and I played. We never quite got to the end, and Sunil must have saved the pieces for later, because I can see the board stored carefully under the occasional table that is laden with books and magazines. I was black. I lost both rooks very early on, an act of carelessness on my part, and once Sunil unleashed his queen, I was in deep trouble.

Now, staring at the board, I can't help thinking about the jigsaw we found when we first arrived at Tony Morse's flat. That, too, had been incomplete, just a teasing glimpse of Nelson's finest moment. No one touched it, no one added to it, and until the cleaning company arrived it served as a kind of *relique*, an amulet against the worst of times. The same applies here, I think. Part of me is tempted to tidy up the chess pieces and return them to their wooden box but, listening to Sunil coughing next door, I realize how important it is to believe in a future for both of us. Leaving the pieces on the board is an act of faith. One day, we'll get to finish that game. And, in all probability, Sunil will win.

Time ticks slowly by. It starts to rain, and then stops again. The sound of a car engine in the street below is a major event. A phone rings somewhere downstairs, ignored. Seagulls dance above the rooftops as the wind gets up again. I have only a sentimental attachment to religion – a decent hymn, the Berlioz Requiem – but by dusk I'm praying for the virus to leave Sunil in peace. I'm back in my mask and visor now, stationed at his bedside, and I know he's seriously ill. Mid-evening, he tries to get up, helplessly clawing at the air, then collapses back again. When I ask him what he wants, what he needs, he gestures wordlessly at his groin. He needs the toilet. Badly.

Somehow, between us, we make it to the loo. I half-close the door, ensuring he's OK, then leave him in peace. During the afternoon, I've found the airing cupboard where Tim keeps his bed linen and now I take the opportunity to strip the bed and fit a fresh sheet. The old one, I ball up and stow in a pair of Waitrose bags, one secured around the other. Think Covid, I keep telling myself. Don't let the virus have everything its own way.

Back down the corridor, Sunil has finished. Given the stench from the loo, he has acute bowel problems on top of everything else, and I help him back to bed, aware of how weak he is, and how short of breath. H, again. Exactly the same story. When I tell him I must take his temperature, he nods helplessly, a gesture of mute compliance.

Taalia has given me a hand-held, non-contact model that looks a little like a gun. I take a reading and shield it from Sunil. His temperature is 104 degrees, which, to me, sounds impossibly high, but a couple of minutes on H's tablet tells me that this degree of fever is still bearable. Just. It's at this point that I hear the lightest knock on the front door. I freeze for a moment, thinking at once of Dessie, but then – out in the corridor – I hear a woman's voice.

It's Taalia. She's brought two boxes of Kleenex and more painkillers. When she asks about Sunil, I tell her he's suffering.

'He has a fever of a hundred and four degrees,' I say.

'That's high.' She looks horrified. 'And so quick, too.'

I nod, resisting the temptation to tell her about the HIV. Instead, I ask her what I should be doing.

'Keep taking his temperature. If it goes any higher, phone for an ambulance. Above a hundred and six degrees he might get convulsions.'

I nod and thank her. I think she wants to come in and take a look for herself, but the expression on her face has already told me everything I need to know. I'm hearing Berndt again, and his theories about courage. Just now, mine has pretty much run out. I've done my best, but the virus has beaten me.

I say goodbye to Taalia, gently close the bedroom door and stand by the window, Sunil's pay-as-you-go phone to my ear. When the 999 operator answers, I give my name and address and ask for the ambulance service.

THIRTY-SEVEN

The paramedics are tramping up the stairs within the hour, a man and a woman. The woman is young, the man much older. Both are wearing full PPE. I show them through to the bedroom. Sunil is hallucinating now, his eyes wild, fighting God knows how many demons. According to the ID taped to his chest, the older of the two paramedics answers to Frank. He studies Sunil for a moment, checks his pulse with his gloved hand, and then takes me back to the sitting room.

'I need his name and details,' he says.

I've been dreading this question, but I know it's inevitable. Since making the call, I've managed to find Sunil's passport. Frank looks at the burgundy cover, and the lines of script across the top. Inside, the laminated page at the front offers the key details. Sunil Salam. Father's name Ishad Mohmood. Born 17/11/1990. Frank makes a note, before asking if there's anything else I should be telling him.

'Yes,' I say carefully. 'He's got HIV.'

'And you're next of kin?'

'Just a friend.'

He nods, curious now, and makes another note when I give him my name and a contact number.

The other paramedic emerges from the bedroom. Despite the visor, I can see the anxiety on her face.

'Hundred and six degrees,' she mutters. 'We need to get a move on.'

Between them, they manage to get Sunil down the stairs. For decency's sake, if no other reason, I've managed to get a blanket round him, but he hasn't even got the strength to keep it on. Twice, on the way down to the street, I retrieve it, and wrap it round him once again, but the third time it falls off, Frank tells me to leave it.

'No one's watching,' he says, 'at this time of night.'

The ambulance is waiting at the kerbside. I put my arm round Sunil as they ready the stretcher, and do my best to comfort him, but I can tell he hasn't a clue what's happening. I put my lips to his ear and tell him he's going to hospital where they'll take proper care of him, and he nods as if he understands but I know he doesn't. Then, with a sudden lurch, he starts to vomit and all three of us pause, just the way you might freeze-frame a moment in a movie, staring at the pool of yellowish gunk at our feet.

'I'll take care of it,' I say. 'You'll need this.'

The female paramedic is helping Sunil on to the stretcher. Frank turns round.

'What is it?'

'His passport.'

Moments later, the ambulance has gone. I watch the tail lights disappearing down the road. There's no traffic around but the blue lights are flashing, reflections jumping from shop window to shop window along the road. I shake my head, knowing in my heart of hearts that I'll never see Sunil again, then I slowly climb the stairs back to Tim's flat. He keeps the bleach under his kitchen sink. Half an hour later, after two buckets of water, I'm still chasing the last of the vomit into the nearby drain.

I get the call from the hospital at just gone four in the morning. It comes from a clerical assistant in A&E. She wants to know my exact relationship to Sunil Salam.

'I'm a friend,' I say again.

'Are you aware that Mr Salam is flagged?'

'What does that mean?'

'It means that we're obliged to notify the police that he's on the premises.'

'I see.' To be honest, this comes as no surprise. 'So, how is he?'

'That's a question I'm afraid I can't answer, Ms Andressen. You might phone back later.' She gives me a number, which I scribble down. When I ask her where the number will take me, she says ICU.

Intensive Care Unit. This is where this story of ours began, I think. Fat Dave coughing his life away on Cynthia's iPad. That grey monochrome morning a week and a half later when a handful of us gathered at the Crem. Dessie Wren's big face at my car window. The little scar above his right eyebrow.

Dessie himself phones at half past eight. Still groggy from a night on Tim's floor, I ask where he is.

'Outside,' he says. 'You didn't recognize the car?'

I go to the window. He's standing beside the VW, the phone to his ear, nursing a tall paper cup with the word 'Costa' on the side.

'You can't come up,' I say at once. 'It's against the law.'

'I wasn't planning to. I just thought you might want to know about your friend.'

'Sunil?'

'Of course.'

'You've come to tell me he's dead?'

'Not quite. I've come to tell you he's very poorly, but then I'm guessing you know that already. I've also come to tell you I hadn't a clue about the HIV.'

'This is for the record? When they hold the inquest?'

'This is for your benefit. I know I'm a bad man in your books, and I know I've pulled some strokes in my time, but even I wouldn't go that far. There was no indication on the Home Office file that he was HIV positive. None. That's a secret he kept to himself.'

'And now, it'll probably kill him.'

'Yes.'

'No guilt? On your part?'

'None, I'm afraid. I'm just sorry it didn't work out.'

'Us, you mean? Staying friends?'

'H. We wanted to bang him up.' He raises the cup. 'Happy days, eh?'

I spend the rest of the morning steeling myself to get in touch with the hospital. When I finally make the call, I find myself talking to a woman who happens to be standing two beds away from Sunil. She checks who I am, and tallies the name against his details, and then tells me he's very sick indeed.

'He's on a ventilator?'

'He is.'

'And do you think he'll make it?'

'It's not my place to tell you, Ms Andressen. Best to phone back this evening. We've just put him on high-dosage antibiotics. This is the nuclear option. Can you hang on a moment?'

I nod, say nothing, bite my lower lip. Then I'm talking to another woman, younger voice. She says she's the respiratory registrar. In view of the HIV, she says, Sunil's prognosis is very poor indeed. Just now, his sats are down in the high eighties, despite hours of ventilation, and there are signs of hyper-stimulation in what's left of his immune system.

'It's doing its best,' she says. 'But don't hold your breath.'

I've been reading about this reaction, more and more common among older patients.

'You mean his kidneys?' I ask.

'I'm afraid so. And his liver. His lungs are shot to pieces already, and we're starting to worry about his brain.'

I nod. Kidneys, liver, lungs, brain. What else could possibly go wrong?

'So, you'll phone me?' I ask plaintively. 'Once he's gone?'

It happens to be Saturday. I spend the weekend waiting for the call, which never comes. I start a couple of Tim's paperbacks, but fail to make any sense of the opening pages. I try listening to the radio, but everyone's talking about Covid. I toy with having one of those soul-to-soul phone conversations with Tim, but I wouldn't inflict this darkness on anyone. And so, in the end, I sit by the window with the blinds down, listening to albums from Tim's collection of Delta blues. Muddy Waters. John Lee Hooker.

Willie Brown. Much of this stuff is beyond plaintive and speaks to me in a language I can understand only too well. This is music about loss, about grieving, and about somehow making it through. Three times, my phone rings and every call comes from Malo. H may have borrowed his phone, I've no idea, but talking to anyone else on the planet is something I simply can't manage. I haven't felt this way since Pavel died, and his was also a death just waiting to happen.

It's Monday morning before I finally get the call from the hospital. It's the registrar again on the ICU, that same voice, and listening to her I can't help wondering how many of these calls she has to make. Sunil, she says, put up a real fight. An induced coma meant that he was unconscious but towards the very end, barely an hour ago, he seemed to be struggling to break surface. Every vital sign, every trace on the bedside rack of monitors, was terminal, no chance of making it through, yet there he was, making a final effort.

'He was in pain?'

'I'm afraid so. We do our best but this virus is truly wicked, especially for someone as compromised as young Sunil. We still have his passport, Ms Andressen, and one or two other odds and ends. The police appear to have an interest in Sunil, so you might want to get in touch with them. Do you have a pen there, by any chance?'

I don't need one. Mr Dessie Wren, I think. And I'm right.

He appears again, late afternoon the following day. This time he comes to the door.

'You've had the cleaners in,' he says. 'Very wise.'

It's true. I contacted the nursing agency for their number after I got the news that Sunil had died, and they turned up first thing this morning. They've spent half a day cleaning around me and now Tim's flat smells like a hospital.

Dessie has a plastic bag in his hand, which appears to be the property of the Queen Alexandra Hospital.

'One or two bits and pieces,' he says. 'I know you're not next of kin, but you're the closest we can find.'

'His family?' I query. 'His mum and dad?'

'They're in Colombo. There are no flights. I'm afraid it's down to you.'

'The funeral?'

'Yes. We've been in touch with his family. It turns out the boy was a Christian. I'd make the call sooner rather than later. The people at the Crem are losing their sense of humour.' He gives me the bag. 'Let me know when you've got a slot.'

'Why?'

'Because I'd like to be there.'

With a nod, and the ghost of a smile, he's gone.

I bolt the door and retreat to the living room. I'm pretty much certain that I have immunity from the virus thanks to the weekend it passed so briefly through me, but just in case I've despatched a swab to the Southampton lab. Now, I empty the contents of the QA bag on to my lap. It doesn't amount to much. Sunil's passport. His watch. The simple silver ring he wore on one thumb. And the little twist of dried ox-hide leather that belonged on his wrist. By now, thanks to his passport, I know exactly how old he was when he died. Thirty years of age. And nothing left but this tiny handful of items.

That night, I watch the TV news. I've decided to serve out the term of my quarantine here in Tim's flat, largely for the sake of my own sanity, and I stare numbly at the screen, trying to make sense of today's stats. In a single twenty-four-hour period, 1,401 people have died. And one of them was Sunil Salam. His passing, so far, has been unremarked but between us, I'm determined to give him at least a modest send-off.

Much later, the news over, I phone Malo's number. As I suspected, it's H who picks up. He starts to demand why I haven't been in touch, why I've ignored all his calls. He sounds plaintive and angry at the same time, something I can't stomach just now, and when I tell him that Sunil has gone, his tone abruptly changes.

'Gone?' he says. 'As in dead?'

'Yes.'

'Fuck.'

'Yes.'

'But he was with us just now. How can that happen?'

I'm tempted to laugh, but I don't. Instead, I tell him that it was complicated, and extremely painful, and that a peaceful death and the word Covid don't belong in the same sentence.

'Bad?'

'Very bad.'

'Fat Dave bad?'

'Probably worse. I wasn't there, but the medics have learned how to be frank at last. He suffered, H. That's all I know.'

'You sound gutted.'

'I am.'

'So, when are you back?'

'A week on Saturday. I'll push for the funeral during the week after. That's all you really need to know, H. Take care, the pair of you.'

To his lasting credit, H makes no objection. Instead he says he's sorry about Sunil, and promises to take care of our own boy.

'Taalia?' I enquire. 'She's still there?'

'Off and on, yeah.' He chuckles. 'And she makes a great fucking curry.'

THIRTY-EIGHT

I spend the next week and a half on Tim's PC. I've mustered the courage to phone him and explained pretty much most of what happened. He's still in Bere Regis, still in love with his mum's veggie patch, and shows no sign of wanting to return to Pompey.

'Treat the place as your own,' he says. 'I'm sorry about your friend.'

So am I. I spend far too long thinking about where I went wrong with Sunil, whether I was reckless to call him out in front of Dessie Wren, and whether he might still have been with us had I not tried to play God. But then I talk to Dennis Mortimer, telling him that Sunil is no longer with us.

'No Marbella?'

'No Marbella,' I confirm.

'Did he ever get the news? Did you ever tell him?'

'No. The morning I dropped by to tell him you'd said yes, he was already ill. I'm afraid there was no way he'd ever make it, and I think he knew that.'

'Best left unsaid?'

'Definitely. But thanks all the same. H thinks the world of you, by the way. Had he ever gone legit, you'd have been his role model.'

Den takes this as a compliment, which it most definitely is, and tells me to take care. The new *Agincourt*, he says, is a big, big ship and I'm welcome aboard any time.

We part, I think, as friends, which – just now – is important.

I have a week and a half to myself, no interruptions, no prospect of entanglements with the darker elements in the city, and I'm determined to use the time to get on better terms with myself. Pavel once told me that writing is the shortest cut to proper convalescence, and because I feel so detached, so adrift, I decide to give it a try.

The trigger, oddly enough, is the lingering smell the deep-cleaning crew have left behind. I recognize this smell from my days in the hands of a neurosurgeon in the weeks that followed the diagnosis of my brain tumour. After the operation, I spent long days in a hospital bed wondering how much life I had left, and that experience has stayed with me ever since. We're all much closer to the Reaper than we might imagine. As the virus has been pleased to confirm.

And so I take advantage of Tim's generosity, and sit at his PC for day after day, trying to recall all those hospital encounters, and then shape what happened afterwards into some kind of narrative. At first it feels odd and hopelessly self-indulgent to devote so much time and paper to my own story, but then I lift another page from the Pavel Survival Guide, and pretend that I'm someone else, someone I've never met before, an outsider charged with getting the right words in the right order. I even, for an entire chapter, write in the third person rather than the first, but then I go back, and change all the pronouns, and suddenly the 'me' on the page is really me.

This, you might agree, is a bit of a revelation but from that point onwards, the writing becomes a surprise and a delight.

When I started, I was writing six hours a day. A week into the book, I'm up at six and in bed by midnight, with brief breaks to secure a slot at the Crem for Sunil. Everything I write is true, has really happened, but this is the first time it makes any kind of organized sense. The story closes with me and my beautiful son on a stretch of springy turf on the Isle of Wight. The sky is full of scudding clouds, and we can see all the way to the Needles. I think it only fair to warn Malo that he might not have a mum for much longer, and what he says in return closes the book. It made me cry then, as it makes me cry now.

The following day, I stow my few belongings in Malo's ruck-sack, and buy a Jiffy bag from the Post Office down the road. The printed-out manuscript, all 330 pages, fits very nicely, and I scrawl the name of the book across the bag in heavy black Pentel. *Curtain Call* will soon be with my lovely friend Evelyn, who was – until her recent retirement – the doyenne of London editors, and I shall await her verdict with interest.

Back at the flat overlooking the Common, I find Malo in rude health. H has had a bit of a relapse, nothing serious, and Malo insists he's got it covered. Dad's trying to run before he can walk, he says. Lovely phrase, totally in keeping with the baby alarm, and if the joke's on H, he doesn't appear to mind.

'You're OK?' He's looking me up and down.

I make the mistake of producing my Jiffy bag and starting to explain about having to put pen to paper, but I realize very quickly that he doesn't really follow what I'm trying to say.

'This is some kind of movie idea?'

'Could be, H. You're in it. Expect the call any day now.'

'Me?' he says blankly.

I change the subject. Sunil's funeral is scheduled for tomorrow afternoon. I'd appreciate us all going to the Crem, and I'm about to pay a call on Tony Morse to check whether we can drive right on afterwards, and go back to Flixcombe without incurring the wrath of Major Crimes.

'You mean leave here? Pompey?'

'Yes.'

H nods, says nothing.

* * *

Tony Morse is expecting me. It's pouring with rain and I'm not up for conducting a conversation by phone from his garden, but Corinne has other plans. She knows that my Covid test has come back negative from the Southampton lab, and she invites me in. Tony is in the downstairs room he evidently uses as a study. It's beautifully proportioned, original plaster work around the ceiling, and the tall window offers a view of his sodden lawn.

'I'm thinking a peacock or two.' He's sitting behind a handsome desk, inlaid with a burgundy leather top. 'Apparently they're more biddable in pairs.'

Biddable. Very Tony Morse.

I settle in the chair in front of his desk. A thin cheroot has been abandoned in a Chinese-looking ashtray, and Tony has a tiny bell at his elbow. Is the comely Corinne awaiting a tinkle or two? Might she arrive with coffee?

She does. Tony finishes making notes on a legal pad, and then enquires about H. I tell him he's getting slowly better, good days, bad days, and might benefit from a return to Flixcombe.

'Would that upset anyone?'

'Dessie, definitely. He thinks you've got the wrong idea about him.'

'I meant anyone who might want to lock us up.'

'Then the answer's no, my darling. Major Crimes have to submit everything to the CPS before they start thinking court, and I have it on the best authority that they're struggling to make a case.' The CPS is the Crown Prosecution Service.

'This is *Plover*? Sammy McGaughy?'

'Christ, no. They got a match on Malo's DNA. That T-shirt of Sean's was drenched in it. Game, set, and match. Didn't anyone tell you?'

'No.'

'Not Dessie?'

'No.'

'Well, let me make your day. Sean will be going down for a long time. That leaves *Avocet*, my darling. Which boils down to H. The bid is to nail him on POCA.'

'*Quoi?*'

'The Proceeds of Crime Act. These days they follow the money. Normally it works a treat, but H has been commendably careful. Forensic accountants charge north of a hundred quid an hour. H is costing them the earth. Back in the day, coppers used to have a sense of humour. Alas, no longer. No, barring some catastrophe, H is home safe.'

'So we can go? Up sticks? Leave?' The prospect is close to overwhelming. No more furtive expeditions. No more afternoons with yesterday's copy of the *Portsmouth News*. No more rubbish television. No more nights on that lumpy sofa, waiting for noises at the door.

'That flat of yours,' I say. 'It was a lifesaver. Literally. If I was allowed to kiss you, I would. Thank you is too small a phrase.'

'A pleasure, my darling. The place is a dump. I can only apologize.'

I nod, saying nothing. Then I ask him who lived there.

'Who do you think?'

I frown. I've had plenty of time to put the clues together: the unfinished jigsaw, the books, the neglect, the damp chill of the place, a life stripped down to the bare necessities.

'A man, definitely,' I say. 'Living alone?'

'Yes.'

'A solitary? A recluse?'

'Yes.'

'Once married? Now widowed?'

'Divorced.'

'And a relative of yours?'

'My father.'

'Your *father*?' I'm staring at him. Me and plots were never best friends, but this is truly a surprise. 'And he'd been there a while?'

'Nearly seven years. He never really got over my mum pushing off. He'd been in the Navy. He'd been used to command. I don't think anyone had ever said "no" to him in his life and it came as a bit of a shock. Did I blame her? Not in the slightest. He was a difficult man, deeply selfish. I tried my best to winkle him out of there, but he'd fallen in love with the view, so in the end I gave up.'

I nod. I can understand an affection for the view, especially to someone who'd spent his life at sea, but I'm struggling to understand why he'd live in such squalor.

'Did you get round there at all? Help him brighten the place up?'

'I tried, but it was hopeless. He was very territorial. He didn't want me anywhere near him. Arrive with a paintbrush and he'd show me the door. That last year of his life, I barely saw anything of him.'

'He had a phone?'

'A landline. When he didn't pay the bill, they cut him off. I bought him a mobile one Christmas and I never saw it again. You were right first time, my darling. Recluse will do nicely.'

I hold his gaze for a long moment until it starts getting awkward.

'Hurtful?' I ask.

'Very.'

I get up and circle the desk before giving him a hug. He's on his feet now, a little unsteady, and I can't help thinking of H. And Sunil.

'Take care,' I say. 'This bloody virus takes no prisoners.'

We say goodbye to Sunil the following day. The nursing agency have let Taalia have the time off to attend, and half a dozen of us gather at the crematorium in the bright afternoon sunshine to await the arrival of his coffin. I've been more than happy to pay for the funeral. There's no cortege because there's no one to fill the undertaker's limousines, but they've done a fine job with the flowers I ordered, and we wait for the coffin. H has acquired two roses from somewhere, and he slips one of them on to the coffin before the undertakers carry it into the smaller of the two chapels. A graceful gesture, I think, and totally unexpected.

The brief service is conducted by a local vicar I've spoken to on the phone. None of us really know anything about Sunil, and my attempts to contact his family in Colombo have come to nothing. Taalia makes a graceful speech about what a lovely colleague she's lost, and then reads a poem in Tamil that none of us understands. Back in her pew, she accepts a Kleenex from Malo and bows her head as the curtains close on Sunil's coffin.

Afterwards, outside in the sunshine, I recognize Dessie Wren as he gets out of his car and comes across to join us. This is where our story began, I think, at Fat Dave's funeral. Another scalp hanging from Covid's belt. Another farewell.

Dessie exchanges a nod with H, and then gestures me aside. Looking at him, I can't help remembering Tony's comment when we met yesterday. Is he really disappointed? Did he really expect anything to come from our brief liaison?

'The lad's ashes,' he says. 'Do you want to deal with them, or shall I?'

I imagine he means arranging for them to be sent to Sri Lanka. Once we've left the crematorium, the three of us will be returning to the Southsea flat to finally pack up and leave. After that, Pompey and I are through.

'I'm going back to London tonight,' I tell him. 'Do you mind taking care of it?'

'Not at all.' His eyes stray to the departing hearse. 'It's probably the least I owe him.'

I don't argue. Instead, I shepherd him a little further away from our little group. Malo is still comforting Taalia. H is in a world of his own.

'Just one question.' I'm looking at Dessie. 'Do you mind?' He shakes his head. 'Why did you really stop me giving all that money to Shanti?'

'Because it would probably have put you inside.'

'And H?'

'Him, too.'

'But wasn't that the whole point?'

'Of course.'

'And Wesley? Was he part of all that? Laying the trap for H?'

'Wesley is easily led.'

'What does that mean?'

Another shake of the head. He won't say. I glance across at H, who's checking his watch. Time to move on. I turn back to Dessie.

'So why were you so generous? To little me?'

Dessie gazes at me, that same smile, that same faint hint of regret.

'Hope springs eternal,' he says. 'Always did, always will.'

'And that boy of yours? Titch? Your so-called godson?'

'That's more complicated.' He smiles. 'You must have been talking to Tony Morse.'

'I was. And unlike you, Dessie, he never lies to me.'

'That's harsh.' He's smiling now. 'Next time, eh?'

H and I make for my Peugeot. H sits in the front beside me while Malo says goodbye to Taalia. She has a car of her own, a beaten-up old thing with scarlet beads dangling from the rear-view mirror, and they share a lingering kiss before Malo re-joins us, folding his long frame into the back seat. Will they ever see each other again? For Clemmie's sake, I hope not, but watching her face as we wave goodbye, I suspect the answer is yes.

At the exit to the crematorium, we find ourselves behind Dessie's VW. We're both signalling for the right turn that will take us back to Pompey, but H suddenly puts his hand on my arm.

'Left,' he says. 'We're going left.'

'Why?'

'Just do it.'

I give him a look. The other rose is on his lap, and he keeps touching the stalk as if to make sure it's still there.

The left turn takes us up the hill, away from the crematorium. H seems to know these roads well. One junction follows another. We go under a motorway, then suddenly we're out in the country, fields of still-green wheat on either side, a glimpse of a rabbit disappearing under a hedge. Then comes a bigger road, occasional traffic. We pass a village called Wickham, and I slow for a tractor towing a huge slurry tank. The car is suddenly ripe with the smell and I glance in the mirror as I overtake, but Malo has his eyes closed and appears to be asleep.

'Right in a hundred metres. You see the big tree there? The oak?'

I do. I indicate right. This is a much smaller road, dense woodland on either side. The road climbs and swoops. H is concentrating now, his eyes on the blur of trees on our left, and he asks me to slow down. Then, without warning, he points at what seems to be a lay-by.

'There,' he says. 'Just stop.'

I do his bidding, and we both get out.

'Malo?' I nod at the sleeping figure curled in the back.

'Leave him be. This won't take long.'

H has made it out of the car now, and he stands uncertainly in the sunshine, his head up, like an animal sniffing the wind. He has the rose in one hand, and he takes mine in the other.

'This way,' he says. 'It's not far.'

I know better than to ask questions. We start to walk. The sunshine has crusted the muddy wheel ruts in the lay-by, and there's a drift of abandoned drink cans and grease-stained take-out cartons in the undergrowth. H picks his way through the rubbish and finds a barely trodden path beyond. We're in single file now. H is in the lead, moving slowly, taking his time, looking left and right, as the road disappears behind us. I can hear bird-song in the branches, and when I look up I glimpse what might be a buzzard, a lingering silhouette against the brightness of the sun. At length, H stops.

'Look,' he says. It's a young deer, the colour of caramel. Motionless, it studies H's pointing finger for a second or two, and then bounds off. 'Good sign,' H grunts. 'Nice place.'

Nice place for what? H won't say. We're on the move again, every step taking us deeper into the wood, then H comes to a halt again, and this time he's looking down. We're standing in what might once have been a clearing, but year after year of growth has reclaimed this space.

'Yeah.' He nods. 'Just here.'

He makes a tiny space among the brambles and the layers of leaf mould with his shoe, and then gives me the rose and bends to tidy his work with his hands, scooping the loose soil to the sides of the circle, like a child on a beach. Looking down, I can see nothing significant, no clue that might be of the slightest interest to H, but he seems convinced. Satisfied with what he's done, he gets to his feet, and asks me to lay the rose in the very middle of the circle. My first attempt draws a brusque shake of his head.

'More to the right,' he says. 'Now up a bit. Yeah, just there.' He wipes the loose soil from his hands. 'Perfect.'

We stand in silence for a moment, gazing down at the rose. There's a question I have to ask, and we both know it.

'Sammy McGaughy?' I ask.

H nods and shoots me a look.

'Yeah,' he grunts. 'God rest his soul.'

Two acts of remembrance in one afternoon, I think. Very Pompey.

AFTERWARDS

It's early August before I have the chance to get together with Tim. My friend Evelyn has come up from East Devon and is staying with me for a while. Tim has taken the train from Pompey to audition for a part in a panto, which is itself an act of faith, and we've agreed to meet in my favourite Italian restaurant.

Tim is late, but it doesn't matter. One of the reasons for Evelyn's visit is the Jiffy bag I sent her back in April, and we've been discussing bits of my first novel ever since, first on the phone, and now face to face. To my enormous relicf, Evelyn thinks *Curtain Call* is a decent read. Even better, she's suggested one or two ways I might consider improving it.

The place that 'consider' occupies in this sentence is the very essence of Evelyn. In a distinguished career, she's helped countless household names to fame and fortune, yet never does she make any lordly assumptions about her own editorial judgements. I'm here to offer a nudge or two on the tiller, she says. The recasting of a clumsy line of dialogue, or maybe a tiny change of narrative direction when the pace begins to flag. If it feels uncomfortable, she insists, don't do it. It is, my lovely, *your* book.

With the waiter lurking for an order, and Tim yet to show up, we're discussing the role that death plays in my debut novel. The book starts with the news that I have the brain tumour which may kill me, and Evelyn likes these opening pages very much indeed. She talks of grace under pressure, and says she loves the way that I've managed to avoid all the girly clichés. Few tears. Absolutely no trace of self-pity. This happens to be exactly the way it was in real life, largely because I needed to hide my numbness, but I take her approval as a compliment. This theme of sudden death recurs throughout the book, with yours truly doing my best to cheat the Reaper of his spoils, and we're discussing a particular scene towards thc end when Tim finally arrives.

I get to my feet and give him a big showbiz hug. This is technically still off-limits but L'Avventura is reliably cool and none of the diners at the surrounding tables register the slightest interest. I make the introductions and thrust the menu at Tim.

'Go for the *acqua pazza*,' I tell him. 'Just trust me.'

The waiter takes the rest of our order and departs. We're drinking my favourite white, Greco di Tufo, and it's Tim who proposes a toast.

'To Jack and the Beanstalk,' he says.

'You got the part? Jack?'

'The Beanstalk.'

Evelyn, who's a great giggler, thinks this is very funny, and within seconds we're all swapping war stories from lockdown. Evelyn has retired to the little seaside town of Budleigh Salterton and thinks that the virus simply made life even quieter than usual. Everyone wore masks. The streets after dark remained empty. And very few people died. Tim nods. Same at his mum's place, he says. Someone in the village took a head count at the start, and another only a week ago, and the two figures were absolutely the same. This sounds disappointing, and I say so. Tim knows Pompey thrives on mayhem and wants all the details. His mum's veggie patch has an undeniable charm, he says, but not very much happens.

And so I do my best to rise to the occasion, court jester among this tight little knot of friends. I spare them the small print of what happened to Fat Dave, and H, and Malo, and Sean McGaughy. I avoid the darker corners of my Pompey story, and the moments when I thought all our days were numbered. Instead, I treat them to choice morsels from the *News*, Pompey's day-to-day chronicle that became indispensable light relief when I needed it most.

The low life who jacked up the new van belonging to a hospice charity and stole the wheels. The scary local bare-knuckle prospect, undisturbed by the virus, still in training for the national championship. The bored rough sleepers who were housed in a city centre hotel, all meals supplied, and terrorized the area for weeks on end. The contract the locals were tempted to take out on the Elvis tribute artist who performed on his garage roof every afternoon. And how the entire city feasted on a stolen recipe for Nando's piri-piri chicken, and all six hundred episodes of *The Simpsons.*

Evelyn enjoys these titbits, and so does Tim. When we've done justice to the food and the Greco di Tufo, Tim asks me how I got on in his flat. Inexcusably, I haven't said thank you, but I've been keeping a present I bought for him, that last day we were down in Pompey, and now I hand it over. It's a stick of Southsea rock, probably years old. The lettering goes all the way through, and we all have a bite. It is, of course, unspeakably sweet, but that's why I bought it in the first place. No one got fat in Pompey by accident, as Tim is the first to point out.

He's been talking to Evelyn about a favourite author of his that she knows very well. Now, he turns to me. He's been back in his Southsea flat for nearly a month and when he first walked in, he couldn't believe how clean it was. I shrug the compliment off, Ms Modest, and tell him I did my best to keep it the way I found it. I can tell he doesn't believe me for a moment, but it doesn't seem to matter.

'That chess game you left under my table?' He's watching me carefully now. 'I'm guessing you were black.'

'You guess right.'

'Then you didn't have a prayer. White more or less intact? Three pawns and your king at the wrong end of the board? Checkmate in three. I'll send you the moves, if you like.'

I shake my head and reach for the last of my wine.

'Sudden death was never my thing.' I risk a glance at Evelyn. 'That's why we stopped playing.'

'We?'

'Me and a friend.'

'Anyone special? Anyone I might know?'

'Sadly not.' I raise my glass. 'Here's to your panto. *Joyeux Noël.*'